Bridgeton

Michael Knoedler

LITTLE CREEK PRESS®
AND BOOK DESIGN
MINERAL POINT, WISCONSIN

Little Creek Press®
A Division of Kristin Mitchell Design, Inc.
5341 Sunny Ridge Road
Mineral Point, Wisconsin 53565

Book Design and Project Coordination:
Little Creek Press and Book Design

First Printing
June 2022

Printed in the United States of America

For more information or to order books,
www.littlecreekpress.com

Library of Congress Control Number: 2022910232

ISBN-13: 978-1-955656-24-5

Cover photo: Wisconsin Historical Society
https://www.wisconsinhistory.org/Records/Image/IM36036

For Mom,

who experienced firsthand

the joys and sorrows of Bridgeton.

RIP

PART ONE

PART TWO

PART THREE

CHARACTERS

Pederson Family

Mickey: primary narrator

Ron and Desmond: Mickey's sons

Matt: Mickey's father

Janice: Mickey's mother

Sharon LeBeaux: Mickey's ex-wife

Dennis: Mickey's older brother by five years

Alberta: Dennis' wife

Margaret: Matt's sister, Mickey's aunt

Grams: Mickey's great-grandmother

Daisy Jensen: Mickey's great-aunt

Sally Jensen: Mickey's cousin, Daisy's granddaughter

Jackson and Erma Jensen: Sally's parents

Stanley: Sally's husband, father of Walter

Joe Rebenick: boyhood friend of Matt Pederson, nicknamed "Dirty Joe"

Hal: Mickey's friend and lover

McPhearson Family

James (Jimbo): close friend of Mickey and Lemon

Doc: Jimbo's father, Bridgeton's only physician

Vera: Jimbo's mother, divorced Doc when Jimbo was seven, remarried to Jack Gordon

Jeremy: Jimbo's older brother by six years

Leslie: Jimbo's older brother by five years

Beverly Shuster: mother of Jimbo's half-sister, Lucy

Lucy: Jimbo's half-sister who died at two months

Shaina: Jimbo's second ex-wife

Kraig Family

Lemuel (Lemon): close friend of Mickey and Jimbo

Orantha Chimes Kraig: Lemon's wife

Bettina, Olivia, and Jezzie: daughters of Lemon and Orantha

Ted: Lemon's father

Lizzie: Lemon's mother

Esther: Ted and Lizzie's oldest daughter

Sarah Ruth: Ted and Lizzie's middle daughter, abducted when she was ten

Little Eve: Ted and Lizzie's youngest daughter

Others

Janie Thomkins, Benny Unertal, Frankie Kronenwetter: Dennis Pederson's classmates

Joanne Michelsky and Kurt Mestanek: classmates of Mickey, Jimbo, and Lemon

Aggie Robinson (Sister Mary Agnes): Lemon's fourth-grade teacher

Melvin Trillup: classmate sent away by the courts because of a gun incident

Debbie Kedrowski: classmate; her mother, Katherine, ran Miss Kitty's brothel

Virgil Lightfoot Gibson: classmate, Ojibwe/Menominee heritage, basketball star

Jonny Lightfoot: Virgil's uncle

Principal Horner: principal at Bridgeton High School

Coach Langford, Mr. Jessup, Gabe Parkinson: teachers at Bridgeton High School

Randy Dover, Peter Stockbridge: basketball players for Wausau High School

JoLinda Showlton: Mickey's former high school student, mother of Ezra

Larry Mestanek: Kurt Mestanek's grandson

PART ONE

European immigrants settled along the Wisconsin River and displaced the communities of Potawatomi, Menominee, and Ho-Chunk through treaties, violence, and thievery. Pineries were one of the first types of immigrant villages. After most of the centuries-old white pines were cut down, paper mills took the place of sawmills in many river towns. Hydroelectric dams accompanied these developments. One can make the case that the twenty-six major dams along the Wisconsin River, from Lac Vieux Desert in the far northeast to the last dam at Prairie du Sac, transformed the lives of the immigrants along Wisconsin's longest river more than any other innovation. The dam at the small town of Bridgeton, constructed by the Bridgeton Paper Mill in 1903, presents an excellent example of this transformation.

From *Life Along the Wisconsin River: An Alternative History* by Virgil Lightfoot and Matthew Michael Pederson. University at Madison Press.

One
Discovery

During the summer after fifth grade, Lemon Kraig and I were engrossed in Landmark history books. In June, we focused on Revolutionary War heroes. Ethan Allen and the Green Mountain Boys. The Swamp Fox. Washington crossing the Delaware River to sneak up on the Hessians. By July, we were on to the exploits of Ulysses Grant, Robert E. Lee, and Stonewall Jackson. One Saturday afternoon, as ten-year-olds, we enlisted in the Union Army as advanced scouts, leading the way down to Skunk Hollow, making sure it was safe for the cavalry. J.E.B. Stuart's Rebs appeared in our sights and we pursued them, skirting the marshes and plunging into the woodlands. Cautious because, the books told us, the Confederate generals were superior to our own. Careful of being outflanked even as we screamed at the ragged grey uniforms just beyond the next grove of white pines.

We normally halted when we reached the rocky banks of the Wisconsin River, but this time the chase continued on the deer trails running along the shoreline, heading upriver toward the dam and Little Bull Falls. We had never gone this far. Creeping along to avoid gunfire from across the river, we hid behind cottonwoods to reload our stick rifles and struggled through blackcap brambles which tore at our sweaty uniforms of faded jeans and T-shirts. We paused at the base of a twenty-foot mountain of boulders and sipped Kool-Aid from our canteen, weighing the odds that the ascent would leave us exposed to enemy fire. Lemon proceeded warily, but when he peered over the peak, he shouted to me excitedly. I joined him and looked downward at the hidden sandscape, my first glimpse of Discovery Beach.

We dropped our sticks and scrambled to the shoreline. The Confederate forces faded away as we wandered around our sandy paradise. The north end of the beach was just as protected by a second set of boulders, and the backside of our haven was bordered with scrub oaks and young red pines, making an approach from that direction improbable. The far side of the river seemed a mile away, but just fifteen yards from us, an elliptical sandbar rose out of the river populated by nothing more than low lying bluestem and false heather. We looked at each other and shook our heads, flabbergasted and joyful. "Where are we, Lemon?"

"We hiked about a mile from Skunk Hollow. I can't hear the falls up ahead. Must be about the same from the other end."

Eager to cool off, we dropped our clothes and waded out to our thighs, dove into the midsummer water a few times and continued to the sandbar where we paraded up and down on the small island—newly crowned princes secure in our river kingdom. Our parents warned us that the dangers of the unpredictable currents lay further out in the main coursing of the river. We spent an hour alternately submerged in the cool waters then losing the chill on the warm sand.

We were putting our briefs back on when we heard a motor, so we grabbed the rest of our clothes and hid behind the boulders. A flat-bottomed river boat with a small outboard eased up to the far side of the sandbar. Janie Thompkins jumped out wearing an oversized man's dress shirt, cut-off shorts, and a straw hat. She was in my brother's class, and while he no longer spent much time with her, they had been part of the same neighborhood gang throughout late elementary school. I hadn't seen her for months and was surprised how grown-up she looked, strutting along the sandbar in our footprints and beckoning brashly to her male companion, who remained at the back of the boat.

She quickly shed her outer clothes, revealing a skimpy red and white striped two-piece, and plunged into the water on our side of the sandbar. The young man jumped from the boat and pursued Janie to the water's edge, eyeing her with delight. He had scruffy, sandy-colored whiskers creating a half-beard and hair much longer than the crewcuts men his age typically wore. He tossed his green T-shirt onto the sand, revealing a hairy chest and the beginning of a beer belly. As we watched him finger the waistband of his yellow swim trunks and deliberate about what to do next, it was clear he was several years older than Janie, probably out of high school.

"Do you know him?" Lemon whispered.

I shook my head. The man slipped off his trunks, demonstrating no embarrassment about his nakedness, and joined Janie in the waist-deep, copper water. They splashed each other, sitting up to their necks. He lunged forward and tried to kiss her, and she backed away, losing her balance and falling backward into the water. He disappeared where Janie's legs had gone under, and after a few seconds, his hand emerged from the water twirling the top to Janie's bikini. Janie laughed. "What are you going to do with that?"

"It's no good unless I have its mate."

He dove under a second and a third time, finally arising with a grin and the twisted bottoms of her swimsuit. Lemon looked at me wide-eyed, and I was speechless as well. Neither of us had seen a naked woman, other than glimpses of our mothers when we shouldn't have been looking. Janie guided herself toward the man until their lips met, and they kissed deeply. The couple kicked the water skyward as they danced back up to the sandbar, his hand clutching at Janie's bottom. Janie spurted ahead to the boat to retrieve two beach towels, and the lovers stretched out on them in view of the shoreline. Before long, he was aggressively kissing her again while Janie giggled and eagerly returned his affections. His hands crept up to her breasts, down to her hips and then to the patch of hair between her legs, at which point Janie pushed him away. "Stop it."

But he wouldn't. He rolled toward her, trying to pin her underneath him. She struggled to her knees, despite his eighty-pound advantage, screaming at him. "Cut it out."

As if propelled by the boat motor, his hands continued to slide between her thighs, until finally, she squirmed away and ran back into the water. He quickly pursued her, so she ran up to the beach, just a few yards in front of us, her shoulders and back side coated with sand. He stopped in knee-deep water, his genitals still in a state of excitement. "Come on, Janie. You know that's why you wanted to stop here."

"Not that."

"You gonna be a cock tease?"

She pointed at his flagging penis. "I don't want that thing in me."

"Then let's get out of here."

"Not until you promise."

"I ain't promising you anything."

He backed up to the sandbar and pulled on his suit, then retrieved two cans of beer from the boat. He stared at Janie while he guzzled the first beer. "Want one?" he yelled.

She shook her head but kept her arms crossed over her breasts and her legs close together. He threw the empty can to the sand, grabbed one of the towels, and punctured the second beer with a church key. "Comin'?"

"Only if you promise."

He shoved the boat back into the current and sneered at her. "See you then," and motored downstream from where they'd come.

Lemon and I quickly slipped into our jeans and walked out to the beach. Janie was still holding herself tightly, sitting in the sand under the lone tree on the beach, a small willow that provided a pocket of shade. "Get her clothes. Let me do the talking," I said.

When she heard my footsteps, she stood up. "Hi, Janie."

"Jesus, what are you doing here?"

"We were on the beach when you pulled into the sandbar. We hid behind the rocks."

"Fucking pervs."

She looked out toward the sandbar where Lemon was gathering her wet suit, dry clothes, and towel. He waded back in, arms above his head, and slowly approached Janie, eyes to the ground. He handed her the towel and dropped her garments at her feet without looking up, and she quickly covered herself. We walked to the shoreline, gazing across the river while she dressed. "What did she say, Mick?"

"Not much. Called us pervs."

"Let's be careful."

We heard her footsteps scuffling in the sand and turned. She wore the cutoffs and buttoned-up shirt that hung to her thighs. Her straw hat was tipped backward at the top of her head as she methodically rolled the wet two-piece in the towel. "How long have you two been here?" she finally demanded.

I didn't want to be the one to let her know, but Lemon spoke up. "From when you got here. We're sorry about what he did."

"He's an asshole."

"Who is he?" I said.

"Eddie. From Weston. We met last week at a wedding dance."

"How old is he?" I said.

"Says he's twenty." She looked downriver. "Think he'll come back?"

She waded in the river up to her knees, contemplating her predicament before pirouetting back to us. Her saucy insouciance returned. "How'd you two get here?"

"Walked from Skunk Hollow," Lemon said.

"That's a ways."

"Figured a mile," Lemon said.

"So you didn't sneak out here to see me and Eddie get naked."

"We were exploring. You surprised us when you showed up," I said.

"But you looked anyway," she said, wearing a naughty grin as enticing as her scanty swimsuit.

"We were worried he might hurt you," Lemon said.

"You're the Kraig kid with the funny nickname?"

"Most of us call him Lemon," I said.

"What's the shoreline like between here and the hollow?" she said.

"Not bad. But you can't walk in shallow water the whole way," I said.

Lemon looked at her feet. "You need shoes or you'll get cut up."

"Shit. My flip-flops are in the boat."

I handed her my sneakers. "Try mine."

They almost fit, but she couldn't squeeze her heel inside. Lemon took the laces from his sneakers and tied them to the ends of my laces, extending them. Then he strapped my shoes to Janie's ankles, and they fit her like slip-on sandals. I put on both pairs of our socks, and we moved as quickly as Janie could walk along the sand, which quickly turned into mounds of rocks and washed up driftwood, then back to sand and gravel again. She needed our assistance to crawl over the trickiest terrain. "You guys come out to that beach much?" she said.

"We just discovered it today."

"Eddie and I should have brought a picnic. Maybe he would have stayed and not gotten so pissed at me."

Halfway back to Skunk Hollow, we heard the motor. None of us waved, but once Eddie spotted us, he eased toward a rocky stretch of shore. There was no place to bring his boat in, so he jumped out into three feet of water and pulled the flat-bottom toward us. When he saw Janie's makeshift shoes, he laughed. "Woulda been a lot easier if you had gotten in back at the sandbar."

"You didn't give me much chance," Janie said.

"You needed a lesson. To know who's boss."

Janie stared at him as if she wished he hadn't come back. "I could go to the cops."

"You wouldn't do that. You were having fun, too."

"Just saying I could. I'm only sixteen."

Her warning got his attention, and he stared at Lemon and me like we'd put the thought in her head. "I won't try it again," he said softly.

"Promise?"

"If that's all you need."

Janie pondered the situation for a few seconds, then slipped out of my shoes and reentered the water, pushing by Eddie without stopping. She would have tipped the boat when she clambered over the gunwale if Eddie hadn't caught it in time. He shook his head at her incompetence and pulled a pack of Chesterfields from the pocket of his swimsuit. He offered us one, but we shook our heads. "I started when I was younger than you guys. Won't kill you."

He flicked his lighter and lit the Chesterfield. After two drags, he smirked. "Where'd you kids come from?"

I glanced at Lemon who said, "We were passing by."

Eddie choked on his inhalation. "Shit. Out here, in the middle of nowhere?"

"Yeah. We're down here a lot," I said.

Eddie couldn't stop laughing. "Were you back at the beach when I was with Janie?"

"Not far away. We came down when we heard your boat take off," Lemon said.

He gave each of us a penetrating once-over. "So you didn't see anything?"

I shook my head. "Just you in your boat."

Eddie inhaled again, raising a skeptical eye. "Don't believe you."

Janie interrupted his interrogation. "Let's go, Eddie. I'm getting hot sitting here."

Eddie pointed at us as he tossed his Chesterfield into the river. "Don't get lost."

He didn't seem much of a danger to Janie as he jumped in the boat and started the outboard. As he eased his way into deeper water, he glanced back one more time before zooming down the river. "Think she'll be OK?" Lemon asked.

"Not sure. I don't know much about this stuff."

I biked by Janie's house each morning and evening over the next few days and asked my brother, Dennis, if he had seen her lately. "Why would I be looking for her?"

"Just wondering. Maybe something happened to her."

"Doubt that. She's like a cat," he scoffed.

"What's that mean?"

"Most people get hurt when they jump into danger. Some walk away without a scar, like Janie."

I saw her the next afternoon, leaning against a black pickup truck parked in front of her house. A flat-bottomed river boat was attached to the back, and Eddie from Weston was standing next to her, poking at her ribs as she laughed and spun away. After ten minutes, he got into his truck and waved to her as he took off. When he approached me, he idled the truck and lit a Chesterfield. "Where's your friend?"

I didn't respond. "Still watching out for Janie?"

"I live just up the street."

"Right, and you were just passing by again," he said as he flicked the cigarette at my feet.

I shook my head and he drove off. I peddled up to Janie. "You OK?"

"Why are you hanging around, Mickey? I don't need a watchdog."

"Just wondering if you went to the cops."

"Eddie's OK. Just has to keep it in his pants. Know what that means?"

"I think so," I said, visualizing Eddie as he stood naked in the shallow water.

"Eddie still wants to know if you and Lemon got a good look the other day."

"What did you tell him?"

"That I ran into you when I was walking back." Then she laughed. "Some boys would have looked away when we took our clothes off. Would have had better sense. Did you see much?"

"Most of it."

"Your first time?"

I blushed. "Maybe you'll remember it then. That's not how it's supposed to go anyway."

"We figured that much."

"Do you guys keep secrets?"

"Lots of them."

"Good."

Lemon and I hiked to Discovery Beach from the dam a week later. It was a shorter walk, but with more vigorous climbing, and we were sweating heavily when we got there. We stripped down and swam around the sandbar before warming up on the hot sand. "What do you think happened to Janie?" Lemon asked.

"Nothing much. She told me she didn't wait for him at the boat landing while he was hitching up his boat. Caught a ride back home with some friends. But she's still seeing him."

We surveyed the far side of the river lined with lush sumac already turning crimson, suspicious that J.E.B. Stuart and the Rebs had returned and were preparing for another assault. Lemon picked up the Hamm's beer can that Eddie from Weston had discarded, and we headed back to shore. He set the steel can on a boulder and found a rock he could hold in his hand. He smashed the blue and white can a dozen times, then slid the flattened metal into his back pocket for our walk back home.

Two
Lucy

I was sleeping on the carpeted floor in Jimbo's bedroom when I first heard the wailing. I rolled over to go back to sleep, but her crying ascended through the heating grate near my head. Jimbo and Lemon were buried in sleeping bags across the floor, still breathing deeply. I rose and slowly opened the door, pausing on the stairs when I heard Doc McPhearson's soothing voice. "I'm so sorry, Bev."

I peered into the kitchen, lit only by the under-the-cupboard fluorescent. Beverly Shuster was shuddering and gasping. Doc's flashlight inspected Lucy, the naked baby on the table—Beverly's two-month-old infant. She lay motionless on her back, in the middle of a turquoise blanket. The movement of Doc's light beckoned as Beverly leaned forward against the kitchen table, her hands clutching Lucy's legs. Stroking them. Pinching them. Lucy was soundless with a dull bluish skin tone. She drew me closer by her inactivity. Beverly rubbed Lucy's belly, pleading with her, "Lucy! Wake up!"

I stood next to Doc as he tried to console her. "She was dead within seconds after she stopped breathing."

"I'd just nursed her twenty minutes earlier."

"It can happen that quickly."

When I reached out toward Lucy, Doc's oversized paw enveloped my hand and pulled it back. Beverly noticed me for the first time and half-smiled through her tears. "Hi, Mickey. It's OK. You can touch her.

Here, let me help."

She cupped my right hand in both of hers. We fondled Lucy's fingers, sliding up her mottled arm to her fleshy neck. Beverly was no longer crying, whispering at my earlobe, "Feel her face."

I looked back at Doc, Lemon in front of him, uncombed blond hair sweeping over his forehead, Jimbo, burly and nearly a head taller than Lemon and I, at his dad's shoulder, both of them fully awake, saucer-eyed in awe at our first encounter with death. Lucy's eyes were half-closed, unfocused. Her mouth barely open at the corners. I caressed her velvet cheek with my index finger. My thumb felt no air from her nose, and the heat fleeing her body seemed palpable. Beverly sang, "Lullaby and Good Night" as she lifted my hand away and scooped Lucy up. She held her near my face, then Lemon's, finally Jimbo's. "See, she stopped breathing. Just like that."

Doc, unnerved by Beverly's actions, spoke very faintly. "Boys," and we moved to the back wall of the kitchen. Three ten-year-olds in white briefs, speechless, lit up by the faint tangerine of dawn edging through the kitchen windows. Doc finally escorted Beverly and Lucy away from us into his office.

We went upstairs and dressed. Jimbo asked if we would stay, but I had to get outside. I glanced at the framed photograph of Jimbo's mother on his dresser, her stern visage with lips almost grimacing, like the camera had captured her at the very moment she'd left Doc and the three McPhearson boys three years ago. Jimbo's older brothers, Jeremy and Leslie, both in high school, had been living with her in Tomah for the past six months. I knew we couldn't leave Jimbo alone.

We walked two blocks to Old Iron, the truss bridge that spanned the Wisconsin River. On the far side, the Bridgeton Paper Mill was lighting up for the day shift. A few men hustled along the wooden walkway to work and stared at us in the five-thirty daybreak. We followed them but stopped halfway along the walkway, dashed across the narrow car lanes, and eased down the slippery ladder to the dam that controlled the cascading water gushing through Little Bull Falls. Since we were six, we'd explored and fished at the root-beer-colored pool below the falls. This time we followed Jimbo to the pair of flat sitting rocks at the southern edge of the pool. Lemon asked, "How long were you there before we came down, Mick?"

"Maybe thirty minutes."

"Was Lucy still alive?"

"Just Beverly wanting her to be."

"She know you?"

"She helps Mom clean house once a month. Just turned nineteen. Her aunt kicked her out when she got pregnant. Lives alone now out on Snyder Road."

Jimbo looked up and finally spoke. "She stayed over last night after she made us supper. Often does when Dad's running late. Lucy must have died in my old crib."

I could hear him crying even though he shielded his face. The river below the dam turned from sheet metal grey to dirty aqua as the engorged citrus sun rose in the hazy morning. We scampered over the boulders to the path along the river, our sneakers and jeans soaked by the spears of mullein coated with river dew. When we reached Discovery Beach and the sandbar, we tossed our clothes into a pile under the solitary willow tree guarding the small beach and swam naked in the shallow tannic waters. After fifteen minutes, we stretched out on the sandbar, the surface grains still moist and cool with early morning, waiting for Jimbo to be able to go back home.

Three days after Lucy's funeral, we pedaled our one-speeds to Beverly's two-bedroom house on Snyder Road. Her lab mix, Pancho, dashed out and yipped at our wheels as we rode up the quarter-mile-long, gravel driveway. Jimbo dropped off his bike and petted Pancho as Beverly strolled down from the front porch. "What are you boys doing here?"

I thought Jimbo would tell her since it was his idea. But he looked away, so I spoke up. "Mom thought you could use some help."

"Doing what?"

None of us knew. "Maybe some cleaning?" I suggested.

She giggled at the thought. "Mickey, you can't even keep your undies out of the dust bunnies under your bed."

I turned crimson as Lemon and Jimbo laughed. Lemon focused on her vegetable garden. "Your butter beans need picking. Everything needs weeding. We can do that."

"What do you know about it?"

"I help Dad take care of ours. He sells down at the market."

"You know what's a weed?"

Lemon nodded and Beverly said, "OK."

She handed Lemon a wicker bucket and left us. Lemon showed Jimbo and me how to reach under the bushes and snap off the yellow pods without yanking up the plants. He pulled the crabgrass alongside the rows, directing us as he scooted around in the garden, clearing the broadleaf plantains and chickweed from her peppers and butternut squash. After we picked the three rows, he showed us how to freshen up the grassy mulch underneath her tomato plants, careful not to knock the green baseballs off the lower branches. Beverly returned with a shovel and sheets from cardboard boxes. "Pull the pigweed along the fence and lay the cardboard down. Cover it over with dirt."

This time she sat on the splitting block nearby watching her chickens scratch for beetles. "Lemon, you know how to gather eggs?"

He nodded.

"There's a bowl inside the pen. Give 'em some water, too. Jimbo and Mickey can finish up with the weeding."

We watched her wander around the front yard, like the chickens in their enclosure, before returning to our tasks. Jimbo dug the dirt while I covered the cardboard mulch. Lemon was running water near the chicken coop, so we washed our hands and had a cool drink. Beverly was slumped into a metal chair on the front porch pushing Lucy's bassinet back and forth. Lemon set the bowl containing four eggs and the bucket of beans on the top step before her, our pitiful offering to her sorrow. “One of the hens has a broken claw.”

She rolled her eyes like she already knew. Jimbo knelt alongside the bassinet and caressed the carved rails up and down, over and over, as Beverly massaged his shoulders. “Used to be yours. Your dad gave it to me.” Jimbo started crying. “Did Doc tell your brothers yet?”

“They won’t want to know. It’s why they left.”

“Maybe they’ll come back now. I never meant for them to go away.”

Jimbo never talked about it. Mom either, though I overheard her arguing with Dad about Beverly. I assumed it was about whether they could afford Beverly’s cleaning services.

We got on our bikes and waved goodbye just as Doc’s red Chevy sedan roared up the driveway. He stopped and jumped out of the car when he reached us. “Jimbo, what the hell are you doing here?”

I didn’t think Jimbo would break down again, but he couldn’t stop himself. He was so much bigger than Lemon and I, but in his grief like our younger brother. Beverly rushed over. “Leave him alone, Doc. Jimbo’s not like Jeremy or Leslie. He’s hurting, too.”

Doc eased off as Beverly continued. “They were helping out. Took care of my garden.”

Doc looked at Lemon and me, understanding we were part of it now. “Then it’s OK. Thanks, boys.”

We biked back toward town, turned in at the cemetery, and stopped at the far edge of the McPhearson family section. An unadorned grey stone, not much bigger than our fifth-grade mathematics textbook, lay flat in loosely packed sod.

Lucy Janine Shuster McPhearson

April 18, 1957—June 22, 1957

She Flew Away Too Soon

Lemon and I waited for Jimbo to cry again, but he surprised me. “I used to caress her face like you did, Mick. Held her in the rocking chair while Beverly cooked us supper.”

He knelt in the fresh sod and placed his hand on the stone. "I could have left with my brothers midyear. Mom expected me to. I told her I would when school ended. Then I fell in love with my sister too much."

Three
Brothers

Jimbo McPhearson was closer to this story than I was, so he should tell it.

In August, a few months after Lucy died, Dad drove me to Tomah, insisting I visit Mom and my brothers before the school year resumed in Bridgeton. I hadn't spent more than a week at a time with Mom since she left us, unlike my brothers who enjoyed Tomah and had been at Mom's since Christmas when she insisted we leave Dad's house to be far removed from the vortex of the pregnancy scandal. We argued when I told her I wouldn't go, but she didn't force me.

I spent the days on my own near the Lemonweir River and slept fitfully on the floor in Leslie's bedroom. Jeremy, who was seventeen, continued to call Beverly a "whore" and "cheap sex." He pushed me around when I objected to his insults, sometimes slapping me in the face. There was no point in telling Mom. She didn't seem to care if her oldest son's language hurt me. Maybe it was because she knew it would bring me so much pain. Leslie was easier to live with but still ensnarled within Jeremy's bitterness. In the end, Mom didn't have room for the three of us and was gone too much of the time with her job at the Monroe County Courthouse. We returned to Dad's house for Jeremy's senior year at Bridgeton High.

Mickey, Lemon, and I biked out to Beverly's a few times, but then sixth grade started, and we didn't think about her tomatoes or chickens anymore. I eagerly moved into Beverly's old room off the kitchen so

Leslie and Jeremy could have privacy upstairs. One evening in mid-September, Jeremy came into my room and rummaged through my books and clothes, most of which were still boxed up. "Want something?"

"Just looking."

He picked up a photo of me sitting in the kitchen rocking chair with Lucy curled up in my arms. He crumpled it and tapped me on the side of my head. "We're a joke around town. Beverly's the cause of all that. Having that fucking kid."

"She and Dad made a choice. Stay out of it."

"What do you know about it?"

"More than you."

He slapped me just above my left ear on his way out, the sting lingering for an hour. His viciousness accelerated over the next few weeks as he kicked and punched me at will. I had bruises on my arms and ribs and could barely put weight on my right thigh, but I was afraid to tell Dad. One night, while I was reading in bed and Dad was out on a house call, Jeremy dragged me outside and locked the door. I sat on the front porch steps, chilled in my pajamas and bare feet. I shouted up to Leslie's room, but he was too intimidated to help. Finally, I slid into my river boots, which were sitting on the porch, and walked the two blocks to Mickey's house. I snuck up the stairs to his bedroom while his mother listened to the radio. Mickey's bedside light was on, but he was half asleep and jumped awake when I touched his arm.

"I need a place to sleep. Jeremy's too mean."

Janice, Mickey's mother, fixed a pallet of quilts on the floor next to Mickey's bed. Dad said I could stay with the Pedersons for a few days, which turned into the rest of that week and then beyond. In the beginning, Dad stopped by after work, but that became too inconvenient for him. Awkward as well, admitting he couldn't protect his own children from each other. He often picked me up on Sunday mornings on his way to the hospital in Wausau. I'd wait for him in the doctor's lounge while he did rounds. Afterward, we'd go out for a late breakfast. "Jeremy's moving into your room."

"Why?"

"Wants more privacy."

I knew it was because Jeremy wanted to come and go late at night without Dad hearing him. "It'll work out best if you stay with Mickey's family until the school year is over."

"What difference will that make?"

"I have an agreement with Jeremy and your mother. He'll go back to Tomah after graduation. You won't have to see him after that."

"I didn't do anything wrong."

"I know. But it's complicated. I owe him, and he has a right to finish high school here."

I stuffed myself with French toast as Dad sipped coffee and pensively observed me. Thinking about his kids wasn't his specialty. "It's OK at Mickey's?"

"Yeah."

"You and Mickey and Lemon getting along?"

I nodded. "Why does Jeremy hate me so much?"

"That's complicated, too. I'm not sure he does. He hates me, and you're getting it."

"He doesn't hit and kick you."

"I wish he'd try. Maybe we could move on if he punched me in the face."

Periodically, I'd go home to get some more clothes. Everything that was mine was sitting in cardboard boxes in Jeremy's abandoned bedroom. My new room. Jeremy's dirty sheets covered the unmade bed, and dust gathered on the dresser. The back door slammed, and voices rose up the stairs. Jeremy and two friends, Jester Grimes and Bobby Tolson, moved into the kitchen, opening and closing the refrigerator as they made sandwiches. If they heard me shift on the creaky floorboards, I could quickly hide in the closet, but they settled in at the kitchen table as I sat motionless on the floor above them, their voices clear, rising through the heating grate, beer bottles clinking as Jeremy explained his plan. "She won't expect it on Friday night."

"Just to scare her, right?" Jester said.

"Throw a few stones against the windows."

"Just to scare the shit out of her?" Jester repeated.

"If she comes out, maybe hurt her."

Bobby's voice joined in for the first time. "I don't want her bringing in the cops. Not after last time."

"It's got to be a quick in and out," Jester said.

"We'll go during the second half of the football game," Jeremy said.

"When the cops are busy," Bobby said.

Jeremy, anger in his voice now, said, "I want her to know what she's done."

They left and I sat on the floor fumbling through my sweatshirts and socks. I pulled out one of my Hardy Boys books and found the picture of Lucy and me in the rocking chair inside the front cover, still wrinkled by Jeremy's bitterness. In two nights, my brother planned to assault Beverly.

On Thursday night, Lemon, Mickey, and I made a plan: Mickey had a BB gun, and I snuck Dad's .22 from the basement. The next night, Mickey and Lemon told their parents we were heading to the high school football game, but we biked out to Beverly's instead. When I told her about the imminent attack, she scoffed. "Just big boy talk."

"Can we stay for a while? Just in case," I said.

"Yeah. I baked today while I was housecleaning."

We ate chocolate cake topped with vanilla ice cream while listening to Fats Domino. After an hour, Lemon suggested we head home, but just then, Pancho started barking from the porch. Beverly brought him inside and turned out the house lights. The three of us stood on the porch, peering into the dark night. Jester Grimes' Buick stopped halfway up the long driveway, and three car doors opened and shut softly. The invaders' low voices paused when Beverly flicked the kitchen lights on and off several times. I crouched down against the porch railings, my night vision finally kicking in, and saw Jeremy's outline against the driveway motioning for the other two to follow. We knelt down as low as we could as they approached the porch. Jeremy beamed his flashlight toward the screen door and windows, but Beverly had slipped out the back. The look of puzzlement on my brother's face, just a few yards in front of me, gave me some pleasure—anything to disrupt the vile certitude he'd displayed over the past few months. Jester started to speak, but Jeremy quieted him with his index finger. Thirty seconds of silence followed. Pancho's low whimpers from the back bedroom of the house were the only sounds. I stood up without saying a word, and Jeremy shined his flashlight on my face. "Jimbo! What the hell!"

The three of them saw the .22 pointed outward. "Jer, this was not part of the deal," Jester said.

"It's my little brother with his BB gun."

Lemon and Mickey arose from their crouch, and Mickey fired his BB gun several times, hitting Bobby in the leg. "Fuck, man. Stop that shit," Bobby said.

Jeremy put his right foot on the first step. "No further," I warned him.

"What're you gonna do? Ping me with a BB?"

I aimed the .22 over his head and pulled the trigger. Everybody jumped as the blast rocketed overhead. Jeremy backed off and held up his hand. "Why are you protecting the whore, brother?"

"She was Dad's girlfriend. He got her pregnant. Our sister died. She's no whore."

Beverly slipped out of the darkness at the side of the house, flashlight illuminating her way, all six of us watching her take her place between Jeremy and me. She stared him down. "Go home, Jeremy. I won't step inside your house again. And leave Jimbo alone, or I'll hurt you."

Her words hung in the blackness until Jester's nervous voice broke the spell. "Don't want to be part of this, Jer."

The three of them eased off quietly, car doors slammed quickly, and Jester backed out to the road and drove off.

Beverly stepped up to the porch. "I think they're done, Jimbo."

"Should we stay any longer?" Mickey asked.

"No need. Jimbo showed Jeremy he means business."

She walked us to our bikes and double-checked the safety on the .22. Part of me expected Jeremy to be waiting for us around the corner, but as we peddled each block, riding three abreast, I finally began to breathe. It had taken me nearly two months of being back in Bridgeton, but the air began to fill my lungs again.

Four
Big Snapper

The last time I'd run into Benny Unertal was at the Bridgeton outdoor swimming pool bathroom. I was peeing, wearing just my suit, and didn't hear him come in until he was standing behind me. He crowded against my backside and shoved his knees against my rear end, forcing me into the urinal. I was small for a ten-year-old and slid in easily. Barefoot in my own piss. Benny's warm urine splashed on my ankles as Frankie Kronenwetter laughed. "Need a better lookout system, Mickey."

This time I was playing under Old Iron, the fifty-year-old bridge that stretched across the Wisconsin River from the village of Bridgeton to the paper mill, Polish Town, and the train station. Mom exaggerated the dangers along the river. "Poison ivy grows along the river like the crab grass in my garden." I believed catching the itchy rash was possible like my brother, Dennis, had with his ferocious outbreak two summers ago. Mom mostly feared that one slip along the turbulent river would leave her in tears for the rest of her life. But the river was too rich in temptation, just a block from our backyard. Dennis fished near the dam at Little Bull Falls whenever he wanted, and there was no reason I should miss out on those same adventures.

I'd just spent fifteen minutes operating with a pointed stick, probing the belly and puncturing the eyes of a carp discarded by a fisherman. I approached the foamy pool just below the dam, lost in a spell conjured by a forbidden spot on the river. I saw Benny and he heard me, despite the rushing water. He looked up from a table-top rock where he stood along the shoreline. His black hair, usually greased back into a perfect ducktail, hung in tangled strands over his unshaven face. He was shirtless and shoeless, wearing only muddied and crimson-streaked briefs. The fist I feared so much at the end of his muscled right arm clutched a silvery knife, the sunlight glittering off of its five-inch blade. He stared at me for another thirty seconds then resumed his work.

I knew I should retreat back over the rocks and up the ladder, but Benny held me there, digging with his weapon. I took ten more steps and nearly stepped on the discarded head of the giant snapping turtle. Benny pressed the writhing torso, belly side up, onto the rock, working the knife above one of the turtle's claws. The four legs squirmed in every direction like they could still ramble away. Without looking up, Benny said, "He's dead. Just doesn't know it yet." He eyeballed me for a second. "Push down on his belly while I cut the claws."

I stood alongside Benny, hands in my pockets, unsure of what to do. The turtle's tail twitched madly, warning me away. "He's immense. Where'd you catch him?"

"Below the pool. Forced a stick across his mouth, and he clamped on."

I thought about the carp, a species whose sole purpose seemed to be to encourage mutilation. "What are you doing to him?"

"Carvin' him up. Once I get his claws off."

He smiled and took a drag from his Camel. "He can't bite, and his claws won't gouge you once they're off."

I pressed down on the snapper's bony underbelly, and, over the next forty-five minutes, Benny dissected it. He amputated the four claws, popped off the hard abdominal shell, harvested the meat from the thighs and neck, and skinned the fat away from the red pulp. He filled a plastic bag sitting next to the cleaned-out carapace with bloody meat. "Ma's not that great a cook. Except for turtle stew."

He washed his knife in the river, licked the cuts on his hands, and sat down for one more cigarette. “You might want to rinse your hands. The stink gets awful after a while.”

I knelt along the pool and cautiously rubbed my fingers in the water. Benny laughed. “Use some sand for grit.”

I hesitantly followed Benny’s orders and tried to scrub the bloodstains from my hands and wrists, looking back at him occasionally. I was still fearful he’d give me a quick shove, and I’d be swept away by the gushing whirlpools below the dam. But he didn’t budge from his rock, gazing off beyond the dam and toward the broad waters of the flowage, apparently enjoying the solitude along the river.

He finally stood and tossed his cigarette butt into the water. He slipped out of his soiled underwear and into his jeans, T-shirt, and boots. “You down here much, Mickey?”

“Sometimes, if Mom doesn’t know where I am.”

“Maybe I’ll see you again.”

That night, while I was drying the dishes, I asked Mom if she’d ever tasted turtle stew. “Just once. Tastes like chicken, only tougher.”

“I was on the bridge today. Saw Benny Unertal catching turtles.”

“I suppose his family eats a lot of game. They don’t have as much as most of us in town.”

Benny and Frankie Kronenwetter approached me two months later as I walked past Tommy Martin’s Pool Hall on Main Street. I thought about crossing over to the library, but it was too late. Frankie grabbed my jacket at my throat. “Little Mickey, out again without your brother. Where’s ‘Denise’?”

Dennis, Frankie, and Benny were all in the eleventh grade. “What should we do with him this time, Benny?”

Benny didn’t say a word, an unlit Camel dangling from his chapped lips. He clicked his lighter open and closed, watching Frankie and me. His knife was sheathed and attached to his black leather belt, and I wondered if the blade still reeked of turtle flesh. Frankie grabbed my Milwaukee Braves baseball cap, twirled it on his index finger, and yanked my hair until my eyes watered. "What the fuck, Frankie!"

I didn't realize the words came out of my mouth until Frankie started laughing uncontrollably. Benny tried not to but couldn't stop himself, nearly choking on his cigarette. "Little pecker thinks he's got balls, Benny."

Benny shrugged his shoulders, cold-faced again as he finally lit his cigarette. Frankie reached down to pull my hair a second time, but Benny blocked Frankie's arm and took my cap with his other hand. "That's enough, Frankie. Let him be."

Frankie pushed me aside and walked ahead, pissed. Benny followed, tossing my cap behind him. As I squatted to pick it up, I watched them go up the steps into the pool hall. I headed toward home, and when I turned onto Pine Street, the soft song came out as unexpectedly as my defiance of Frankie Kronenwetter. "Benny Unertal's huntin' turtles, Benny Unertal's guttin' turtles, Benny Unertal's eatin'—Mama Unertal's stew."

Five
Mary Agnes

This is Lemon Kraig's story, though I had a hand in it.

It had been a long winter, eating up half of April. When spring finally arrived, it was difficult sitting at the desks of our fourth-grade classroom. Sister Mary Agnes was just as antsy as we were. She opened the eight-foot-high, double-hung windows as often as she could, but if the wind from the west was strong, as it was most days, our sheets of mimeographed paper would blow around the classroom like maple leaves in autumn, much to our delight, and to Sister Mary Agnes, too. But Sister Mary Cecilia, the principal, would come in and scold us if there was too much laughter.

Mary Agnes gave us an extra recess on occasion. No other grade had that privilege. She would often take a swing when we played softball, running the bases in her black lace-up nun shoes, or she'd turn one end of the long jump ropes so more girls could double Dutch. More often, she circled around the playground, her oversized rosary beads clicking with each stride, pretending she was watching us. I knew she wasn't.

She had dismissed us several minutes early on Friday, May 17. I was halfway home on my bike when I remembered I'd forgotten my baseball glove. When I reached our classroom, the door was shut, so I turned the knob, expecting it to be locked, but when the door swung open, I witnessed one of the most amazing sights I've ever seen. Sister Mary Agnes stood at the wide-open back window, the strong breeze blowing fiercely into her face. Her black veil and white coif sat on a desk behind her, and her neck-length brunette hair was blowing straight back as she leaned out of the window into the gale.

I was stunned, thinking the wind had blown off her headdress. Sneaking as quietly as I could to my desk, two rows from where she stood, I knelt to reach my glove under the book tray. One leg of the desk was caught in the strap of my glove. I lifted it as gently as possible, but the desk teetered as I grabbed my mitt and slammed down onto the dull brown tile flooring. Mary Agnes turned to me, a look of ecstasy that I'd never seen on her face. Saintlike. "Lemuel the King. What are you doing back here?"

"Just needed my mitt for the weekend."

She didn't seem to notice that her head was naked, and I thought about leaving without asking, but couldn't. "What happened?" pointing to her head.

She laughed loudly. "I had to take it off and feel the wind through my hair. You weren't supposed to see. Thought I'd locked the door."

I nodded and backed out of the classroom as she tucked her hair back under her veil.

A week later, Mickey and I were clothes-pinning baseball cards to our bicycle spokes when Mary Agnes came biking by. When we looked up, she waved. "That's her, Mickey."

"Mary Agnes?"

"Yup."

"How does she keep it on her head?"

"Not sure. Some kind of clips. Sometimes you can see bobby pins."

"Did she really have hair?"

"About as long as Mom's."

"Must be hot under there. I figured they must shave their head or have a crew-cut at best."

Two days after the school year ended, she biked by again and stopped near our driveway. "I'm headed across the river. Want to join me?"

Mickey and I followed Mary Agnes' fat-tired, one-speed to Old Iron, our wheels rattling across the boards on the walkway. She led us past the paper mill and the new houses along the Polish Town back roads. She turned to climb up the steep hill to Pillerton Park, but a third of the way up, Mickey and I were walking our bikes. Mary Agnes kept on going. She was sitting on top of a picnic table when we approached her. Sweat poured down from our hair across our eyes, but Mary Agnes' face was perfectly dry. Mickey asked, "How did you do that?"

"What? Ride up the hill?"

"No. Not sweating like a waterfall?"

I interrupted. "Mick."

"It's OK, Lemuel. Mickey's not been around us much."

Mickey blushed. "We're trained to never show we are making much effort. Like the Virgin Mary, I suppose, during childbirth." She pulled out her soaked white handkerchief. "I dried off before you arrived."

We looked down at the Wisconsin River for a few minutes. Mickey pointed out the sandbar and Discovery Beach, still visible underneath the late spring canopy. "You boys go there on your own?"

"As long as nobody knows. It's the best. Our private beach," I said.

"My girlfriends and I had a special place along the Wisconsin River south of here when I was growing up. I think about it a lot."

She said it with a longing on her face that made us feel like part of her was breaking in half and that we couldn't dare interrupt her recollections. After a few minutes, she stood up. "Ready?"

We glided down the winding road, trailing behind Mary Agnes, wondering if her veil was strapped on tight. Midway across Old Iron, she stopped and suggested we head down to the beach. Mickey looked at me like the sky was falling and the universe would never be the same. We leaned our bikes against the railings, dashed across the narrow car lanes, slid under the bar on the other side, and scampered down the ladder. We led her to the trail along the river, stopping at the turtle pool for a few minutes before racing through the battlefield of mulleins. She kept up with us, giggling over our shoulders. The river was high but not dangerously so when we reached the beach. She took off her black shoes and thin black socks, lifted her robes above her knees, and eased into the water calf deep. We were wearing shorts and waded in up to our waist. She cavorted in the water like she was dancing the polka at a local wedding, splashing and laughing, not minding she was soaking her robe and our shirts. Mickey went out a bit deeper and plunged under surfacing near the sandbar. She smiled at me, and I followed Mickey. After fifteen minutes of diving off of the edge of the sandbar, we stood next to her in the water, dripping from our clothes. "Do you ever get to swim in summer?" Mickey asked.

"Only at the convent in La Crosse. We have an indoor pool there. Long enough to swim laps."

"What do you wear?" he said, eyeballing the saturated skirt of her robe.

"Take a guess."

"Not skinny dipping?"

She laughed harder than I'd heard her all school year. "Black suits. But more skin than we can show at any other time."

We sat on boulders in the sun until our feet dried, shoed up, and walked back. We were about to saddle up on our bikes when Mickey asked, "How do you stand it?"

She laughed. "Which part of it?"

"Not diving under when it's hot."

"It's a sacrifice to God."

When we reached Bridgeton Public Library, she pulled over. "I'm leaving tomorrow for the summer. Enjoy yourselves, boys. See you in late August."

But Mary Agnes didn't come back. After two weeks of school, I asked my fifth-grade teacher, Sister Mary Rita, where she'd gone, but all she'd tell me was that Mary Agnes had been reassigned. A month later, while I was in the office paying for my lunch, I saw a pile of flyers for the Franciscan Order of Nuns sitting on the counter. Recruitment propaganda. It was not unusual in the 1950s for a pious Catholic girl to go directly to the convent out of eighth grade. I found the address of the convent in La Crosse and sent a letter addressed to "the nun in charge," explaining how much I liked Sister Mary Agnes, formerly of St. Peter's Grade School in Bridgeton, and that I wanted to send her a letter. It took four more letters to the convent and frequent pestering of the nuns at school before Sister Mary Rita sat me down after school in early February. "Lem, I've been asked to speak to you. You must stop inquiring about Mary Agnes."

"I just want to write her a letter."

"Well, you can't. She's no longer with us. That much I can tell you."

"Where did she go?"

"She left. Nobody knows."

Mary Rita sniffled. "We all miss her. She was my best friend here."

"Maybe she went back home."

"Don't know. She visited her family in the summer, somewhere around Stevens Point."

"What's her name—in real life?"

"Aggie. She kept her name when she joined us. Aggie Robinson."

After school, I hustled to the Bridgeton Public Library and looked through the Stevens Point phone directory. There were twenty-three Robinsons listed. Over the next week, I wrote to them all and received just three responses. Two said they didn't know Aggie Robinson, but the third said she was his brother's daughter and included their address in Wisconsin Rapids. I sent Mary Agnes a letter asking her to tell me why she had disappeared.

In early May, nearly a year after I had discovered Mary Agnes with her naked head extended into the westerly breezes, Mickey and I pedaled home from the slough down by the cemetery and set our bikes on our front lawn. As we walked into the living room, I was telling Mickey a joke about the loaves and the fishes that I'd heard in church. He stopped listening and pointed behind me. Mary Agnes was sitting on the sofa across from Mom, sipping lemonade. She stood up and laughed like she had countless times during our fourth-grade lessons. Her hair was pulled up under a Green Bay Packers cap, and she wore a pink flannel jacket over a navy blue T-shirt and rolled-up jeans. I'd rarely seen a girl wear jeans, except for the country girls from Halder. Mary Agnes' jeans looked like men's pants the way they hung on her trim torso. She strode over to us and shook our hands. Mickey was just as amazed as I was.

"I guess I owe you an explanation, Lemuel the King. Would you like to walk over to the river?"

My mother nodded. I didn't think she knew about my efforts to locate Mary Agnes, but she must have from the way she smiled at me. The three of us headed across Old Iron, not saying much until she stopped us halfway. "Let's go down to the beach."

When we reached it, Sister Mary Agnes removed her boots, rolled up her jeans above her knees, and waded into the water. Mickey and I thought it was too cold. She told us to sit on the rocks along the beach. "Boys, I've never talked to a former student about leaving the convent. But, Lemuel, you deserve to know after hunting me down like you did."

She brushed some wet sand from her feet and sat between us. "There's not much to say other than I had to go. And it had a lot to do with the two of you. When you discovered me that day with my veil off and the wind blowing through my hair, I realized how much I missed the way things used to be. And, Mickey, when you asked me how I could stand it, not diving under the cool water in hot weather, I made up my mind."

"You can just do that? Leave whenever you want?" Mickey blurted out.

"When they want you to go, it makes it easier."

"Did you do something wrong?" Mickey asked.

She stood up and walked along the shoreline. "Did I hurt her feelings?" Mickey whispered to me.

"Not sure."

She approached us again with an earnest look on her face, like she was about to explain a mystery of the Catholic faith. "To answer your question, Mickey, no, nothing wrong as much as it matters to me. But since I'm not in charge, it's not for me to say. They said I was a bad influence."

"Everybody loved you last year," I said.

"You and the rest of the kids were not the problem. It was the other nuns. And I think my superiors were right about that. So, it was best that I left."

"I thought being a nun was something you did for the rest of your life," I said.

"It could have been, but I'm not cut out for that life."

"What will you do now?" Mickey asked.

She laughed. "You guys ask more questions than anybody else I know. That's good. Shows you're curious."

She laced up her six-inch high work boots and shook the sand from her jeans. "I don't know what I'm going to do."

"From what Lemon says, you were the greatest teacher, so maybe you ought to continue doing that."

We walked back home, and Mom asked her to stay for supper, but Aggie said she had to get her parents' car back. She shook our hands, said goodbye with a hint of hesitation, and drove off. After Mickey took off home, Mom asked me to bike up to the A&P for hot dog buns. As I rounded Pine Street, I pulled up alongside Aggie Robinson's white Chevy station wagon parked a block from the bridge. She was standing on the grassy bank just above the river, and I watched her as she took out a red bandana and wiped her eyes and nose. I pedaled off before she could notice me.

Six

All You Have Is Hope

Everybody was thinking about it and, at the same time, too intimidated to say much about it. Because of it, the village council shut down the swimming pool for July and August. We brought dimes to school each week to help cure it, but it could still be lurking around the corner in the gymnasium or ascending from the urinals in the boys' bathroom as we splashed our pee onto the discolored porcelain. Waiting to attack us in the next mouthful of air we inhaled. A cloud of fear hovered over Bridgeton just like, we were told, it hung everywhere in the world in 1956.

We didn't dare call it by its name. To personalize it even in that common way was inviting it to join us at the lunch table in the commons or near our desks in our fifth-grade classroom. When Kurt Mestanek, who sat just ahead of me in our row by the windows, missed a week of school for a tonsillectomy in December, I was convinced it had taken him away permanently, and I would be forced to view his specter for the rest of the school year. Kurt and I were friends only during the school day, but on those nights during his absence, I talked to him under my warm bedding for an hour before I fell asleep, begging his forgiveness for not playing with him more at recess time.

A Depression-era photograph of former President Roosevelt sitting pensively in his wheel-chair was mounted on the front wall of our classroom, monitoring our thoughts, in startling contrast to the one next to it, of President Ike standing vigorously and grinning triumphantly in his World War II uniform. Whenever Mrs. Deffield assigned me to count the March of Dimes donations, I scrutinized every ten-cent piece, hoping I'd find more Roosevelts than Mercury Liberty Heads. The prevalence of Roosevelt disks would validate the optimism we were encouraged to display about our futures, allowing us to believe again in those words on the coins: "In God We Trust."

Jimbo willfully blocked it from his consciousness. If he allowed it to slip into his imagination for even a few seconds, he was asking it to be his companion, letting his guard down in the process. Though he was nearly a foot taller than everyone in our class with more natural muscle than most of us would accumulate in a lifetime, Jimbo was mouselike in his timidity. When words about it escaped my thoughts on occasion, he snapped at me to "shut it." His trepidation consumed him.

On the other hand, Lemon wanted to understand it, and he was smarter than anyone else in fifth grade. He eagerly read the medical journals in Doc's waiting room each month, even before Doc got to them. He told me about the scientists laboring away twenty-four hours a day in the most prestigious laboratories in Pittsburgh and Cincinnati searching for a vaccine. Since even the best scientists couldn't protect us from it, Lemon was looking elsewhere. He spoke about it openly on our way home from the skating rink at Dessert Park.

"I'm lucky I go to St. Peter's," Lemon confessed. "Maybe that will keep me safe."

"Safer than the rest of us at the public school?"

"Shit, Mickey. The laws of probability are such that some people will get it, so you need an edge to protect yourself. We get to pray anytime during the day. All you can do is hope."

"Maybe I'll start going to church more on Sundays."

Lemon shook his head, discounting my pious intentions as unsubstantial. "If Sister Mary Cecilia has the slightest inclination it's nearby, the whole school goes down on our knees. Does your teacher make you pray ten times a day?"

"Not even once."

"Normally, it doesn't matter where you go to school. This time it does."

"What about Joanne Michelsky?"

"She must have gotten sick before we started asking Jesus to protect us."

We reached Willow Street, the short cut home, but we'd have to pass in front of the Michelsky house. Lemon didn't pause at the corner but turned around when he noticed I was lingering. "Come on. Let's take the long way."

"I'm going down Willow."

"For Christ's sake, Mick. It could get you, and you're not even Catholic."

Lemon didn't waste another word of warning. He ran up to Eighth Street while I took a dozen uncertain steps. Bing Crosby's baritone filled the air from the speakers at the skating rink. "When I'm worried and I can't sleep, I count my blessings instead of sheep." My hockey skates circled my neck, the blades bouncing on my chest, as I moved more quickly toward Joanne's house. Doubting my decision, I dashed to the other side of the street and peered at her house, which was dark except for the kitchen nightlight. Was she in there? Barely moving? Could it pass through the door, skitter across the snow-crusted street, and find me?

Hunched over beside the snow banks, I raced down the icy sidewalk toward the far corner, the edges of my skate blades gouging into my parka, punishing me. Lemon was waiting outside the front door to his house. "What did you see?"

"Nothing."

"Nobody's seen her in months. Maybe she's withered up like that paralyzed raccoon we saw by the river, waiting for it to kill her."

"Let's ask Jimbo," I said, despite knowing his reluctance to discuss her.

We walked up to the McPhearson house, our shadows accompanying us in the clear moonlight. Jimbo's dad, Bridgeton's only physician, had regularly been inside the Michelsky home. "Is Doc around, Jimbo?"

"He's on a house call."

"What's he told you about Joanne Michelsky?" Lemon asked.

"That it's none of my business."

"Is he afraid to go into her house?" I said.

"He isn't scared about crap like that. He learned that in medical school."

Jimbo slept over in my bedroom a few days later, as he did on many Friday nights. Doc was frequently at the hospital in the evenings, and Jimbo's brothers were with their mother in Tomah. As a result, Jimbo was often alone and needed a companion. As our evening of silliness wound down near midnight and fatigue slipped into our conversation, I asked him why he was so frightened about it. He started to say "shut it," but before he could finish, I heard him sniffling. I waited until he turned back toward me before I said anything more. "You don't have to say. Just if you want to."

"I'm sure it'll get Dad. He's around sick people all day. In his office or their homes."

"They say it gets mostly kids."

"I'll be up shit creek. I'm not like you and Lemon, with two parents. I'm never going back with Mom. It'll just be me."

"Have you told your brothers?"

"Just Les. He told Jeremy, and he called me a big baby."

"What about Doc?"

"I can't tell him. It'll just get him faster."

I was too young to know how to comfort him, so I rolled over in my sleeping bag. Just before I fell asleep, I told him I wouldn't bring it up again. He reached over and slung his arm on mine. "I won't tell you to 'shut it' anymore."

I asked Mrs. Deffield if she thought we could do anything more about it. “My friend, Lemon Kraig, says they’re praying like crazy over at St. Peter’s.”

“You can pray anytime you want while you’re sitting at your desk. I’m not sure that will stop it, if you’re meant to get it.”

“What about Joanne Michelsky?”

“You should pray for her.”

“Was she meant to get it?”

Sobered by my question, she responded slowly. “I didn’t mean it like that, Mickey. Despite our precautions, some people will be infected. Some recover with a limp or a weakened arm. But sometimes it’s worse.”

Three nights later, I was alone at Dessert Park. Lemon was at church, pleading with God and St. Jude during the fifth day of a novena. The temperature had risen during the day and settled at forty degrees, softening the surface ice and slowing our skating speed by half. At seven-thirty, there were just three of us left on the rink. Chet Parker who sharpened skates and ran the concessions in the lodge spun a batch of recent hit songs: “Rock Around the Clock,” “Maybellene,” and “Ain’t it a Shame,” but none of them propelled my blades any faster. Then words I hadn’t heard in months poured out of the speakers. “Have faith, hope, and charity. That’s the way to live successfully.” As the lyric repeated itself, I edged closer to making up my mind, though I wished Lemon was with me so I could discuss my dilemma with him.

I trudged toward home in full deliberation. The low-hanging clouds and cold mist enveloped the sounds of the evening: pickup trucks rattling across Old Iron maintained the beat; Ella Marie Jansen’s high-pitched screaming directed at the boys who threatened her with a face washing of slushy snow formed the background vocal; and Tennessee Ernie Ford’s preacher’s sermon booming out of the speakers cautioned all of Bridgeton about the burdens of “Sixteen Tons.” The skates hanging from my shoulders felt that heavy. The warm winter air loosened the glaze that had been shellacked on the sidewalks for weeks, making each step more slippery than usual.

I stopped at the corner of Willow Street again and willed my legs toward Joanne's house. I stepped haltingly up to the porch and knocked. Lights came on in the entry way, and Mrs. Michelsky opened the door, her front covered by a soiled apron. She looked at me like I was making an incomprehensible mistake.

"Mickey. What are you doing here?"

"How's Joanne?"

"Come in. She's in her bedroom."

For the first time, I wondered how Mrs. Michelsky could still be standing since she was in the house with her daughter all day, but I followed her in and stood in the kitchen. She offered me a brownie, but I wouldn't touch it, my knit hat and chap mitts firmly in place. "She might be awake. Would you like to see her?"

She ushered me down the hallway past the sewing room. Mrs. Michelsky ran a seamstress business out of her house, but her tailoring mannequin was undressed, and the ironing board folded up. We stopped at the doorway to Joanne's room, the bedside lamp illuminating the right side of her wan face. "You have a visitor, honey."

Joanne tried to turn, but only her head moved, her face not expressing the least bit of surprise. Maybe it had driven even that possibility out of her. I could feel her looking at my skates. "How was the ice, Mickey?"

Her voice emerged out of a cavern of quiet and isolation like this was the first time she'd spoken in months. Her words barely resonated through the mentholated air in the house. "Too warm tonight. But it's been slick for weeks."

"I've wanted to skate all winter."

"Just like last year when we played tag."

"You always caught me even though I had faster skates."

With a great deal of effort, she rotated her face away. Her ivory leather figure skates balanced on a hook near her bed, a Christmas present from last season. They likely would have fit her this year. Mrs. Michelsky touched my shoulder, turning me back to the kitchen. "She's tired, Mickey."

I nodded and Mrs. Michelsky released me into a bitter, cold drizzle, her throat catching as she thanked me for visiting. "You're the first friend who's stopped over."

I hung my skates in the entryway inside our back door and sat down to remove my boots. I rubbed my cheeks and around my lips, then rushed to the bathroom and ran the shower. Mom knocked. "Mickey, are you OK?"

"I got all sweaty running home."

I scrubbed my face relentlessly until the water turned cold and put on clean pajamas. When I walked into the living room, Mom looked up from her magazine, startled. "What happened to your face?"

"Nothing."

"Looks like it's on fire."

"Do you think if I pray, I won't get it?"

"Get what?" Mom asked.

"And be like Joanne Michelsky?"

"Her mother just called. Said you stopped by."

"I shouldn't have."

"She said Joanne was glad you came."

"She didn't look happy."

"How could she. I wish you would have asked before you went."

"Will I get it now?"

"There's always a risk."

I lay awake that night, moving my legs and arms every ten minutes, listening to Mom crying on the other side of my bedroom wall. Dad reassured her, reaffirming what Mrs. Michelsky reported on the phone, that I hadn't gotten within fifteen feet of Joanne. When I fell asleep hours later, I dreamed of Joanne's four-poster bed sliding around on the ice at Dessert Park. Joanne had her skates on and repeatedly attempted to sneak out of bed, to catch up to me as I glided away, but each time her feet came close to the sparkling surface, it pulled her back. Her mouth moved in anguish, but I couldn't make out the words even as I skated closer and closer to her, near enough that it could easily capture and torment me like it did Joanne.

A week later, Lemon Kraig waited for me after school. "Joanne went to the hospital. She's going into the iron lung."

"Damn."

"I'm not sure what God's up to."

"Lemon, I went to see her last Wednesday."

"What! Her mom let you in?"

"I talked to Joanne."

"Why did you do that?"

"You told me all I had was hope. Must be the same for her."

Joanne died in late March, two months after my visit. Our class went to the funeral and sat behind the students from St. Peter's in the crowded church. I watched Lemon throughout the ceremony, Joanne's empty spot in the pew next to him. But he didn't sing along with the hymns or march to communion with the rest of the fifth graders from St. Peter's. That night thirty of us showed up at Dessert Park. It was to be the last cold night of the season. We formed a chain and skated around the rink for an hour. I was the final link, holding onto Lemon with my right hand, Joanne with my left. She wore her flowered flannel nightgown, the blades of her ivory skates glistening, newly sharpened on Chet Parker's grinder. On one turn, she disengaged from my hand and rushed to center rink leaping into the air and landing perfectly on her left foot, completing the acrobatic turn with a minute-long spin. Then she quietly rejoined the chain, the rest of us still somberly attached to each other, hoping we would not lose another from our circle of classmates. While I waited for

Lemon to change into his boots, she skated up to me one last time and curtsied. "Thanks, Mickey. Remember me next time."

On our way home, Lemon announced his intention to transfer to the public school. "Now? There's only a couple of months left in the year," I said.

"Mom doesn't want me to, and Dad says maybe next year. But I wish I could do it tomorrow."

"Why?"

"I don't believe in God anymore. Not after what happened to Joanne."

"Even if praying keeps you from getting it?"

"It's still not fair."

In October, a month into sixth grade, a poster of Dr. Jonas Salk appeared on our bulletin board with the triumphant headline: "The Fear Is Over! See Your Doctor Today!"

Seven weeks later, the thirty of us in our class marched the four blocks to Bridgeton City Hall. Lemon, who had been with us at the public school since September, moved back in line to stand with Jimbo and me as the queue crawled toward Doc McPhearson and the county nurse. Closer and closer to losing the fear. Jimbo stoically bared his fleshy bicep and took his medicine. When his father pulled the syringe out of his arm, he said, "It'll be all right now, son." Lemon barely winced when Doc injected him with the magical vaccine and didn't turn his eyes from the procedure, acknowledging that science had triumphed over his former beliefs.

When it was my turn, Doc said, "I know you took a special interest in Joanne. She'd want you to live for her sake." As the needle entered my arm, I pictured Joanne's polished skates glowing and flickering like votive candles on the wall in her bedroom.

Seven
Tea Party

We had just three more days remaining in our tumultuous sixth-grade year. Before that milestone, there was a much bigger one for seventy-nine young men and women of Bridgeton—high school graduation set for Sunday mid-afternoon. Jimbo's brother, Jeremy, would be celebrating the end of his rocky high school years. Their mother, Vera, who had moved to Tomah almost four years ago, was in town for the day and overnight, staying with us. She and Mom had maintained their friendship, especially with Jimbo living in our house over the past year. Vera could have slept at Doc's, in Jimbo's unused bedroom, but there was too much lingering ill will. The memories of Doc's affair with Beverly, Lucy's death, and Jeremy's abuse of Jimbo were nearly palpable within those walls. Vera knew more about Jeremy's volatility than Doc did because of the information Mom gave her, but Lemon and I were the only ones to whom Jimbo told the complete story.

Jimbo was still my roommate for three more days, but he was eager to resettle into his old room at Doc's. Since March, he'd been crossing off each day on a calendar near his bed. During his stay with us, Jimbo had rarely seen Vera other than for a week at Christmas and Easter weekend. He spoke to her on the phone in Dad's basement office on Sunday nights, but that was mostly him listening to Vera for fifteen minutes. Mom said they'd eventually have a lot to talk about.

Mom organized a late morning brunch on the day of graduation for the three of us and our mothers. None of us liked the "lady food": unsweetened ice tea, chicken salad sandwiches cut into triangles, and Mom's special lime Jell-O with chunks of celery and carrot. But we were expected to be there and enjoy our mothers' conversation about how the "vagaries" of life swept through every place, even a village as small as Bridgeton; how life could change dramatically whether your eyes were opened or closed; and how none of the three women ever expected to have a son graduating from high school. Little of their conversation seemed relevant to eleven-year-olds itching to get outside on a gorgeous, seventy-degree day.

Vera talked about the unpredictability of being a doctor's wife in our small town. Doc was always short of cash because he did too much doctoring for free. She had an assortment of memories I'd never heard before. Lyle Densmore bartering a side of beef from a sickly cow after Doc performed an appendectomy on Densmore's daughter. The meat was too tough except in boiled-down soup. The weekly visits from the "chicken lady," who faithfully delivered a freshly butchered chicken every Wednesday for a year because Doc was treating the "chicken lady's" mother. The McPhearson family got so weary of eating chicken that Vera gave the birds away. "Free" gallons of Altenburg milk, delivered every other day in glass jugs at the McPhearson's doorstep until a two hundred dollar medical bill was worked off. At least the milk was something the McPhearson family consumed. Vera made us laugh with her story-telling. Even Jimbo broke into a grin, and he'd heard most of the tales many times before. While she regaled us with her family's history, I could almost see why Doc would have wanted to be married to her.

Vera's memories were inching closer to the day she abandoned Bridgeton, leaving Doc and the boys, and Mom sensed it. She changed the subject to the graduation party, and Lizzie Kraig congratulated Vera on her upcoming nuptials. Jack Gordon was an accountant for a chain of banks in the Tomah area and made more money annually than Doc would see in several years of taking care of his patients. Vera described the extravagant home Jack built for her and his two kids, one of whom was in our grade.

Jimbo wouldn't talk much about Jack, other than he didn't like him or his kids. He didn't want to attend the wedding in late June but knew he had to. He was still fearful that Jeremy might seek his revenge over the incident at Beverly's house last fall once Jimbo was cut loose from the protective web of Bridgeton and the people watching out for him.

We endured an hour of lady chat and wanted to head out to the river for a few hours before Jimbo was scheduled to go to the graduation ceremony. I cleared my throat a few times and pointed to the clock on the mantle. Mom smiled and was about to let us go when Vera strolled back to center stage. "Jimbo, before you leave, I want you to thank Mrs. Pederson for all she's done this year."

"He calls me Janice. And he thanks me almost every day. He's more polite than either Mickey or Dennis," Mom said.

"That makes me proud. But I'd still like to hear him say it."

Jimbo looked at me like I should be helping him get through this. He stood up, something he knew his mother expected. "Janice, you've been very good to me. I know you didn't have to do it. So, thanks. You kind of saved me."

"It's been a pleasure, Jimbo."

Vera turned red-faced. Jimbo was sincere and polite, but having her son acknowledge Mom as something better than his real mother tripped a switch in her. "And thank Mickey, too, for sharing his room," she said briskly.

Lemon and I started laughing until our moms shushed us. Jimbo said, "Mom, that's not how we do it."

"Doesn't matter. Say it."

Vera was getting irritated, and Lemon and I could feel the change. "Get it over with, and we can get out of here," I whispered to Jimbo.

Jimbo nodded, understanding he had to make some peace, but his resentment toward his mother was bubbling up. He glowered at her as he said, "Mick, thanks for being my brother. You helped me out in a hundred different ways when I was all alone."

He meant it but didn't say it because he wanted me to feel good. He stared at his mother, challenging her. Vera's need for some level of retaliation reached a new level, but she masked it in a way even I had to admire. "I haven't told you, Jimbo. Might as well be right now. You're moving back with me next week. Jack and I have plenty of room in the new house. For all of us. You can make some friends in Tomah over the summer, so you'll know the kids when school starts in the fall."

The shockwaves reverberated around the room. Jimbo reached into his reserve of resiliency that had been mostly depleted during the past year. "That's not the plan, Mom," he said softly.

"Doc's agreed. Leslie will come back here to finish his last year. But you've got no reason to stay. You can start over in your new home."

"I can't do that," Jimbo said with more force, speaking for us all.

Vera's triumph rippled across her face. "It's time. I want you back."

Jimbo paused, his rage gathering force, then he exploded, "Jesus, what about the last four years. You just took off and left us. Now I'm used to it. I don't want to live with you and Jack."

He stormed out of the tea party while Lemon and I looked over at our mothers who were too stunned to say a word. Finally, Mom nodded and we followed him out.

Even though Jimbo was already pedaling away on his bike, we knew he was headed to the same place we gathered when anything went wrong. We caught up to him on Old Iron, climbed down to Little Bull Falls and sat on our favorite rocks. Jimbo wouldn't look up at us. I figured he was crying, but when he finally glanced up, he revealed a visage of fierceness and pure defiance, like when he fired his .22 over Jeremy's head. I could envision him running away from Tomah and hitchhiking back to Bridgeton, over and over, until Vera finally got the message.

We rode back to Doc's house. Leslie and Jeremy were already at the high school, and Doc was getting dressed, so we waited until he came downstairs. He was surprised to see us there, in ambush formation. "Jimbo, not going to graduation?"

"Don't think so, Dad."

"Figured you'd gone with your mother. She'll be—disappointed if you don't show up."

"Was it your idea, Dad?"

Doc knew right away. "You moving with her to Tomah?"

The three of us nodded. "Nope. It's all her. But she's your mother. She deserves some of the years with you before you and your brothers drift away."

"What about the years he's spent here, Doc?" I said.

He chuckled at my determination. "You and your parents going to take him in again, Mick? Is that what this is about?"

Lemon came to our rescue as he often did. "Doc, he's got more people here than he has in Tomah. Mickey's family, my family, you, Les."

Doc pondered Lemon's argument, always more respectful of Lemon's ideas than Jimbo's or mine, but didn't say a word until he looked at his watch. "Shit, we'll be late."

"He can't go dressed like this," Lemon said.

Doc looked at our muddy jeans and sneakers. "Been down at the river. OK. I'll drive you over to Mickey's."

We sat silently in the back seat of Doc's sedan until he pulled into our driveway. "Hurry up. If you're not back in five minutes, I'm leaving. Then you can deal with your mother on your own."

Jimbo sat on his bed, tucked into the nook of my bedroom, still riveted by his bitterness. "He's your only chance, Jimbo," Lemon said.

"No, he's not," but he took off his jeans and T-shirt and changed into clean clothes.

It turned out, Jimbo was right. Doc couldn't save him this time.

Maybe he didn't have the courage to stand up to his ex-wife. When we strolled into the graduation party at Doc's house later than most of the guests, Jeremy was laughing with his friends and wouldn't have noticed if Jimbo was there or not. We ate two pieces of chocolate cake and sipped some lemonade as we snuck out back. "Let's get out of here," Jimbo said.

It was dark so we didn't initially notice the three lawn chairs in the middle of the backyard, but when we did and realized it was our mothers talking, we crouched down as Mom spoke. "Vera, Lizzie and I know what it means to love our kids. And it must hurt like hell to be separated from them."

Lizzie Kraig joined in. "We can't tell you what to do. But we love Jimbo like he's one of our own. We're not his mother. More like his aunts. Bridgeton has held him together since you left. You must have had good reason to leave, Vera, or you would never have done it. You're sensible like that. But Jimbo's got people here. Even though Doc is sometimes the least of them."

We could hear Vera's sniffles and her halting words. "Do you know how it feels—to see him love you two more than he loves me? Mickey and Lemon are more his brothers than Jeremy and Les. I want him back. I want to restore my family. It starts with Jimbo."

"He'll always love you. But if you force him to go, you'll lose some of what's left. Are you ready for that?" Lizzie said.

Vera got up from her chair, heading toward us, but we were still invisible to her. When she bumped into Jimbo, she stumbled and nearly fell. Jimbo, already a few inches taller than his mother and nearing one hundred and fifty pounds, rose up and grabbed his mother to keep her from tumbling, as effortlessly as if he were lifting a five-year-old girl. Vera held on, and without intending to, for an instant, they looked like they were supporting each other. Maybe they'd not done this for each other in years. Vera broke down further into tears and clutched Jimbo as hard as she could though he barely responded to her embrace. She gripped him by his shoulders, standing him straight in front of her. "You don't want to go, do you?"

"Mom, I can't go. I don't know if you understand that."

I wasn't sure what Jimbo meant, but he was determined to make his case. "Everything's here. It's my home. Where my friends live. I'm moving in with Dad again when Jeremy goes back."

"Is that it? Jeremy?"

"He's part of it. The bad part. I want to stay for the good stuff, Mom."

Lizzie and Mom stood alongside us as we listened to Vera weep like she'd just lost her one-year-old. Jimbo enclosed her fingers in his hands that were already as big as an adult's, but he held his mother's hands as tenderly as if his half-sister Lucy were still alive and swaying in his arms. He didn't break down as he had for days after Lucy died. Living away from his family for nearly a year had toughened him up in a way that I hadn't noticed during all the months he slept just ten feet away from me in my bedroom. It was as though he had been scheming at night, long after I'd fallen asleep, about what he'd need to do to keep his real family intact if he were ever threatened with its dissolution. Maybe Vera saw this or, just as likely, she gave in just as she had let him stay on with Doc years earlier. Vera kissed her son on the forehead. "OK, then. Just don't forget me. That would break my heart."

We left Jimbo and Vera sitting on the lawn chairs in the McPhearson's backyard and walked the three blocks home, our mothers a few steps behind us. Lemon and I wanted to go back and retrieve Jimbo, so when we reached our driveway, we turned to ask. We didn't have to say a word. Lizzie laughed. "I told you, Janice."

"The back light will be on. There's school tomorrow. Everyone's got to get up," Mom said.

Eight

Dirty Joe – Part One

Joe Rebenick was a Bridgeton legend, but the three of us had rarely seen him. Twice we caught glimpses when we were on Old Iron, and he was fishing at the dam. More recently, he flashed by when we were biking near Dessert Park, scurrying into the woods with a bundle over his shoulder heading down a ravine toward Skunk Hollow, like a red fox when he detected the presence of humans. I heard him at our back door a few weeks after Jimbo moved back into Doc's house, talking with Dad, but when I peered out the kitchen window, I could only see a sun-bleached, brown fedora covering his face. Their voices were low, occasionally chuckling, but I didn't dare join them.

Mom was waiting for Dad when he came in after twenty minutes. "What did Dirty Joe want this time? More cash?"

"He's got his own money. Inherited everything from his parents. I've told you that."

"Why do you give him more then?"

"Sometimes he borrows ten or twenty from me until I can get to the bank. I always get it back."

"You shouldn't have let yourself get hooked into managing his money."

"We were neighbors growing up. I played with him just like Mickey does with Jimbo and Lemon. He's harmless."

"The women are complaining about him hanging around the playgrounds. Mrs. Strosnek claims he exposed himself."

"He wouldn't do that. Even if he's not right, he wouldn't do that."

When Dad and I were alone, I asked him about Dirty Joe not being right. "The war. We were together during basic, and he ended up in the Philippines. Spent over two years in a Japanese prison camp. Hasn't been the same since he came back."

"Does he work?"

"Lemon's dad hires him once in a while when he's got some carpentry work. For the most part, he doesn't have to. His parents left him with enough, but they made sure he couldn't get at it."

"That's why you take care of his money?"

"He'd fritter his wealth away if I let him. Drinks enough as it is using his allowance and what people give him. He spends most of his time by himself."

"Where does he go?"

"In the winter, in the heated garage at his folk's old place on Jefferson Street. Turned the single-car stall into his version of an apartment. He doesn't use the house much other than for storage."

"What about when it's warm?"

"Not sure where he goes. Different camps along the river."

Later that summer, Jimbo, Lemon, and I were exploring behind Skunk Hollow. As we were resting under the cottonwoods near the river, Jimbo was the first to smell the smoke. Thinking it might be a forest fire, we followed the scent trail. Over Coyote Ridge and down in the hollow, we glimpsed a campfire. We watched from behind a stack of boulders and saw two small tents, a clothesline draped with shirts, trousers, and socks, a table built of driftwood, a big stack of firewood, and two stools near the campfire. Dirty Joe was bustling about in shorts and flip-flops, checking a pot of steaming food over the coals of a well-established fire pit. When the wind blew our way, we could hear him humming as he read a book under the shade of the oaks and hickories.

We made our way as quietly as we could. Joe stood and gazed at us when we were halfway down, watching us clamber about, before settling back onto his stool. He nodded when we reached the edge of his campsite. "Walleye stew in about fifteen minutes. Be happy to share."

His dark hair was long and wet in back, and his thin black beard hung to his sternum, covering most of his hairless chest. His skinny legs looked like toothpicks running down from his army-issue boxers. He felt the clothes on the line. "Just washed them down at the river." He chuckled. "Took a bath, too. Hardly recognize me as Dirty Joe. Give me a few days, and I'll darken up again."

He lifted a bottle of clear liquor like he was thinking about offering it to us. "Your daddies would never forgive me if I gave you this. But it won't be a surprise when you tell them I'm drinking. It's what I do."

"Dad doesn't know where you live in summer."

"Been here for a few weeks. Nice spot. Not far from the river. Mosquitoes are bad most everywhere I go, which is one reason I stay dirty. They like me less."

He filled three tin cups with stew. "Only have one spoon. You can drink most of it. Use your fingers for the rest."

The mix of potatoes, carrots, onion, and fish was too hot to sip, so we set the cups down. "Where'd you catch the walleye, Joe?" Jimbo asked.

"Downriver a bit. There's a nice hole."

"We've seen you from the bridge a few times," I said.

"Yeah, I know. I've watched you at your beach. That's a beautiful spot. One of my favorite bathing holes."

We ate our stew and cleaned out the cups in a basin of water. "We better go. Thanks," I said.

"Come anytime. I like visitors. Truth be told, you're the first this season."

We returned a half-dozen more times over the next few weeks and brought him cans of beans or fresh plums and peaches, which he appreciated. Joe was right about the dirt. Most days his face was as grimy as the river mud. He gave us a shopping list and ten dollars for our next visit. "Save me the trouble. Nobody in town likes it when I show up. This way I can just stop into the liquor store near closing time."

Two days later, loaded down with ketchup, pork chops, potatoes, oranges and bananas, we approached Dirty Joe's camp. There were signs of disturbance everywhere. Coals from the campfire were scattered about, both tents were ripped to shreds, and food stocks were thrown into the woods. The few clothes Joe had that he wouldn't have been wearing were tossed aside, his bedding in a tumbled pile caught in the brambles. Lemon noticed a trail of blood, and we followed it toward the river. We found Dirty Joe near the shoreline, collapsed in a heap, unconscious but breathing. When we rolled him onto his back, Lemon discovered the puncture wound underneath his crimson-stained undershirt. Lemon took off his blue T-shirt, ripped it into thin strips, and stuffed them into the hole in Joe's chest. Joe moaned as Lemon pressured his wound. "Joe! Joe! Can you hear me?" I shouted.

There was no response as he slipped into deeper silence. "What should we do, Lemon?" Jimbo asked.

"We've got to get him out of here."

Jimbo took off without a word. I assumed he was heading back to town—over a mile away, but he was back in ten minutes, a pistol in his hands. "Where'd you get that?"

"Thought I saw it near his tent. We might need it."

It was the first time I thought about us being in danger. "There's no way anybody can drive down here. We can try to carry him back," Lemon said.

"He must weigh over two hundred pounds," Jimbo said.

The only exit was downriver at the landing, a mile away. Jimbo said he'd go, but just then, we heard an outboard coming our way. Jimbo and I waded out into the river up to our thighs, but the boat's motor seemed to cut away. "Shit," Jimbo said as we listened.

He pulled the pistol from his belt and fired it into the air. Nothing. He fired again, then three more times, finally drawing the outboard toward us. A DNR boat with two green uniforms headed our way. The shoreline was too rocky to land the boat, so we talked to them out in the water, explaining that Dirty Joe was barely alive, but the greenies just wanted to talk about the gun. Jimbo handed over the weapon and they examined it. "Where'd you get it?" one of the greenies demanded.

"Found it at Joe's camp," Jimbo said.

"Smith and Wesson Victory. Looks like World War II issue," the other greenie said. "Why were you firing it?"

Jimbo and I glanced at each other, annoyed at their idiocy. "Joe might be dying," I said.

They looked at us as though this was a ruse. "Show us."

We pulled the boat as close to shore as we could get it. Lemon had been listening to our conversation and shouted, "Over here."

One of the greenies jumped into a foot of water and ran over to Lemon and Joe. He quickly clicked on his walkie-talkie, demanding an ambulance at the landing in ten minutes. Knowing it would have to come from Wausau, that meant at least thirty.

Lemon held the boat while Jimbo, the greenies, and I lifted Joe to the boat. One of the greenies jumped in while the rest of us eased Joe to the gunwale and rolled his body over the side. The greenies yanked Lemon in beside Joe and told Jimbo and me to walk back. We watched the boat disappear around the bend and headed back to Joe's camp. We examined the ransacked mess more closely but didn't see anything more unusual than we'd observed in a rush the first time, so we hurried to Jimbo's house.

Dirty Joe was on a gurney in Doc's office, and Doc had already cut off Joe's shirt and was carefully extricating the bloody packets of Lemon's T-shirt from the wound, interrogating Lemon as he did. "Was he ever conscious?"

"No. We found him by the river. A trail of blood the whole way."

He tossed the bloody strips into a trash can and poked around the wound. The bleeding had been stanched considerably by Lemon's work, despite the jostling Joe underwent getting to the ambulance, but Lemon still went through a dozen gauze pads soaking up the blood as Doc probed around in the wound. "The puncture wound's not bad. But it's deep. Hard to know if it's reached his heart."

He cleaned the wound with saline and antibiotics, stuffed it with clean gauze packs, and covered the bandages with long strips of adhesive. The ambulance men came back in from their cigarette break, and Doc told them to take Joe to St. Mary's. They suggested Doc catheterize him for the trip. Jimbo and I removed Joe's boots and socks while Doc cut through Joe's muddy trousers and urine-stained underwear. He handed me the pieces of clothing, and the smell from his dirty boxers was so strong I turned away as I set them on the trash container. I kept waiting for Doc to tell us to leave, but he'd already recruited Lemon as his assistant and didn't mind us being there. He quickly inserted the tubing through Joe's shriveled up penis, but Joe didn't whimper or budge. When Doc was done, he motioned to the driver who covered Joe with several wool blankets.

Doc and Lemon cleaned up the medical supplies, and as Jimbo and I gathered the remnants of Joe's clothing, Doc said, "You did good, boys. Maybe saved him. Put the clothing in a bag. Cops might want to have a look."

He called the hospital and Sheriff Menderson and briefly explained what happened. He nodded several times before he hung up.

"I'm headed up to St. Mary's. You three better stick around. They'll be wanting to question you about the crime."

Nine
Dirty Joe – Part Two

Doc called an hour later, and Dirty Joe was alive but still unconscious, heading into surgery. We waited for the police in Doc's kitchen, but it took another two hours before two county detectives finally interrogated us. They looked at us skeptically, having a hard time believing we might have had a hand in Joe's rescue. "What did you touch at the crime scene?" the chubby one with a blond crewcut asked.

"Just the pistol," Jimbo said. "But we've been down there a lot, and somebody really messed things up."

Like the greenies, they wanted to talk more about the gun, "Did you have the pistol with you when you showed up at Joe's?"

"I found it underneath his bedding, in the brambles," Jimbo said.

"Why'd you shoot Joe," the tall detective with a moustache said, more a statement than a question.

I looked at Lemon and Jimbo, all of us wondering why the detectives would be accusing us. Hadn't they been to the hospital and talked to Doc?

"Tell us the truth, boys. It'll be easier if you do."

"He wasn't shot," Lemon said. "It's a puncture wound."

"How do you know that?"

"Pretty obvious. Doc confirmed it."

"The gun's been fired."

"Jimbo fired it to bring in the boat, the one with the greenies," I said.

The detectives smirked like they'd caught us in a trap.

"How many times?"

"Five," Jimbo said.

"Why were you visiting Joe in the first place?"

"We discovered his campsite when we were roaming around near Skunk Hollow. Visited him a bunch of times after that. Usually, we brought him some food," I said.

"Did you want to hurt him?"

We understood we needed to be cautious. "If we wanted to hurt him, why'd we rescue him?" Lemon pointed out.

"Think you're pretty smart, Kraig? Knowing a little bit about doctoring."

None of us responded. "How much money did he have?"

"We didn't see any more than what he gave us for groceries. Ten bucks," Jimbo said.

Dad walked in just then. "Officers, you should have called me when you decided to talk to the boys."

"Just friendly questioning. They're not at any risk. We're just getting to the money."

Dad snorted. "Joe's money?"

"Yeah. Figure that's the most likely reason he was attacked."

"He's living in a camp in Skunk Hollow. Why would anybody want what he's got?"

"Story goes, he's got a lot of money stashed away."

"I take care of it. His family directed me to in their will. Joe gets twenty-five dollars a week."

"Maybe he had more than you know?"

"Doubt that, unless there's something he's been hiding. He spends most of what he's got on drink."

"Does your boy know that?"

Dad was confused. "Know what?"

"That Joe might have had twenty-five dollars?"

Dad laughed at them. "That they'd stab him nearly to death for his allowance, then get the rangers to rescue him? Want me to check their pockets?"

"The boys were the last to see him. That we know. We have to follow every possible lead."

"I guess you do. Cause what you're suggesting makes about as much sense as me robbing Mickey's piggy-bank."

The detectives left after that. By the next morning, they'd arrested Benny Unertal and Frankie Kronenwetter. The two of them had been seen by mill workers under the bridge the morning of the stabbing with knives and cash in their pockets. Besides, they'd been in trouble with the law on numerous occasions.

Joe regained consciousness two days later, but Doc said he wasn't talking to the detectives, and he couldn't remember a thing about the attack. Doc took us up to see him on Sunday morning. Joe was sitting up in bed, tubes flowing into his chest and arm, the catheter still running out of him. He nodded to us as Doc examined him. "Surgeon said you'll be OK as long as the chest wound doesn't get infected. The knife missed your heart and aorta by half a breath. You're a lucky man, Joe."

"Where am I gonna go?"

"You'll be here for another week, at least. We'll find someplace after that."

"Maybe back at my camp."

Doc laughed. "Camp's destroyed. Maybe you didn't hear. The boys want to visit for a while. I'll be back in an hour to pick them up."

Joe smiled when we crowded around his bed. "You get my groceries?"

"Left them when we got there," Jimbo said. "Something else took priority."

"How'd you find me?"

"Lemon saw the blood trail to the river," I said.

"You stuffed my wound, Lemon?"

"That was easy. Getting you out was the hard part."

"Figured I was a dead man when they skewered me with that knife."

We all paused. "Who're you talking about?" I asked.

"Two guys."

"Benny and Frankie?" I said.

"Mighta been. It was early morning and still dark."

"Jesus, Joe, you gotta be more specific than that," Jimbo said.

"Told the cops I don't remember. Maybe that's the best I can do."

"But if it's not Benny and Frankie, they're still out there," I said.

"I don't think they got what they wanted."

"What's that?" I asked.

"Go down there and find out."

Later that afternoon, we returned to Skunk Hollow, carrying a shovel, even though Joe said he'd left one at the camp. We took our time, approaching his demolished camp from the far side of Dessert Park. Joe said he buried it behind the hickory tree where he tied his clothesline. Jimbo dug just a foot before he hit the parcel wrapped in plastic, but we didn't want to open it there, figuring the cops or the men with the knives might be watching. We raced back out to Dessert Park, taking turns carrying the shovel, crouching down behind the shelter, our chests pumping with anxiety, listening for footsteps. After fifteen minutes, we slowly unwrapped the package. There was more money than any of us had ever seen.

Joe hadn't told us what to do with it, so we took it to my house. Dennis was mowing the front lawn, and Mom was working a shift at the hospital. Dad was cleaning the inside of his old truck but didn't look up as I leaned against the open door. "Joe said you visited. That was nice." Dad spent an hour with him that morning after we left.

"Yeah. He told us something," Lemon said.

Dad laughed, finally giving us eye contact. "Like who tried to kill him?"

"Come on, Dad. This is serious."

"I know. The cops arrested the two kids in Dennis' class."

"Joe doesn't know who did it," I said.

"Or wouldn't say," Dad said.

"But we found this. Figured you should take care of it."

Dad opened the package and counted the three thousand dollars. "Damn. Where'd you find it?"

"Dug it up by Joe's camp. He told us where. Figured that's what the guys were after," Jimbo said.

"Come on. Let's go see him."

Joe was snoozing, so we went down to the cafeteria and had an early supper, killing nearly an hour until he woke up. When he saw us, he grinned. "Matty Pederson. And the boys. Twice in one day. Am I dreaming or what?"

"Hey, Joe," Dad said as he opened the package. "Where'd you get the money?"

"Sometimes I don't spend all you give me."

"Not three thousand dollars you don't."

"Momma had some hidden. Told me not to tell anyone. Not even you."

"You must have told somebody."

"Maybe somebody overheard me bragging. At Kennedy's Pub. That was pretty stupid."

"Not one of your brightest moments. When was that?"

"Two weeks ago, if I remember right. The days are kind of blurred. Went up to Kennedy's to get some refills."

"Who was there?"

"Can't recall. Jimmy Kennedy would know. He's the one who kicked me out."

"What do you want me to do with the money?"

"You weren't supposed to know, Matty. Now what am I gonna do?"

Dad laughed. "Same as you've been doing, Joe."

The same two detectives arrived at the hospital an hour later and looked at us like we'd just escaped from jail. They arrested two men from Wittenberg by the next morning, and Benny and Frankie were released. Dirty Joe spent the next three weeks at our house, but Mom didn't know what to do with him. He kept wanting to sleep in our tent, in the backyard, so finally, we set it up. I fixed up a cot with plenty of blankets and pillows and asked him if he wanted me to sleep in the tent with him. "What for?"

"Just to have someone. That's what we'd do."

"Haven't had that since the military. It's OK if you want to. Lemon and Jimbo can come, too."

Dad had Dirty Joe's keys, and we went with him to check out his garage apartment. It needed a thorough cleaning, so Dad paid us ten dollars each to make it sparkle. He spent most of Joe's three thousand dollars on a new shower stall, refrigerator, and furnace unit and hired Lemon's dad to install three double-hung windows for ventilation.

We went down to Joe's camp, which was no longer a crime scene, and gathered what was salvageable: blankets, cooking utensils, a few books, cans of food, the clothesline, an axe, and a few sets of clothing. We washed his clothes at the laundromat and hauled a dresser down from Joe's old bedroom in the house next door.

When it was completed and Joe was ready to be on his own again, we walked Joe over. He wasn't surprised. Somehow, he'd heard what we were up to and didn't seem impressed. He said it was a bit too civilized for his taste and wanted to know if we'd brought the tents up from the camp. We reminded him that his assailants from Wittenberg had shredded them. "Guess I'll have to get a new one," Joe mused. "The garage will be OK for now. Until I finish healing."

A few weeks later, Jimbo and I went to see Joe. The garage was locked, and we looked in the windows, but there was no sign of him. We wandered down to Skunk Hollow, but his old camp was empty and still disheveled. We decided to hike up to Discovery Beach. We splashed through the shallows reliving the events of the county fair in Wausau, and when we turned the last bend, we saw Dirty Joe sitting on a log. He had set up his new tent under the lone willow tree on the beach. He had a campfire going and nodded like he'd been expecting us. "Figured I might as well set up closer to my bathing hole. Hope you don't mind me invading your privacy."

Jimbo and I stripped down and jumped in the water. "How long you gonna stay, Joe?" I asked.

"Not sure. You know, your dad and I used to come to this little beach when we were your age."

"He could probably find you, then, if he wanted."

"Don't tell him I'm here. I need to get away from things for a while."

PART TWO

Life in Bridgeton was always more than the grid of village streets and county roads, more than the houses, farms, businesses, schools, and churches that demarcate any city or village in Wisconsin. Those are merely the dots on a map. But when a patient entered my two-room home office, or, more particularly, when I stepped into the kitchen of the farmhouse where a patient lived, the mysterious space between the dots filled in. In my profession, the drama of human existence unfolds in the realms of sickness and fear and hovers between life and death, coming alive when a doctor treats his patients in this traditional way.

From *The Lives of Small-Town Doctors of Minnesota and Wisconsin: 1925—1975*, (Chapter Five: “Doc McPhearson”). Dr. Lemuel Kraig, editor. University of Minneapolis Press.

Ten
Little Lemon

Lemon had three younger sisters—Esther, Sarah Ruth, and Baby Eve—all named after characters from the Old Testament, just as Lemuel was. Ted Kraig was enamored with the book, but more as literature than scripture, even though the Kraigs were faithful members of St. Peter's parish, other than Lemon, who fell away after fifth grade. His dad understood Lemon was wise enough to think for himself, despite his age.

Esther was quite the opposite. She stayed after school to help the nuns at St. Peter's and was invited to the nuns' residence on weekends. She wore an authentic nun's habit, coif, and veil every Halloween night for three years running. Lemon was worried she might run off to the convent after eighth grade. Little Eve was the youngest by five years. An accidental child, though Catholics had an abundance of those in the 1950s. Eve followed everyone around, insisting she was old enough to be included. It didn't matter if it was Esther or Lemon, Jimbo, and me.

But she never trailed after Sarah Ruth. Nobody did. Sarah Ruth was a child "of her own mind," as her aunts, uncles, and teachers said of her. She bore an uncanny resemblance to Lemon. Same flaxen hair, blue eyes, and broad smile with a split in her front teeth. She walked and ran just like him and talked in the same energetic voice, though usually, her utterances were fewer than ten words long. They shared the same excitable hand gestures like a pair of goldfinches fluttering over a birdbath. Lemon tried to deny the similarity, but Jimbo and I kidded him relentlessly, until he finally acknowledged what everyone could see. Jimbo called her Little Lemon.

Sarah Ruth wasn't nearly as smart as her brother, but nobody was. It was hard to tell how bright she was because of her single-minded and fierce loyalty to the patterns she followed every day. Anything out of the routine upset her equilibrium. As a result, she resisted the free-flowing games we organized in the backyard or basement of the Kraig home, preferring to be by herself.

When Sarah Ruth was ten and Lemon, Jimbo, and I thirteen, Sarah Ruth disappeared. She was playing by herself in the backyard, something she often did. When Lemon went out to get her for lunch, she was gone. Lizzie Kraig was at work at Wausau Mutual, and Ted was gardening at his family's farm north of Bridgeton. Lemon called all the homes he suspected Sarah Ruth might be visiting. No luck. Lemon, Jimbo, and I spent the afternoon biking around town and along any side road Sarah Ruth might have mistakenly taken. We scoured the city parks, checked the labyrinths in the basement of St. Peter's Church, and searched the pine forest behind the Bridgeton swimming pool. We queried kids headed to the library and adults on their way to the store, but there was no sign of her.

We stopped back at Lemon's house, fueling up on sandwiches and milk. Lizzie was home from work talking to Chief Edwards in the living room, trying to exude confidence. Little Eve was crying while Esther comforted her, fingers intertwined in prayer. As we listened to Lizzie and Chief Edwards talk, we began to understand the fear that undermined every guess about Sarah Ruth's whereabouts. The inexorable and mysterious flow of the Wisconsin River. We had all been warned of its dangers since we were young enough to walk, but we never thought about the hazards as we played along the water's edge. The Kraig's backyard was just two blocks from the riverbank.

Lemon had heard enough of the fears, so we headed back out, this time to ferret around in every place we knew along the river. We walked the shoreline from the cemetery to the bridge, in the process, discovering hideouts we'd never seen before. We snooped around every cluster of rocks near Little Bull Falls. I refused to watch the water pouring over the dam, thinking the half-submerged body of Sarah Ruth might roll over the top, like a fallen pine tree on its journey from Eagle River to Prairie du Chien. We searched the area below the dam, all the way to Discovery Beach, our voices hoarse from calling out to her.

We returned to Lemon's house for flashlights, determined to spend the night looking for her. Mom had come home from the hospital as soon as she heard the news and was cleaning up the supper dishes in the Kraig kitchen. Lizzie, normally the calmest of women, was beside herself, sniffling, trying to comfort Esther and Little Eve who were weeping uncontrollably. A pair of rosaries were discarded on the coffee table. Mom pulled me outside. "You need to come home, Mickey. You've done your best for the day. You can pick it up again in the morning."

"She's out there, somewhere, Mom. She can't spend the night by herself."

"Ted's looking every place you could imagine. The police are searching with their dogs. Jimbo can spend the night. Make plans for tomorrow using every bit of knowledge you have about the river."

Jimbo and I talked for an hour in my room. We fell asleep without sensing it coming upon us and woke up as dawn was sneaking around the back porch. Dad was already up, and Ted and Lemon were sitting in the kitchen, strategizing. No one wanted to utter the words of despair. The three of us biked toward the river as the sun was rising over the backyard, with single-minded intent, finding Dirty Joe.

We figured he'd be camping out, as he did throughout the warm weather months. We tramped through the dewy grounds of Skunk Hollow, past several campsites Joe had used over the years, but there was no sight of him. We walked back to town and pedaled to his garage apartment and were surprised to see his laundry hanging from a clothesline running from the corner of the garage to a gigantic maple tree. Joe was sitting on a lawn chair out front of the garage, catching the morning sun, a bowl of hot oatmeal on his lap. He nodded. "Hey, boys. Out early."

"Figured you'd be down in a camp," I said.

"Was until last week. Fell and broke my collarbone. Holed up here for a few weeks."

"We're looking for my sister, Joe. Checked down by your old camps in Skunk Hollow."

"Sarah Ruth. Police came by last night. Wondered if I'd seen her."

"Any other old camps along the river?" Lemon continued.

"One or two. I'll go down with you in a bit. But Lemon, you ought to be home, helping out. I'll go down with Mickey and Jimbo."

"Nothing to do there but cry and fret. Listening to the adults not talking about her drowning," Lemon said.

"I understand. Still, that's the best place for you. When they find her, you can let your buddies know."

Lemon finally agreed and pedaled off home, relieved to think that in Joe's mind she was still alive, but Lemon was wrong about Joe. "I didn't want him with us," Joe said. "We might run into Sarah Ruth. Odds are she'll be washed up. He shouldn't see that."

He was the first to speak this bluntly about her fate, and the words caught us off guard. "Why did the cops come, Joe?" I wondered.

"The usual. Because I'm an ornery drunk, thinking I might have made off with her. Or worse. I'm an easy target."

We made a bundle of sandwiches and filled two quart jars with water which we wrapped in towels. Jimbo loaded our lunch into Joe's World War II knapsack, Joe slid his right arm into his harness, and we headed off to the woods beyond Skunk Hollow. We skirted around Trillium Woods and stood before Jonserud Marsh, ablaze with marsh marigolds. We circled around it from both directions, fearing the worst whenever we passed by the deeper water. Joe led us to an old camp just up the rise from the marsh, but there was no sign of Sarah Ruth. We walked the river shoreline all the way to the landing. Fifteen trucks were parked there, a few still unloading their boats to join the river search party. Joe waved to one. “Hey, Robby. Looking for the Kraig girl?”

“Yup. Hope I’m not the one to find her. The river’s high from last week’s rain, so she might be a ways downstream.”

“We’re checking the shoreline,” Joe muttered.

We left Robbie and sat on a fallen log eating ham sandwiches. “What’s Sarah Ruth like?”

“Unusual. Something different about her,” Jimbo said.

“Could she walk five miles?”

“Probably. When she decides to do something, she’s determined. No one can stop her. She’s focused like that,” I said.

“But she’s never been along the river down here?”

“Don’t think so. No reason to come this far. Maybe under the bridge once or twice. Not any further,” Jimbo said.

“I’ve been thinking. It’s a long shot. There’s a place, must be two miles beyond here. One of my best camps. A good-sized cave just a short distance from the river.”

We walked in a southerly direction, downriver, and the deer trail petered out, forcing us to bushwhack through brambles or into the woods away from the river. Joe always brought us back toward the water when a trail resumed. Periodically we’d hear a motor from a boat and deep-voiced men yelling, “Sarah Roooth! Sarah Roooth!” Their vocal emphasis elongated the last syllable, their pleas echoing across the valley of the riverbed. Sometimes, multiple voices from different skiffs seemed to call out to each other with her name. Halfway to the cave, we found a child’s shoe, half-in, half-out of the water, a cheap sneaker from Woolworth’s, sole and heel worn down. It looked like the one Lizzie described, a hand-me-down from Esther.

We identified shreds of cotton caught in berry brambles a short distance later. Joe fingered them. “Fresh enough that it could be hers.” Twenty yards more, just below a hill laden with sharp sandstone rocks, Joe pointed to drops of blood. We followed the trail of scarlet for another quarter mile until Joe pointed toward a thicket of scrappy willows and cottonwoods. "The cave's up there another twenty yards."

The cave was so well hidden that we would have walked right past it if Joe hadn't stopped. We had lost sight of the blood on the last part of the trail, but now we saw bigger splats. Joe stooped down, led us inside, and flicked on his flashlight to illuminate the deep recesses of the fifty-foot deep cave. We saw Sarah Ruth motionless on her side, faced away from us in the far corner. We scooted back toward her, Joe struggling with his shoulder injury, stooping at the same time as the ceiling of limestone was less than four feet in some sections. Joe scanned the cave with the light, and we saw remnants of his old camp. Joe was the first to touch her, feeling for a pulse on her neck. "She's alive, by God," he yelled. "Help me turn her."

Sarah Ruth mumbled and moaned as we repositioned her onto her back. We emptied Joe's backpack, stuffed it with our shirts and the towels, and placed it under her head. Jimbo held the flashlight as Joe examined her, and he seemed to know what he was doing, which surprised me. Sarah Ruth's face was dirty and streaked with blood, but mostly from scratches. The blood we'd been following came from a tear on her left forearm, which was still oozing, but mostly stopped. "Needs to be wrapped," Joe said.

I suggested ripping up the towels, but Joe scanned the cave with the light focusing on his old campsite. He scrambled forward in the cave and yanked several rocks free from a nook in the wall. He pulled out a package wrapped in plastic and followed the light back to us, where he unwrapped the bundle. "First aid kit. Left it here thinking I'd be back. Coyotes took it over the next spring."

"This still their den?" I asked.

"No sign of them. Lucky for Sarah Ruth."

He cleaned the gash with a bottle of disinfectant and wrapped it tightly with gauze and tape. "Will need a few stitches," he said.

In the dark, none of us had noticed her right foot, the one without the shoe. Jimbo focused the light on it, and the ankle was swollen to twice the size of the left one. Joe tenderly felt the tissue around the swelling, and Sarah Ruth winced audibly. "Hell of a sprain. Might be broken. Don't know how she made it this far." He sat back against the rock wall, his palm on Sarah Ruth's forehead. "A little warm. Not too bad."

I could see he was contemplating a way out. "Best way to get her back is in one of those boats out there. Go down to the river. There's a little beach just a bit further up. Big enough for a boat. One of them will come by. I'll stay with her."

We followed the deer trail down the river, found the beach, and waded out into the water. Jimbo's baritone rang out, over and over, "Found her. Found Little Lemon. Got her."

I reminded him most people didn't know Sarah Ruth by the moniker he'd given her, and he corrected himself. We took turns shouting for fifteen minutes before we heard a boat. Tim and Brad Haberman, father and son, who lived a block from the Kraigs, heard our shouting and motored in. Tim called out, "She alive?"

"Yeah, maybe a broken ankle," Jimbo yelled back.

We pulled the boat to the sand, and all four of us dashed up to the cave. Joe shined the light as we ducked inside. We scooted back and saw Sarah Ruth sitting up, halfway through one of the ham sandwiches. "She's guzzled a quart of water. Seems OK, but she's talking kind of crazy. Maybe you boys can get more out of her before we move her."

Jimbo and I watched her delicately nibble around the crust of the bread, then tear it off, taking in tiny bites, which was her usual style. Sarah Ruth was idiosyncratic in how she ate everything. I'd gotten used to it through so many meals at the Kraig household, but here, knowing how famished she must be, it seemed out of place. "Little Lemon, how'd you get here?" Jimbo asked.

"Jesus."

She confused us. "Did you walk the whole way?" he continued.

"Jesus brought me."

She had the same response to almost everything we asked as she finished her sandwich and wiped her hands on her shirt. "Need my wet rag," which was the usual way she ended her meals at home. Joe came over. "Sarah Ruth, we're gonna move you down to the river. Tim and Brad have their boat. They'll get you back home."

She nodded, still distracted by her dirty hands. Jimbo unpacked a towel from the backpack, wet it, and handed it to her. She smiled, like cleaning her fingers was the most important task in her life. We stood her up, perched on one leg, and Jimbo and I carried her to the cave entrance. The five of us lifted her out through the narrow opening and down to the river. Jimbo accompanied Tim and Brad after we loaded her into the boat while Dirty Joe and I watched them head up to the landing. "She give you any explanation about what happened?" I asked him.

"Pretty much came back around to Jesus. Same as with you guys."

"What do you think she means?"

"No idea. Traumatized maybe. She religious?"

"Not as much as her older sister, Esther."

"What's wrong with her?"

"Not sure. She's not retarded. Lemon's been researching what it might be since it's gotten worse."

"Hard to believe she would have marched from the Kraig house all the way down here. Most kids would have quit long before she did."

I put on my T-shirt and slid the water jars in the backpack while Joe reconfigured the sling around his collarbone. "How'd you learn to do first aid, Joe?"

"In the prison camp at Cabanatuan. After the death march."

"Where's that?"

"Philippines. Was there for almost three years. They made me the medic because I was the only one healthy enough to get around."

"What was it like?"

He looked at me for a minute, wondering if he should say more. "Your dad wouldn't want me telling you about it. Maybe when you're older, if I'm still here."

When we got back to the landing, half of the vehicles were already gone. Word had spread quickly among the boaters. Joe's friend, Robbie, was finishing up with his boat and gave us a ride back to Joe's garage. I pedaled over to Lemon's, but the house was empty, so I went over to Jimbo's. He was waiting for me on the front porch. "Dad sent her to St. Mary's right away."

"She say anything more on the way to town?"

"Lots of Jesus talk again. This time she started talking about a man with long hair who drove her to the landing."

Sarah Ruth spent a week at St. Mary's, her left foot in a cast. Near as anyone could speculate, she broke her ankle when she fell on the rocks, where we'd found her shoe. She received five stitches in her arm. Doc told Joe he'd done well attending to Sarah Ruth and wondered if Joe might want a part-time job. Joe laughed. "Got one. Surviving."

"What's your full-time work?"

"Drinking."

While Sarah Ruth was in the hospital, Lemon spent hours with her and pulled the facts from her mostly unintelligible explanations. He was the only one who could translate Sarah Ruth's confusing language. She described a man who called to her two blocks from the Kraig house and convinced her he'd just seen a miracle. He needed Sarah Ruth to verify it and lured her into a canary-colored Chevy. With her proclivity for memorizing strings of numbers, Sarah Ruth recalled the license plate number. He drove her to the landing and led her downstream, but when he showed her the miracle, she bolted, running further downstream, mumbling to herself, needing to get away from him. She didn't remember when she fell and broke her ankle and gashed her arm, but she didn't linger after it happened.

When she thought she heard his voice near the river, she crawled inland until she found the cave.

"Jesus" was apprehended three weeks later, near a boat landing at Nekoosa, further down the Wisconsin River. Fishermen were suspicious of a bearded man in a yellow Chevy eyeballing their kids. Chief Edwards showed us his picture. He looked like the painting of Jesus hanging from the wall in Esther's bedroom. He had long hair, a brown beard, azure eyes that seemed to care, and a slight smile on his thin, rosy lips. Esther took the painting down and hid it in the garage. She didn't have the nerve to throw it away, but she abandoned her obsession with the nuns.

Jimbo and I discovered Lemon in Doc's office a few months later, reading a medical textbook. "You shouldn't be in here, Lemon," Jimbo said.

"Doc's out on a call. Said I could sit and read."

"What are you looking up?" I asked.

"I think I found something to explain Sarah Ruth."

We sat down across from him. "It's just a short paragraph. Describes her to a T."

"What is it?"

"Something called autism."

"What can you do about it?"

"Nothing. Just live with it."

Eleven
Memorial Day

After rescuing Sarah Ruth, Dirty Joe achieved a level of celebrity status he mostly abhorred. He could tolerate his saloon mates stopping at his garage apartment with six-packs of Pabst Blue Ribbon or a quart of Jim Beam, but when their wives dropped by with hamburger casseroles and lemon cakes and the Bridgeton City Council invited him to a special meeting for their Citizen of the Year award, he decided to disappear again. He invited the three of us over for a farewell meal to clean out his refrigerator. “Where are you headed?” I asked.

“Maybe back to the cave, now that the coyotes have abandoned it.”

“Long way to replenish your supplies,” Jimbo said.

“That’s the downside. On the other hand, I don’t have to carry as much stuff since I’ve got the cave to keep me dry. Last time I was there, the fishing was good. Just down from the beach where Sarah Ruth was picked up. Plenty of walleyes.”

Joe made us take some of the food donations back home. “Want us to check your place once in a while?” Lemon asked.

“Mickey’s dad’s got a key. You can work it out with him.” Joe sat down next to Lemon. “How’s Sarah Ruth doing?”

“Better each day with the foot. Doc says she’s likely to have some aftereffects.”

Joe nodded like he knew too much about the subject. "She will. Be gentle with her."

That was the last we saw of him for three months. When I checked his place, there were signs he'd been back, and I always left him a note, but I didn't lay eyes on him until Halloween night. Lemon and I were accompanying Little Eve trick-or-treating. A dim light lit Joe's garage, so I hung back until Lemon and Eve turned the corner, then I knocked on his door, though it took five minutes before he opened it. "Get in here. Don't want the kids to think I'm home. Didn't buy any candy."

I could smell alcohol on his breath, but that didn't limit his hospitality. "Was it you who popped in to check on the place?"

"Mostly. Dad trusted me with the key. I saw signs you'd been around."

"Probably on a liquor run." He looked at me intently. "Kid, don't ever let it take control of you. It just kills you with its niceness."

"Going back down to the river?"

"Getting too cold. Might stay here this time."

Joe opened another can of Pabst. "You better go, Mick. Your dad would be upset with me if he knew you were here and I was drinking."

I didn't think any more about him until a week later when he knocked at our back door just after supper. He and Dad sat outside, even though the chilly night air was dropping into the thirties. At one point, Dad came in for two jackets and motioned to me. "Maybe you should come out, Mick. Put your winter coat on."

Joe slipped into Dad's lined denim work coat. Then he turned and saw me. "The boy shouldn't hear this, Matty."

"Why not? It's his school."

Dad explained while Joe looked away. "Your principal visited Joe. Wants him to give a speech to the student body next week, on Veteran's Day. What do you think about that?"

"What would you talk about?"

Joe shrugged his shoulders. "Somehow, he heard I was in the prison camp in the Philippines. Wants me to recount those memories for all the kids in the gym."

"Joe thinks it might be too much for the little kids. What do you think, Mick?"

"It would be different. Usually, the middle school band plays a bunch of patriotic music, and the old soldiers talk about saving our country. But nothing about a prison camp."

"Told you, Matty."

Dad smiled. "What if I call the principal? Tell him you'd like to speak to an older group. In a regular class."

"That would be better. Still have to convince me I should do it."

"Come to my history class. Mrs. Glass is always talking about wars," I said.

Joe continued to show up at our house over the next few nights, and he and Dad sat outside in the chilly air or took a walk. On the fourth night, we had just started supper, so Mom invited him in. She'd begun to have a change of heart about Joe over the past few months. While we ate pot roast, she said, "Joe, can I make a suggestion about the school talk?"

Joe looked up, still a bit intimidated by her. "Get a haircut. Trim your beard. Make sure you're cleaned up."

Joe looked at Mom like she'd just desecrated his mother's grave. Dad intervened. "I think what Janice is saying is that if you look presentable, in a more conventional way, the kids might be less distracted when you tell your story."

Joe nodded. "Wish I still had my uniform. Maybe that would impress them."

Dad disappeared into the basement and returned with his navy uniform he hung in the storage room. "We were the same rank, more or less. Try it on."

Joe stood and Dad slipped the blue jacket over Joe's shoulders. The sleeves came down to the middle of his palms, but the rest hung evenly. Joe snugged the buttons. "Bit more belly than I had when we went through basic."

Dad smiled. "We all have."

Joe examined the trousers. "These will never do."

"Just a pair of dark trousers. Do you have any?"

"Yup. From Dad's funeral. Still have the black shoes, too."

On Veteran's Day, we sat in the gym for forty-five minutes for the usual presentation, which could have been the same as last year. When we returned to our classroom, Joe was standing near Mrs. Glass' desk, but even I might not have recognized him on the street. His hair was much shorter and combed, he was clean-faced with a few razor cuts, and his fingernails were trimmed and cleaned. Dad's uniform jacket was buttoned tightly as if Joe wore it every week. He looked smart, like he was headed to a military funeral. Dad stood next to him, dressed in the navy blue wool suit he'd worn to the paper mill that morning. Mrs. Glass introduced Joe as "Mr. Joe Rebenick," for those of us who didn't know him, but most everyone in town still referred to him as Dirty Joe, even after his role in the rescue of Sarah Ruth. Joe leaned against the podium while Dad slipped away to the back of the room.

Joe started off slowly, hesitating with each phrase, recalling how a group of his friends joined the navy shortly after the Japanese attacked Pearl Harbor. He stumbled through his words, looking up to the ceiling for assistance. They ended up at the same training base in California, and Joe was in the rush of troops that entered Manila Bay trying to stop the Japanese. He snuck into Corregidor and ended up with the troops on the Bataan Peninsula, where he was captured by the emperor's men when the American troops retreated. But as he began to describe the Death March, the details became sketchy, and his voice faltered. I wanted to get up and hold his hand. When he stopped mid-sentence, Dad rejoined him in the front of the room. Joe hadn't even made it to Cabanatuan.

Joe retreated to Mrs. Glass' chair, head bowed nearly to her desk while Dad took over. "Joe was one of my best friends growing up in Bridgeton. We played along the river, attended this same elementary school, graduated high school, and went our separate ways. I was finishing college at Stevens Point when Pearl Harbor got hit. Joe showed up at my doorstep and convinced me we should join the navy right away. We got split up after basic, and he was captured, just as he told you. He spent nearly three years in a Japanese prison camp at Cabanatuan under the worst possible conditions. He lost lots of friends to disease, malnutrition, and the unbelievable cruelty of the Japanese. But we didn't know that at the time. You see, when my friends told me Joe disappeared after the Battle of Bataan, most everybody assumed he was dead. But we didn't have a body, so he became one of the many MIAs."

He paused and looked around, wondering if we knew what an MIA was, then he continued. "I was in combat for six months. Guadalcanal was my main mission. It was just terrible. I had to listen to the screaming of the wounded and dying all around me. I can barely talk about it after all these years. Even to my sons. I took one to my belly."

He stepped forward and pulled his suit coat aside, touching his white shirt to the left of his belly button. I'd often seen his war scars, but he refused to tell me about the specifics.

"I was lucky to get pulled out. After two months of recovery, I was assigned to deskwork in San Diego for the rest of my tour. I wrote a lot of letters to families informing them their son or husband was missing or in the hospital. Sometimes they were notifications of death. Can you imagine getting one of those?"

His question was rhetorical, but none of the thirty-two kids sitting there had the least thought of interrupting Dad. "It was a sad, sad job writing those letters to folks just like your moms and dads, informing them they'd never see their loved one again. I kept praying I'd never have to write one to Joe's parents."

Dad paused and wiped his eyes with his handkerchief, looking briefly over at Joe. "I got married on leave while I was recovering, right here in Bridgeton. My first son was born while I was still in San Diego. All that time, Joe sat in his prison camp. Three times a day, I checked the updated list of the dead. Looking for his name but not wanting to see it. One day, February 3, 1945, I had just come back from a walk during my lunch break. It was a gorgeous day in San Diego. You could see the whitecaps on the Pacific Ocean in the distance. I'd been thinking about what kind of a life I'd be living when the war ended because lots of people were talking about that. The big bombs at Hiroshima and Nagasaki were still over six months off. But it seemed like the horrible stuff might finally end. Life could go back to normal."

Joe raised his head like Dad had never told him these details before. "I sat down at my desk and read about the joint American and Filipino raid at Cabanatuan. American GIs were liberated, even though hundreds had died in the years of the camp. A few hours later, we started getting lists of survivors. When I saw Joe's name, I stood up and yelled and hooted as loud as I could. Just like you might when you unexpectedly get the best Christmas gift you could imagine. Everybody in the office thought I was crazy, but I was so relieved. Like I'd been holding onto something for three years and could finally let it go."

He paused, regaining his composure. "It took many months before Joe showed up again in Bridgeton. The war was over, and I was just beginning my job at the mill. He walked into my office with a smile on his face. But it was a different smile than he had when we were kids growing up along the river. None of us from the war ever smile like we used to. I gave Joe a big hug and took him out to lunch.

"Some of you have seen Joe around town over the years. Maybe some of you heard about him getting stabbed or rescuing Lemon's sister last summer. He's one of us, but he's never been the same. Nobody who's come back from Korea is the same either. And if any of you have to go off to war, and I sure hope you never have to, odds are you won't be the same when you return. That's what happens to veterans. When you're done listening to all the glory-filled recollections on Veteran's

Day about serving our country, don't forget about people like Joe and me. Soldiers who still carry the war within themselves. It's an awful thing."

Dad shook Joe's hand, and the two of them marched out of the classroom. We didn't say thanks or clap our hands—didn't have time. It ended that abruptly. Mrs. Glass didn't know what to say, so she told us to go out to the playground for a while.

A few days later, I stopped at Joe's apartment. It was locked up, and there was no sign of him. I told Dad but he already knew. "I drove Joe to the Greyhound terminal in Stevens Point yesterday. He's heading to Daytona Beach, Florida.

"What's he going to do there?"

"He's got an old navy buddy who's been asking him to come down for years. Joe saved his life in the prison camp."

"How long will he be there?"

"He might stay the winter."

"You worried about him?"

"If I was worried, I wouldn't have taken him to the bus. Joe's been taking care of himself for years."

"What about money?"

"I gave him three months allowance. And a hundred extra for an emergency."

Joe sent a Christmas card wishing us well and called Dad each month to talk about money. I forgot about him as winter shifted into spring. The school year wound down and Memorial Day weekend appeared, announcing the beginning of summer. Jimbo, Lemon, and I watched the Memorial Day parade from the library steps. It wasn't much. A fire engine led the way, followed by seven veterans in full uniform, rifles on their shoulders. The high school marching band played "My Country,'Tis of Thee," and Police Chief Edwards waved from his squad car. The eighth-grade band came next, massacring "America the Beautiful." Finally, forty veterans wearing assorted pieces of their old uniforms brought up the rear: Jerry McCready in his wheelchair, Jimmy Kennedy pushing him along, some looking crisp in their army jackets, others barely able to gather them around their bellies.

We were about to bike out to the cemetery for the traditional reading of the Bridgeton soldiers lost in war and the twenty-one-gun salute, but we paused at a perplexing sight. Joe Rebenick, twenty yards behind the group of vets, stumbled a bit as he walked up Main Street. He wasn't trying to catch up, just moving at his own pace and not always in a straight line, wearing Dad's U.S. Navy jacket, rumpled khaki pants, and untied sneakers. Dad wasn't at the parade. Otherwise, he would have rushed out to retrieve Joe. Joe noticed us straddling our bikes, and he nodded and saluted in our direction. Then he continued his pursuit of the parade.

During the reading of the names, Joe stood off to the side, leaning against a white pine not too far from the slough that ran in back of the cemetery. When the seven soldiers hoisted their rifles for the salute, Joe stood to attention. But as the first round of seven shots went off, he half-crumpled to the ground. After the second round, he slumped down to a crouch. After the third, he disappeared into the woods.

He came around to the house that evening, and Dad suggested they go for a walk by the river. Joe saw me sitting on the porch, watching, and motioned for me to come along. Nothing much was said until we got halfway across Old Iron. "Matty, it's never gonna work for me here. I hadn't been drinking for almost three months. Get back here for two weeks. Bottle's got me again. I'm going back to Daytona."

"Still have a place back there?"

"I can stay with my buddy until I find another apartment. Same as this past winter."

"Same deal with the money?"

"Put the old house and garage up for sale. When it goes, I'm gonna buy a place in Daytona somewhere. Until then, yeah, same deal with the money."

Joe's property sold in September, and Dad and I went through his belongings in the garage and took what Joe might want. There was some valuable furniture in the house that Joe had never used. He told us to sell what we could and give the rest away. Dad kept a bedside table from Joe's childhood bedroom that Joe might want someday, but in the meantime, I could use it.

By December, Dad had tied up all the loose ends of Joe's finances. Joe's Christmas card arrived on December 23, and it didn't say anything more than "season's greetings, hope you're well." Dad stared at the check for $13,500 made out to Joe's name and the envelope with Joe's address he intended to send it in, both of them sitting on the kitchen table. "Jan, want to take a trip to Daytona Beach?"

"When?"

"Sometime during the holidays."

"We can't do that, Matt. It's Christmas. I'm working shifts for all the girls at the hospital who are spending time with their families. It's my year for that."

"What about you, Dennis?"

"Got plans for skiing at Indianhead. Have shifts at the market, too."

"Sounds like just me and you, Mick."

"Can Jimbo and Lemon come?"

"Why not. Drive down and spend a few days on the beach. Get back for New Year's Eve."

We loaded up the station wagon with Joe's belongings and left at five on Christmas morning. We stopped in Louisville, made it to Daytona the next evening, and found a motel on the beach with cut rates for the holidays. The ocean was too cold for swimming but just fine for splashing. Joe had to work during the day as a cook at The Wave, a breakfast and lunch restaurant in the tourist section of the city, but he took off work on our final day. Dad asked him to entertain us for a few hours while he took care of some business, so Joe took us out for lunch at The Wave. Three-course meal on the house.

Dad returned in the afternoon. “Did I check out, Matty?” Joe asked.

Dad nodded. “Let’s go to the bank.”

They deposited $13,500 plus Joe’s allowance for the next year.

Jimbo, Lemon, and I stayed up until three that night while Dad slept in a separate room so he could rest for the drive. We fell asleep again after we packed up the station wagon, and by the time I woke, we were two hours south of Atlanta. Jimbo and Lemon were still sleeping in the back, and Dad was sipping coffee from his thermos cup. “Staying awake, Dad?”

“I’m good, Mick. We’ll stop for lunch when I have to gas up.”

“What did Joe mean about you checking up on him?”

“I talked to his sponsor at AA and his old navy buddy.”

“Why?”

“Wanted to make sure. It’s a lot of money to hand over. If he’s still drinking.”

“Did it all check out?”

“One hundred percent.”

“Was coming down here because of Joe’s parents? Wanting you to watch out for him?”

“Mostly.”

“Mom wanted you to go, right? She wants the best for Joe.”

“Both of us want things to work out for Joe.” He laughed. “But she wasn’t that crazy about us leaving on Christmas morning.”

I poured him another cup of coffee. “Dad, you did good on Veteran’s Day. Saving Joe like that. Telling your story instead.”

“I didn’t think I’d have to. I wanted to hear about the prison camp. Joe’s never told me much about it.”

We pulled into a gas station. There was a small park nearby, and Dad got some groceries and joined us at a picnic table. Jimbo, mouth full of a salami sandwich, said, "Got to tell you, Mr. P. This is the best Christmas I've ever had."

"Pretty good one, I agree."

"When we loaded up back in Bridgeton, I figured Joe would be coming back with us."

"Nope. He's happy living away from Bridgeton."

"How come people like you and Ted Kraig didn't leave?"

"Didn't need to, I guess."

Twelve
Junior Snow Boys

It started on a Sunday night, January 16, and continued without a halt for twenty-six hours. Reports came in every few hours on radio station WSAU: eight inches, foot-and-a-half, twenty-seven inches, just shy of four feet. Heavy, wet masses of impassable thickness. Cotton clusters became as heavy as iron pellets as the storm extended into Monday afternoon. Saturated drifts whistled up to our living room windows. The radio newscasters warned us about keeping small children inside so they wouldn't disappear beneath the blizzard-driven mounds. The telephones were tied up all day. Bernice Shantz, the party line operator, chastised us if we tried to call our friends. "No personal calls. Keep the lines free for emergencies." The snowfall finally blew eastward, leaving us with sixty-six inches of new snow—Bridgeton's biggest snowstorm since 1898.

By noon on Tuesday, Bridgeton village plows began to clear the streets so the dairy farmers could get their milk to the cheese factories and essential workers could attempt the drive to work. Everybody who had chains put them on their trucks and cars, but it didn't make a difference for many. Mill workers by the score, dressed in snow pants and their tallest boots, skied or snowshoed across Old Iron, laughing and shouting as they took the place of cars. They packed extra food on their backs and joined several dozen papermakers who had spent the last forty-eight hours at the mill, stranded since the blizzard hit.

School, which was rarely called off, was closed Monday through Thursday, but it was a heyday for shoveling. Twenty of us seventh and eighth graders from town met at city hall. Two other teams of high school boys had gone out earlier, and now it was our turn to get instructions from Mayor Keltenburg. We were officially titled the Junior Snow Boys, though five girls joined us during the first hour. The homes of senior citizens and the infirm were shoveled out first. We mutated into a swarm of hornets descending on driveways, swinging our black metallic instruments, a symphony of percussive grunting as we lifted and threw the snow over impossibly high peaks. We cleared the snow from the street to the entryways, making sure every door could open. Old women tapped on the windows in thanks, and the most gracious brought us cookies and hot chocolate.

The Snow Boys piled back into the school bus and headed to the next house three blocks away. Ten driveways, twenty front porches, thirty doorways—we stopped counting as our repetitive exertions reduced us to automatons. By mid-afternoon, we gathered in the warming house at Dessert Park skating rink, inhaling platters full of hot dogs and chips. Klug's Department Store brought us new leather mitts with woolen liners. Chet Parker gathered our wet ones and suspended them from a clothesline that ran from wall to wall inside the warming house. The wood stove was cranked to ninety degrees, and we stripped down to our long johns and T-shirts and sprawled out on the warm cement floor. Our sweaty socks dried and crusted on our feet, but nobody had thought to bring a second pair. Our biceps and back muscles calmed down, no longer twitching from load after load of the densest snow any of us had ever shoveled. After an hour-long break, we headed back out to the streets.

Doc McPhearson drove up to the school bus in a borrowed pickup truck with a plow affixed to the front and honked at us. Lemon, who'd been assisting Doc with house calls since Doc's hand injury last summer, talked with him for five minutes and called me over. "Doc's got to check on Mrs. Rangerford."

"Out on Johnson Road?"

"Yeah. Wants us to come along in case we need to shovel our way in."

Jimbo and I followed Lemon, tossed our shovels in the back, and crowded inside the cab next to Doc. "You guys have any energy left?"

"Jesus, Dad, is the road even plowed?" Jimbo said.

"Don't know for sure with all the drifting. But Mrs. Rangerford's daughter called me. Her mother doesn't answer. She's been sick."

"She's eighty-eight. Has some congestive heart failure," Lemon said.

"Maybe she's just asleep," Jimbo said.

We followed the Marathon County plow out Johnson Road, creating a single lane with enormous difficulty. Our tire chains slipped on the icy snow closest to the pavement, but Doc was careful whenever we started skidding. We were barely crawling along at ten miles per hour, and even that seemed too fast, pausing whenever we got too close to the backend of the plow. It took forty-five minutes to go five miles. The county plow went up the Rangerford driveway, stopped fifteen yards from the house, backed out, and waved us in. Doc parked where the plow tracks ended, and we jumped out and began shoveling while Doc waited inside the warm truck. It took another twenty minutes before we got close. Doc surged ahead of us, the last three yards in chest-deep snow with Lemon right behind in his tracks. Doc had to pull him through the final drift onto the porch. Lemon moved the snow blocking the front door while Jimbo and I shoveled to catch up, sweating again, like we'd never dried off during our afternoon break. When we opened the door, the interior was barely warmer than the fifteen-degree, late afternoon air. Lemon was trying to get a fire going in the cold wood stove while Doc was in the bedroom alongside Mrs. Rangerford. "She's cold," Lemon said. "Don't know if she's nearly dying from her weak heart or because she's freezing to death."

"Damn, doesn't she have a furnace?" Jimbo shouted.

"Not working. We tried."

We ripped up newspaper and cardboard and tossed in a small pile of pine kindling. The first attempt went out. Lemon looked behind the stove, flipped the damper, and the downdraft wind gushed through the stove's chamber as I lit another farmer match. Jimbo and I blew on the embers, and the kindling finally caught, but there were not enough small pieces to keep it going. Jimbo dashed out to the porch and found a stack of firewood under a three-foot weight of snow. He called me out, and we shoveled furiously, reaching the canvas tarp covering the wood. Jimbo yanked out more kindling and small pieces of oak and loaded my arms. I spilled them at Lemon's side and raced out for more. We hauled in ten loads, with some big lunkers to keep the fire going overnight. "How is she, Lemon?"

He shook his head, fearing the worst. Doc called out. "I think she's got a pulse. Her cardiac system is so broken down it's hard to tell. She's too damn cold."

We carried a mattress from the second bedroom and spread it near the wood stove. Each of us took one of Mrs. Rangerford's limbs, boosting her with the layers of quilts to the pallet on the floor. We piled on blankets from the other bedroom while Jimbo tossed more oak into the stove. When the temperature rose to fifty degrees, we took off our parkas and spread them on top of her. Doc checked her heart and pulse. "I think she's coming back."

The high beams from the snowplow shined up the driveway in the early dusk, and two figures jumped out, racing and slipping through the pathway we'd shoveled to the house. Laura Skalitsky, Mrs. Rangerford's daughter, and her son burst through the door. "How's Mom?"

"Coming around. The house got too cold for her," Doc said.

Laura cleaned up the kitchen. Miraculously, the water was still working. We moved some furniture out of the living room and slid Mrs. Rangerford's bed out near the fire. We lifted her off the pallet on the cold floor, which was easier with two more sets of hands, and after another thirty minutes, Mrs. Rangerford began talking in a confused way. "Where's Lenny?"

"She means Dad. He's been dead for two years," Laura said. "We tried to get to her to move in with us earlier this winter. She wouldn't leave. Now we'll have to take her."

We dressed again in our Snow Boy clothes and brought in more wood for the night. "We're heading back. Call me if she gets worse. We'll get the ambulance out in the morning," Doc said.

Laura was crying and laughing, overwhelmed by what we'd done and what she'd have to go through next. "Thanks, Doc. And you too, boys."

As Doc backed out of the driveway, the three of us clung to the sides of the truck, pounding on the windows if he was sliding into deep snow. We only had to shovel out one time. Johnson Road now had a broader lane, and we made it back to Bridgeton at twenty miles per hour. Doc drove us to the McPhearson house, and Lemon and I called home while Jimbo heated up meatloaf, boiled potatoes, and a can of pork and beans. "Helluva job you did at the Rangerford's, boys. I know you're tired. But if you can, head outside when you're done eating. Walk around town. It's just amazing. Might never see another snowfall like this one," Doc said.

After dinner, we bundled up and wandered the streets. The moon was two days from full, lighting our way. Every home looked smaller, some no bigger than doghouses beside the mountains of snow. Gigantic spruce trees bowed under the snow, humbled, almost defeated. Main Street was dark except for Wilke's gas station. We stopped and took off our knit hats to listen. The winds carried the scratching of metal shovels against sidewalks and the grinding of steel snow plows reaching for the pavement.

I was the first to hear the music. "Tequila" by the Champs, our current favorite song at the skating rink. We went to our homes and retrieved our skates. Over one hundred people had come down to the rink with shovels in hand. Moms and dads, high school sweethearts and kids like us, all of Bridgeton following the snowplow across the barely visible ice. The rink lights atop snow-covered poles combined with the moonlight to light the way. Snow crystals glistened like jewels. Some sections of the ice were already open, and a few kids were skating, and by nine, it was clear enough for all of us. Hockey players and figure skaters chased each other around, taking turns racing toward fifteen-foot snow banks, then leaping and diving into them, laughing hysterically at the snow mascara and icy powder on our faces. Chet kept spinning the songs. "Witch Doctor," "At the Hop," "Bird Dog," "Catch a Falling Star." We knew the words and sang and skated until our ankles wouldn't support us. At eleven, Chet played his traditional closing song, "Auld Lang Syne," Perry Como wishing us good night as we held hands and sang along.

We walked slowly back to Jimbo's house along River Road, our thigh and calf muscles spent. Jimbo slipped and fell and remained stretched out on his back in the middle of the snowy road as if he had no intention of ever getting up, laughing like we were tickling him to death. We joined him. Three near corpses, side by side, giddy with fatigue, staring up at the moon. Lemon was the first to stand up again. He offered me a hand, and I nearly pulled him back down. I grabbed Jimbo's left mitt, Lemon his right, and we pulled him up into our chests. Snow Boys of Bridgeton clutching each other.

Never been another night like it.

Thirteen
Dad

Mom took on an evening shift at the hospital with five days a week guaranteed and better pay, which we needed after Dad's surprise layoff from the Bridgeton Paper Mill. Corporate turnover had earned him his promotion to vice-president ten years earlier, but the sale of the mill in April brought in a new team of executives. All but a few of the men in town continued with their per hour jobs as though they never knew the mill was under new ownership, but salaried positions, like Dad's, played out by different rules. He'd told me more than once there was a risk moving up the corporate chain. But when that risk caught up to him, it was as though he'd been blindsided on a lazy weekend afternoon.

I'd never known him to be without work, most of the time sixty-hour weeks. His anger mellowed a bit as summer wore on, and he helped Grandpa out at the telephone company. Despite our economic uncertainty, we rented a lake house for a week in August near Minocqua, our first family vacation in years, and, for a few days, we all got along without any worries about the future.

Then Dennis left for his first year of college at Stout, and Mom resumed work from two to midnight. I started eighth grade, but Dad had nowhere to go. When I returned home after school, uncertainty filled every room of the house. I heated up the casserole Mom left for us, set the table, and raced through my portion of the hot dish. Occasionally, I looked up at Dad during the meal as he sipped on his second or third whiskey sour, but he spoke very little and wore a distant, distracted look. His charcoal whiskers, which were headed toward a thick salt and pepper beard, only added to his forsaken attitude.

I hadn't ever been alone with him like this on such a frequent basis. He felt it, too. He began skipping out most evenings, usually to Kennedy's Pub, leaving me with the dishes, and returned near my bedtime. From my upstairs bedroom, I would hear his loud grumbling if I hadn't cleaned up the kitchen thoroughly and waited for his grunt as he collapsed into his recliner with the evening newspaper before shouting, "All good, Mick?"

"Good up here, Dad," I replied, anticipating his next question. "No phone calls."

Five weeks into our new routine, I returned home one evening from Lemon's. The house was quiet, and I assumed Dad was at the tavern. Bobby Darin's "Dream Lover" was spinning in my head from the 45 Lemon and I had been listening to for over an hour. I peed, brushed my teeth, examined the zits on my forehead, shrugged at the hopelessness of controlling the outbreak, humming as I headed toward my bedroom. Dennis' desk lamp was lit, and Dad sat there rummaging through my brother's papers. I stood at the doorway, wondering if I'd done something wrong, unsure how to talk to him without Mom as a buffer. "Hi, Mick," he said without looking up.

"Didn't think you were home."

"Yup. Just out walking tonight. Wanted to be here."

He was barefooted wearing a baggy white T-shirt and khakis from J.C. Penney, a fresh towel over his shoulder. "Everything OK?" I said.

"Good enough. Thanks for cleaning up the kitchen."

I was puzzled by his gentle tone. "Come here."

I took two steps toward him and stopped. He smiled and looked up. "I'm sorry you're afraid of me."

"I'm not really." It was only partly a lie, but Dad was more right than not.

“We don’t know how to talk, do we? Without Mommy here.”

“She’s easier.”

“Maybe I was gone too much.”

“You had to be, right?”

He was amused by my explanation. “You’re just too damn nice, Mick. Dennis tells me to fuck off when I jump on him. I know how to respond to that. But you just take it.”

I’d rarely heard him curse unless he was angry, though there’d been more of it over the summer. “Turns out, I’m only good with bar talk like that when I’m trying to be friends.”

What could I say? “Would you sit with me for a minute? Unless you’d rather be in your room.”

I sat on Dennis’ bed, and he turned the desk chair toward me. “How do you like your brother’s room?”

I didn’t understand. “It’s fine.”

“Would you like it? It’s bigger than yours. I can move his stuff.”

“Where would Dennis go?”

“He’s not coming back except for vacations. Maybe next summer if he can latch on at the mill. But they won’t be hiring for months.”

“Geez. He’s just off to his first year of college.”

“I told him not to come back.”

He chuckled at my incredulous look. “And I’m going tell you the same thing. When the time comes, of course.”

“But he’s part of the family.”

“I know. And Mommy knows, too. But we’re in agreement about this, even more since I lost my job. There’s no future in Bridgeton. Life here is like Old Iron, that damn old bridge I’ve walked across all these years on my way to the mill. Obsolete. Barely functional.”

“But I like it here. I’ve got my friends.”

“You’re too young to get it, Mick. That’s why I decided to start telling you now. I kind of sprung it on Dennis over the last few months. He was still pissed at me when he left. You probably noticed. But that's why."

"You came back after college, Dad."

"Got me there, buddy. But I'm not too old to admit my mistake."

"Why did you?"

"Grandpa's expectations. He wanted me to work with him, but I drew the line there. Got a management position at the mill right away. Everything seemed to be in place. Now look at me. Forty-three years old. No prospects except going on the dole with Grandpa."

"Must be other stuff you can do."

"I'm sure it'll work out. I'll find something in Wausau or Point that fits me. I'm looking every day. I'll commute. But Mommy's working in Wausau, and if I get a job there, I've got to ask: why don't we live there, too? See what I mean, Mick? There's no damn future here."

I nodded but didn't understand much of what he was telling me. "Better do my homework and get to bed."

"OK. See you tomorrow."

I didn't have any homework. I just needed to get away from Dad. I stripped down to my underwear and sat on the edge of the bed, wondering if I'd ever see Lemon and Jimbo after we moved. I listened to Dad's movements as he ran the upstairs shower, dried off, walked by my room in his robe and down the stairs to his bedroom. The house was quiet again, something I struggled to get used to. I got up and peered into Dennis' room, wondering if he'd return for my birthday in a couple of weeks like he said he would, even if Dad didn't want him. I heard creaking on the steps and turned around to see Dad in his pajamas. He put his hand on my shoulder. "You're not really thinking of taking his room, Mick. He'd fight you for it. He's coming back for homecoming in two weekends. We'll celebrate your birthday then."

I was confused with no idea why he was talking like this, as his hand guided me back to my room. He pulled back the bedding and sat next to me as I snuggled in. “Need to read for a while?”

I shook my head. “When I was your age, Grandpa was gone even more than I’ve been. He never put me to bed, even when I was little. I’m a little better than that. But not much.”

“You don’t need to be here. I’m good.”

“I want to.”

We listened to the ticking of my clock and the wind blowing light rain against my window screen. “What I told you before about Bridgeton….”

“Yeah.”

“I meant it, but in a theoretical sense. You know what that means?”

“Odds are that it should happen, in the big picture. But sometimes it doesn’t.”

“Right. That’s very good. Your teachers tell you that?”

“Lemon’s always talking about theory and probability.”

Dad was impressed. “You could do much worse than hanging around with Lemon. Maybe he’ll pull you along in his draft.”

He looked at me, unsure if I understood him, but I’d already figured out that part of spending time with Lemon. “If I continue to be his friend, some of his smarts might rub off on me. Everybody knows Lemon could be studying calculus if he wanted to.”

“You know, Mick, you’re much smarter than Dennis was at your age. Maybe you should stick around and teach me something.”

“Dad, I really like Bridgeton. I love Old Iron and the places along the river.”

“Me, too. Don’t listen to a bitter old man like me.”

“You’re not that old.”

He laughed for nearly a minute, but the joy turned sour toward the end. “Just bitter. I need help with that, too.”

Fourteen
Fragments

I began to feel the change during the winter of eighth grade. Mom picked up extra shifts at St. Mary's Hospital after Dad lost his job at the Bridgeton Paper Mill, and he and I were often alone in the evening. He told me stories about growing up in Bridgeton, "escapading" along the Wisconsin River, as I did with Lemon and Jimbo. He had five or six companions, but it was Dad, Joe Rebenick, and Fleecy Fortney, more often than not. Then he drifted into how they ended up in the War in the Pacific. Fleecy perished in Okinawa, and Dad and Joe came back damaged. He even related the specifics about the horrors of Guadalcanal and how he received his gut wound, much of which he kept from Mom and Dennis. After years of hiding the scars from the war, he wanted one of us to know the entire truth about his months in combat.

The change followed me through that summer before I entered high school. Lemon was assisting Doc McPhearson most days, shadowing him and taking notes due to Doc's arm injury, while Jimbo was learning to drive tractor and work the hayfields out at Kurt Mestanek's farm. Dad lined up some work for me, assisting Mrs. Rosen, who lived two blocks away. She was seventy-two and had broken three toes on her left foot, stumbling over a broken sidewalk. She needed regular help with grocery runs, yard work, and house cleaning. I was efficient at the first two but slacked off on the third. Her daughter, Tia, came up every weekend that summer, and sometimes she and I pooled our resources on bigger jobs in the backyard, giving us time to talk.

Tia Rosen was a professor of psychology at the University of Wisconsin in Milwaukee, but she wrote crime novels on the side. After I showed an interest in her writing, she told me how her thoughts came together to make stories, something I hadn't thought about before. She said she'd pay me fifty cents an hour, my going rate at Mrs. Rosen's, to write something, anything, as long as it didn't read like something my teachers would expect. But every time I started with an idea, my brain locked up after the first couple of sentences.

One day, she suggested I sit at the patio table while she weeded her mother's perennial flowerbed. She set a pad of paper and her fountain pen in front of me. "Write down whatever comes to mind."

What flowed out was very brief and definitely not a story, but Tia read it to herself and smiled. "Don't ever throw this away." She could see I was skeptical, even if she was complimenting me. She sat down next to me and read my words out loud.

"At some point during this past year, the phrases in my head got longer. More than a couple words. But not quite sentences. Fragments. Enough to keep the conversation going when I talk to myself. Like that voice in my head wants to tell me things I don't understand. Extending my thoughts. Fragment after fragment. Kernels of explanation. Slices of detail.

"My days are different now, compared to when I was nine or ten. Life used to be pretty much all action. Simple words and short phrases would do. Now, the activity has slowed down. And my voice wants to tell me things in a more complicated way. Maybe someday, we'll be talking back and forth in complete sentences."

I'd mostly been listening to Tia's rich alto voice while she read, not paying much attention to the thoughts behind my words. "Do you have any idea what you were writing about?"

I thought she was making fun of me, so I didn't want to say. "Not really, but you told me it could be about anything."

"What you wrote about is what happens when we get older. How we observe things becomes more complex and sophisticated. We need to reflect more. Not always, but usually. It's complicated and best explained by the stream of thinking you call fragments."

I nodded, though I wasn't sure what she was talking about. Then she said, "When I was nine, your dad's sister, Margaret, had her face and neck burned in a Halloween accident. She disappeared for the rest of fourth grade. I thought maybe she'd die because of the way people were talking about her. She didn't return to school until the next fall. Looked completely different, of course. Scarred all over her face, neck, and parts of her arms. Even before this terrible accident, she was a shy girl, but it was impossible to get her to talk after that. Even when we were working one-to-one, she wouldn't say a word. Our teacher, Mrs. Sundby, tried to prepare us for Margaret's return, making sure no one laughed at her. But getting us to accept her was more difficult and took time. She asked me if I'd be Margaret's helpmate in class. Margaret would be missing school from time to time for ongoing plastic surgeries and needed someone to help her catch up."

Mrs. Rosen's voice interrupted us. "Tia. Would you come in here?"

Tia yelled back. "Be right there, Mom. Just finishing up."

She shook her head, knowing her mother could wait. "Margaret missed two weeks in November, so I took her homework to the house. Your grandparents' place on Second Street. Margaret was sitting in a rocking chair in the living room. Her neck was bandaged up to her chin, where she'd had the new surgeries. When I explained what she had to do with her math and reading, she looked at me and started talking. From silence to words. Just like that. Your grandmother came into the room and stood behind the rocking chair, bug-eyed in astonishment, joy plastered all over her face."

"How come?"

"Margaret wasn't talking at home either. This was the first time anybody heard her speak since the accident."

"What'd she sound like?"

"Even though her throat was burned in the accident, her vocal tissue was intact. So, I'm sure her voice sounded much the same as it had a year earlier. But no one had heard her talk or sing or shout for so long."

"Do you remember what she said?"

"Not specifically, but it came out as three- or four-word phrases. Like Margaret was relearning how to speak."

"What do you think happened?"

"I talked to Mom about it. She used to be a schoolteacher. She said Margaret was talking all the while she was silent, but just to herself, inside her head, in fragments of speech. She was too traumatized to let it come out. She went through so much pain and was so disfigured. When the sounds emerged from her scarred face again, she was like a different person. She'd become a new Margaret."

Tia watched me. "Do you know your aunt very well?"

"I try to be her friend. I know she gets lonely. She was hospitalized several times for that. Dad's close to her. Takes her to breakfast every Saturday morning."

"When I was writing one of my books, I wanted to create a character who'd undergone a drastic physical change. I thought about Margaret and even asked her if she'd mind. She laughed at me. 'Are you going to make me a scary monster?' I promised her I wouldn't. She'd be mysterious but misunderstood. Almost invisible, living secretly with a housekeeper who preserves her privacy. Most of the characters don't know she's alive, even though she influences their actions. Until the end, when the private detective discovers the scarred woman in her house."

"What'd Margaret say?"

"That I should write about someone beautiful instead."

"Sounds like her."

"Yeah, but it broke my heart to hear her say that."

"Did you write about her?"

"In my third novel. I called her Margaritte. She's one of the few good characters in the story. The detective cries at the end when he meets her, which he's not supposed to do."

"Why not?"

"Tradition. A hardboiled private detective doesn't go soft, unless it's for a sexy girl who walks into his office wanting to hire him. But this time, he melts when he hears Margaritte speak through her scarred lips."

"What's the detective's name?"

"Lex Sharapelle."

Mrs. Rosen shouted out more vigorously. "Tia! Mickey! Could you please help me?"

She didn't like being alone for long if there were people around the house, but I'd learned to take my time responding to her anyway. Usually, she'd order me to sit and then she'd talk about her past, as though she didn't care if I got my work done. It was worse when Tia was around. "Coming, Mom." She chuckled. "She probably doesn't need much."

"She usually doesn't."

"You can take off, Mick. I could use your help tomorrow with the back gate if you've got time."

I was halfway out of the Rosen yard when Tia called me back and handed me the piece of paper on which I'd written my words. "Hold on a minute. I've got something for you."

I stood on the front porch and reread what I'd written but was still unimpressed. Tia came out the front door holding a book. *Woman with the Scarred Face: A Lex Sharapelle Mystery*. "Not sure you'll be interested. But give it a try if you want."

I asked her about the author, Sean Daly. "It's my pen name."

"Why don't you use your own?"

"Crime novels are a man's world. It's the only way I can get my books published."

I folded the paper and stuffed it inside the cover flap, and that night opened up Tia's detective novel. She'd written a note inside the front cover, "Sometimes complete sentences are overrated. Your friend, Tia Rosen."

I started reading. "Priscilla Richards strutted into my office on a Thursday morning. Dark crimson stiletto heels. Violet silk stockings. Tight, black-and-white polka dot skirt stopping mid-thigh. Pale blue muslin blouse through which I could see the outline of her nipples. Dark eyes that could have read my secret files without opening them up. Tangled, red hair that matched her shoes. She smiled through tangerine lips. 'Mr. Sharapelle, my husband is Terry Richards. He's been missing for two weeks. I don't care if he's run off. Just find out if he's dead.'"

I flipped to the back pages, searching for the woman with the scarred face and found her on page one hundred seventy-four. "She rose out of the rocking chair and turned to face us. Black silk scarf covering her head and the edges of her face. Green turtleneck sweater up to her chin. Dark glasses with golden frames staring at us. A sliver of a nose under tortured scars. Strands of disfigured skin where her lips should have been. Her words escaped out of a dark cavern, like she hadn't spoken of him for decades. 'I tried to save Terry. After he found the money. But it was too late.' She took three steps toward us, removed her glasses, and slid the scarf to her neck. Thin black hair grew out of a battlefield of twisted skin on her scalp. Silver streaks of tears ran down her disfigured cheeks. 'He didn't know I was still alive. That I still loved him.'"

I thought about Margaret and a boyfriend she had in college, Joe Stanish, wondering if Tia Rosen ever met him. I opened the piece of paper I'd written on earlier in the day, turned it to the blank side, and started writing.

Aunt Margaret lost part of her face when she was nine years old. Spent the rest of her life looking for it.

She went trick-or-treating, costumed as a ghost. A sheet of white muslin draped over her head with holes cut out for her eyes, nose, and mouth. The fabric hung below her knees. Grandma Pederson tied a purple bandana around Margaret's neck, snugged tightly and double-knotted, to keep the ghost skin in place. Margaret held a Halloween lantern. A votive candle inside a carved pumpkin to light the way. Her younger sister, Mary, carried the canvas candy bags. It was a balmy evening for late October. Gusty currents swept through the Wisconsin River valley into the streets of Bridgeton. The sheet billowed at Margaret's thighs and chest. The ghost skin flew outward, grazing the pumpkin, sliding against the flame. The edges of the muslin caught fire, and the specter was soon ablaze. Margaret dropped the pumpkin and tugged at the sheet of fire that torched her head and chest. The double-knotted bandana did its work. Mary clutched at the burning material, but it was too hot to the touch. The two of them raced down Second Street toward home, screaming in unison while the flames consumed the fuel. The fire died out when they reached the front door. The blackened sheet on Margaret's face and scalp and the incinerated bandana on her neck were coated with residues of Margaret's skin.

Years later, Grandma refused to discuss the accident. Other than blaming herself for what happened. Dad warned Dennis and me about bringing it up, but there was no need. I saw Margaret several times a week when we visited our grandparents. I rarely noticed the scars on her face, neck, shoulders, and hands. She'd always had them. One of her ears was missing its top half, but she heard me clearly when we played gin rummy.

Margaret was a classy lady. She graduated from Loyola University in Chicago on an academic scholarship and had a steady beau from Lake Forest, Joe Stanish. He traveled to Bridgeton to ask Grandpa for her hand. Grandma told Grandpa to inform Joe that he should go back home. She would continue to protect Margaret, making amends for Halloween night. I was at my grandparents' house when Margaret stood alongside Joe and his silver Pontiac, completing their goodbye. He held her hands as she wept, tenderly touched the scars around her eyes, and caressed the skin along her cheeks to ease her sorrow. When he kissed her, I wanted to believe he would return again and again.

Margaret began working in the office at the Bridgeton Telephone Company that Grandpa started thirty years earlier, accounting for gains and losses and making sure the federal loan payments were made on time. I stopped in to visit her on the way home from school. She always had a bowl of Hershey's Kisses on her desk. When I reached for one, she offered me, instead, two squares of Belgian chocolate hidden in her desk drawer. She walked me to her office door, hugged me, and told me to enjoy the rest of the day.

Margaret had several stacks of catalogs from the Hudson Bay Company nesting around Grandpa's house. She purchased her clothes from The Bay in Montreal when she vacationed there each September. She wore the beautifully tailored, ankle-length, indigo wool coat and the knee-high boots trimmed with fox fur as she shoveled snow alongside me. She traveled alone to Ireland and Norway to see relatives and studied French for two months in Paris. Grandpa paid for everything.

I became more aware of her scars when I was eleven because of her lipstick. She invited me to her bedroom and showed me her new cabinet. Handcrafted slots for the hundreds of metal tubes of lip paint. From the deepest purples to the most brilliant reds to the most succulent oranges. I watched her casually apply a shade of scarlet, wipe it off, then coat her lips with a new color. She told me it was labeled "Burnt Persimmon." The colors created the illusion of intact lips surrounded by distorted, stretched skin. Plastic surgery done in the Depression years had little sophistication. When she smiled into the mirror, her glamorous lips encircled her perfectly straight, white teeth.

Margaret loved to swim in the village pool. She dove from the springboard like a kingfisher gliding down from a willow along the Wisconsin River. I watched her from outside the fence during adult swim, gracefully launching off the board and emerging at the cement wall that divided the adult section from the children's. Backstroking up and back for miles. More often than not, Margaret was the lone swimmer in the pool.

She was determined to teach me to dive. I kept landing on my belly, and my friends laughed at me. One sultry evening, we jumped into the pool, joining fifty others trying to stay chilled in the warm water. Few people in Bridgeton had air conditioning in the 1950s. She stood at the side of the pool, near the twelve-foot-deep section and demonstrated her dives over and over, never creating a splash when she arrowed into the water. I got better throughout the hour, gaining confidence. When I surfaced from my last dive, a boy and a girl stood behind Margaret. They were my age, though I'd never seen them before. They were laughing at Margaret as they pointed to her neck and face. Margaret ignored them as the boy ran over to his mother sitting on a nearby bench. His mother stared at Margaret and grinned. More amused than her children.

I sat on the edge of the pool. Margaret wrapped her white Hudson Bay bath towel around her face and neck. Just her eyes were visible. The girl tugged at the back of the towel and pulled it free. Margaret's scars were naked again. The lifeguard, who sat ten feet above us in her chair, glanced down as Margaret retrieved the towel from the wet cement. She resumed her job, watching for misbehaving children at the far end of the pool. Margaret restored the towel around her head and shoulders. The boy rejoined his sister, and together they jerked the towel again. Margaret, anticipating their attack, held on fiercely. The boy didn't see me approach and was off balance when I pushed him. He fell backward onto the cement walkway, scraping his elbow. His mother jumped up and ran at me. "What are you doing! Leave Paulie alone!"

The lifeguard quickly climbed down from her tower and checked on Paulie, but he burst free from her arms and clutched my neck in a wrestling hold. The lifeguard attempted to pull him off me. But the two of us fell into the deep water. Paulie released me as his fears took over. I surfaced, and he stayed under. Margaret dove in and pulled him up. Her scarred arm supported him under his neck. Paulie, gasping, looked up at Margaret. "Let me go, you freak."

The lifeguard completed the rescue. Paulie's mother comforted him even though he'd swallowed no more than a few teaspoons of water. Margaret gathered her clothes and towel and disappeared into the changing room. She emerged fifteen minutes later, eyes blurry. Only part of that was from the chlorine.

She didn't say a word as she drove me home until she pulled over a block from the house. "Do you know that family?"

"Never seen them before."

"Me, either." She rubbed her face and neck. "Most people at the pool know me. Doesn't bother them."

"I'm sorry about what they did."

She smiled, a trace of lavender lipstick on her teeth. "Let's get a burger at the A&W."

"Sure."

While we waited for the carhop to deliver our food, she twisted the rearview mirror toward her and applied a thick coating of the same lavender lipstick. "Maybe if I'd had more of this on, they wouldn't have noticed."

Usually, she would quickly apply her lipstick without needing her reflection to guide her. This time she worked the purple paste over and over, staring intently at her face. "Never seems to bother you, Mickey."

She removed a purse-size package of Kleenex from the glovebox and dabbed at the smudge at the corner of her mouth before turning the mirror back in place. She focused her vision straight ahead, now using a tissue on her eyes. "They just don't know about you, Margaret. Probably hadn't seen anything like it before."

The carhop returned with our burgers and French fries and could see Margaret's distress. "Everything OK?"

Margaret couldn't respond, so I leaned toward her window. "It's good. Thanks."

Margaret didn't unwrap her burger and only nibbled on the French fries. Gradually, her tears were replaced by a look of stony determination. She pulled out of the parking lot slowly and crawled along River Road at fifteen miles per hour despite several cars blaring their horns as they passed us. She pulled into an overlook of the Bridgeton Flowage. "You're a lot like your dad, Mickey. You're both caretakers."

"Grandma watches over you, too."

Margaret chuckled. "She sure does. She wouldn't let me go when I had a chance."

"What do you mean?"

"I wanted to go to law school in Chicago. She made me come back here."

"How could she do that?"

"Daddy was on her side. Said the law was no place for a woman. Back then, I didn't think I could continue in school without their support. But I wish I would have stayed. There are thousands of freaks on big city streets. Nobody there cares if I'm ugly or not."

"Couldn't you go back now? On your own?"

"It's too late. Daddy would fight me even more. Mom has some coronary issues. I'd probably break her heart if I left. Maybe it would kill her. Nobody would want that, not even your dad." She laughed. "Things were much simpler when I was twenty-two."

A speed boat zoomed by with a water skier dancing on a single ski. "Your dad was the only one who stuck up for me after I graduated from Loyola. He knew I'd be happier in Chicago. Boy oh boy, he and your grandpa got into some fierce arguments."

Margaret unscrewed her lipstick case, touched her bottom lip with the tip of the lavender paste, and held it there for what seemed a minute before returning it to the case. "You never seem that sad," I said.

"I try to be happy. Maybe if I lived all alone in a big house. Down a long, long driveway."

"You could have your own swimming pool."

"A housekeeper would do all my errands. I would read and draw and take walks. I wouldn't have to see anyone. I could be invisible."

"Wouldn't you get lonely?"

"I'm used to being alone. Done it all my life."

Fifteen
Melvin Trillup

The Brick was a one-story, country grade school rooted like a bunker into Tenman Bluff on the far side of the Wisconsin River. We could observe the activity at the school from the rolling river banks in Bridgeton, as pickup loads of Brickies drove up to 4-H Club meetings and monthly potlucks. The school was the community center for nearby families, most of whom worked dairy farms, managing herds of two dozen Holsteins from dawn to dark. Melvin Trillup's family was different. They raised Dorset and Hampshire sheep, the same as their forebears had in Wales, and abstained from most neighborhood socializing. Melvin was the only one of the five Trillup children who hadn't been homeschooled.

Though the Brick was just two miles from the center of Bridgeton, the river divided us, and townies seldom interacted with Brickies. Consequently, when the Brickies settled into ninth grade with the rest of our classmates from St. Peter's Catholic school and Bridgeton Elementary, they stood out like newly arrived immigrants. They congregated into a pod and propelled themselves like a colony of algae throughout the high school building as if there were some invisible glue binding them to each other.

This sense of the Brickies being travelers in a foreign country was exacerbated in Melvin's case because, by a genetic quirk within the families of the Brick community who propagated children in 1947, he turned out to be the only boy in his class of seventeen. The adhesive that connected the female Brickies to each other didn't extend to Melvin. His predicament was further aggravated by his size. He was the smallest boy in our class of eighty-two students, not even five feet, less than one hundred pounds, and barely sneaking into puberty. His buzz-cut and peach fuzz sideburns added to his childlike appearance. As a result, he wandered the hallways of Bridgeton High alone, seeking a safe corner where he could take a deep breath.

He landed in third-hour Algebra 1 class with Lemon and me. Bridgeton High did not believe in accelerating bright kids, but Lemon was so brilliant that he was teaching the class more than Mr. Lattimore after just a month. Lattimore often sat in the back of the classroom with a cup of coffee, amused to have an additional break in his schedule. He nodded approvingly as Lemon swept the strawberry-blond hair from his eyes and offered private tutoring lessons to every student who was having difficulty factoring binomials, something he had mastered in fifth grade. We were utterly confident in Lemon's abilities. He had a knack for reaching kids with the fundamentals of algebra that Lattimore had forgotten long ago, if he had it to begin with.

When Lemon noticed Melvin lagging, he adopted him as his class project, convinced that Melvin could master algebraic equations and linear inequalities and earn a B. At first, Melvin could barely figure out enough to get a D-. I did the dirty work as Melvin's partner through the grind of daily homework, and sometimes I struggled to understand it myself.

Melvin was also in our English and physical education classes. We assisted him in English as much as we could but were handicapped by Mrs. LeFore, who did not have the same permissive attitude about students helping each other as Mr. Lattimore. In gym class, with a mix of ninth and tenth graders, the task was both simpler and more complex—keeping the tenth-grade thugs from harming Melvin. We enlisted Jimbo in the endeavor. Jimbo had reached most of his adult stature by the end of eighth grade, an imposing specimen nearly six feet, five inches tall, two hundred thirty pounds, most of it natural muscle. Despite his size, he understood being bullied more than anyone I knew.

We weren't nearly as successful in PE as we wanted to be, and Jimbo and I were hauled into Principal Horner's office on several occasions. Our crime: insubordination by interfering with a teacher's authority. Coach Langford didn't care if his football players shoved Melvin into the bleachers or forced him under the showers with his clothes on and didn't want any of us taking up Melvin's cause.

Jimbo bloodied the nose of the coach's son, Casey Langford, when he and his hoodlum friends stripped Melvin down to his briefs and attempted to duct tape him to the shower stanchion. Coach Langford turned Jimbo into a tackling dummy that afternoon at football practice, which so angered Jimbo that he quit the team the day after Coach promoted him to a starting position on the varsity defensive line. But we couldn't protect Melvin all the time, even if he was earning a well-deserved C in algebra. He began to show up late for class with a torn shirt or wet trousers around his fly where Casey Langford and his friends urinated on him. Or his feeble attempts to fight back would result in a cut lip.

When Melvin began skipping PE class, Coach Langford would send Lemon and me to find him. If we did, we never forced him to return, taking him, instead, to Mrs. James' office. She was a new counselor in the building and one of the few teachers who wanted to protect Melvin, though she discovered the high school staff was too intimidated to back her when she spoke out. When Melvin went AWOL all day, Lemon took matters into his own hands by tutoring him after school and convincing a few teachers to permit him to take exams to the Trillup home, where he proctored Melvin's efforts.

Coach Langford wouldn't tolerate this coddling. He silenced Mrs. James and convinced Principal Horner to threaten Melvin and his family with truancy. Lemon and I were at the Trillup's when Police Chief Edwards delivered the ultimatum. Melvin's mother meekly nodded her head, but Lemon challenged him. "Dave, who's going to make sure Mel's safe at school?"

Dave Edwards, first cousin to Lemon's dad, could only shake his head. "Sorry, Lem, that's not my job."

Melvin returned to school—for a week. When Lemon and I visited him at home during his second episode of absences, Melvin showed us his guns—a .22 and a double-barrel shotgun. He liked to hunt, but trap shooting was his passion. He had a collection of trophies on the living room mantle that he'd won at local and regional contests, competing against trap shooting veterans. We followed him out to a field of clover behind the house tucked between two pastures of grazing sheep where he'd set up a shooting range, and he demonstrated how to launch a clay by swinging the throwing arm of the trap thrower. An orange disk, five inches in diameter, soared through the air and landed half a football field beyond us. "Which gun do you use?" Lemon asked.

Melvin retrieved a second shotgun, a single-barrel, Browning Auto-5, and exulted, "Special for the sport. Let me show you."

He stepped back and waved at me to yank on the throwing arm, releasing another disk from its nest. Melvin snapped off a shot, and the pellets from the shotgun blast shattered the clay. Lemon propelled a clay from a second machine twenty-five yards away from me, and Melvin pulverized it. Then we sent two clays flying at the same time, and Melvin fired. Two shots, two clays down. "That's called a double trap," Melvin said as he reloaded his rifle.

Lemon and I took turns at the trap throwers over the next hour, and Melvin missed only three times, reloading after every five shots. He was machinelike in his near perfection, fully determined to demonstrate his expertise. As we biked the three miles back home, Lemon wouldn't say a word, and when we reached his driveway, he kept pedaling with me. We stopped outside Jimbo's house, and Lemon led the charge up to Jimbo's room. Jimbo was listening to the radio, half-asleep. "Jimbo, Melvin might do something if things don't get better."

"What are you talking about?"

"We just saw him shoot clay targets. Like a robot. A perfect marksman."

"He's good. I've seen him shoot. What's wrong with that?"

"The cops will make him come back to school again. Nobody can keep him safe all day, and everyone's got a breaking point."

"Nobody breaks like that, Lem."

"What if he's thinking about it?"

It was funny how we trusted Jimbo with this type of stuff. The real stuff. We thought he was our expert. He shook his head. "We'll protect him when we can and hope that fucking idiots like Casey Langford find a new target."

When Melvin returned the next week, he marched through the hallways with a composed glare and the same level of intensity we'd seen when he annihilated the clays on his shooting range. His stony resistance was so focused in algebra class that he worked on just a couple of problems. I didn't push him to do more. He attended PE but retreated to the top row of the bleachers, refusing to participate. For the first two days, Coach Langford let him be but ordered him to change clothes and shoot buckets with the rest of us on the third day. "Didn't bring my shorts and gym shoes," Melvin said.

"Play in your street clothes. But get your ass off my bleachers."

Jimbo climbed to the top of the bleachers and stood next to Melvin. "He's on my team."

Coach was in a surly mood, not only irritated by Melvin's behavior but still angry with Jimbo for quitting the football team. "OK, McPhearson, your team against Casey's. The rest of us will watch."

It was brutal from the first possession. Casey and his football buddies fouled us the moment we touched the ball. Jimbo smashed Casey with an elbow to his neck as he attempted a layup. Casey targeted the back of Melvin's head with the ball when Melvin stood motionless and unsuspecting, just three feet away. The ball snapped his head forward into Bobby Resonte, who shoved Melvin to the floor and tromped twice on his back. Jimbo leaped into Casey's face, screaming at him, shoving him, his rage out of control. Lemon and I were barely able to hold Jimbo back. Coach Langford's whistle finally interrupted the play, and he ordered Jimbo to the principal's office. Jimbo hustled to the locker room with Melvin in tow and Lemon and me in the rear. We changed clothes, making sure Melvin didn't run out on us. The four of us strode through the gym like a posse of outlaws from a Hopalong Cassidy movie. Principal Horner didn't believe our complaints, so we accompanied Melvin home to make sure his mother heard the real story before the school called with their invented one.

Melvin wasn't in algebra or English class the next day. There was no word of him until the three of us strolled into the locker room after lunch, late for gym class. Melvin was perched on a stool, his back against the wall, his semi-automatic shotgun aimed at the rest of the class. Most of the boys were half-dressed in their gym clothes, and several were naked, reaching for towels. Coach Langford attempted to settle Melvin down in his usual manner. "Your ass is gonna be in jail, Trillup. Put the damn rifle down."

Melvin was thinking only about retaliation against everyone in PE class, and maybe the world, who treated him unfairly. With only a few seconds hesitation, Jimbo advanced into the middle of the confrontation, standing tall between Melvin and the crowd of boys, next to Coach Langford, as though he'd planned this intervention weeks ago. "Mel, who do you want me to take out?"

Jimbo looked down at Coach, six inches his junior, though Coach's belly pushed him near Jimbo's weight. "Coach Langford? I'll take him down right now. So you don't have to."

Melvin was unaffected, hands steady on the shotgun, and nobody doubted it was ready for action. Jimbo moved to Bobby Resonte's side. "How about Resonte? The fuckhead who stomped on you yesterday." Bobby looked afraid, wearing nothing but his white briefs. I wondered if they'd turn yellow.

Jimbo shifted over to Jackie Schaffer, another bully. "What about Dickface Schaffer?" Jackie mouthed a "fuck you" toward Jimbo, but Melvin was unfazed.

Jimbo shoved his index finger into the bare chest of Casey Langford. "Is this the asshole you need me to take care of? I'd love to do it. Just nod your head."

Melvin responded with a slight grin, and Jimbo could see the change. "Yeah, Casey Langford? Biggest turd in school, right, Mel?"

Melvin's grin became a full smile as he engaged with Jimbo's show. "I'm gonna do it, but then it's over, OK? Just say, 'yeah,' and I'll take care of him."

Melvin nodded twice, and we could see his lips moving. "First you gotta agree. But then we're done," Jimbo insisted.

Melvin nodded with gusto now, and his voice cracked as he said, "He's the one."

Jimbo pointed to Casey's jockstrap twisted around his groin, half in place. "Straighten yourself out."

Casey obediently packed his genitals into the pouch of the jock, waiting for Jimbo's next command. "You ready, Langford?"

"Knock it off, McPhearson," Casey's dad shouted.

"Be careful, Coach. Melvin's got the shotgun."

Jimbo didn't deliberate any longer. He uncorked an uppercut into Casey's solar plexus, a thud so pure and sweet it couldn't have been a more perfect punch. The air went out of Casey like an inflatable Santa that had been unplugged, and he was on the floor, gasping, reaching for any drops of oxygen we could offer as he curled into a fetal position. He finally caught a bit of breath and heaved deeply, forcing the beans and franks from his lunch to erupt. The nearby students backed off from the mess as Casey rolled into his own vomit.

Jimbo stood in front of Melvin. "I took care of him. Just for you. Now, give me the shotgun."

Melvin pulled the rifle away from the class and, almost smirking, said, "Until somebody else takes his place."

Quicker than Jimbo could put his hand on the rifle, Melvin had the stock between his ankles, the barrel under his chin, and his thumb on the trigger, like he'd practiced the maneuver at home. Nobody was paying attention to Casey moaning on the floor. Coach Langford was out of his element, speechless. Jimbo crouched down on one knee, a foot from Melvin, as calm as I'd ever seen him. "You have to keep your promise, Mel. Only fair, right?"

Lemon stood behind Jimbo. "Come on, Mel. Give it to Jimbo."

Melvin shook his head, defeated. "We need you around here, Mel," I said.

He gave me a quick glimpse, knowing my words were a lie and believing there was no way out. Chief Edwards and Principal Horner conferred pensively near the entrance to the locker room, but nobody interfered with us. Then Jimbo started crying. "My brother used to beat me. Just as bad as you get it. I felt like shit."

Melvin's hands started shaking, thumb still on the trigger. Jimbo leaned forward and spoke so softly nobody could hear him except Melvin, Lemon, and me. "He kicked me. Pounded me. I had bruises all over my body. Wanted to get back at him so bad. I understand, Mel. I do."

Melvin had to be wondering how his muscular hero who had just crushed Casey Langford with one blow could have ever been anyone's punching bag. Jimbo delicately touched Melvin's boyish chin and cheek, and Melvin's tears rolled over Jimbo's thick fingers. Jimbo gently took the shotgun, clicked on the safety, and slid it across the cement floor toward Chief Edwards. Edwards immediately checked to see if it was loaded. Everyone saw the five shells drop into his left hand.

Jimbo helped Melvin off the stool, almost carrying him, as he led him out of the locker room. They walked across the gym floor, Jimbo's right arm over Melvin's shoulder until Sheriff Menderson stopped them, turned Melvin around, and cuffed him in bracelets that almost slid off his slender wrists. Menderson accompanied Melvin out to the squad car, and Jimbo quickly headed up the hallway. Lemon and I ran to catch him, but he was already in Mrs. James' office. We could hear him sobbing through the door.

Lemon and I left school and wandered along the shoreline of the river. "How did you know he'd bring the rifle to school, Lem?"

"I didn't. But I knew he'd break. Anyone of us would have."

"Did you think Jimbo could stop him?"

"Wasn't sure. But he was the only one who had a chance."

Lemon's dad was at their house when we arrived. The school hadn't called yet, so we told him what happened, and after he silently listened to everything we said, he immediately drove off. Dad arrived an hour later from the paper mill and took me home. He wanted the details but only the truth. I told him everything, pausing only when the words caught in my throat, "Glad we don't have guns. In case anybody gets that angry."

"I've got a couple, Mick. Never shown them to you or your brother. I saw what they could do when I fought at Guadalcanal. That was enough."

The next day, Mr. Lattimore was back in front of the classroom teaching Algebra 1, and Lemon was nowhere in sight. He wasn't in English class either, so I didn't see him until lunch time. "Where'd you go, Lemon?"

"Dad got me moved up in classes. Algebra 2, Chemistry. Principal Horner is letting me take PE class independently. Dad said, 'If the bullies are going to run the show, then get out of there as soon as you can.'"

"What's that mean?" Jimbo said.

"Might finish high school early. In three years. Not sure."

"Shit. All I got is a rescheduled PE class," Jimbo said.

"No days out for gut-punching Casey Langford?" I said.

Jimbo laughed. "Langford came to see Dad last night, yelling and cursing his ass off behind the closed door of Dad's office. He threatened to sue Dad and beat the shit out of me. When he was done, Dad asked him if he needed a new physician for his wife who is seven months pregnant. That calmed him down a bit. Dad suggested bringing Casey in, so he could examine his abdomen. Coach left after that."

Jimbo's new schedule put him in my eighth-hour history class. When he walked in, everyone stopped talking. "Where should I sit, Mr. Harris?" Jimbo asked.

Mr. Harris, who was only a few inches taller than Melvin, motioned him to the front of the classroom and stood up from his chair. Dwarfed by Jimbo, Mr. Harris reached up, shook Jimbo's hand, and started clapping. Everyone joined in, and the applause and whistling went on for almost a minute. Jimbo never liked attention and turned away. When they were done, Jimbo said, "What about Mel?"

We fell silent as Jimbo took a desk behind me.

Melvin Trillup spent the next two weeks at the Marathon County jail. There was no juvenile section in 1961, so he was mixed in with drunks, petty thieves, and dads who weren't paying their child support. Our fathers visited Melvin's parents and offered to pay for a good lawyer, and, after the initial court proceeding, Melvin was placed at the Mendota Mental Health Center in Madison. He never returned to Bridgeton High School.

Melvin stayed in touch with Jimbo and invited the three of us to his wedding ten years after he disappeared from Bridgeton. Life had spun us in different directions during the intervening time. I was teaching social studies at Eau Claire Memorial High School, and Lemon was in his second year of residency at the University of Minnesota Hospitals training to be an orthopedic surgeon. Jimbo was limping along as a mechanic for American Airlines in St. Louis, still battling PTSD four years after his discharge from the Air Force. A plum-sized chunk of shrapnel had blown out his left knee at one of the many battles near Chu Lai and shortened his tour in the war Lemon and I had been able to avoid. He was among the first GIs to receive knee replacement surgery, but he was not the same guy we knew so well in high school.

Melvin asked Jimbo to be his best man and told him nothing was off limits when he gave his toast at the reception dinner, but Jimbo knew he couldn't mean it. Instead, Jimbo, speaking softly through his thick, black beard to a crowd of one hundred guests at the Madison Elks Club, recalled the years growing up in Bridgeton at a much simpler time when neighbors accepted neighbors regardless of differences. He described how smoothly Melvin adjusted to high school in Bridgeton before transferring to a new school in Madison. He ended by detailing the Central Wisconsin Trap Shooting Tournament he witnessed in eighth grade. Melvin won first place and was celebrated with his photograph on page one of the sports section of the *Wausau Herald* holding a trophy almost as tall as he was. Not many at the wedding knew about the trophies as Melvin had given up trap shooting after he was sent away.

Later in the evening, Melvin took some time to chat with us. He was only a few inches taller than he'd been in ninth grade, not more than thirty pounds heavier, and had a wispy moustache and shaggy, brown hair covering his ears. Seeing us look down at him again must have taken him back to those troubling months in Bridgeton. "If I had my druthers, I'd be six-foot, like you guys. But as Popeye says, I yam what I yam. My height kept me out of Vietnam. Being a shrimp finally paid off." It sounded like a quip he used with a lot of people.

With little prompting, he turned the clock back ten years and told us about his life after a nine-month hospital stay, completing his last three years of high school in Waunakee, living with the Jorgenson family, who treated him like one of their own. He earned an associate degree at Madison Area Technical College. After bouncing around with some accounting work, he was now the business manager at the Madison office of the U.S. Postal Service. He hadn't been back to Bridgeton since he was escorted out of town in handcuffs when he was fifteen and saw his family only when they visited him at his home in Middleton. He rattled on with five minutes of nonstop, compressed information but then suddenly ran out of things to say. It was hard for us to keep the conversation going without posing the questions we needed to ask but were reluctant to utter. He gave us another few seconds before he said, "Better give some time to the other guests."

He shook our hands with firm resolve, like he was about to fire at a clay disk hurtling through the sky, and started walking away, but then paused and came back. "That was a terrible day, back in Coach Langford's class, when I brought the shotgun."

He hesitated for just a few beats, knowing we were entitled to the explanation. "I still think about it almost every day. It's always there, even though I haven't talked about it since I left the hospital. Nobody could possibly understand why I did it. Even if I gave them all the reasons, they still wouldn't add up. Nothing would, except to call me crazy. Maybe you guys have an inkling. You were there and witnessed some of the crap that led up to it. But even with that, it still doesn't make sense."

He turned away toward the roomful of his wedding guests, gathering his nerve, before looking each of us in the eye. "Some days, I still wonder why I didn't pull the trigger, because I meant to. Wanted to. It wouldn't have mattered if I had taken somebody with me. That's all I could see that day."

His eyes flickered upward to the ceiling like we were alongside him in his daily ruminations about the locker room at Bridgeton High School. "The details were fuzzy for months afterward. Some still are. But I've wanted to tell you guys about it for years, knowing you were there trying to stop me."

"Do you remember Jimbo taking the shotgun away?" Lemon asked.

He looked into Jimbo's face. "I can still hear the sound of your voice pleading with me to give it up. But the specific words are foggy."

"What about Jimbo punching Casey Langford?" I said.

"I never know if what's in my head is what I saw or what Jerry, my therapist, told me about what happened. I know he spent a day in Bridgeton talking to people."

"We spoke to him one afternoon," Lemon said.

"Jimbo filled me in. Wish I could remember that punch more vividly. Jerry said he would've given a hundred bucks to have seen it." He smiled at Jimbo. "You doing that for me. Casey rolling around on the floor in his own puke." Then he turned serious again. "You getting that shotgun away from my head."

His tears started, and he wiped them on his cuff-linked sleeve. "I sent a letter to Casey and his dad, apologizing."

"For what?" Lemon said.

"It was part of the program at the hospital. Trying to resolve my anger."

"But you must be pissed at them. Even after all these years," Jimbo said.

Melvin looked at him like Jimbo was seeing through every façade he'd erected since that day. "Suppose so, but what's the point?"

Jimbo, still searching for a way to purge his bitterness over what he'd seen and done in Vietnam, lashed out. "Sometimes, you have to make a fucking point."

Melvin nodded. It was just the two of them now. "My clearest memory is you asking me which one I wanted you to take down. I had no idea what you meant by that—if you were going to take the gun from me after we settled on Casey and shoot him yourself. Then you belly-punched him. While everyone must have been watching Casey, I kind of blacked out. I don't even know how the barrel of the shotgun ended up under my chin. When I came back, you were kneeling in front of me, crying, touching my face, begging me to stop."

He shook his head like he had gone too far on his wedding night when memories like this had no place. "Man, that was a bad day. If my wife knew about it, she'd probably leave me. Have me locked up again."

He touched Jimbo's beard with his right hand. "I used to ask Jerry every week why you did it. Because you and I were barely friends."

"It could've been Mickey or Lemon. I just took my turn," Jimbo said softly.

"Jerry told me I owed you. That I couldn't ever give up until I paid you back."

Jimbo affectionately enclosed Melvin's fingers in his enormous mitt. "The medic who hauled me out of Chu Lai took care of your debt. Save your payment for your wife and kids."

Melvin half-smiled through his tears. "Never asked you. Would you have slugged Coach if he'd been the one?"

"He had that enormous beer gut. Wouldn't have had the same effect."

We laughed, but Jimbo continued, stone-cold sober, his fist now gripping Melvin's firmly. "I should have smashed him. Right in his goddamn teeth. He deserved it more than the rest of them combined."

Melvin's wife approached, her wedding gown unpinned and loose around her waist. We could see she was halfway through her pregnancy. Melvin introduced us again, and she thanked us for coming. "Not many here from Bridgeton."

She could see her husband had been sniffling. "Honey, are you alright?"

Melvin nodded. "We were just talking about the old days. These guys saved my life one time. Especially Jimbo."

She grinned at us, full of joy and innocence. "That was so nice of you."

She had no idea what Melvin was referencing, and we didn't want her to know. Instead, she led Melvin away to the parquet dance floor, and he held her hand, confident in his love. Melvin Trillup did not seem like he was faking it. The five-person band started up again, and the lead singer announced it was the moment for the bride and groom's special song, the band's cover of Elvis', "Can't Help Falling in Love." Jimbo grinned as Melvin pulled his wife as close to him as her baby bump would allow, both of his arms around her waist, the lyric about wise men and fools washing over us. Jimbo was pleased with himself, and it took enormous persuasion in those years getting him to be that way. "What you told Mel earlier. That wasn't close to the truth," I said to him.

"It wasn't that far off. You and Lem watched over him, too."

"But we wouldn't have done what you did."

"Somebody's got to do the shitty stuff, Mick. Otherwise, things fall apart, and we can't go on."

"Was Vietnam like that?"

"That was different. Something the government tried to make me do. Getting that shotgun out of Mel's hands was personal. I needed to stop him. If he'd started shooting, everything about us growing up in Bridgeton would have been shattered." He slung his arm over my shoulder. "You understand that, too."

I nodded as we watched Mel twirl his wife three times when the band segued into "All Shook Up." I poked Jimbo in the ribs. "You never would have slugged Coach."

He turned and kissed me on the cheek. "Who knows? I wasn't myself that day."

Sixteen
Miss Kitty's

Not a week went by without someone referencing Miss Kitty's. Tight-jeaned classmates drove by her house at night, pausing on Rib Hill Road to glance into the upstairs windows, the ones we assumed were bedrooms, always dimly lit and curtained with heavy drapes. Occasionally, one of them regaled us with his adventures of sneaking into the premises, hidden behind an eight-foot-high cedar barrier, where he then witnessed through the downstairs windows spectacles of women performing feats so provocative that he reached the most explosive orgasm in his life. Rumor was, you had to be twenty-one to get an "appointment" at Kitty's, just as you had to flash your ID to get into a bar. But there were countryside taverns where the bartenders didn't check your age, and we hoped Kitty's might be the same.

This keen interest made life very complicated for Debbie Kedrowski, who lived at Kitty's with her mother, Katherine. Debbie had been in our class since fifth grade, but once we understood, by eighth grade, what Miss Kitty's allegedly was, Debbie became an instant pariah to many. Most of the girls went out of their way to avoid her. In contrast, the most daring and lustiest of the boys befriended Debbie hoping she'd reveal house secrets. With an air of a woman in her twenties, Debbie smiled at their inquiries but wouldn't say a thing.

It was early September of eleventh grade, and Jimbo was on an enforced break from his starring role as a two-way lineman on the football team, recovering from a separated shoulder. On a Saturday evening, he and I were fixing dinner at his house, something we often did on weekends when Mom worked her evening shift at St. Mary's Hospital. Jimbo, who had become quite adept at cooking over the past five years, grilled the marinated chicken on the side patio. A Chevy Impala pulled into the driveway, and Debbie Kedrowski exited the driver's door and assisted a woman about forty-five from the passenger side. The woman leaned on Debbie, limping, as they entered Doc's office. Jimbo handed me the tongs for the chicken and dashed out to get his dad who was building a table in his woodshop. Debbie came out of the house a few minutes later and found me cooking. "Where's Doc, Mickey?"

"Jimbo's retrieving him. He'll be there in a minute."

Debbie scanned the sizzling chicken. "Better turn those pieces in the middle. They're catching fire."

As I flipped the chicken breasts, Debbie retreated back inside. I wanted to listen in just as Jimbo would be, but somebody had to watch our supper. Jimbo reappeared with Debbie a few minutes later. "It'll be a while. Might as well sit out here with us."

Debbie picked up the second set of tongs and worked the chicken. "What are you doing tonight?" Jimbo asked, quite brashly.

"As you can see, Mom'll need help. Some TV. The usual for a Saturday night."

"*Gunsmoke*?" I asked.

Debbie smiled like a knowing actress. "Maybe. I know what people say about our place."

"Just like the Long Branch Saloon has more going on than drinking and gambling," Jimbo said.

"You think that's what happens at our house?" Debbie teased but with a bit of an edge now, though Jimbo and I still enjoyed it.

"The kids at school think so."

"Don't believe all the rumors."

"Any reason we shouldn't?"

"I could invite you out to the house sometime, if you're not too timid. You'd see that Mom and I are just an ordinary family trying to get by."

Dad walked in with a bowl of potato salad. He recognized Debbie and nodded. "How's the chicken doing?"

"It's ready," Jimbo said. "Dad's treating Debbie's mom inside. Said to start without him."

I handed out the paper plates, including one to Debbie, but she resisted. "Mom and I will get something later."

"We've got plenty," Dad said as he scooped servings of salad and bacon beans onto her plate.

We settled into our meals, Jimbo passing around the paper towels for the greasy chicken, the four of us eating in silence until Dad broke the spell. "Your mom OK?"

"Slipped on the stairs. Her foot's swelled up."

As if on cue, we heard Doc's voice from the front steps cautioning Katherine about extraneous activity. "If it feels the same on Monday, let's get some x-rays."

"Over here, Dad," Jimbo yelled out.

As they came around the corner of the house, Katherine paused and winced while Doc fiddled with the height adjustment on the crutches he'd given her. "Hey, Katie. Come join us," Dad said.

Katherine glanced down at Debbie, nearly done with her food, then over at Dad, thinking the same as me, how all of this would get translated by the neighbors when word got out that the "boys" hosted Miss Kitty and her daughter for a barbeque. She was more concerned about Mom than Dad was. "I think we better go."

Jimbo fixed a plate and topped it with tinfoil. "For when you get home."

A few days later, Debbie was standing at the bus stop after school, and Jimbo and I stopped on our way to his car. The temperature was in the low nineties, humid as mid-July, and Jimbo and I had stripped off our damp T-shirts as soon as we walked out the front door. Debbie's blouse was unbuttoned to her brassiere. "I think you missed the bus. You can still catch it at the Brick," Jimbo said, referencing the elementary school across the Wisconsin River. "We'll drop you."

Debbie sat between us in the front seat of Jimbo's Fairlane. She smelled of eight hours in high school classrooms, tangy from the perspiration saturating and resaturating her clothing, even if she'd done nothing more than sit in a near-comatose state while our teachers rattled on, oblivious to the heat. It was the same stink Jimbo and I had, but it was intoxicating emanating from her body. The breeze through the open windows caught her auburn hair, blowing it across my skin. More than anything I wanted to feel her bare shoulders up against mine.

We caught up to the bus halfway across Old Iron. "We can take you all the way home if you want," Jimbo said.

"If you've got time. I usually drive, but Mom needed the car to go to the hospital."

"Foot any better?"

"Not much. Swelling's down with all the icing, but she still can't put any weight on it."

Jimbo passed the bus and the Brick and headed out to Rib Hill Road. When we pulled up alongside her house, she invited us in. "You can park behind the house."

The tall cedar gate was open, but the Kedrowski Impala was gone. Miss Kitty's had two back doors, and Jimbo and I slipped our T-shirts back on as Debbie led us through the one on the left into a kitchen that could have been the one Mom took pride in. A single dirty coffee cup rested in the sink, and the counters were cleared except for a plate of fresh chocolate chip cookies. Late afternoon sunshine lit up the turquoise and lemon décor, and cool air blew in from a window AC unit. Debbie tossed her books onto a desk in her bedroom, down a short hallway.

"Hungry?" she said, already rummaging in the refrigerator, pulling out bread and cheese. She heated a large griddle over two stove burners and buttered one side of a half-dozen slices of dark bread, set three of them on the griddle, shaved cheddar cheese from a two-pound block, cut a fresh garden tomato into thin strips, and placed layers of cheese, tomato, and a second handful of grated cheese on top of the bread already sizzling on the griddle. By the time she topped each sandwich off with the second slice of bread, the stacks were ready to flip. She turned down the heat then quartered eight-inch pickles. "Milk or water?"

We were too amazed by the deft coordination of her cooking performance to answer, so she plunked ice cubes into three glasses and filled them from a pitcher of lemon water. "Have a seat," she said, smiling.

"You've made grilled cheese sandwiches before?" Jimbo asked.

"Cooking's one of my jobs around here. Not unusual to make ten at a time." She was about to coat the inside of the sandwiches with mustard when she paused. "Spicy or yellow?"

"Whatever you like," I said.

"Most people don't like the spicy."

I'd tasted plenty of grilled cheese sandwiches before, but none like Debbie's. The cheese and tomato fused into the type of sandwich you'd expect for ten dollars at the Wausau Club. "The grated cheese makes all the difference," she said after we'd complimented her again on her creations.

Jimbo paused halfway through. "Your dad around?"

"I see him from time to time, but he doesn't live here. Mom inherited the house from her aunt, which is why we moved back to Bridgeton when I was ten. She grew up in these rooms."

She placed the cookies in front of us and slipped away to the bathroom down the hall. We followed her steps and peeked into her bedroom. The bed was neatly made with a dozen stuffed animals sleeping on her pillows. Two wall posters, one of Annette Funicello hugging Frankie Avalon, the other of Steve McQueen perched on his Triumph motorcycle, adorned the walls on either side of her bed. We shook our heads at how normal things looked and sat back down as she came out. "Bet you're dying to see the rest of the house," she said.

Jimbo nodded. "We'd be one up on everybody else at school."

She led us through a double-action door into a living room furnished with four love seats and one long sofa, all coated in deep crimson leather. Three coffee tables rested in front of the furniture with clean ashtrays stacked six-high and car racing magazines fanned out neatly. We followed her across the dark green carpeting up the stairs to a traditional layout of a series of four bedrooms with one large bathroom midway along the hall. Each bedroom was painted a different color: ochre, blood-orange, indigo, and violet, with a double bed topped by a spread that matched the color of the walls. The bedside tables had two drawers and small lamps with darkened shades. Generic paintings of ocean or desert landscapes were the only decorations on the walls, and the scarlet carpeting was freshly vacuumed. All of it cast a spell that reminded me of the clean motel rooms my parents and I had walked into after check-in. It was hard to believe anything very risqué could happen here.

We returned to the kitchen, Jimbo just as puzzled as I. We were attacking a few more cookies when two women burst through the back door, both around thirty, carrying large handbags, dressed for the weather in Bermuda shorts and loose blouses. Neither wore makeup, and their hair flowed freely, though damp from the humidity. They could have been moms picking up their kids after school or working at a church bazaar. They were surprised to see us sitting with Debbie. "Hey, Debs, who are your friends?" the dark-haired one said, like an eagle-eye auntie watching out for her ward.

"Guys from school. Mickey and Jimbo. They gave me a lift when I missed the bus."

We looked at them, not sure if we should say hello. "I'm Zel," the dark-haired woman said, offering her hand. "Madame Stuck-up is Bridget."

Bridget laughed and reached for a cookie. "Not too many, girl. You know what happens," Zel chided her. "Is your mom around, honey?"

"Not back from the hospital."

"Let her know we're upstairs."

Debbie nodded and the two women sashayed by us to the living room area. We watched Debbie who quickly rose to clean up the mess from the sandwiches. After ten minutes of agonizing silence, Zel returned, her hair now spiraled on top of her head, her eyes mascaraed into a lady of the night. "Bring us a pitcher of ice water, Debs. It's going to be a hot one tonight."

After Zel departed, Jimbo asked nonchalantly, "Debbie, want to clear up the rumors? Just for our benefit."

Debbie shrugged, figuring she might as well let us in on the secret if she had any intentions of inviting us back. "Mickey, you look too young to get in." Giving a closer eye to Jimbo's two-day growth of dark beard, she added, "You might slip by if you had a fake ID."

"Can any man walk in?" I said.

"We've got security, and Mom interviews every potential customer. Most of the johns are regulars and show up by appointment. Everyone prefers it that way. They enter through the other back entrance, by the way. None of them comes into our living area."

"Anybody we'd know?"

She raised her eyebrows. "Yup. That's as far as I can go. Mom would kill me if I gave names."

"Would you tell me if my dad's a customer?" I asked.

Jimbo and Debbie giggled. "He seemed to know you at the barbeque the other night," I said.

"He's old friends with Mom. Seen me with her. Not like we're recluses."

"Ministers or priests?" Jimbo asked.

"You'd be surprised."

Jimbo continued to push it. "Anybody from school?"

She hesitated before saying, "Just one."

"Student?" I said.

"Nope."

We rattled off the names of the likely male teachers, but she shook her head after each one. We couldn't think of anybody we'd missed. "You're forgetting someone."

"Eddie, the custodian?"

"Other direction."

"Principal Horner?"

She lit up like she'd been dying to tell someone. "Jesus. I can't believe it," Jimbo said.

"Not so much anymore. Used to be a regular."

We heard a car pull into the back. "That'll be Mom with some groceries."

We went out back to help. Katherine was still on crutches, and an older man was helping her to the house. "Hi, Deb," he said. "It's not broken."

"Thank God," Katherine said.

We set the groceries on the counter, and Deb put the food away. She introduced us to Richard, the security man, then started on another round of grilled cheese sandwiches as we slipped out the back and drove to town.

We were both intrigued with Debbie, especially Jimbo. He asked me if I'd be offended if he pursued her, and I told him he had rights. He saw her every day for two weeks until his shoulder healed enough to resume football practice. Three weeks later, Debbie gave me a lift home after school. We hadn't talked much since Jimbo began romancing her, and, as we sat in her car in front of my house, she asked, "Want to come out for a sandwich?"

"If you can bring me back to town."

She displayed her skill with the griddle again, this time with turkey and Swiss. Same process, the same level of perfection. I asked her how things were going with Jimbo. "It's over. Whatever it was."

"What happened?"

"We were sitting at the kitchen table last Saturday evening. Somebody came in the customer door. As soon as he heard his dad's voice, he got nervous. I told him to relax. Doc comes out periodically for medical screenings of the girls. Maybe he was here to check Mom's foot. Jimbo asked the inevitable question: Did Doc come to the house to be with any of the women? I didn't want to lie. Mom's been seeing him once a month for years. Her only client. Bartering for his medical care. She likes him and knows he's become a confirmed bachelor since his wife left him."

"Want me to talk to Jimbo?"

"What could you say?"

She was right. I would have done the same as Jimbo if Dad were a regular at Miss Kitty's. "Does your mother ever force you to see anyone?"

"Don't be so stupid, Mick. It's her business. Her workers want to be here."

"Sorry."

"She would never let me, even if I wanted to. She expects me to go to college and make something different of myself."

Jimbo was the one who brought up his break with Debbie. "I haven't been thinking about her much. Disappointed but no heartache. It was more a fantasy than anything else."

"How's that?"

"Got caught up in the idea of having sex. Being in that house, walking through those bedrooms. I could almost smell the juices. I'd jack off thinking about Debbie and me in the room that's painted dark orange. We'd be in her house after school. She'd lead me upstairs and seduce me."

"Would it have been the first time?"

"Not quite, but this would be the real thing. Not jammed up in the backseat of the car or in my bedroom wondering if Dad might walk in. We'd be in a room created specifically for nudity and sex. Damn, it was arousing to think about it."

"You tell Debbie that?"

He looked at me like I'd just flunked a grade, then smiled affectionately. "Turns out, she's not that kind of girl. A virgin just like you."

I nodded. "That's kind of what she told me, too."

"You asked her if she's done it?"

"Just if her mom puts pressure on her to be one of the ladies of the house."

He laughed. "Not scoring too many points with her, Mick."

"I think we're still friends."

"More than I am."

"Must be lonely."

"For her or for horny guys like us?"

"Debbie mostly wants someone to talk to. She doesn't have any friends at school. Now that you're out of the picture."

"Maybe her best friend is one of the ladies. Like Zel."

I thought about Debbie, at home on a Saturday night, listening to music in her bedroom while men and women were touching each other in completely uninhibited ways on the other side of the house. "Maybe you can be her friend. Invite her over to your house after school," Jimbo said, chuckling as he did.

"Yeah. I'm sure Mom would approve. But you could have been that guy. Doc would have understood."

"Shit. When I heard Dad's voice in the parlor at the Kedrowski's, it was like a cold shower. Put Willy to sleep, thinking Dad could be in one of those bedrooms."

"Debbie told me about your dad and Katherine. Sounds like they're good friends."

"That would have made it worse. Him sitting at the kitchen table with Katherine, drinking a beer, deciding it's time to go make love in Katherine's bedroom, on the family side of the house. Right across from Debbie's room. Like that would work out. Dad and me, having a father-son outing at Miss Kitty's."

We laughed uncontrollably. "By the way, Mick, you have my permission to go after her."

"As if I needed it."

A few weeks later, on another Saturday night, Mom was working another weekend shift at the hospital while Dad and I watched the weekly episode of *Gunsmoke*. When the show ended with Marshall Dillon joking with Doc and Miss Kitty after he'd arrested yet another varmint, I asked Dad if he liked the show. "It's not bad. Ends too predictably most of the time with the marshall catching the bad guy without as much as a scratch."

"What about Miss Kitty?"

He looked at me. "Which one?"

"On the TV show."

"Pretty good character. Wish they had more episodes showing Marshall Matt and Kitty having their affair. Would be more realistic."

"They're lovers?"

"She's a prostitute and owns part of the Long Branch Saloon. Runs the other bargirls you see in the background. Dillon's a decent guy, and Kitty's a smart gal. They'd make a good couple. If only they showed it more."

"Maybe they're just friends."

Dad laughed deeply. "And maybe the sun won't come up tomorrow. Always a chance."

"What about the other one?"

"Other what?"

"Katherine Kedrowski?"

"She's harmless. Provides a service. Mommy wouldn't agree. Between you and me, some men need that sort of thing. I saw a lot of whorehouses in the military. Never took advantage. I promised Mommy I wouldn't when I went off. Was faithful about that."

"What kind of guys go to places like Kitty's?"

"Single men who want to be certain that if they spend money on a date, she'll end up in the sack. Frustrated married guys. Could be a young buck like you wanting it for the first time."

I didn't know what to say to that. "Too blunt for you, Mick?"

"Sort of."

"It's the way the world works. Always has. Why do you think they call it the world's oldest profession?"

"What do you mean?"

"There'll always be a place like Katie Kedrowski's. There were a couple of brothels around Wausau when I was growing up. We'd probably be better off if they just legalized the whole thing."

"How do you know Katherine and Debbie?"

"Went to high school with Katie Spurley. See her around town occasionally. Debbie's usually with her. Lots of people won't talk to them. Seems silly to me."

"Mom doesn't care?"

"That I talk to an old friend?"

"That it might not be right, considering."

"We've agreed to disagree on that one."

A few months later, a group of local ministers got agitated about Miss Kitty's and tried to shut it down. They appeared month after month before the Marathon County Board, petitions in hand, and wrote letters to the *Bridgeton Times* and the *Wausau Herald*. It took more than a year before they achieved their goal. A few months after that, Principal Horner saluted us on graduation night with a speech about integrity and decency. Debbie Kedrowski wasn't there. She and her mom disappeared midway through our final semester.

When I asked Dad what he thought about the hullaballoo, he shook his head. "Wish the damn priests and ministers would get upset about something that really mattered."

Seventeen
Sally's Teeth

Dad's aunt, Daisy Jensen, lived in Knowlton, six miles south of Bridgeton. Knowlton grew up as a "pinery" settlement, four sawmills turning acres of white pines into timbers and board feet, located where the flowage of the Eau Pleine River shoots into the Wisconsin River at Lake Dubay. After the extinction of the ancient pines in the 1930s, there wasn't much left in Knowlton except Crazy Lou's Bar, St. Francis Xavier Catholic Church, and a dozen homes along the water. And, of course, the Knowlton General Store—three-quarters general goods, the other quarter a tiny branch of the U.S. Postal Service. Daisy was the post mistress, though sometimes, when we dropped in on her, she would cross over to the far side and sell us an eight-ounce bottle of Coke and an ice cream sandwich while the store clerk was out pumping gas, in the process, violating federal government regulations.

Daisy's husband died when she was in her forties. Her only son, Jackson, was off "gallivanting," as Grandpa Pederson, Daisy's brother, often said. Jackson's wife, Erma, and only child, Sally, struggled to survive in a north-side apartment in Chicago while Jackson sent money when he found work. However, postcards from places like Amarillo or Carson City were the more likely correspondence. No one reminded Daisy of this situation without risking tears or anger, depending on the day.

When Sally was sixteen, Erma passed on after a quick bout with pneumonia. Sally hadn't seen her daddy in years and didn't know how to reach him, so she turned up at the train station in Bridgeton to live with Daisy. I had met her but a few times in my life, and Dad hadn't seen her for more than five years. Though she was the only passenger to disembark from the train that rainy afternoon, we still inquired to make sure she was Sally Jensen. She'd grown up that much. Lanky at just a few inches shy of six feet, her mousy brown hair in a ponytail, and skin as clear as a prairie sunset with a few splotches of freckles, but as likeable as we remembered her when she answered our questions about the six-hour train trip. When I kidded her about being as tall as I was, she laughed, and I saw her teeth for the first time. I don't know what had gone wrong. Some were missing, and others wildly crooked. They looked like they would cause great pain if she bit into an ear of corn. They upset her natural beauty so much I had to look away.

We loaded her three suitcases and several large packing boxes into Dad's old Chevy pickup and drove quietly to Daisy's house. Dad offered his condolences about her mother, and Sally thanked him, but she had no interest in extending the conversation. We hauled her things into the spare bedroom while she and Daisy conferred in the kitchen. When we were done, we could see both Daisy and Sally had been crying, so Dad declined the invitation to dinner and drove us back home.

A few days later, Sally picked up where she'd left eleventh grade at Lane Tech High School, this time with us at Bridgeton. She was a year ahead of Jimbo and me, but she shared many of Lemon's classes in his accelerated program, so he took her under his wing. After Lemon, she turned out to be the second smartest person in school, chasing him for top grades in anatomy and physics.

After a few weeks of busing back and forth to school, Daisy asked Dad if Sally could stay over at our house twice a week to participate in rehearsals for the school musical. She'd arrived too late to get one of the leads but was in the chorus of *Oklahoma*. She had a majestic soprano voice that Lemon could never top. It rang out on opening night in the old high school gym, louder and purer than those of any of the other prairie girls looking to fall in love. She should have been Laurey Williams sitting in the cardboard surrey in the middle of the stage.

By the time the musical was over, Sally was staying at our house most school nights. Dad set her up in Dennis' old room as though she'd lived with us for years. She cleaned the house and bought groceries if Mom hadn't gotten to it and was more polite with my parents than I was, which was to be expected of a house guest, but it felt genuine with Sally. After a while, she was making supper several nights a week with Mom still nursing on the surgical floor during the evening shift at St. Mary's. Some nights Lemon would come over, and they'd do homework, and when Jimbo joined in, the four of us played hearts. Jimbo could make her laugh at jokes Lemon and I no longer found funny, and uninhibited laughter was something Sally was hesitant about, despite her eternally upbeat nature. But she forgot herself as we giggled in the privacy of our basement den.

Sally spent a few hours with Great-Grandma Pederson several days a week. Grams was ninety-three, living in her little house on Sixth Street, next to the old harness shop. Sally fixed her a meal for the next day and cleaned the messes Grams no longer noticed. I went with her occasionally, but Sally took on the chores with love, not obligation as it was for me.

The school year ended, and Sally went back to Knowlton though I'd see her once in a while at Grams. I told her Dad spoke to a dentist in Wausau checking on the cost of repairing her teeth. After Sally went in for the consult and Dad saw the estimate, he realized he couldn't afford the thousands of dollars it would take to make her teeth right. Daisy had very little to contribute, and there was no point in doing just a partial redo. We all felt bad, but Sally took it in stride. "I'm used to it," she said. "So, nothing's changed."

When the next school year resumed, Dad insisted that Sally come back with us. We didn't realize how much we missed her until she settled into Dennis' room again. Lemon wasn't around much, as he'd enrolled in college courses in Stevens Point during his final year in Bridgeton. Sally auditioned for Julie Jordan, the lead in *Carousel.*

Jimbo, who was singing the part of Jigger Craigin, told me she was leaps and bounds ahead of everyone else. Mrs. Loudin had to give her the part, and Sally was more pleased than I'd ever seen her until she heard the backlash from the jealous girls in the chorus: "What will she do when she has to smile on stage!"

She told Mrs. Loudin she'd miss too many rehearsals helping Daisy with Grams, who was in decline, and took a part in the chorus instead. Dad suggested it was a mistake, that she deserved what she earned, but it didn't seem to matter to her. She was determined to be cheerful, simply knowing she was good enough for the role.

Sally's migraines kicked in more that year and almost kept her from the four-night run of the musical. When the pain afflicted her, she hid away in Dennis' room, shades drawn, as though she'd moved back to Knowlton. Jimbo often brought her homework to the house and would talk to her quietly while he sat in a chair near Dennis' bed. The headaches ran for two days, sometimes three, every few weeks, but she never stayed away from her shifts at Grams.

Sally competed in vocal competitions on many Saturdays in winter and spring. Mrs. Loudin became her biggest fan as Sally accumulated a dozen gold medals and helped Sally apply to colleges. Some days, while I waited for her after school, I'd sit in the back of the choir room and watch Sally rehearse, her eyes closed, with just a slight flutter. The melodies captured my imagination even if the words to the pieces by Schubert and Puccini were incomprehensible. Sally's soprano soared to a place I could dream of but never reach, where she could forget about her mother and father and her responsibilities as a caretaker.

Senior prom approached, and I spoke to Jimbo. "You know how much she likes you. Do her a favor."

"I like her, too, more than any other girl in school. But just as a friend. Make sense?"

"Not like you haven't gone out with girls who are less than beautiful."

"Why don't you take her?"

"She's my cousin."

"Once removed," he said.

"Is it her smile?"

"Mostly. Just can't visualize kissing her. Pressing up against her teeth."

"At least you're honest."

Jimbo gave Mark Swiderski twenty dollars to take Sally to the prom. On the afternoon of the dance, Mark called and said he couldn't make it. It was the first time I'd seen Sally cry. His rejection confirmed everything she held inside. I called Jimbo, who went to the Swiderski house, but Mark's mother said he was fishing near Merrill and wouldn't be back until late. Jimbo was beside himself with anger though he calmed down before he went in to see Sally. "Just heard. What a shithead."

"It's OK. I'm over it."

"Nobody gets over crap like that."

Jimbo was trying to find a way out before he had to say yes. "Know any other girls going stag?"

"Don't worry about me. It's not your problem."

The soft spot inside Jimbo was breaking down. "Could I take you?"

"Because you feel sorry for me?"

"As a friend."

"Not if you don't want to be with me."

"I'm asking, Sally. Don't break my heart."

She laughed. Jimbo was the only one who could bring out her full smile so easily. "What time are we supposed to be there?"

"Dinner at The Palms at six-thirty. Dance is at eight."

"I'll be back."

Sally's pale blue prom dress was simple with golden daisies to honor her grandmother. It was the same dress she'd wear to the graduation ceremony two months later. She insisted on it, even though Mom was willing to buy her something more extravagant. Sally was practical that way, never wanting to look too good. Jimbo showed up in his only suit coat, tight-fitting since he'd gotten it for eighth-grade graduation, with a pair of his dad's suit pants that almost matched. He apologized for not having a corsage, but Sally didn't care.

Dad and I snuck into the dance for an hour, hiding in the back row of the bleachers, blending in with the crowd of parents who were so proud to see their children posing as adults. The band kicked into a string of doo-wop hits, and Jimbo pulled Sally out to the gym floor. Jimbo was the best dancer in school, despite his gigantic size, and Sally was almost as good, like they'd spent hours at the Arthur Murray Studio in Wausau. The other kids parted and gave them center stage, clapping as Jimbo peeled off his suit coat and flung it into the crowd, his undersized white shirt untucked and soaked with perspiration. Neither one took a break for the fifteen-minute long sequence of songs.

When the band finally slowed down and played "Will You Still Love Me Tomorrow," the two of them danced closely together, moving around the floor gracefully, holding hands, Jimbo's arm around Sally's waist, hers on his shoulder, unlike the other pairs that barely shifted out of place. Dad smiled. "We should go before they see us."

Sally came in at eleven, in a rush. I was waiting for her, watching a late-night movie on our fifteen-inch Sylvania. "How'd it go?"

"Wonderful. Most of the kids are going to after-prom parties. Jimbo's taking me out to the river instead."

She rushed upstairs to change and came down in trousers and a sweatshirt, jacket over her shoulder. Jimbo drove up and she raced out. When Sally returned at one-thirty, I was in bed, half-asleep, half-wanting to talk to her. She was in and out of the bathroom in a minute, and I could hear her sniffling through the wall between our rooms. I knocked on her door and her crying softened, but when I rapped a second time, she responded faintly with one word that kept me up for the rest of the night. "Tomorrow."

She came down at nine the next morning, fully dressed, and could see I'd been waiting for her, but she headed out the door. "I'm helping out with Grams all day."

"Want a ride?"

She wouldn't look at me. "The walk will do me good."

I biked up to Jimbo's, but he was asleep and grumbled as I shook his shoulder. "Come back in the afternoon. I was up until dawn."

He stopped at the house an hour later. "Couldn't get back to sleep. Thanks for waking me up, asshole."

"Want to talk?"

"Let's go down to the dam."

We clambered down the ladder underneath Old Iron. The turbulent, April waters from the Bridgeton Flowage roared over the dam and crashed through Little Bull Falls as we sat on the weathered boulders along the shoreline. Jimbo was warming up to his explanation. "I really tried to be nice. In every way. But I fucked up, I guess."

"What happened?"

"We had a great time at the dance. Sally's terrific on her feet. I saw you and your dad there, so that's no surprise to you."

"You weren't supposed to notice."

"She hadn't been invited to the parties afterward, so I took her down to the old sawmill, by the benches. The river was noisy with spring runoff, and the walleyes were jumping like crazy. I told her about us playing on the river since we were boys, and she laughed at the stories. She said she heard about me paying off Mark Swiderski and that it didn't matter. She explained her plans for next year, studying voice at Stevens Point and commuting from her grandma's in Knowlton, which is all she and Daisy can afford. I told her she should have been Julie Jordan. The character fit her so perfectly, sucking it up even if things weren't fair. She said she'd been raised to take care of people. Had to. Then, out of nowhere, she started singing 'If I Loved You,' that song from *Carousel*, softly like she was in character as part of the show. I hummed along, singing the words when I remembered them. I told her to sing out and pretend the river was ten thousand people who'd paid admission to hear her. Man, she's got a voice. We sat on the bench like we were starring in the play. I was Billy Bigelow, singing the duet with her. I could feel her wanting to fall in love. Wanting me to kiss her."

"Geez, you should have stopped singing with her."

"I did and told her how much I liked her, but as a friend. That I didn't want to be romantic. She said she knew. She'd given me enough hints over the past few months. I couldn't be so dense not to figure her out. I told her I could be pretty stupid sometimes."

I laughed, but Jimbo could only shake his head. "I could feel her heart breaking. Never wanting to smile. Feeling she was repulsive when she did. Mick, I didn't know what to do. Then one of those idiotic Jimbo impulses came to me. I asked her if she'd ever been kissed. She giggled and said she was still an ugly duckling waiting to turn. I told her I'd be honored. She said it couldn't be out of pity because that would crush her. It was the sweetest kiss I've ever given. No teenage lust. Just tender lip to lip that lasted for fifteen seconds. She got up, went over to the river, and got pretty close to the edge. I followed her and said something pathetic like, 'not gonna jump, are you?' She shook her head and said she was just wondering if it would ever happen to her."

Grams took another downturn, and Sally missed most of the last month of school taking care of her. One night in mid-May, I went up to Grams' house. Sally was sitting at the kitchen table, reading, her homework spread out before her. "How's Grams?"

"In and out."

"Getting your school work done OK?"

"Yeah, other than calculus, not that hard."

"Aunt Daisy around?"

"She went back to Knowlton. I'm spending the night."

"You mind missing so much school?"

"It's fine. Better for my migraines. Less stress."

"I brought your mail."

It was just one letter from Washington University in St. Louis, and she set it aside like it was junk. "Want something to eat?"

"Dad and I just had supper."

"He's a good cook. I've learned a lot watching him prepare food."

"Sally, open it."

"It's just another rejection."

"Give it to me then."

She opened it and started smiling, unfettered joy gushing through her crooked teeth. "What'd they say, Sal?"

"They're taking me. Full scholarship. Room, meals, tuition."

"Let me see."

She wasn't exaggerating. I knew enough about colleges to know what a plum she'd just nabbed. I hugged her, and she wouldn't let me go until the shoulder of my T-shirt was saturated with her tears. "You OK?"

"Nobody really wanted me before for what I am."

Eighteen
Virgil Lightfoot Gibson

Virgil Lightfoot Gibson showed up at Bridgeton High on the first day of our senior year. He corrected teachers whenever they called his name for roll. "Lightfoot, not Gibson." Most teachers ignored him, but Gabe Parkinson was one of the exceptions. Jimbo, Virgil, and I took Advanced American Issues with Parky that semester. He was a stickler for calling students by their last name, telling us it was preparation for college.

Parky steered us into discussions about how America deals with minority groups, past and present. No matter the group, no matter the timeframe, it was always a bleak interaction. We reread what our tenth-grade U.S. history textbook stated about the end of slavery and discrimination after the Civil War. Or how native tribes were generously given prime real estate when forced onto their reservations. Then he showed us alternative documents that revealed what our textbook left out or deliberately chose to omit. "Be skeptical of what you think you know," was Parky's mantra.

He taught us about our ancestors, the Menominee and Ojibwe and Ho-Chunk, not the Germans or Norwegians or Irish, how treaties between the tribes and the government were made and broken over and over. Sometimes they were made in good faith until waves of new immigrants pushed the government to break their "good faith." Until there was no good reason for the tribes to believe that any treaty would survive. "Neither side knew what would happen down the road," Parky explained. "Making history is not about foresight. It's about adapting to the here and now. You don't realize what you've done until decades later."

Virgil Lightfoot outpaced Parky when we discussed Native American issues. Virgil believed his ancestors were fiercely determined but undermanned by the limits of their technology and genetic resistance. If they'd had the same weapons as the Europeans, they would have survived as co-equals even if the white settlers didn't like them. If his ancestors hadn't succumbed to European diseases, their numbers would have held strong, and if his forefathers didn't have such susceptibility to alcohol, they would be as powerful as any state today. "SOL," Virgil said bitterly. Most of us didn't know what that meant, so Parky explained.

Parky invited Virgil to give a short talk about his ideas, and Virgil showed up the next day without any notes, just a paper bag. He stood before us at Parky's lectern and pulled out two full quarts of Jim Beam whiskey. "This is why you won."

We all laughed while Parky escorted Virgil and the booze to the office. Principal Horner was livid. "What the hell are you doing, Gibson?"

"Lightfoot, sir."

Virgil opened one of the bottles and took a swig. "It's Coke. I was making a point."

Parky told us what happened when he and Virgil returned to class, laughing at his own rush to judgment.

Virgil didn't say much in any other class, just completed his work without complaining, like the rest of us, good enough to get by with a B and be admitted to college, and in Virgil's case, making sure he was eligible for sports. All the coaches were salivating over Virgil's natural talent. He was six feet, four inches tall, one hundred eighty pounds, quick as a marten, and leaped like a whitetail. He had no interest in football or track once he found out that Coach Langford was the head coach. Nor did he show up for after-school pick-up games organized by the basketball coach, Mr. Jessup, though he planned to go out for the team in November. At day's end, he sat in his battered green pickup truck at the far corner of the parking lot, waiting for his twin sister, Jennifer, to get her books. After she arrived, they disappeared somewhere west of town, re-emerging at five minutes to eight the next morning.

One evening in January, as Jimbo and I checked out his new color television set, Virgil pulled into the driveway and helped an older man to Doc's office. Then he vanished, back to his truck. We went out to get him. "It's cold, man. Come inside," Jimbo said.

Virgil was skeptical, even though Jimbo talked to him every day at school. Virgil was the best player on the basketball team, and Jimbo was the first big man off the bench. Reluctantly, he left his truck and came inside. I asked him if the older man was his father or grandfather. "Uncle Tommy. My mother's brother. Jennifer and I live with him and his wife."

"Where'd you live before?" I said.

"Been around. Keshena or Lac Courte Oreilles most of the time. My family belongs to both tribes. Uncle Tommy said we needed to graduate from high school. Do something other than drink our lives away. If I complete my full load of credits this semester, I can finish in May. Same with Jennifer."

Virgil stood up and tilted his head back slightly, nose to the air. "There's something here."

"What do you mean?" I said.

"I have some power to know about places. Something bad happened here."

"Like what?" Jimbo asked.

"Probably someone died. Maybe in your dad's office. Might be nothing. Can I walk around?"

Jimbo nodded and Virgil paced through the kitchen. "Here, too."

He walked into the bedroom where Beverly used to sleep years ago, now filled with boxes of Doc's supplies. "It's strongest here."

Virgil sat on the old bed. "What happened here?"

I explained about Beverly and Lucy. "Nothing violent with them? Because I also feel anger."

Jimbo told Virgil about his brother beating him. "Can I walk through the other rooms?"

We led him upstairs. "Much better here."

Jimbo's bedroom was only semi-chaotic. His bed was unmade, and his dresser drawers were pulled out, but the rest of the room was neater than Jimbo usually kept it. Virgil sat on Jimbo's desk chair and smiled. "Harmonious. You're lucky this is your room."

"How do you know?" I said.

"Just a gift I have."

"Is that what you do before each game starts? When you sit on the bench while we're shooting around?" Jimbo said.

"Kind of the same. Getting a sense of the place and the night. Whether I should shoot or defend."

"I don't get it," Jimbo said.

"The spirit tells me about each school. Even the gym at Bridgeton changes from game to game. Some nights I know I can score. Other times, I know I will miss too often, so I focus on defense."

"Then you tell Coach Jessup?"

"Right."

"He lets you get away with that?"

"I told him before the season that's how I am. If he didn't like it, he could sit me on the bench. Other coaches have done that. So far, Jessup's been pretty fair."

I didn't understand. "You don't go to enough games, Mick," Jimbo explained. "Against some opponents, Virgil scores twenty or thirty points. Other games he hardly shoots, but he holds the best player to almost nothing."

"Never been able to do both in the same game," Virgil said.

"How'd you get Coach to make sure the PA announcer introduces you as Virgil Lightfoot?"

"Told him that's my real name. Gibson got added later on. Made sense to him."

Virgil looked at a photograph of Jimbo, Lemon, and me from fifth grade. Jimbo was much bigger than I was, even then. "Why do they call you 'Crush'?" Virgil asked.

Jimbo wouldn't say, so Virgil looked at me. "Something happened our freshman year. Jimbo punched Coach Langford's son so hard he collapsed."

"Why?"

"He was an asshole. Bullying our friend," Jimbo said.

"The school let you do that?"

After I told Virgil how Jimbo had gotten the shotgun away from Melvin Trillup when he was threatening to shoot up our physical education class, he looked at Jimbo with a new set of eyes. "You have big powers, man."

Doc came out to retrieve Virgil and told him his uncle needed to rest for a few days. He gave him some medicine, and Virgil escorted his uncle to the truck. Virgil returned a few minutes later with a bag of wild rice, partial payment for Doc's services.

Our world changed just a few weeks later. Virgil's sister, Jennifer, worked at the Riverside Café, and her shift ended on a Friday night, but she had to wait two hours for Virgil to pick her up after his game in Medford. Three boys from Wausau offered to give her a lift home. They'd been friendly to her while she waited their table, so she took the ride. They headed to a cabin in the woods instead. The three took turns—two holding her down while the third raped her. Afterward, they dropped her two miles from the Riverside and told her "to get lost, squaw." She walked to the café but sat out in the cold for an hour, ashamed to go back inside, until Virgil picked her up.

Virgil took her to the Bridgeton Police Station the next morning, and

Chief Edwards called in the Marathon County cops. On Monday, Virgil and Jennifer went to the district attorney's office. The cops identified the perpetrators, all Wausau High School basketball team members. Two of them were starters, including Randy Dover, Wausau's best player, third-team all-state the previous year. The boys had been bragging around school, making no attempt to cover up their actions until their lawyers told them to stifle it. The district attorney gave in claiming there was not enough proof to proceed with charges. It was a case of she-said versus three-of-them-said. But more telling than that, Jennifer was Native American, and most telling of all, Randy Dover was the son of Rex Dover, owner of the paper mill in Rothschild.

Virgil missed school for several more days, and when he returned, it was to help his sister. He insisted the teachers give him her homework to complete at home. When two of them refused, Jimbo pressed them for it, and his reputation forced their cooperation. Virgil skipped the next two basketball games and returned for the regular-season finale but seemed lost on the court. He tried a few shots and missed them badly. The player he was guarding drove by Virgil's flailing arms for layups all night. Bridgeton lost by twenty points.

The next day, Virgil showed up at Jimbo's and asked him for a ride to Shawano as his truck couldn't make the trip. He suggested I come, too, to keep Jimbo company during the wait. Virgil was glum and silent during the two-hour ride and when we dropped him off at a trailer home five miles outside of Shawano. He told us to come back in a few hours while he talked to his friend. When we returned, we sat in the driveway for fifteen minutes until an older woman came out of the trailer and waved us to the door. The inside looked lived in by lots of people. The kitchen was clean, and freshly baked bread and cake cooled on the counter. Newspapers and books covered the sofa and end tables. A Collie paraded past seeking our affection. Virgil came out from the bathroom, hair slicked back and wet, eyes clear and smiling broadly. An older man, about sixty, joined us from a back bedroom. We sat at the kitchen table, and the woman served us bowls of food. "Venison chili from our woods," the old man said. The woman passed a platter of cornbread, and Virgil explained, "Jonny's my uncle. Tommy's brother. This is his wife, Edna. Jennifer and I lived with them for a while after our parents split up."

"You two take care of Virg?" Jonny asked.

"Not much. Just a favor, driving him out here," Jimbo said.

"I think we fixed him. Cooked out the bad stuff. Maybe he can do something for you now."

On the drive back to Bridgeton, Virgil explained, "I lost my powers after my sister was attacked. I thought it was because I couldn't do anything to help her. Jonny's my power father. He restored me."

"How?"

"We took a sweat."

Virgil explained about a sweat lodge and how it could help heal people. "Jonny said I was too angry. That I didn't lose my power. It was hiding."

"Can you feel it now?" I said.

"Doesn't work so good in cars."

"Is your uncle a Lightfoot or a Gibson?" I asked.

"All Lightfoots on my mother's side."

"Are you gonna continue with the team?" Jimbo asked.

"I'll talk to Coach. Explain what happened."

In the 1960s, the annual state basketball tournament was still run as a one-class competition, with every school having a chance for the one gold ball. Big schools trounced smaller schools in the preliminary rounds, but it was rare when the opposite occurred. Bridgeton first played Marathon City, one of the smallest schools in the area. Virgil played offense and scored thirty-two points before sitting out the last five minutes of an easy victory. Jimbo added seven, but it was one of his best games all season. The next two games against Plainfield and Rosholt followed the same pattern, and Bridgeton, surprisingly, was one of the few small schools still in the competition in the state. In the fourth game, we played Wisconsin Rapids, a high school with fifteen hundred students, not a top-notch team, but with one great player who could carry the team if he got hot. Virgil played defense that night and held him to eight points, and Bridgeton won by seven.

There were two games left until the state tournament in Madison, but no one expected us to get there or be competitive in the next contest against Wausau, a school six times our size, ranked third in the state. The *Milwaukee Journal* had just proclaimed Randy Dover all-state, and another of the boys who assaulted Jennifer Lightfoot, Peter Stockbridge, was unanimous all-conference. It was impossible to say Wausau was our big rival because this was the first time we'd played them in fifteen years. But it was David vs. Goliath, nonetheless, and, for Virgil, much more.

The game was played in the field house at Wausau High, and our fans were outnumbered five to one. I eyeballed Virgil during the pregame, sitting on the bench, feeling the place, standing and smiling as he approached Coach Jessup. Jessup laughed heartily and slapped Virgil on the shoulder.

In the first minute of the game, Eddie Raybold, Bridgeton's best inside man, went down, screaming in pain, holding his knee. Coach Jessup ran out and waved to Doc McPhearson at the end of our bench. While the game was interrupted, Virgil pulled Jimbo off to the corner. Within my view, Virgil untied his trunks, pulled out a small leather pouch and indicated Jimbo should tie it to the strings of his shorts. Jimbo looked bewildered but followed Virgil's orders, tucking the sack inside his trunks.

Jimbo substituted for Eddie Raybold, who sat next to Doc on the bench, shoe off, knee iced, done for the night with the game tied at four. Randy Dover drove the lane with Virgil in front of him. As Dover's shot went off, both players spilled to the floor. The referee called Dover for a charge. Virgil brought the ball up court, and Dover shuffled his feet to stay in front when Virgil shifted quickly to his right, then back to his left. Dover reached out as Virgil scored a layup and committed his second foul less than three minutes into the game. Dover sat on the bench, sulking, pissed that he'd been treated unfairly, while Wausau's coach howled at the referees. Wausau's focus turned to Peter Stockbridge, playing down low, Jimbo's man to guard, though Stockbridge had a three-inch height advantage. He dribbled the ball twice and pivoted around Jimbo, rolling to the basket as Jimbo reached out to block it. Jimbo's legs, normally two oaks rooted in the earth, lifted like the birch trees in Frost's poem freed from the ice, and he tipped the ball away, soaring two feet into the air. Everybody on the bench cheered while Coach Jessup looked on in amazement. He'd never seen Jimbo go vertical by more than a few inches.

The game went back and forth. Wausau's defense was unbelievably tough, but they couldn't stop Virgil. He went for twenty in the first half, and Bridgeton was ahead by six at the break. Randy Dover was back on court in the second half, determined to go it alone, but Virgil stuck with him, and Dover missed six shots in a row, ones he normally would have made without Virgil shadowing him. His coach ordered him to pass the ball, and Dover's teammates brought Wausau back to even. It was late in the fourth quarter, and Virgil was singlehandedly keeping Bridgeton in the game. He had forty-one points, scoring in every imaginable way, while Dover had just three points and four fouls. Stockbridge dumped in seventeen, but it could have been thirty if Jimbo hadn't blocked him from the rim so effectively.

With twenty seconds left and the score tied, Stockbridge tapped a loose ball to Dover, who drove the full length of the court, assuming it would be an uncontested layup, putting Wausau ahead for the first time. Virgil loped behind Dover like he was barely moving as he narrowed the distance. As Dover lifted off his left foot for the score, Virgil leaped from the foul line and pinned the ball against the backboard as soon as it left Dover's fingers. He hung in the air, looking down at Dover, grinning, and landed with the ball in his hands. He quickly called timeout while three thousand Wausau fans screamed for goaltending. The referees consulted and talked to both coaches affirming a clean block.

Bridgeton had the ball out at side court with thirteen seconds left. Three Wausau players chased Virgil's dribble, blocking him from the hoop, but he drove anyway, torquing his body to avoid a charge. With three seconds left, he dropped the ball to Jimbo, who was stargazing at

Virgil like everyone else, never expecting to get a pass. Jimbo fumbled the ball and nearly kicked it out of bounds but finally pulled it to his chest, extended his thick arms, and flipped the ball off the glass as the buzzer sounded. The Bridgeton bench players raced to their teammates, burying Jimbo beneath their joy.

I watched Dover and Stockbridge, staring at Virgil, who had taken it upon himself to defeat them, playing both ways. It was the last thing they expected on this night. Wausau's coach told them to shake hands, but Virgil shook his head in disdain before he was swarmed under by his teammates.

Later that night, I asked Virgil what he'd given Jimbo. "Nothing much. Just a pouch of herbs."

"Must have worked."

"I wasn't wearing it. Couldn't have been much," downplaying his power.

"How'd you know you could play both ways tonight?"

"Uncle Jonny called me up before the game."

Bridgeton lost the sectional final two nights later. Virgil played both ways again and scored thirty-seven points. Jimbo moved like he was stuck in the mud and fouled out in the third quarter, but not many of us cared. The victory over Wausau had been our state championship game.

Jennifer returned to school for the fourth term, and Virgil watched over her like a raptor, but she wanted him to. Both graduated, and Virgil was accepted into a new program at the University of Minnesota in Duluth focusing on Native American studies. I was headed to the state college in Eau Claire with an undeclared major.

We lined up on graduation night, taking our turns parading across the stage. The boys had a tradition at Bridgeton. When each of the guys walked across the stage, the rest of us would shout out his nickname. Lemon had come back to watch and joined the seniors in the salutes. When it was Jimbo's turn, we shouted out "Crush," and Jimbo smiled despite himself. When Principal Horner called out Matthew Michael

Pederson, the boys didn't know what to say as they'd never known me as anything but Mickey. Virgil's name came near the end, and every one of us stood up and stamped our feet and chanted like a drum, "Lightfoot, Lightfoot," as loud as we could. Virgil laughed and bowed to us. He had brought more to our school spirit in one game than we'd had in four years.

Later that night, Virgil and his sister stopped into the graduation party at our house, cohosted by my parents and Doc McPhearson. At one point, I pulled him aside. "Is your spirit strong tonight?"

"If I need it."

I led him up to my bedroom. "Let me sit for a few minutes."

I went downstairs and retrieved Jimbo and Lemon. When we returned, Virgil looked at us. "Harmonious. Like Jimbo's bedroom."

We slipped out the back and headed over to Lemon's basement bedroom. Virgil was amazed when he saw all the scientific instruments and medical equipment. "Medicine man. Do you heal people down here like Doc?"

"Hope to someday," Lemon said.

It didn't take Virgil long to sense Lemon's room. "It's almost the same as yours," he said to Jimbo and me. "How long have you been friends?"

"Since we were five," Jimbo said.

"We have a special place. A small beach along the river. You should see it sometime," I said.

"We could do a sweat. That way, you'll never forget it."

Jimbo and I walked to Discovery Beach with a shovel and a pitchfork the next day. We gathered as much firewood as we could, dug a fire pit three feet deep, and collected twenty cantaloupe-sized stones and laid them in the pit. A few days later, the four of us hiked down to the beach, sharing the load for Virgil's portable sweat lodge: bundles of thin willow branches, blankets, and a canvas tarp. When Virgil saw the beach, he indicated we'd set up the lodge near the willow tree with the door facing eastward toward the river and dug a hole in the sand as the center focus of the lodge. Lemon and I managed the fire while Jimbo and Virgil lashed the willow branches together with the leather straps Virgil pulled out of his knapsack. They covered the structure with overlapping layers of blankets and topped it with the tarp. "Now we have to wait for the rocks to heat up."

"How does it work?" I asked.

Virgil threw two more logs onto the fire. "When the stones are hot enough, we'll carry a dozen inside with the pitchfork, into the middle, where I dug the shallow pit. Heat from the rocks warms things up. We take our clothes off and sit on the towels inside for an hour. Sweat our asses off until we can't stand it."

We laughed. "It'll be special with the river, dashing into the cold water afterward. You won't believe the feeling. If we were all tribal members, we'd chant inside. Maybe play some drums and talk about our sadness or troubles. It's a special ceremony for us, but Uncle Jonny gave me permission to set it up with you. Since you have become my brothers and will respect it. We'll sit quietly and talk a little bit about peaceful things or something on your mind that's important to distract ourselves from the heat. Cleaning our spirits and getting rid of the shitty stuff. Sooner or later, one of us will make a break for it and run into the cold river."

It took two hours for the rocks to heat up and for the lodge to reach the necessary temperature. We set our clothes in piles away from the lodge and crawled inside. The space was dark and tight, barely tall enough as we sat shoulder to shoulder surrounding the pit of hot stones, slippery skin on our right and left. Virgil asked us to recall something good that had happened to us along the river, and we took turns telling him stories about how Lemon and I had discovered the beach and how the three of us had come back many times when we were out exploring. I could almost hear him smiling in the blackness. "No need to talk anymore. I can tell you guys are like us when you are here."

The silence took over. I heard a kingfisher diving into the river, a few squirrels scrambling overhead in the willow, and the river rushing by. It didn't take long for me to stop thinking and simply feel the heat, listening to my heartbeat. We passed around a jar of warm water. "It's important to drink," Virgil said.

Virgil splashed some water on the hot stones, and the steam rose, making the heat more intense. Lemon was the first to dash out with Jimbo on his tail, splashing and whooping loudly as they swam out to the sandbar. Virgil waited for me to break. "Anytime, Mickey. I'm ready."

We burst out of the lodge, running from the shore into four feet of cinnamon-colored water, plunging under, surfacing, and diving under again. I knelt in water to my neck as my vision reeled. Red, green, and purple ribbons stretched out in the sky like northern lights. Shadows danced on top of the water to the piano notes of a jitterbug. Virgil touched my head, making sure I was OK, then left me to join Jimbo and Lemon on the sandbar.

Time shifted, heading backwards. Two boys coming upstream. Dirty Joe and my dad, Matty Pederson. Nine-year-olds. Naked. Hairless bodies. Splashing and giggling. Joe looks over his shoulder at youthful versions of Lemon, Jimbo, and me. All five boys coming toward me. Stopping a few feet away. Waving. Fading. Disappearing.

PART THREE

What happened to us? Much the same as transpires with most friends we make when we're young. We journeyed away from Bridgeton and stayed in touch occasionally. Lemon healed broken bodies, Mickey tried to inspire teenagers with his wisdom, and I floundered about for several decades until the fibers of cherry and walnut and maple found their way under my skin. Slivers of joy and satisfaction inching into my soul. And then, about the time life should have taken the three of us to distances far removed, from where we wouldn't see each other except at the funerals of our mutual acquaintances, life spun us around and turned us inward just enough to draw us together again.

From *The Woodworker of Bridgeton*, a blog by James E. McPhearson.

Nineteen
Sally's Wedding Gift

Despite missing so much school her senior year, Sally Jensen was still at the top of her class. She told Principal Horner that Marjorie Thomas, the salutatorian, should give the student address at graduation, that she hadn't been in Bridgeton long enough to earn the honor. Grams died in June, and Sally moved back to Knowlton for the summer. She took off to St. Louis in August, and other than a few visits during her early years in college, I lost track of her, though she continued to stay in touch with Dad. She graduated from Washington University and headed to the University of Chicago in a PhD program in art history. I'd finished college at Eau Claire and was teaching social studies at Memorial High when her wedding invitation arrived.

Dad called that night, barely able to contain his enthusiasm. Sally's father was still gallivanting in whereabouts unknown, so she requested Dad walk her down the aisle. Her fiancé, Stanley, came from old wealth and was already a partner in a prestigious law firm. His family was paying for the wedding, including our lodging at the Palmer House in downtown Chicago. On Saturday, July 7, Holy Name Cathedral was packed, with most attendees from generations of wealth, which made me squirm a bit considering the humble background I shared with Sally. Aunt Daisy and Dad, Mom, and I were the only relations of Sally in attendance.

Sally was brilliant in ivory as she nearly waltzed down the aisle, a lace veil shielding her face. Dad had to hustle to keep up with her. Stanley ceremoniously flipped the veil over her head at the altar, and she smiled at him. The light pouring through the stained glass windows glistened and flashed, exploding off her teeth. She'd had them fixed.

As we went through the greeting line, I couldn't keep my eyes off Sally. I thought about her opening the letter from Washington University at Grams' house, her happiness unbounded then, too. I yearned for her to start singing musical theater songs like she used to when she cleaned our kitchen after supper. We hugged, and I wanted her to talk to me for an hour so I could continue to stare at her teeth. The restoration must have taken years and more money than Aunt Daisy ever had in her bank account, but it couldn't have been done any more perfectly.

"Hi, Mickey. So happy you made it. I have something for you. Can you meet me for breakfast tomorrow morning? Early, before the day gets crazy?"

The next morning, she wore a pale blue dress that reminded me of her senior prom and graduation outfit. "It's the same," she laughed when I mentioned it. "Just needed a little alteration."

She wanted to know about Lemon and Jimbo, but I was distracted and finally had to ask. "What happened, to your mouth?"

She projected her million-dollar smile. "Most people I know have no idea. I've hidden all the pictures of the old me. Never even shown them to Stanley."

"When did you get the work done?"

"I lived in the home of one of my voice instructors the last two years at Wash U. She needed someone to help with her mother, who was nearly ninety. After her mother passed on during my final year, my instructor took me to the best restorative dentist in St. Louis. She paid for the whole thing. Said it was a gift for the love I gave her mother before she passed."

"Like skipping high school and taking care of Grams. It all paid off."

"My migraines pretty much went away, too. The dentist said they might have had something to do with the tension created by my crooked teeth."

"How many of your old ones are still in?"

"All the molars. Half of the other ones. It took forever, and I stayed in St. Louis an extra year to finish it."

"You look astounding. But you always had a great smile."

She blushed. "You guys were so good to me." She handed me two letters. "One's for you and Lemon. The other's for Jimbo."

I didn't open the first letter until I visited Lemon a month later. Sally gushed on for two pages, thanking me for sharing our home, Lemon for challenging her academically, and both of us for being the two most decent human beings she could imagine meeting in high school. She said she'd met lots of people as good as we were since she left Knowlton, but none better. Lemon and I were embarrassed by her goodwill.

Jimbo was in the Air Force and had been back from Vietnam for a year, still trying to get his knee right. He'd just completed his fourth surgery, this one at Walter Reed, so I decided to drive out to Washington D.C. The last time I'd seen him was at the hospital at Camp Pendleton just after his return from Chu Lai, and he'd been in an irritable mood, forcing me to cut my visit short, so I was skeptical about what I might find this time.

He was getting physical therapy most days, hobbling around on crutches, in a great deal of pain and misery. I slept on his couch for a couple of nights, cleaned up his messy apartment, accompanied him to the hospital, and watched him drag his beer belly through the exercises as he cussed out most everyone who tried to help him. On my final night, I tried to ease his mind so that he would read Sally's letter. I asked him out to dinner, but true to his mood, he declined. "Rather stay in. Get some takeaway. I'll pay you back."

"Jimbo, as an old friend, I'm worried about your drinking. Jack Daniels all day?"

"Better than the alternative. I know how to work my way out of alcohol. But anything with opium scares me. Had enough of morphine coming out of 'Nam. Easier to be angry and drunk."

"Do you see anyone socially?"

"People in physical therapy count?"

"Friends?"

"You're the first in months."

I shook my head. "Sorry about not calling more."

"Don't be. I'm not much to be with—as you can see."

We talked about Lemon, Bridgeton, and Jimbo's family who didn't see him much. Part of me wanted to cry. Instead, I told him about Sally's wedding. "No shit. Now, that surprises the hell out of me. New teeth, rich husband, PhD. Jesus, Julie Jordan has come a long way."

I couldn't remember who she was.

"The lead in *Carousel*. The role she should have had in high school but turned down. Unlucky in love to say the least. Kind of like Sally always thought she'd be."

I handed him a picture from the wedding, of Sally standing with my family, smiling broadly, so full of authentic happiness you'd never imagine her father had run off when she was a kid, and her mother died when she was sixteen. He studied it like she was a phantom he never expected to hear about again. "She wrote a letter to Lemon and me. She was very gracious."

"She mention me?"

I pulled the envelope from my shirt pocket. "This one's just for you."

He looked at his name on the stationery and set the letter on top of his glass of whiskey. "Not sure I can deal with any more heartaches."

"Maybe it's good news."

“You open it. Look it over. Let me know.”

I scanned the first paragraph. “You’ll approve.”

“Read it. You were always good at interpreting, making something better than it is. But skip anything that’s bad.”

> Dear Jimbo,
>
> I’m guessing if you’re reading this, Mickey’s told you about the wedding and seeing my altered appearance. So, I don’t have to break that news to you. Which is good since I suspect you haven’t given me much thought since I left high school. That would only be natural.
>
> Wasn’t the same for me. All through college and a few years after, our “date” carried me along. I’d see other couples or observe a cute guy with curiosity or even desire, and wonder if I’d ever have that kind of luck. If you taking me to senior prom on a date you never intended to go on, would be all there was. Especially the hours afterward, along the river, when we talked like we cared about each other and you made me sing “If I Loved You” because I should have been Julie Jordan. And, of course, the kiss. So tender and generous. I know it was against your will because you didn’t really mean it. But it was all I had. And it brought me great joy most of the time. Sometimes sadness.

“Better stop,” Jimbo interrupted. “Don’t like the way this is going.”

“Be honest. You once told me if she had nice teeth, you’d consider her. But you couldn’t imagine your tongue inside her mouth.”

“Don’t remember that.”

I quickly scanned the rest of the letter. “I’m going to continue unless you want to read it to yourself.”

“Go ahead.”

> When I emerged from my cocoon, at twenty-four, living in Chicago, the world was a different place. Nobody knew me there. From before. I had so much smiling stored up. I’d grin at total strangers, and they’d respond like they’d never seen anyone glitter like me.

Stanley was sure taken in. He asked me out before anyone else had a chance. Took me to places I couldn't afford, like the opera and the theater, because he knew I'd love them. He kissed me for the first time near water, just like you did. An evening walk along Lake Michigan. It was much briefer than yours. He didn't ask me like you did. Or threaten to push his tongue into my mouth like you probably did with other girls. But he didn't kiss me out of pity, because I'd never been kissed and maybe never would be, which was part of why you kissed me so sweetly. Later, he proposed to me even after he knew all about me growing up in meager circumstances but not knowing how I used to look.

I didn't think I'd be able to write this note. Ever. To thank you for letting me love what you were in my mind for all those years. For taking me out to dinner or to a movie when I went by myself. You weren't actually there. I'm not quite that daft. But you were present enough to remind me it was possible.

By the way, I tried out for Julie Jordan in a St. Louis Theatre Guild production. Was runner-up and sang the part of Carrie Pipperidge instead. As you may recall, Carrie weds successful but dull Enoch Snow and lives happily ever after. Stanley's not dull, by any means. Nor is he my runner-up. But he is my second chance. I'll never forget what you did for me, making me feel just a little bit desired. I needed that so much at the time.

All my love. Forever.
Sally

A grin forced its way through Jimbo's sour disposition. Just barely. He picked up his glass of whiskey, looked at me, and set it down without drinking. "I know I should cut back. I can if I need to."

He stared at the photo from the wedding again. "Tell me how she sounded when she talked. Her voice was so musical. Sent me over the moon."

"Beautiful. Just like I recalled from the two years she lived with us. She'd often lift off into song while making supper or cleaning up the kitchen. I don't know where she learned so many tunes, but every night it was something different. Dad and I would sit in the living room and shake our heads, marveling that we were so damn lucky to have her around."

Jimbo smiled at my reverie. "Yeah, she could sing the shit out of everything she tried."

"She even led a singalong at the wedding. After the meal was over, when people were giving toasts."

"No kidding. What kind of songs?"

"A couple of Beatles songs. Then she sang one by herself. Starts with, 'When you walk through the dark.' Some church song, I guess. Many of the older people knew it and sang along as much as they remembered the words, but Sally didn't need anyone helping her. She was a soaring bird, going solo."

"That's from *Carousel*, dummy. When Billy Bigelow dies. Francie Gollon, who played Nettie Fowler, couldn't hit the notes, so they asked Sally if she'd sing it in the show even though she was in the chorus. You don't remember?"

"I guess I should."

"'You'll Never Walk Alone.' She blasted it out. Gave you goose-bumps. Everyone stood up and cheered. You honestly can't recall that?"

"I remember the people cheering for Sally but not the song."

Jimbo clutched the photo in his right fist, drifting back to our high school days, a look of contentment on his face. Then he leaned toward me. "I must have done a few good things back then."

"You were everybody's hero, man."

He took it in, half-wanting to deny it. "Please help me up."

I pulled him to a standing position and handed him his crutches. "It hurts a lot."

"Maybe this operation will be the one. They told you the replacement process was your best hope."

"I'm not talking about the knee."

"What is it?"

"Being alone. I'm not very good at it. Been that way since high school."

"You could see someone at Walter Reed."

"Just started. Having you here helps."

"Want me to stay a few more days?"

"Yeah. I would if you can tolerate me. I'd like you to come to my counseling session tomorrow. You game?"

I nodded. "I'll go get some food."

"Let's go out instead. There's a burger joint up the street."

Twenty
Marriages

In October of seventh grade, the blade of a table saw ripped through the tendons on Doc McPhearson's right hand while he was cutting a plank of maple for a cabinet he was constructing in his woodshop. Throughout the many months of his recovery, he hired Lemon to sterilize equipment, take notes on patients, and, on occasion, assist him with direct care. Doc never fully regained the use of the hand, and Lemon continued to be his shadow through his three years of high school.

When Lemon enrolled at Marquette University as a sixteen-year-old, he was undecided about a career in medicine or engineering. He became an orthopedic surgeon, which, to my mind, is a combination of both fields. During his residency, he took a turn in the surgical unit at Kingston Public Hospital in Jamaica and befriended Orantha Chimes, a surgical nurse. A few months later, he joined the orthopedic department at the University of Minnesota and sponsored Orantha's stay in Minneapolis. She first completed her certification as a fully-licensed American nurse then entered medical school two years later.

When I met Orantha for the first time, I was stunned. Not just by her blackness, though she was as dark a woman as I'd ever talked with. I assumed she was white from everything Lemon had told me about her. Never once did he even hint about her skin color, just that he'd met her in Jamaica and was in love with her, which was shocking enough, as Lemon never seemed remotely interested in women, other than as friends.

Growing up in Bridgeton in the 1950s, Lemon and I had limited experience interacting with anyone who wasn't Caucasian. There were always a few Menominee or Ojibwe in school, but Virgil Lightfoot was the only one I got to know. The Simpson family adopted two Korean children, but neither was in our grade. Our worldview expanded in college, especially for Lemon when he worked in a clinic in the low-income section of Milwaukee. Black students were still scarce in Eau Claire, where I earned my teaching degree, and were mostly on campus as athletic recruits. I befriended Johnny David, a tremendous high jumper and scholar, who said he felt like he was walking into the University of Mississippi some days, the way people looked at him.

To say I had worked through any inbred prejudices toward people different than I would be an exaggeration, but I refused to believe those prejudices might be a fixed part of my nature. It took time to appreciate differences, even for well-reasoned adults. You never knew what might bubble up when dealing with someone outside your tribal group.

As Orantha, Lemon, and I ate dinner, I realized she was brilliant. A first-rate thinker. And listener. Her intelligence practically radiated off of her ebony sheen. Later that evening, Lemon and I spent a few hours together. He needed to know what I thought of Orantha. "She might be smarter than you," I said.

"She is. That's the first thing that attracted me to her."

It was hard for me to hold back. "Did you think of mentioning ahead of time that she's black?"

He smiled. "I could have, but I wanted to test you. I've done the same with Ted, Lizzie, and my sisters."

"Did any of us pass the exam?"

"Everyone, more or less. Just startled in different ways."

"Orantha's OK with your experiment?"

"She trusts me. Now she trusts you, too."

"Who's next?"

"I think the lab work is over. I'll tell Jimbo before he meets her. Because I want both of you to stand up at the wedding."

"How soon?"

"Within the year. We have to work it out with her family to make sure they can be here."

"How do they feel about you?"

"They've come to accept me. It's more losing their daughter to another country than any skepticism about me."

"You sure she's the one? Not like you've played the field."

"I'm positive even if I'm a novice in the game."

I'd never doubted Lemon and wasn't about to start now.

"Will you be my best man?" he asked.

"My privilege. But I think it will mean more if you ask Jimbo, given how he's been."

"Hadn't thought of that. You're right. Co-best men, then."

Six months later, Orantha and Lemon were married. In the first year of her OB/GYN residency, Orantha gave birth to Bettina, as dark as her mother. Olivia, two years later, light brown. The third, Jezzie, could have passed for white.

I had dated very little in high school, other than the few months I saw Debbie Kedrowski. I had a year-long affair with a girl from Superior during my junior year of college, which had no chance of lasting as she could never break away from her high school boyfriend. I met Sharon LeBeaux a few years out of college at a party hosted by the history department at the university. She was new to Eau Claire, hired to direct student housing, raised in Grand Rapids, Michigan, in a blue-collar family, and her dad was a longtime union activist. Our romance was feverish and quick to culminate in an engagement. Dad and Mom urged me to slow down, but Sharon was steering the momentum, and I was along for the ride, enjoying being a bit out of control. Sharon wanted kids right away, and I saw no reason to hold back. Ronnie and Desmond were running around in our refurbished older home before Sharon and I got used to living together.

We socialized with Lemon and Orantha in the early years of our marriages. The meetings were mostly playdates for the kids with an occasional formal party at Lemon's home. After the last gathering, at which Lemon had been saluted for his charitable work with a free clinic, Sharon refused to make the two-hour trip again. She argued it was too much trouble hauling the kids off to the Twin Cities or a bother getting a sitter, claiming her weekend time was for our children, in our home, and discouraged me from visiting Lemon's family as well. I suspected something had percolated up from Sharon's past but didn't want to address it, knowing it might be too ugly.

When I accepted Lemon's invitations after that, I stayed overnight in the guest apartment above his garage, which saved a late-night argument when I returned to Eau Claire. It was easier dealing with Sharon's sullen looks the next afternoon. I saw Lemon a half-dozen times a year, often the two of us having a Saturday lunch at a St. Croix River restaurant, midway between Eau Claire and Minneapolis. It was something I needed to do because he continued to connect to the core of my life, but each time, I paid the price dealing with Sharon's anger.

When the boys were fourteen and ten, Sharon announced she was taking a new job, back in Michigan, at Grand Valley University with significantly better pay and just a few miles from her family. "You didn't tell me you were in the market."

"I was always looking. Didn't know how serious this one might be. I interviewed when I took the boys over for Easter weekend."

"What about me? I haven't had a chance to think it over."

"I don't want you to come. Our marriage isn't working out."

The last statement was not a complete surprise. Disagreements over many issues had crept into our lives over the past six years, her antagonism over my friendship with Lemon being just one of them. But none of the rancor seemed strong enough to bring about divorce, splitting one of us from the kids. That's how little I knew about Sharon. "Is this a timeout? Giving me a chance to decide if I want to join you later?"

"No. I'm calling it quits."

"What about the boys?"

"They'll come with me. I spend more time with them."

Even if that was true, it wasn't like I was an absentee father. "A judge will have to decide that."

"You sure you want to go that route?"

"Absolutely. This is their home, where they go to school. They've established friends."

"I want them near my family. So they can grow up knowing their grandparents better."

"Sharon, what's this really about?"

"Lots of things. Do I really need to go through them all?"

"Lemon and Orantha at the top of that list?"

"What if they are?"

"You've never told me why you dislike them so much."

"Yes, I have."

Over the years, she had mocked what she perceived as their pretentiousness, do-gooders swimming in easy wealth, and she believed that Orantha looked down on her and only accepted me because I was Lemon's oldest friend. "What you've offered are bullshit explanations. Exaggerated nonsense."

She looked at me, debating whether to be straightforward or not, finally accepting she might as well be at this late stage. "I don't think that's the way families are meant to be."

I scoffed at her. "That Orantha's black and their kids are mixed race? That a white guy from Bridgeton would marry into that?"

"It's not the way I've been raised. It's just wrong."

Her full display of bigotry took me by surprise. I'd been told by many people that you never know what resides in the heart of an individual until she encounters her worst fears, and that's what this was for Sharon. Orantha represented something that threatened her vision of family life. Of course, it didn't make any sense; that's what blind prejudice is.

"You're just parroting your old man. Des and Ron couldn't possibly agree with it."

"You'd be surprised."

We asked the boys the next day. Ron, full of certainty at just fourteen, lashed out. "Whites marrying niggers is wrong."

Sharon objected to the epithet, but not the spirit behind it. "Ron, you know better than that."

"Grandpa says it. You don't tell him to shut up."

"What do you think, Des?" I said.

"I don't know." He was not hiding his feelings and was genuinely perplexed.

"Do you want to go with Mom?"

"I wish we could be together, but Mommy says this is for the best."

"But do you want to leave?"

He shook his head and cried while Sharon comforted him.

You could have blown me over with something lighter than a feather to realize I'd been such an inept father. There was no need for further discussion. I'd lost their souls. Worse, Sharon had poisoned them. I went out for a drive and sipped a pint of Jack Daniels as I walked the shoreline of the Chippewa River. I returned home after midnight and spent the night in the guest room. When the moving van showed up three weeks later, I reminded Sharon to leave everything I'd set aside and to take our bed with her. I didn't care if she discarded it later.

I drove over to Lemon's that day. Orantha had taken the girls to see her family in Jamaica, so I settled into my usual digs in the guest area above the garage for a few days. Lemon was busy with surgery, leaving before I got up and not returning until after dinner. I had plenty of time to think things through until, finally, I had a desperate need to take some baby steps in my new life. I met Lemon for lunch on the third day, but he wanted to talk about Jimbo instead. "What do you think about us driving to St. Louis?" he asked.

"Jimbo's expecting us. Even if this marriage is a low-key affair, he still wants one of us to stand up for it."

"We did that the first time. We've paid our dues."

"People make mistakes. Deserve a do-over. What if I needed you down the road?"

"This is different. When it's so obvious it's not going to last."

We had met Shaina when Jimbo drove up to the Twin Cities six months ago, and her needs were so profoundly apparent we hoped Jimbo would discover them once the novelty of the relationship wore off. But it hadn't, and now he was about to complicate his mistake.

"You're probably right. But lots of awkward marriages survive. Jimbo might surprise us," I said.

Lemon laughed. "He'll surprise us. I'm always grateful for that. But not with this marriage. Unless he's willing to be miserable for the rest of his life."

"He can't be that desperate. Should we tell him what we think?"

"That's crossing the line. Sure way to lose his friendship."

"Wouldn't you want your friends to identify a mistake you were stepping into?"

"Of course, in the best of all worlds. But it doesn't work that way when lust and infatuation get mixed together."

On the drive down, Lemon wanted more specifics about what happened with Sharon. I'd given him the briefest sketch a few weeks earlier, but he was too smart not to read more deeply between the lines. When I told him what Ron had said, he looked at me. "Jesus, Mick, how did you put up with that for so long?"

"For the first few weeks, I gave myself an out. I convinced myself that Sharon was so clever at hiding it that she fooled me. But that's giving me too much credit. It was right there all along, staring at me, but I didn't want to know the truth. Now it's too late."

"It would destroy me if I lost my girls."

"No different for me. I'm not sure I'll ever see Ron again. I have some hope for Des, but probably not after he spends a few years in Grand Rapids."

"Any regrets?"

"My best assessment is to avoid gazing backward. I'll never get moving if I do."

"I mean about choosing my family and me? There was another option, and most people would have taken it. At least until your kids grew up."

"I love Orantha, and your girls treat me like their beloved uncle. I couldn't have ended our friendship. Not for anything. Not even for my kids. And that's what Sharon would have demanded."

The words sounded strange coming out of my mouth, but I hoped my boys would understand. Des, at least. I owed them something better than they would get from their mother, even if I couldn't see them much because of it.

Lemon's words interrupted my sad reflections. "I'm not sure I could have done the same."

"It was about integrity. I know you believe in that. If you had to, you'd make the same decision."

"I don't think I'm that strong."

"You'll never find yourself in that situation, Lem. And I don't want to ever again."

Twenty-One
Out of the Blue

A few years after my divorce, I converted half of my basement into a studio apartment complete with a separate entrance. The house had four upstairs bedrooms, and the basement was mostly superfluous space. My plan was to rent it out to college students and bring in some extra income. But in the back of my mind, I was hoping that, down the road, Des would visit for more than a week at a time and even enroll in college at Eau Claire if he had his own place. In the meantime, I made the leap and brought a stranger into my home, and, after the first year, it became a way of life. Len Platoff was the second tenant, a business major who worked evenings at UPS, quiet as a twelve-year-old dog, with no apparent private life. We said hello in passing, and I invited him to dinner a few times, but he didn't seem interested in getting to know new people or have much of a knack for human discourse.

So it was a complete surprise when I came home from school on an October afternoon and saw him laughing and conversing effortlessly with JoLinda Showlton as they cleaned out the back of his pickup truck. JoLinda was one of the most memorable students in all my years of teaching. Smart but not showy about it, coming from a lower-income family but not humbled by it or intimidated by those who had more. She was so authentically living through the joys of being a teenager that it seemed almost inevitable that a calamity would come her way, so we could watch her deal with the flip side of life with as much natural aplomb. That was precisely what happened in her tenth-grade year when her mother was run over by a gravel truck while biking in the early morning on a busy county road. JoLinda was in my American history class at the time and seemed to recover remarkably well and quickly, though the vitality she'd displayed so readily and transparently before the tragedy took several years to take hold again, something I was able to witness in my seniors honor course.

The ease with which JoLinda and Len touched each other as they hosed down and swept the truck bed, her hands grazing his lower back and his fingers gliding across her ass, made it obvious they were lovers. My years of enforced practice observing similar behaviors with the teenage couples at work gave me assurance about my judgment. But this was different. It was taking place in my backyard, likely to be followed by its intimate denouement in my basement an hour later. I was so startled that I almost went into the house without speaking until JoLinda broke the spell. "Hi, Mr. P."

"JoLinda, where have you been the past few years?"

"Housecleaning work to support school. Still living with my dad—most of the time."

"How close to finishing?"

"Halfway. Been a slog."

Len was watching us intently. "Did you know JoLinda was one of my students in high school?"

He shook his head, retreating to his usual level of communication with me.

"JoLinda was one of my favorites. Treat her well, Len. Anything less will disappoint me."

I saw JoLinda a few more times through the fall, and just before Thanksgiving, Len came upstairs to talk. "Would you mind if Jo moved in with me for a while?"

"Lease is for one. What's going on?"

"Not getting along with her dad. They need a break from each other for a while."

"Let me know if it's more than a few weeks."

JoLinda informed me a few days later that she needed to move in permanently. "What's the problem with your dad?"

"Complicated. He doesn't want me spending time with Len. So I'd really appreciate you letting me stay."

"It's fine. Everything OK with Len?"

"For now. It's not always easy in such a small space."

"You looking for some more housecleaning work?"

"Always."

"Add my place to your list."

"How soon?"

"Whenever you've got time. Maybe you can get your own place if the work picks up."

I saw her in the nearby IGA a week before Christmas, forlornly scanning the tomato sauce options. Her usual exuberance had been wiped clean from her face. I could have passed by without saying hello, but her daily presence in the basement apartment had brought her front and center from the recesses of my memory. The thoughts were not lust-filled in the least. More of a parent hoping his daughter was making smart choices. "What are you doing over break, JoLinda?"

"Not sure. Len is heading off tomorrow to spend a couple of weeks with his family in Rhinelander. I've got lots of cleaning jobs. It'll go fast."

"What about Christmas?"

"Something will come up. I usually see Dad's family."

But nothing worked out. Two days before Christmas, as I was helping her move my living room furniture for vacuuming, she told me she'd be spending Christmas alone. My only option was to invite her to Bridgeton for three days though it took a great deal of persuasion before she finally agreed. She was quiet on the drive over, curled up in the backseat of my Toyota rather than wanting to carry on a conversation, other than having me stop for a bathroom break in Abbotsford. Mom and Dad were gracious about hosting JoLinda, putting her up in Dad's basement office, providing her with some privacy. JoLinda didn't eat much and said even less. I was almost embarrassed for her as she was usually so effervescent. On Christmas Eve night, Mom sat down with me. "We need to talk about your friend."

"Sorry she's so out of sorts. It's rough being alone for the holidays."

"Do you know she's pregnant?"

That thought was the furthest thing from my mind. "It's not yours, is it?"

"No, Mom. I swear to God."

"You're not a believer, Mickey."

"On your name then."

She looked at me, wanting to believe I wasn't bedding down one of my former high school students. "How did you find out?"

"I suspected the moment I saw her. Nurse's instinct. When I heard her vomiting in the bathroom, I put two and two together. I'm the first person she's told."

"What did you tell her?"

"She needs to talk it over with her boyfriend—since you're not the dad. She's at four months."

JoLinda and I drove back to Eau Claire after Christmas dinner. I couldn't put her through the embarrassment of being around Mom and Dad any longer, even if they'd begun to treat her like one of their own. We chatted off and on, but she was still quite dispirited. "When will you talk to Len?"

"I was going to tell him before he went to Rhinelander, but he was in such a rush. He's got an old girlfriend back there. I don't know where we stand."

"Use my phone when you call him. Don't worry about the cost."

"Thanks."

"And feel free to spend as much time in the house as you need. You might get pretty lonely in the basement."

"Your mom was so nice. Made me wish I still had one."

"She's good that way. She told Dad, in case you're wondering. He's normally very friendly but not as enthusiastic as he was after he found out. They were disappointed we left."

"Didn't they think it was weird?"

"They assumed I'm the father. Is that bizarre enough for you?"

She laughed for the first time since we'd left Eau Claire.

JoLinda called Len the next day. I was nearby when she did and could feel his anger running through the phone lines. He showed up a few days later, berated JoLinda some more, left her with three hundred dollars for an abortion, and didn't return until the day before the spring term was to begin. JoLinda hadn't used the money and wasn't sure what she would do when the baby was born. She asked me if I'd help her talk to Len again, so we gathered in my living room. Len was still pissed, even after JoLinda apologized several times for something that was as much his doing as hers. "You told me you were on the pill, so none of this makes sense."

"I was. The doctor said it isn't foolproof."

"Why are you so intent on fucking up both of our lives?"

She started sniffling. "She isn't sure what to do, Len," I said.

"It's not that complicated. She can get it done right here in Eau Claire."

"You know it's more than that," I said.

He waited for her to stop crying. "I'm not going to support a kid that I don't want when all you have to do is go through the damn procedure. I'll take you down there, for Christ's sake."

He got up to leave. "I've packed up your stuff. We're done if you hadn't figured that out."

After Len kicked JoLinda out of the apartment, I set her up in the best of my guest rooms. She decided to take the semester off and figure out what would happen after the baby arrived in early June. In March, my principal called me in. "Mickey, I'm not sure what sort of relationship you have with the Showlton girl, but I'm getting heat about it from several school board members."

I wasn't surprised. Eau Claire had sixty thousand people, but it was much like the village of Bridgeton, just with more bells and whistles. I explained the situation, and he smiled. "That's not how it looks from the outside."

"What's wrong with helping her out?"

"It's about appearances. You've been around long enough to know that."

I was familiar enough with my rights as a union employee, so I simply said, "With all due respect to you and your bosses, you can fuck yourselves."

He laughed. "Figured you'd say something like that. I'm not offended in the least, though I'm not flexible enough at my age to try what you're suggesting. But I'll relay the message in more professional words."

Jo and I developed a routine throughout the late winter and into the early spring. She kept fit with walking and her housework, shared supper with me most nights, went to bed earlier than I did, and was still sleeping when I went off to work each morning. Mom drove over in early May to make sure the house was set for a new baby. Jo still had minimal contact with her dad, though her sister, Hazel, came over most weeks, sometimes staying for dinner. When I asked Jo why she wasn't living with her sister, she said, "She didn't want me when I split up with Len, and then I got comfortable here. It's still OK with you, Mickey?"

She'd finally gotten over the hump and stopped calling me by my surname, though she still referred to Mom and Dad by theirs. Despite her comfort living in my home, she refused to discuss her life after the baby was born. I told her to finish one thing at a time and that she was welcome to stay as long as she wanted.

The college semester ended in mid-May, and Len disappeared without a goodbye. He left me his address so I could send him his security deposit, but given the state of the apartment, I had no intention of delivering on that promise. Jo cleaned the place but didn't tell me, and when I went down the next Saturday morning to take care of Len's mess and saw what she'd done, I nearly broke down in tears. How Len could have deserted such a fine young woman dumbfounded me. The least I could do was give her Len's security deposit.

I accompanied Jo to the hospital when she went into labor, coached her through the birth of Ezra Michael, and brought her back to the nursery in my home after three nights in the hospital. Mom came over for two weeks during the last days of my school term. After Jo and Ezra were asleep on Mom's final night, she asked me what I was going to do about my guests. "Haven't thought about it, to be honest. Just wanted Jo to get through it."

"She's decided to give him up."

"To whom?'

"That's where she's stuck. But she knows she's got to disconnect soon, or she'll never do it."

"Think she'd let me adopt him?"

Mom looked at me like I was crazy. "How would you manage?"

"I don't know, but I really love the kid. I don't want her to leave. If I take him, she'll have reason to come back."

She held both of my hands. "Are you in love with her?"

"Of course, but not how you're thinking."

"I was thinking she was your replacement child."

"Yeah. I'll be in misery when she leaves."

"If you're serious about Ezra, talk to her before something else happens."

I procrastinated for another week before asking Jo what she thought. She assumed I was kidding, but after I convinced her I was serious, all she said was "maybe." We went on as roommates and parents through the summer, and every time I asked about Ezra, she gave me the same answer. One lazy afternoon, as I gently rocked Ezra to sleep, she asked me about the two boys in the photos displayed around the house. "They're mine," I said.

"Where are they?"

"With their mother in Michigan. She took them away four years ago."

"I wondered why you live in such a big house. Makes more sense with four of you."

"It was too big even then. It hasn't been a home for years—not until you and Ezra settled in."

"How old are your kids?"

"Ron's a few years younger than you are. Des just turned fourteen."

"When do you see them?"

"Des will be visiting for ten days in August. I hope you're still here so he can meet you and Ez. Ron refuses to come back even for a few days. It's a sad story. I don't talk about it with many people."

"You feel like it's your fault?"

"It might be hard for you to believe, but I had very little to do with the separation."

She could see my sadness welling up. She peered into my eyes and soul and understood my sorrow, though she should have been too young to have that level of compassion. Maybe losing her mother and learning that the twists of happenstance can be very cruel had awakened that sensitivity. She rubbed the back of my hands that held her baby. "When I see you holding Ez like this, it's obvious you've got a lot of love burning inside you."

"I wasn't this good with Ron and Des. Not nearly good enough. That's why I want to try with Ezra, to show everybody that I can be better at it."

"It must break your heart knowing your boys are out there."

I nodded. "Not a day goes by without a little bleeding. It's my great failure in life."

Jo took Ezra from my arms, tears running down her cheeks, as she headed off to the nursery. I stepped outside so she wouldn't see me cry. The conversation felt like the final interview by an adoption agency, and I had no idea if I passed muster. A few weeks later, Jo's sister stepped up. She and her husband hadn't had any luck getting pregnant, and they took Ezra in, first as guardians while Jo went back to school, then by December as a full adoption. Jo moved back home with her dad. They'd reconciled after Jo made him a grandfather for the first time and turned Ezra over to Hazel.

My basement apartment had remained empty after Len left, but as parting gifts, Jo found a new tenant and came over every other Saturday for breakfast and to clean my house. I was getting used to being alone again, discovering it was just as difficult this time around after Jo had interrupted my years of solitude. But it was my lot in life. I asked Jo if she regretted handing Ezra over to Hazel. "Every day. I can see him when I want, but I'm no longer his mother."

"You'll always be his mother."

"Of course, but I want him to grow up saying that to Hazel. It was the best thing."

"I wish it had worked out another way."

"I know you do. I called your mother, and we talked it over before I took him to Hazel's."

"She tell you not to let me adopt him?"

"No. She ran through the pros and cons. She believes you'd be a great dad if you had another chance and said she'd be delighted to have Ez in your family. But I wanted him in mine."

"Makes perfect sense, Jo."

"Please don't hold it against me."

How could I? She'd given me days and days of hope when I least expected it.

A few months later, I drove over to Bridgeton, expecting to visit with my cousin Sally. I'd seen her just a couple of times since her wedding, but never for long. Over the last year, she'd been spending a night or two with my folks every month when she came up from Chicago to see her grandmother, Aunt Daisy, who was in Greenfield Nursing Home near Wausau. "You just missed her. Has to get back early, so she's going to sit with Daisy for a few hours before she makes the long drive," Dad explained.

Sally was peering out the window in Daisy's room, her back to the door, and didn't hear me come in. I peeked over at Daisy, swallowed up in white sheets and a turquoise blanket. The attendants had positioned her on her left side, and her right eye was shuttered as though a summer home had been closed down for the winter. She was breathing slowly but not deeply. "How is she, Sally?"

She turned in full surprise. "Mickey! It's been so long. When you spoke, I thought it might be Stanley."

"Sorry to disappoint."

"Hardly. My mind had drifted off."

Her wedding was fifteen years in the past, and the smile that had illuminated her future that day had dimmed considerably. Her brown hair hung loosely instead of in the ponytail she used to wear in high school, and it was greying at the edges. Much of her prairie girl optimism had been replaced by a furrowed glance. Life had delivered a few kidney punches when she wasn't looking, just as it had to the rest of us. She looked down at her grandmother. "She doesn't have more than a few weeks. Could happen tonight. She's that close."

"Are you ready for it?"

"She's given me time. I've been distracted, so that helps."

"With what?"

"It's too complicated. You don't need to hear about it."

We sat next to each other, Daisy to our left. The room had experienced death before and would again after Daisy left it. We were marking time until the next round. Sally filled me in on the past few years, earning tenure this past winter at Northwestern in the art history department, enjoying it and wanting to travel to Austria to pursue some research, but unwilling to plan for it until Daisy's passing. "Was it any different when your mom died?"

"She went so quickly. I came home from school, and she was already unconscious in the hospital after a week of declining health. Died overnight. I never got to say goodbye. Grandma and I have said our farewells a half-dozen times. Each one different, but both of us aware it might be the last."

"Stanley ever come up with you?"

"He did a few times after we got married when she was still at the house in Knowlton. He was embarrassed by her poverty. I never thought we were poor when I was staying with her. We got by, and she could always fix me a good meal. He wouldn't spend the night. Insisted we stay at a motel. The first of many arguments about Grandma."

"What else?"

"I wanted her to live with us during her last years. He wouldn't hear of it. So, here we are."

"Sorry."

"Do you think you came from humble beginnings?"

"We had it better than you and Aunt Daisy. Bridgeton seems outlandishly small now when I come back, even though it's grown into a suburb of Wausau. It's humbling to know I came from that. But it's what I knew, and I still have grand memories."

"I don't think Stanley would have married me if he'd known the full extent of my past. During our courtship, it was just me telling him about it. Seeing it firsthand turned out to be different."

Daisy uttered a low moan. "Has he seen Aunt Daisy like this?"

"We haven't been talking much."

"Is that what's distracting you?"

She nodded. "I almost told your dad. Figured he'd be a good listener. But I couldn't."

"Can't be that bad."

She smiled for the first time, her teeth glittering when she did, despite her sorrows. "You sure you're up for my heartaches, Mick?"

"Go ahead."

She slipped her hand into mine. "Remember, a few years ago, when I told you I was having trouble maintaining a pregnancy? Miscarried after the third month. Over and over. Six times. Until the doctor told us to stop trying."

"Yeah. You said that Stanley felt worse than you did. Something I didn't believe, to be honest."

"I wanted to adopt. He wouldn't hear of it, not with a stranger's kid."

"Where's it stand now?"

"He had an affair with a legal secretary he met at a conference. Went on for quite a few months. Then he had a brainstorm and talked her into carrying his child, paying her off, and letting us adopt the kid. Letting *him* adopt the kid. He didn't tell me any of it until the baby was born. Said he didn't want to complicate things if something happened during the pregnancy or if she changed her mind."

"Jesus. He just showed up with the kid?"

"Out of the blue. Gave me two days' notice. Painters and carpenters came in to fix up the spare bedroom. Introduced me to the nanny. Expected me to play along as the joyous mother. Telling everyone it was a traditional adoption."

"Which was what you wanted, so how could you say no?"

She started laughing, but tears accompanied her smile as she patted my hand. "You're ahead of me in the story. Like you've heard it before."

"What are you going to do?"

"It's been four months. We've had baby showers, and Stanley's parents have shown him off to their friends."

"What's his name?"

"Stanley made that choice, too. Named him after his dad. Walter. Same name as Grandma's husband. I could have kicked him for that."

I handed her the box of tissues, and she used them as she stood and looked out the window. A black front was moving in from the west, and her drive back to Chicago would likely be in heavy rain. I joined her, my arm around her shoulder. "I won't sleep next to him. Feeling him up against me in the night."

"If you keep that up for long, he might tell you to get out. Men do that."

"I'm supposed to put up with it?"

"He still seeing her?"

"He says no. Not sure I believe him."

"He might be thinking what he did was for the marriage. Planting the seed and harvesting what you wanted."

"He said that. Almost word for word. Like I should thank him. I'm supposed to get over how Walter's come into our lives and raise him like my own."

Daisy moaned again and started mumbling. Sally held her grandmother's hand in her open palm, Daisy's fingers waggling back and forth. Sally placed her other hand inside Daisy's fingers, and Daisy closed her hand. She moaned again, like she was trying to speak and uttered a syllable that sounded like the number four. Then she slipped back into unconsciousness, her chest barely rising and falling.

Sally looked up at me. "One of these times, she'll stop breathing."

"What was she saying?"

"Probably the word 'forgive.' It's about my dad. Her son, Jackson. I haven't seen him in years. Not sure he's even alive. Grandma's forgiven him for being such a shit. Wants me to do the same."

"How'd she get over it?"

"Said she'd done the best she could raising him. That she wasn't responsible for him. She wants to die with all of that cleansed out of her."

We sat quietly watching Daisy inhale, pausing as if she were holding her breath, then exhale. I anticipated the deep waters of death would drown her during one of those transitions. Sally asked me about my divorce. "Irreconcilable differences. My ex is a hater, and I don't want to be."

"You couldn't forgive her?"

"Not for what she's doing to our boys."

"How long has it been?"

"Almost four years."

"Does it still control you?"

"I've let most of her go. It's just the boys now. Are you thinking of leaving Stanley?"

"I've got a job interview next week in Philadelphia."

Sally asked me to step out while she said goodbye to Aunt Daisy, and I walked around the parking lot until she came out to her car. "Let me know what happens."

"I will."

Aunt Daisy died a week later, and Dad helped Sally with the arrangements. A group of thirty-five gathered at St. Francis Xavier Church in Knowlton and the nearby cemetery. Daisy was interred next to Walter Jensen.

Sally spent the night with us in the old house on Pine Street. I figured it might be one of her final visits, so we talked before she went to bed. "I canceled the job interview. I'm not ready to move on."

"What about Stanley?"

"I don't know. I intend to mother his child. Make Walter my own, if I can. That's all I can promise him. I can forgive Walter. He has nothing to do with it."

Twenty-Two
Women and Men

When Debbie Kedrowski Hopkins strolled into the Friday evening festivities at our twenty-fifth high school reunion, no one was more surprised than I. None of us had seen her or even heard about her life since she vanished midway through the final semester of our senior year, in the middle of the ugliness over her mother's brothel when evangelical ministers went berserk in a frenzy of righteousness.

Her hair was still reddish, faded into a light strawberry hue, twisted into a bun. She was fifteen pounds heavier, like we all were, but carrying it well and surprisingly sure of herself as she looked out at the crowd. A few former classmates stopped and said hello to her, but nobody lingered. Not much different than in the hallways of high school back in 1965. When she stepped outside to the deck of the Riverfront Pavilion, I followed her, two beers in hand. She pretended she was surprised when I called her name, and we embraced gingerly so I wouldn't douse her in brew. "I was hoping you or Jimbo would show up."

"Jimbo will be at the dinner tomorrow. You staying for that?"

"Not sure."

I offered her a beer, and she responded by pulling a pint of Canadian Club from her purse and pouring a generous dose into her cup of Pepsi. "To old times," she said, and we tapped plastic cups together.

She gave me a ten-minute tour of the past twenty-five years: setting up home in Oshkosh after she and Katherine vanished during the night when gunshots shattered the downstairs windows of Miss Kitty's, graduation from Marquette University in three years, her first job in the marketing department at Miller Brewery where she met her future husband, three kids in six years, and currently half-owner of an advertising firm in Waukesha, living her version of happily-ever-after. She asked me what happened to my marriage, somehow knowing about my divorce, but I didn't want to say much. "One of those things. Seemed better than it was."

"Any kids?"

"Two boys, but I don't see them much anymore."

She was telling me about her children when two women approached us, their faces disguised by a new weight class and hairstyle. The taller of the two didn't waste time with a civil greeting, shooting her barb straight at Debbie. "What are you doing here? I know you didn't get an invitation."

The shorter one nodded through her double chin, providing moral support. Debbie and I were startled by the ferocity of the greeting, but before we could think of a simple retort, the tall one spoke again. "I've wanted to call you a slut to your face since eighth grade. After all these years, that might be too nice of a greeting."

Debbie recognized her before I did. "Patty Cherwinski. I can see your social acumen hasn't improved any."

"Whore."

"I knew your dad. Thursday was his night when you and your mama thought he was bowling. Served him whiskey and Coke at the house. Had a funny-looking cock, but you've probably seen it. Tiny thing, but he made it work."

Patty tossed her beer at Debbie, half in her face, the rest dribbling down the front of her pale green dress. I slid between the two and escorted Debbie to the far side of the deck. When I looked over my shoulder, Patty's husband was pushing her in the opposite direction. We kept walking toward the parking lot. Debbie was crying now, using my handkerchief to wipe off her face. "Memory of a fucking elephant," she said.

"Was she like that in high school?"

"She and twenty other girls."

Debbie opened the pint of whiskey and offered me some. I took a sip to be polite, but the bottle was nearly empty, and as we walked toward the river, I could see she'd had too much to drive. "Did Patty's dad come out to your place?"

"Not a regular, but he saw Bridget on occasion." She laughed. "Never saw him naked, but Bridget described him to me. The cock talk was just for effect."

"Did the job."

She continued to clean herself off, but the fabric covering her breasts was soaked. "What do you want to do?" I asked.

"Can't stay, obviously. Guess I'll go back to the hotel."

"I'll drive you. Where are you lodging?"

"Holiday Inn in downtown Wausau. What about my car?"

"We'll figure it out tomorrow."

Halfway back, she asked me to drive by her old place, so I turned down Rib Hill Road. The grey siding was now white, the cedar fencing around the parking area was cleared away for a grassy backyard, and a sign for Murray's Bed and Breakfast was posted out front. "Have you heard about these changes to your place?" I said.

"Just that it sold."

"Several times. Been a B&B for ten years. When I heard a family from Merrill converted it, I figured it was a perfect setup."

"Separate living quarters. See what you mean."

"Wonder if they repainted the rooms?"

She laughed and asked me to pull over on the roadside just ahead. She opened the door and dashed across Rib Hill Road toward a small woodlot behind the garage. I gave her ten minutes before I followed, the flashlight from my glovebox illuminating the dark night. She cut a lonely figure in a clearing of the trees, her arms clutching herself tightly. Her crying was audible.

"What's wrong?"

"The old maple is gone."

I scanned the surroundings with the light. "Looks like they timbered the lot not long ago."

"That was my marker."

"For what?"

"My journals. I buried them in a plastic container to keep Mom from reading them. Didn't have a chance to get them when we left so suddenly. Everything about growing up here was in those pages."

"Maybe in the daylight, with a shovel."

"I'll stop back tomorrow."

I accompanied her into the Holiday Inn and asked her if she wanted to sit in the bar. "Yeah, if you've got time. Let me go change."

I wasn't sure how long I wanted to stay, but it seemed only decent to spend a bit more time with her. After what we had for those intense three months when I first learned what sex meant, at least to the teenage version of who I was. Getting that far with Debbie hadn't taken long after she broke up with Jimbo. Maybe he'd primed the situation for both of us. In the beginning, it was always after school when her mother was away at her physical therapy appointments, and always in Deb's room. Afterward, in a daze, I stared at the poster of the grinning face of Steve McQueen sitting on his motorcycle, his masculinity revved to peak form, trying to figure out if he was laughing at my juvenile attempts at sex or because I'd just enjoyed something almost as good as racing his Triumph.

Debbie told her mother after our third time, without seeking my permission. The women of the house found out soon after that and treated me like a prince each time I stepped into Miss Kitty's, imparting some unbelievably frank advice about becoming a better lover in the process. Zel told me in confidence, "Nobody's much good at it until you get to triple digits. Even then, it's a lifetime of learning." She turned my face redder than Dad did when he talked about sex. She pestered me after a month. "Getting better at pleasuring her with your tongue?" confiding that I should to satisfy Debbie.

Another of the women, Wanda, was curious about how quickly I could regain myself for the second or third go-around. "It's so sweet, you two starting off as virgins." Another of my secrets revealed. "Lucky not to have to use condoms," she added, unlike all but the most favored of their customers. They all thought Deb was fortunate to be on the pill. "Wasn't like that when I was sixteen," Zel remarked, reminiscing as we sat at the kitchen table. It got to the point where I imagined all of them, Miss Kitty included, eavesdropping at the closed door to Debbie's bedroom, applauding if we made any noises. Sometimes, I couldn't get hard thinking about them. It didn't seem to affect Deb as she mocked my "provincialism."

I couldn't talk it over with anyone. I hadn't told Jimbo how far things had gone and figured he might hold it against me. Dad was a possible candidate, but he probably would be scandalized about my silly predicament, despite his open mind about such matters. These long-ago memories stirred me up more than I had been in years, and I wondered what Debbie had in mind.

She finally joined me at a corner table. "Sorry to take so long. Took a quick shower to get rid of the stench of the beer. While I was in the shower, I started laughing about the run-in with Patty. Must have been amusing watching the catfight."

"Funnier after the fact. I was worried you two would get into a hair-pulling thing."

She sipped on another whiskey, slurring a few words, but it didn't take her long to get to her point. Maybe she'd thought about it in the shower. "Would you come up to my room for a while?"

"What do you have in mind?"

"Talk more intimately. Wouldn't mind reliving old times a bit."

"Thought that was over when I broke it off."

"You mean when I did."

"You're too drunk to remember."

"Hardly. You got freaked out fucking me in the house when the women were around. Mom warned me you were in over your head anyway."

She was drunker than I thought, so there was no point in arguing. She was at least half-right anyway. "What about your husband? What's his name?"

"Leo. Things aren't going so well there. We haven't had sex for over a year."

"Hard to believe that, the way you're coming onto me. It'll get better if you stay with it."

"Doubt it. Not after he discovered what Mom used to do."

"How'd he find out?"

"I got tired of keeping it a secret from him."

I laughed. "Wish I'd been a fly on the wall during that conversation."

"It was one-sided. He walked out when I tried to explain."

"Most husbands wouldn't want to hear that news."

We went up to her room. I wasn't sure of my intentions as I hadn't been with a woman since Sharon left over four years ago. As we stretched out on the king-sized bed, I thought about Zel and wished she were here to give me some coaching. "You been with many women since we did it?" Deb asked.

"My ex and a couple of others."

"How'd they compare?"

"You were better."

"You just flattering me to get my panties off?"

"Doubt you have any on."

She laughed and quickly lifted up her skirt. Yellow bikinis. "Was just kidding."

She turned to me, mouth slightly open like she used to do back at Miss Kitty's, when she wanted me to start. I kissed her deeply, but something was holding me back. I opened up her blouse. No brassiere, but even kissing her there didn't trigger anything. I thought maybe I'd been away from it too long. We took off our tops. Her breasts looked much the same despite three kids and twenty-five years of gravity's effects, but I couldn't generate any arousal and didn't want her to discover that. I backed off and sat up. "We should stop."

"Because I'm married?"

"I think that's it. Doesn't feel right."

"Give it more time. You'll come around."

I was already buttoning my shirt. "I'll get going. Catch the last hour at the reunion."

She covered herself with the bedspread. "Just this once, Mick. For me."

I stood over her wanting my exit to be as graceful as possible. "Where are your keys? I'll get the car back in the morning."

"Sure you won't stay?"

I shook my head. "In my purse."

I didn't know how to say goodbye, knowing it would be the final time I'd see her like this, so I shuffled toward the door. "I'll call you about ten."

She began pleading again, but I walked out before she had an opportunity to change my mind and headed out into the night air. It was turning cooler but still comfortable without a jacket. I was alternately puzzled and angry. Not being able to retrieve something as essential as that desire caught me unaware. Would the same thing happen the next time I reached an intimate situation? Before I knew it, I'd walked a mile up Grand Avenue. I glanced around the neighborhood but didn't recognize any of the storefronts. I stepped into a tavern that was darker than most and was greeted by Frank Sinatra singing "One for My Baby." The bartender set a napkin before me. "Tap. Just a small one."

"Only have the one size."

I sipped it but knew more liquor wouldn't help me figure out what happened, and I wouldn't find the answer back at the reunion. Had Sharon screwed me over that thoroughly? Her parting blows: took our kids, our furniture, our bed, and stole my libido in the same move. A man stood next to me. "Mind if I sit here?"

"Go ahead," but I was still lost in my bewilderment.

"You from around here?"

I didn't want to talk. "West. Eau Claire. You?"

"Moved here a few years ago. When I got hired at the two-year campus."

"Professor?"

"Yup. Biology."

"I teach high school. Social studies."

I still wasn't giving him much eye contact, and he picked up on my mood. "Sorry to bother you. Can see you're not here for that."

I finally turned to him. He was about my age, short beard, hair thinning and a few pounds extra like me. "Sorry. Something just happened, and I'm trying to figure it out."

"If you want to lay it on me, I'll listen. But don't want to intrude."

Why not? Who else would I confide in? "I was with a woman, who I used to see years ago. We got intimate, but nothing worked."

"You talking about the mechanics?"

"What drives the mechanics."

"You been in here before?"

"No. Was wandering around after I left her and stumbled in here."

"Take a look around."

"Be right back."

I walked to the bathroom, checking things out both ways. Forty men standing at the bar or sitting at tables and booths. No women. Shit. Of all the gin joints. I laughed at myself as I sat back down, and he could see I had figured it out. "Had no idea, and I used to live around here. Hadn't given much thought to Wausau catching up with the times."

"It's the only establishment in town. No reason to be too amazed."

"Hope you don't mind me being here. All things considered."

"Free country. Maybe your mechanical bent has changed."

"Doubt it, but I'm open to suggestions."

"She your ex-wife?"

"My first affair. From high school."

"Is there an ex in the picture?"

"Pretty far out of the frame. Haven't been with anyone since we split and assumed things would come back automatically."

"They probably will. Give it time. I used to be married."

"What happened?"

"Might be the same as you. We lost interest in each other."

"Some of that for me."

"Then I turned in a new direction. Found the attraction did wonders for my mechanics."

"In places like this?"

"Sometimes. Want another drink?"

"I've barely touched this one, but let me get you one."

We talked about teaching for an hour, and when I glanced up at the clock, it was past eleven, too late for the reunion, and Mom and Dad would be asleep. Still, it seemed like the moment to leave. "Hey, I should get going."

"Me, too. Want to walk by the river? They've fixed up the walkway. Pretty slick."

It was odd strolling alongside him, knowing what he wanted, but I hadn't said no. We sat on a bench staring out at the river, and I tossed a stone into the water. "I grew up about this same distance from the river."

"Whereabouts?"

"Bridgeton. You know it?"

"Just to drive by."

It was difficult to sit there with the tension building, and I wasn't sure why I didn't walk away. He broke the spell. "I see a bit of myself in you."

"How's that?"

"I wasn't sure at first either."

His thigh pressed against mine lightly, and I felt something stir. "I haven't thought about it before."

"Never?"

"Can't say never. But never realistically."

He placed his hand on my arm. "That OK?"

I felt more arousal. "Yeah."

He slid his hand to my thigh. "My name's Tom."

"Mickey."

"My place is just a couple of miles from here, and I live alone. Do you have time?"

I had no idea what to say, and Tom saw that. "No pressure. I know it's a lot for the first time."

The new desire was surging through me, and I moved my hand to his. "I'm curious."

"Then let's try it."

It was after two when I pulled into the driveway. Dad left the back porch light on, and the bedside lamp lit my old room facing Pine Street. I'd moved past fatigue into something new, so I walked over to Old Iron. The rumor was that the bridge would be gone in two years, replaced by something modern that could handle wider traffic. I stood midway across the wooden walkway. The night was black, too overcast for sky glow, and I leaned my head over the iron railings toward the sound of Little Bull Falls. I could tell the river was running low from the quiet flow over the dam. It would feel like an abyss if I didn't know it so well. I reached into my pants pocket for the phone number Tom had given me and was tempted to let it drop into the dark river. I shook my head, searching for regrets, but had none.

I staggered over to Doc's house at nine the next morning, washed out on exhaustion and confusion. Jimbo's truck was in the driveway, and I heard him puttering in the woodshop. "Hey, man. When did you get here?"

"Got away from St. Louis early. Made it to the reunion for the last few hours. You were conspicuous by your absence."

I filled him in on the specifics of the fight between Debbie and Patty Cherwinski, and we both laughed. "Girls will be girls."

"She'd taken care of a pint of whiskey, so I took her back to her hotel in Wausau."

"You must have done more than drop her off. To be gone all that time."

"She wanted to relive old times, but it didn't feel right. Her car's still out at the Riverfront Pavilion, and I told her I'd get it back. You up for a good deed this morning?"

"Sure. Afterward, we can get a late breakfast."

I called the hotel, and Debbie woke up after twenty rings. I told her Jimbo would bring the car up in thirty minutes—and to make herself presentable.

Jimbo drove us out to the Pavilion in his truck, and I handed him the keys to Debbie's car. He gave me a puzzled look in return. "Thought you'd drive it and I'd follow," he said.

"When I called Debbie, she said she'd like to visit with you for a while. She'll bring you back afterward. I'll drive your truck back to Doc's."

"Shit, man. What's going on?"

"She needs a friend, just like in the old days. I've already done my part."

"You sure about this?"

"Just go. You'll have a good time. Promise."

Dad was emptying the trunk of his car when I returned home. "Coming or going?"

"Aunt Penny is downsizing to an apartment in Merrill. Mommy's already up there. I'm making space for her Goodwill donations."

"When will you be back?"

"Late afternoon." He shut the trunk. "I forgot to tell you that Debbie Kedrowski called a few days ago. Wanted to know if you'd be attending the reunion."

"Saw her last night. Did you tell her about Sharon and me?"

"Just that you were single again. Debbie asked about it. That a problem?"

"Not at all. Just wondering how she knew."

"How's she doing?"

"About what you'd expect, given she's married with three kids."

"She say anything about her mother?"

"Still in Oshkosh, where she set up after they left here. Part owner of a restaurant and still works there as a hostess."

"Do you ever think of Debbie, given she was your first girlfriend?"

"I hadn't until last night."

"I dated her mom for about a year in high school. Didn't want to tell you when they were living around here."

"That why Mom didn't want you talking to her?"

"Had more to do with Katherine running a brothel. But, yeah, Mom was concerned. Sometimes the first love dies hard."

"I don't think I loved Debbie. It was just a physical thing."

Dad smiled. "That can linger, too. Are you seeing anyone in Eau Claire?"

"Nope. Still in recovery."

I took a nap and was finishing a late lunch when Jimbo walked in. He grabbed a beer and led me to the screened porch. "Thanks for the tip, Mick."

"How'd it go?"

"We talked for a while, then she invited me to bed."

"That bluntly?"

"Pretty much. Said she wanted one of us this weekend. Might as well be me since she struck out with you."

"That didn't turn you off?"

"She thinks about me from time to time because we never completed what we started."

"Was it everything you imagined?"

"I'm sure it was more than I imagined when I was seventeen. I haven't had much since Shaina. In any event, got my ashes hauled."

"She would have been my first in a long time."

"Since you split up with Sharon?"

"Yeah. Not much over the past four years."

"Missing it, or have you started to forget?"

"Not sure. It's difficult beginning again."

"Hard finding someone. Harder keeping her."

I thought about the hours I spent with Tom after I walked out on Debbie. "You're right. Easier to just let it go, sometimes."

Jimbo finished his beer and leaned forward, his thick beard trimmed for the reunion, grinning like the cat with the canary feathers stuck in his teeth. "What?"

"Debbie and I had an interesting conversation. After we were done."

"That can happen. At least you didn't bolt right after."

"Couldn't do that. She was driving me back. She recalled her affair with you. In endless detail."

"You knew we went out for a few months after you broke up with her."

He started laughing. "But not about all the sex, man. Hours and hours of it, orgasm after orgasm. All the positions you tried because she was so curious. 'The best sex she's ever had' sort of thing."

He turned my face crimson, which was his point, and it took a while to think of something to say. "I don't think it was as interesting as she told you. We were both starting out."

"Was for her. She couldn't stop reliving it. Got embarrassing as the details piled up."

"You don't need to tell me."

"Even told me about your special move, coming in from the backside."

"Make you feel a bit inadequate?"

"Shit. Not like you wrote the manual. But when she suggested we take another tumble, it felt like I was behind you in line. Told her I needed to get back."

"Sorry you had to experience that."

"Why'd you keep it a secret?"

"Didn't know I wasn't supposed to. Figured you might not want to hear about it."

"I might have gotten jealous. I was way more sexually agitated than you were back then. At least I thought so until today."

"Water under the bridge, then?"

"Long past the bridge, buddy. But a good story between us. Lemon doesn't have to know."

"Not sure he's interested in stuff like that."

I walked him out to his truck. "Want to drive to the dinner together?" he asked.

"Yeah. I'll walk up around six and say hello to Doc."

I wandered around the old house. There were pictures of Dennis and me at all ages in most of the rooms. The loneliness I often felt crept back in. I called Grand Rapids hoping to speak to Des. Sharon answered and said he was gone for the day. I told her to say hello to him. Ron, too.

I almost began to cry, feeling that forlorn, and it surprised me, as I normally didn't sink this low into the blues. I looked at the phone number Tom had given me, wondering if this was my new destination. I dialed it, and he said he could be free tomorrow afternoon. I told him I'd drop by.

Twenty-Three
Forty-Eight

We turned forty-eight in 1995. The events of March, April, and May of that year smacked us around like a tornado churning in off the western prairies, turning a hardwood forest into toothpicks. Just when we didn't think we'd recover enough to go on, something uplifting would arrive on an unexpected breeze allowing us to regain some lightness in our footsteps. The heartache subsided. Then our next breath would be sucked out of us, and we'd be spun around again. We were lucky to have each other.

It started off with my brother, Dennis, losing his father-in-law. He did all he could to support his wife, Alberta, but he couldn't pull her out of her grief until their son, Derrick, and his wife, Sandy, presented them with their second grandchild three weeks later. Derrick asked me to be Sean's godfather, even though I didn't profess the faith Sandy did. Derrick didn't care about my religious tendencies. He knew how I'd lost my sons, Ron and Des—his first cousins—and wanted me to climb back into our family nest, taking on some aspect of parenthood with his child. It was such a generous overture, and so surprising, that I pledged my intention to honor their gift.

A month after that, and completely without warning, Orantha's father passed on in Kingston. She was beside herself, and Lemon could do little for her, especially since he had come to love his father-in-law so deeply. Lemon's family boarded the plane to Jamaica—minus Bettina, who was eight months pregnant. Lemon asked me to look in on her during the week of his absence, and I called her every day and drove over from Eau Claire on the weekend.

A few weeks later, my closest friend on the staff at Eau Claire Memorial High School, Charlie Fitzsimmons, dropped dead on a Monday morning during his history lecture. I was teaching in the classroom next door and heard the students shouting for help. By the time I reached Fitz, he was already turning blue. Despite our best efforts performing CPR, and the quick intervention of the rescue squad, Fitz was DOA when the gurney wheeled him away from our lives. Teachers and students alike went into shock, and I was unable to teach, like many of my colleagues, even though we stood in front of our students and pretended to conduct our lessons. Fitz's funeral gathering filled the gymnasium at school. I was consumed with meditations on the uncertainty of life as I prepared my eulogy and couldn't escape from my words in the subsequent weeks.

Bettina was just a few days from her due date when I got a phone call from Al Barlow, Jimbo's supervisor at American Airlines. Jimbo had been AWOL from work for three days and didn't respond when Barlow called his cell. Barlow discovered Jimbo curled up on his living room couch, half-asleep, half-drunk, a fifth of Jack Daniels nearly empty on the coffee table. Jimbo barely responded to Barlow's greeting, four days of facial growth adding to his disheveled appearance. Barlow knew Jimbo lived alone, so he dug around in Jimbo's desk looking for a family contact. My phone number was the one he had discovered.

I called Lemon. Orantha was back home, but he was reluctant to drive down to St. Louis with the birth of his first grandchild so imminent, until Orantha insisted he go. On the way down, we talked about our options. The most sensible was for Jimbo to come clean about his problems and for us to get him whatever help he needed before we zoomed back home after a day or two. We understood the improbability of that set of dominos falling into place.

Jimbo was as Al Barlow described him, now with additional layers of whiskers. Most of his dishes were dirtied and scattered about the kitchen, and the living room, bathroom, and both bedrooms were even worse, like burglars had flipped them. There was no open booze as Al had removed all the beer and spirits he could find in the house. Jimbo peered up from his doze. "Want to talk?" Lemon asked.

"I should. Since you took the trouble to get here. Let me get cleaned up first."

We straightened up the living room and did the dishes while Jimbo showered. He joined us, standing in the kitchen doorway, watching us clean up his mess. His dark hair was speckled grey and slicked back, longer than I'd seen it on him in years. He had a few razor nicks on his chin and neck, and his belly extended his grey T-shirt over his belt buckle. He shook his head as he watched us, with a look of embarrassment and resignation, and poured a cup of coffee Lemon had brewed. We sat down at his kitchen table.

"Al Barlow said he'd count your absence as sick leave," I said.

"I've got plenty accumulated. Have only missed a few days since Dad died."

"So it's not about your job?" Lemon said.

"I'm not in love with my work like you two, but it's good enough."

"What is it?" Lemon asked.

"Did you hear my mom passed away last week?" Jimbo said like he was talking about yesterday's rain. We shook our heads, Jimbo being one of the few who would have told us. "Sudden. Brain aneurysm. Nobody got to say goodbye. Not even her husband."

"Shit. You could have called," I said.

"What would you have done?"

He was right. Neither Lemon nor I would have flown to the funeral in Clearwater where Vera and Jack had retired. "Did you stay down there long?" I said.

"Just an overnight. Got a motel room near the funeral home."

"You and Jeremy still on the outs?" I said.

"We've always been."

"Nothing like this happened after Doc died?" Lemon said.

"That's right. And he meant more to me than Mom ever did. I guess it's the finality of it. That I'm completely alone now. No wife or kids. I speak to Les a couple times a year. You two. My work-mates."

"Your supervisor cared enough to find you and call me up. That's something," I said.

"Of course. I'm not a numbskull."

"When did the meltdown start?" I said.

"As soon as I got back. Maybe I should have stayed in Clearwater for a few more days."

"Drinking much?" Lemon said.

"The bottle Al found had been sitting there since I got back from Florida, but he was mistaken when he thought I was drunk. This time is different from any other mental health curses I've dealt with over the years. Even when I've had my go-rounds with depression, I got on with life. The day after I got back from Florida, I woke up from a nap and couldn't move. Like it was pointless to get up and continue with my routine."

"Do you need to see somebody?" I said.

"Not sure."

Lemon's phone rang. Bettina was in labor and headed to the hospital. "You should go back. I'd feel terrible if my mess kept you from being there," Jimbo said.

Lemon was antsy, wanting to drive right back to the Cities, looking to me for help. "If I stay, will you drive me back to Eau Claire? Spend some time at my house?" I asked Jimbo.

Jimbo refilled his coffee cup, smiling for the first time. "Damn, that's good news. Grandpa Lemon. So proud of you, man."

"Didn't do much. Just holding her hand at this point."

"Who's the dad?"

"Her college boyfriend. Not sure they'll get married or if she'll be on her own. That's the only pisser."

"You'll make it work."

"Trying to."

Jimbo looked at me. "I like your offer, Mick. We can leave anytime. Let me square it with Al first."

We went out for an early supper before Lemon took off, and Jimbo continued to interrogate Lemon about Bettina and the baby. "She didn't want to know the gender. Wants a boy to break the spell of girls."

"She moving back home, so you and Orantha can help?"

"For a while."

Lemon glanced at me, both of us understanding how therapeutic it was to see Jimbo so distracted.

Jimbo and I took off the next morning in his Chevy pickup. We engaged in small talk on the way, but I was hesitant about pushing him, concerned I'd trigger him back to the depths. Just north of Peoria, he asked me to drive while he slept the rest of the way. The moment we stepped into my house, Lemon called. Bettina had given birth to a baby girl. Lemon and his three sisters, three daughters, now a baby granddaughter. Orantha was finally feeling life again after the ordeal with her father.

We went out for dinner, both of us drinking ginger ale, and by the time we got back, I was ready for sleep. "You OK if I go back to work tomorrow?"

"I won't do anything crazy. You don't even have to clean out your liquor." He was working at regaining my trust. "I'll spend the day preparing for your examination."

"You that sure it's coming?"

He smiled like he used to back in middle school. "I'd lay a year's salary on it, Mick. That's what you do for me."

I was laughing with him now. "Why don't we postpone the exam and you come to school with me? I'm discussing the Vietnam War in two of my classes. Won't put you on the spot. You can sit there and listen and yell at me if I'm going astray."

"Let me sleep on it."

When I rolled out of bed, he was preparing breakfast, showered and shaven, dressed in clean jeans and a button-down shirt. "This mean you want to go?"

He served me some coffee. "It'll fill my day."

Somewhere on the way from the teacher's lounge to my first-hour class, Jimbo disappeared. I found him twenty minutes later in the woodshop talking to Jerry Ruess, our veteran shop teacher. "If you don't mind, Mick, I think I'll hang out with Jerry."

Jerry was amused by this stranger strolling about his classroom, examining the different woodworking projects. "I could use an extra hand."

Jimbo was more exhausted than I was that evening. "Fuck, those kids take it out of you. I'd forgotten the types who get scheduled into shop classes. Hats off to you assholes who try to teach them."

He insisted we grill out on the patio, wanting to remind me of his barbequing talents, and by the time we cleaned up and watched television for an hour, it was nine, and we were ready to knock off. After another day of this routine, Jimbo asked if he could finish the week. We still hadn't taken time to talk, but I could see Jimbo feeling better each day.

My phone rang at five on Saturday morning. It was Lemon again, sobbing like I'd never heard him. Sarah Ruth was dead in his parents' home in Bridgeton. She'd overdosed on her sedatives while Ted and Lizzie were vacationing in New York City. Little Lemon had just turned forty-five.

Jimbo and I forged a new plan. On Monday, we'd drive to Bridgeton in two vehicles, spend the night at my parents' house, and after the funeral, Jimbo would head back to his routine in St. Louis. Knowing our time was running out, we finally got around to it Sunday night. I started out easy. "What's happening with the woodshop at your dad's old place?"

Doc had created a probate mess for Jimbo and his brothers three years ago when he split up his property, making Jimbo the sole heir to his woodshop. The house couldn't be sold as long as Jimbo retained the shop, and Jimbo didn't want to get rid of the shop and lose the memories he had of working with Doc on cabinetry projects. "I kept it for two years."

"Did you finish that cherry end table your dad started?"

"I'd set up to finish it. Run the machines to make sure they worked. Lay the hand tools on the workbench. Nice and pretty. Then I'd freeze up. Like Dad's shop wasn't really my own. Stupid of me to keep the place so long."

"Who bought the house and shop?"

"The renters grabbed it up. Money's been dispersed to Les and Jeremy."

"What about the equipment and the tools?"

"Most of them are back with me in St. Louis."

"Tell me about your mom."

Jimbo paused as I shifted directions. "I was shocked when she passed. Figured she'd go for many more years, maybe outlive me. She was always so damn healthy. I hadn't seen her since Dad's funeral. We talked once a month, but I hadn't visited after they moved to Florida. I never really knew her again after she moved out when I was seven."

"Was this shutdown anything like the months after Vietnam?"

"Not really. As much as I can remember."

"What would have happened if Lemon and I hadn't shown up?"

"I've always been resilient. Probably would have gotten up in another day or two and called Al to see if I still had a job."

"He must like you. To go to all this trouble."

"He's an AA guy. We've talked. He'll want to save me now."

"Must be more than that?"

"He's my best friend at work, but we're not close beyond that."

"You scared about going back home?"

"Some of the demons are pretty resolute. This week helped. You're always good for me, Mick. Putting me back on a better path and spending time with Jerry in the shop was a blast. Haven't laughed like that in years."

"Maybe you need a woman in your life?"

Jimbo laughed. "Haven't been very successful with that. You know my quandary. Not easy to live with, but terrible at living alone."

"I'm not much better."

"Does being close to Lemon help?"

"Sometimes. But we often go for months without seeing each other."

"But knowing he's just two hours away keeps you right-side up."

"He'll need us now. He's always felt responsible for Sarah Ruth."

"That's what I really need. Remembering someone's got it worse than me."

"Truth in that. Did you have these blue spells back in Bridgeton?"

Jimbo looked beyond me into his past. "Some. Started in eighth grade. Got worse during our last two years in high school. I kept most of it from you and Lem."

"I thought what happened to you in Vietnam was the trigger."

"The war added some more layers, but it was there before that. Feels organic now. I can't remember not dealing with it. But I hate being reliant on medication."

"What do you think alcohol is?"

"You're right. I don't drink more than a few beers each day when it's going smoothly. Maybe I'm a low-level medicator."

"That's why I've pretty much stopped drinking. To make sure alcohol wasn't getting me through my loneliness."

"Hits you, too?"

"Often enough. Never as bad as you, but a sense of helplessness sometimes."

Jimbo picked up a framed photograph of Ron and Des when they were still with me. "Things any better with your boys?"

"Just with Des. We talk every few weeks. Last summer, I visited him in Lansing where he's going to college. He let me sleep in his bed while he took the couch."

"No kidding. How'd it go?"

"Just a beginning. He was pretty nervous about having me around for a few days."

"I'd be, too, after all those years and the bad blood with your ex."

"At least it's something. Do you ever wonder if things would be better if you had kids?"

"Maybe, but that wasn't in the cards. My sperm count is too low to make babies."

"No, shit. How'd you find out?"

"Shaina and I rutted like rabbits for a year. When nothing happened, we both got checked. She was fine, but big ol' Jimbo wasn't man enough."

"You know it has nothing to do with your masculinity."

"The urologist reassured me with that argument. But it didn't work with Shaina. Wanting kids was the key reason she married me, and she didn't want to mess around with treatments when they discovered my infertility. All for the best anyway. We weren't a good match in practically every way, other than for having good sex."

The memory of talking with Lemon about Shaina popped into my mind. "I was going to tell you that before you married her."

"What stopped you? Getting a laugh from me going through more misery?"

"I conferred with Lemon. He didn't think that's what friends should do."

"That was decent of him. Still, since you two had it figured out, you could have saved me some pain."

"Maybe lost you when you got angry."

The conversation waned as we both reflected on what had gone wrong in our past. Just as quickly, waves of sorrow over those blunders and the people who'd been dying in our lives ran through me. "Damn, this has been a hell of a stretch," I said.

My tears came unexpectedly as I told Jimbo about Fitz, and soon he was crying, too. We babbled on for ten minutes about missing people, but for Jimbo, it was the memories of Doc that wounded him most. That and not having anyone else.

"You've got people, Mick. You're lucky."

I didn't want my sorrows to send him back to where Lemon and I'd found him a week earlier. "I'm always here, Jimbo. Willing to hear you out or make a visit. Whatever you need."

His laughter broke the spell. "Then I'd have to admit I need somebody."

"I made that confession to Lemon a few years ago. Said he'd always back me."

"Bridgeton buddies. That's not how things were meant to work out. We're supposed to move on from that boyhood stuff."

"If we weren't such good friends, maybe. What else do we have?"

"You're right, and I appreciate your offer. Do me a favor?"

"What's that?"

"If I don't call or drop by, will you reach out? I'm not sure how good I'll be about remembering."

"Enough said."

There was more sorrow for me at Sarah Ruth's funeral than I'd experienced from all the rest of the sad events that spring. Maybe it was the tender memory of finding her curled up in the rear of Dirty Joe's cave when we were thirteen and understanding she could still have been that helpless, more than thirty years later. Lemon could not console his parents enough and could barely talk to express his sorrow. Little Eve, his youngest sister, presented the eulogy at St. Peter's Catholic Church instead. Nine months pregnant with twins, after years of trying, Eve waddled up to the altar. Jimbo and I, sitting next to Mom and Dad, grinned madly at the sight of her. Our memories of Eve were so dear: the tomboy running after us, fiercely determined to be older than she was, utterly defiant when she was told to head back home. She'd grown up to become Sarah Ruth's best friend. A nurse who watched out for her. Now she'd have to support Lizzie and Ted, who might never forgive themselves for leaving Sarah Ruth for those few days, even if Little Eve had dropped in to see her just hours before Sara Ruth emptied her bottle of pills.

Her ten-minute speech had everyone crying and laughing. She never mentioned Sarah Ruth's battle with autism and loneliness, dwelling on her quirks instead. Her unique style of chewing the crust free from her sandwiches. The extreme orderliness she maintained in all the bedrooms of her siblings after they'd moved away like she expected them to return that evening. Her penchant, once she discovered authors she loved, to read every novel they wrote, obsessively, from the first to the last but never out of order, harassing the librarians when they couldn't get the book she wanted. Her extraordinary devotion to Little Eve during her pregnancy, cleaning Eve's house weekly and preparing the few recipes she knew how to cook, over and over. There were plates of brownies everywhere in Eve's kitchen that Eve snuck out of her house each morning for her coworkers at the hospital.

Little Eve gave no signs of breaking down, determined to salute her sister with the joy often missing from Sarah Ruth's daily life. She reached the end, recalling her sister's twenty-four-hour disappearance when she was ten, how everyone in Bridgeton searched for her, shouting out through every park and from every inch of shoreline, calling to her from boats cruising slowly up and down the Wisconsin River. Eve reminded us of the chant that rang out that day all over town, that was later adopted by the Kraig family whenever they came home and beckoned to Sarah Ruth: "Sarah Roooth, where are you?" and of Sarah Ruth's delight in the playful way the family showered this affection. Eve paused for the first time, and Jimbo and I could see she was losing her composure. We had to rescue her. We stood and called back to Eve, "Sarah Roooth, where are you." Lemon turned back to us, smiling, standing, chanting the same. Then Esther and Lizzie and Ted Kraig. Mom and Dad. Friends and relatives. Good citizens of Bridgeton who had searched for Sarah that day. "Sarah Roooth, where are you?" Eve conducted us from the stage now, standing in front of the lectern, as though a baton were in her hand as we summoned our lost friend. Ted and Lizzie giggled at the absurdity of it all. Veteran parishioners from staid St. Peter's congregation chuckled, despite themselves. The organist in the choir loft pumped notes to keep the rhythm. Father Cashon finally joined in, too. As our beseeching to Sarah Ruth wound down to Eve's slender voice, Jimbo and I started clapping loudly, others following, the stained-glass windows rattling from the applause. Little Eve laughed as she clapped and stamped her left foot, then suddenly looked down at the moisture soaking her feet while she held her belly. Orantha was the first to realize her waters had broken and rushed to the altar. Lemon and Orantha helped Eve's husband escort her out of the church to St. Mary's Hospital.

The spell of our springtime sorrows had been broken. Finally. As we ate our luncheon in the church basement, word came through of the birth of the twins. Healthy baby girls. No one had to guess what their names would be.

Twenty-Four
The Knapsack

After Dad died at age seventy-nine, three days after a massive heart attack, Joe Rebenick flew up from Daytona Beach. I picked him up at the regional airport, and he insisted I drop him at the Longstreet Motel, but I refused and took him to the house. Mom hugged him like a childhood friend she hadn't seen in decades. Joe was embarrassed and reticent. "Janice, you don't need me in the house. Mickey knows better than that. You should, too."

"We set you up in the basement in Matt's office. It's equipped with a sofa bed and a bathroom. And, Joe, you're never in the way."

Mom had spent time with Joe after he left Bridgeton when she and Dad vacationed in Florida. She'd long been over her distaste for him, appreciating him as Dad's oldest friend. I hadn't seen him since I was thirteen, on the beach at Daytona. He looked a bit older than seventy-nine, some of it no doubt from his debilitating stay in the prison camp, but most of it due to those ravaging years of drinking. He told me he'd been sober for decades. His last relapse was in Bridgeton when he practically fell down drunk bringing up the rear in the Memorial Day parade thirty-seven years ago.

Joe became less of himself just being back in town. He hid out in the basement most of that first day and stopped into the wake for just a few minutes, taking off when he saw the line of people. He sat by himself during the funeral at the Unitarian Church in Wausau. Pastor

Jacobson agreed to provide a non-denominational service. Dad had never regained any religious zeal after World War II, despite Mom's urging.

During the gathering at the house after the funeral, Joe was skittish, up and down the stairs to his basement headquarters or perched on a stool in the corner of the kitchen. He was agreeable with the few people who were curious about his years in Florida, but he didn't initiate any conversations. An hour after we'd come back from the burial, he asked me to step outside. "Mickey, do you still have a bike in the garage?"

"Wouldn't be in good shape. Where do you want to go?"

"Back out to the cemetery. I'd like to say goodbye to your dad. In a quiet way."

I understood. I was planning on the same before I went back to Eau Claire in a couple of days. "I'll take you. Won't get in your way."

I parked at Dad's plot, soil still moist from the interment. "If you want me to wait, I'll walk around for a while. Or I can pick you up later."

Joe was nervously fingering a folded piece of paper. "Give me ten minutes. Maybe twenty."

I walked off searching for the gravestones of people I had once known, glancing periodically at Joe, who had unfolded the paper and was reading from it.

He left the next afternoon. Mom handed him a check for seventeen thousand dollars at the airport, the remains of his inheritance that Dad had invested and managed for over fifty years. Joe smiled for one of the few times over those two days. "Matty was always good for it. Lent me money on the principal anytime I needed it."

"It's yours now, Joe," Mom said. "Matt was so proud you turned your life around."

Joe lived another seven years. Neither Jimbo nor Lemon could join me for his funeral in Daytona, and Mom said she was too old to make the trip. Well over a hundred people showed up for the service, which was held in the basement of a Baptist church where Joe attended AA meetings for decades. Joe didn't want a traditional funeral, but those who loved him, many of whom were Friends of Bill, insisted on saluting him. They told their best stories, and I added a few. Nobody there had heard about his near-death experience after the stabbing in Skunk Hollow or his brush with fame after he led us to Sarah Ruth in the cave near the Wisconsin River. The attendees wanted me to tell more about Joe's life in Bridgeton, but I was reluctant. I didn't want them to know that throughout the years I'd known Joe, he was mostly under the influence.

On my way out of the gathering, Loretta, Joe's partner over the past twenty years, stopped me and said she had something for me. She drove me to their place, a beach bungalow with a beautiful vista of the Atlantic Ocean tucked between two four-story apartment buildings. "Must be sublime in the morning sun."

"That's why Joe bought it. It's worth a lot of money now, with all the development. I'll keep it as long as I can manage. It's his gift to me."

"From what I know, he didn't have anyone else."

"Except for your family back in Bridgeton. He didn't like to talk about the old days. Worried it would set him off."

"Did he ever open up about his experiences in the Philippines?"

"Not even the vets at AA could get that out of him."

"You know he was in the prison camp at Cabanatuan."

"For three years, right?"

"He never told me the full story. Dad either."

She handed me a black plastic trash bag. "He wanted you to have this."

I pulled out Joe's old World War II knapsack, not looking any worse for wear than it had when Jimbo carried it full of sandwiches and bottles of water during the search for Sarah Ruth. Inside, there were three envelopes. One was oversized, containing a collection of photographs of Joe standing with Dad and me on the back porch, that Mom must have snapped; of Joe, Jimbo, and me after discovering Sarah Ruth, that the photographer from the *Wausau Herald* had taken for the front-page story after her abductor had been apprehended; and an assortment of Joe with Jimbo, Lemon, and me on our Christmas trip to Daytona. Dad had shot most of a roll using Joe's Kodak. There was one I took that day of Dad and Joe, the Atlantic in the background, Joe's arm around Dad's shoulder, the orange glow of sunset on their faces.

Joe enclosed a check inside one of the smaller envelopes, made out to Janice Pederson, for $10,000. "There's a note taped on the back," Loretta said, touching my hand.

I carefully pulled it free. "Thanks, Janice. For making me part of your family."

"Mom doesn't need it. And she'd be embarrassed to take it."

"I know. I spent time with her when your folks visited. I could tell she's not the type to want gifts like this. I told Joe the same thing. He said she can give it away." Loretta squeezed my hand. "Or give it to you."

"Did he leave you with enough?"

"Yes. He managed his money very well. Something your dad taught him."

The third envelope was addressed to Matty Pederson. Joe's scrawl was written across the seal. "Wait to open that one. Find a good time and place." Loretta laughed. "For one thing, it's almost impossible to read. I offered to type it up for him, but he didn't want me to touch it. He said you'd know what it was."

While I waited for my flight the next day, I unsealed the envelope and began to read Joe's note but quickly stopped. I could see it would be too much for me. I refolded the piece of paper and returned it to the envelope. After I was back in Eau Claire for several days, I spent a few hours with the letter.

That summer, at our fortieth high school reunion, I read it again to Lemon and Jimbo.

Dear Matty,

Never in a million years did I think you'd go before I did. When I got the call from Mickey, I was so shocked I couldn't move out of my chair for the afternoon. Because you deserved to have more years than me. To live it out with Janice and the boys and their families.

I don't know what I'm going to do when you don't call next month. To talk about my money. Our money, because it's like you are giving me a gift each time the check arrives. It's no longer savings Momma set aside for me. That's why I've never wanted you to cash out the account and deposit it in my bank down here. Because then you wouldn't have a reason to call me and I'd lose contact with my best friend. The only one who connects me to the old days.

My thoughts often drift back to Bridgeton and the river. At the oddest times, day or night. And you're usually there. Sometimes, I'm by myself camping along the river in those years after the war. But I try not to think about those moments when I was drinking so much. The best reflections are about you and me as boyhood friends inventing escapades out of pretty much nothing. Taking turns leading the way.

When Mickey and Lemon and Jimbo found me camping that day in Skunk Hollow, and we shared some walleye stew, it was a bit like our time together. I realize now, that was the beginning of me becoming something new. Took a long time. Alcohol is a motherfucker. But I loved the time with the boys during those months. Reminded me of us, Matty. Those golden years before we got wounded forever by the war. We were never quite the same afterward. Just like you told those boys in Mickey's history class that day. When you took over for me after I couldn't go on. That was the final day in Bridgeton for me. When I knew I had to be somewhere else, to become something else. I know I came back to town again and made a fool of myself one last time. But that moment in Mickey's grade school classroom made me see

> something. I had to stop forcing Matty Pederson to watch over me. It wasn't fair to you. Sooner or later, you'd give up on me if I continued drinking. I had to leave Bridgeton to get sober. And stay away. I know you understand that. But sometimes I miss knocking at your back door for one of our evening chats. I long for that so much.
>
> It's a hell of a thing growing up, isn't it, Matty? To lose what's so pure about life. I think about that all the time.
>
> I don't suppose I'll be able to stop remembering you, during whatever time I have left. Maybe I'll call Janice to see how she's holding up. And I sure won't forget Mickey and Lemon and Jimbo. Though I was always worried about Jimbo. Life shat all over him as a kid, way more than anyone deserved it. Hope he's alright.
>
> Matty, since neither of us believes there's something more after we die, this is the end. It came too quickly. I never got to say goodbye. Figures that you wouldn't let me see you in a vulnerable state. Near death. It was always your job to be my caretaker. Not the other way around.

I looked up, barely keeping back the tears. Lemon, with a half-smile, shook his head, muttering, "Man, oh, man. That's one beautiful eulogy."

Jimbo was stone-faced like someone had startled him beyond recognition, and he rose from the chair and quietly departed from the motel room. "What's that about?" I asked Lemon.

"Not sure. Maybe Joe's reference to him in the letter. Maybe Jimbo being Jimbo."

"I bet Joe wanted to read this at the funeral. He could have. It was kind of an open mic at the service."

"Must have been twenty people who got up that day."

"He didn't have the nerve," I said.

"Maybe had the nerve but was convinced people wouldn't have understood. Joe was pretty much an outcast in Bridgeton."

"Not many people knew that Dad was Joe's financial caretaker all those years."

"Probably thought he was getting assistance from the government. Being a vet."

I called Jimbo and let it ring to voice message and hung up. He returned a few minutes later. "You OK?" I asked.

"Yeah. Joe's note just flipped me upside down for a few minutes. Like I didn't know who I was."

"Because he mentioned life crapping on you as a kid?"

"A little. But I never thought of myself as a victim. Joe either. He never seemed to feel sorry for himself."

"When we knew him, we were kids, and he was drinking to cover up," Lemon said.

"Funny what people do when bad stuff happens," Jimbo said.

"How did you handle it, Jimbo?" Lemon asked.

"Like I said, not that much happened that was bad in the big picture. When Mom and Dad got divorced, I was too young to understand. I stayed in Bridgeton, in my old house, went to the same school, like nothing had changed. It only seemed bad when I had to visit Mom and realized she and Dad still had lots of antagonism toward each other. Since I've been divorced twice, I understand splitting up is what happens when the wrong people get together and can't get over the hard times."

Jimbo cracked open a can of beer. "Later, when Dad took up with Beverly and my brothers freaked out, I couldn't understand their anger. I loved having Beverly around. More than being around Mom, that's for sure. And when Lucy was born, it was a genuine gift. I was crushed when she died. But that's just life reaching out and hurting you, naturally. Jeremy beating me up was different. Nothing natural about it. He hated Dad, so he hit me. Total bullshit. I've never forgiven him for it. He's never apologized. He's not my brother anymore. But something good came out of that. Spending that year in your house,

Mick, was one of the best things that's ever happened to me. Thinking back, it really straightened me out. Your mom and dad were the best."

I nodded, but he didn't need my approval to go on with his musings. "Later, the Vietnam stuff fucked me up. Still gets me sometimes. But that happens to lots of people in every generation. Like Joe said about Matt and himself. Societal shit-job."

"Ever wish you weren't alone?" I asked.

"Doesn't everybody who is? Lemon, you're one of the fortunate ones. But being alone is not life shitting on you. It's just another way to wind down the years. Until we go."

Not much we could add to that. "I guess that's why I walked out earlier. Dying scares the hell out of me. I'm man enough to admit that. The fucking end. How could it ever be?"

"We just turned fifty-eight. Long way to go, Jimbo," I said.

"I know. Maybe I'm just jumping ahead. But how could I never see you guys again?"

We knew what he meant. Same as Joe meant in his eulogy to Dad. We were lucky, just like Joe and Dad had been.

Twenty-Five
Bridgeton Redux

Lemon never forgot about Aggie Robinson. Like many of us do with a favorite grade school teacher, he fell in love with her as a boy, but unlike most schoolboy fantasies, Aggie became a real friend to Lemon.

She settled in the Twin Cities area a few years after leaving the Franciscan nuns and taught middle school for thirty years, maintaining close contact with Lemon, especially when she taught his daughters in the Wayzata schools. Lemon looked out for her when she lost her partner, Betty Portzen, and especially during the last two months of her life after she developed pancreatic cancer when she was eighty-one. Aggie asked Lemon to administer her will, though most of it went to the charitable organizations she was involved with over the years.

She left a gift for the two of us, a package wrapped in butcher block paper. As we sat together, late at night on her funeral day sipping whiskeys, Lemon set Aggie's legacy before us and proceeded to tear off the paper to reveal a ten by twelve-inch wooden jewelry box fastened expertly with ten strands of twine. We paused a moment while Lemon refilled his glass with a finger of whiskey. "We didn't drink much in high school. Not like the other guys."

"Me, you, and Jimbo. We walked a pretty straight line. For the first two years anyway. After that, you weren't around much."

"Have you heard from him lately?"

"I suggested he meet us in Chicago in a few weeks."

Lemon and I had established an annual tradition of an extended springtime weekend in one of the cities in the Midwest. Over the years, Jimbo had joined us on occasion. "What did he say?" Lemon said.

"He'll think about it. He's depressed. Trying his best."

We sipped a bit of whiskey in tribute to both Jimbo and Aggie.

"Open it, Lemon."

The twine was bound so tightly he struggled to cut it off. The box contained nothing more than three inches of sand. "What the hell," Lemon said.

I dug in and pulled out an envelope with our names on it and handed it to Lemon. "You read it. You deserve the honor."

> Dear Boys,
>
> I came to life when you took me to Discovery Beach. After we visited it that first time, I went back and dug up this sand. It's had a prominent place in my bedroom wherever I've lived since. Be so kind and take it back to the beach. Mix my ashes with it. Thank you for this last favor.
>
> Your dear friend,
Aggie Robinson

We stopped in Bridgeton on our way to Chicago and had lunch with Mom at the old house on Pine Street. I tried to convince her to move to an apartment closer to me, but she declined, again, chuckling as she did so. We toured the town for twenty minutes. Much of it had changed, particularly over the past twenty years. A dozen streets had been added and filled with newer homes for those commuting to Wausau and Stevens Point. Modern schools had taken the place of the buildings where Lemon, Jimbo, and I attended. Even St. Peter's Church had been replaced. The paper mill was still there, some of it recently remodeled, despite its uncertain future. The village, now a city, had exploded from thirteen hundred when we grew up there, to nearly five thousand.

Old Iron was gone replaced by a girder structure so settled into position that not many would have guessed it wasn't the only one that had ever connected the eastern and western sides of the river. There was no way to get down to Little Bull Falls without climbing over a ten-foot fence, so we drove to the other end of town, retracing our memories for the back way to the river and Discovery Beach through Skunk Hollow. The woods getting to the river was overgrown but clear of fences as we scrambled through the underbrush, both of us carrying a backpack, Lemon's with Aggie's ashes and mine with the box of sand. When we reached the river, we took turns pulling the clumps of last season's burdock out of each other's clothing, then headed upstream.

It was much the same as the walk from over fifty years ago. Everything was smaller, naturally. The river, which used to seem a mile across, was not more than forty yards in some places. Some of the boulders seemed steeper along the bends in the river, but that was mostly due to us being older. When we sensed we were close, we took off our shoes, rolled up our pants, and walked the last fifty yards against the current.

The beach looked remarkably the same as well. The sandbar of times past was gone, replaced by another further out. In reality, the beach had always been tiny, barely big enough for five or six people to stretch out their towels which was why it had never become a popular place for visitors. The ever-changing dynamics of the Wisconsin River had done little to rearrange this bit of shoreline since our last visit. It was still tucked away and perfect.

The temperature was about eighty degrees, and we were surprised how warm the water was for mid-May. We did the only thing that seemed right, stripped down like we had the last time we were there, after high school graduation when we sat in Virgil Lightfoot's sweat lodge.

We walked out to the sandbar, set the boxes down, dove under three times, our genitals shriveling in the water, mixed the ashes and sand and took turns releasing handfuls into the Wisconsin River and saying goodbye to Aggie Robinson. Then we relaxed in the shallow water, as tannin-colored as it had been when we were young, and watched her float away.

As we sat on the beach drying off, Lemon asked, "What are you going to do?"

"What do you mean?"

"You're not getting married again. Ron might as well live ten thousand miles away. You've reconnected with Des, but odds are you're never going to move close to him. You're retired and still living in your oversized, aging house in Eau Claire. When are you going to see all that?"

He caught me off guard as he often did. It never seemed fair, but that was his gift. "It's just what it is. Time has left me there."

"We left Bridgeton years ago. You come back to see your mom or if there's a reason like this. Time doesn't make you stay anywhere unless you want it to. Besides, do you have a better friend than me?"

I looked away so he wouldn't see my tears and embarrassment. When I glanced back, his eyes were watery, too. "Neither one of us will ever forget this little beach, but we don't have to be here to remember it. Get a place in the Cities so I can see you every week."

It took nearly a year before I sold my house and moved into a condo in downtown Minneapolis. Lemon and I took turns inviting Jimbo to visit us, but he took his time, and there was no good explanation for his hesitation. He was retired as a mechanic for American Airlines and not in a relationship, unless he was keeping it a secret. Nothing held him back except his unique state of unhappiness and inertia. St. Louis wasn't even that far.

We would have dropped our persistent pursuit if Jimbo didn't enjoy our friendship so much. It wasn't just rehashing the old times in Bridgeton, though there was no denying those formative days were at the heart of our affection. There was an additional force now, an extension of that early bond focused on and energized by our contemporary lives, but that was something Jimbo didn't always trust or couldn't fully accept. Even after all the times we helped him out of his dark spells, he inevitably retreated back to his isolation and his reticence about revealing much of his private life. He rarely talked about how many authentic friends he'd made and kept since he left Bridgeton. I figured it was fewer than I had and that wasn't many.

He finally called me on a Saturday in early April and said he was driving up the next day. Lemon laughed. "What if both of us were leaving town tomorrow? Think he'd still come?"

Jimbo parked his ten-year-old F-10 pickup outside my condo and announced he'd rather stay in my second bedroom than at Lemon's, if that was OK. "Lemon and Orantha will be disappointed," I told him, speaking the truth.

"There's just too much life there. Orantha's so nice. Their daughters drop by with the grandkids."

I understood. Sometimes Lemon's happiness and good fortune were a bit overwhelming. Jimbo unpacked his duffel into my extra dresser, hung his toiletry kit in the second bathroom, and after a week, did his laundry. I ate breakfast before he got up and left most mornings to do errands while he slept in. He went out by himself for the afternoon after making a series of calls without telling me where he was headed. We made supper together or ate with Lemon and Orantha and spent quiet evenings with me reading and Jimbo searching his computer. I began to feel like we were ten once again after he moved into our house in Bridgeton because his brother was beating him up. I closed my eyes as we sat in the living room of my condo and recalled the nights we lay in my old bedroom, reliving the events of the day before sleep took us away, often mid-sentence.

After two weeks, Jimbo informed me why he'd been so secretive. He was house-hunting in the Twin Cities. "When you moved here, I started thinking about it. But I've got my woodshop to think about."

He hadn't mentioned doing any woodworking since he'd moved Doc's tools and equipment to St. Louis over fifteen years ago. "When did you get serious about that?"

"You remember the spring of 1995. I was done in after Mom died and spent a week in the woodshop at your old high school."

"Then we went down to Sarah Ruth's funeral."

"Right. When I got back home, I started puttering around in my garage and realized I needed to build a bigger shop. I set it up over the next year, but something still wasn't right. Then I remembered that end table Dad started working on before he died. I brought it into the house and set it on my kitchen table. Just looked at it for a few weeks, examining the possibilities. Waiting for a signal, I guess. Maybe for Dad's permission. One weekend, I took it out to my new shop and worked on it until it was completed. That was the beginning. Haven't stopped since."

"How much time do you spend doing it?"

"Most days. Sometimes I start working in late morning, and when I look at the time, it's evening. It's still just a hobby. But I can't give it up. Just like Lemon can't give up supervising residents in surgery."

"What do you create?"

"Little things usually. Boxes and cutting boards. Some chairs and a few tables. Sometimes I make stuff just to see if I can. I keep some of it but mostly give it away to neighbors and old workmates."

"But not to Lemon or me?"

Jimbo smiled, his private world slipping out. "Then you two would pester me about it. Maybe you'd think I was happy again. Finally doing something I enjoy."

"Asshole."

"I used to think you got a perverse pleasure seeing me so miserable. Not way back in Bridgeton when I first started dealing with my depression. But later, when I came back injured from the war. After my marriages failed, and I didn't have anything except my airline work."

"Always wanted you to be happy, man. Just like I wanted you to bunk with me during sixth grade."

"Most of me understood that—the reasonable part. But I just couldn't believe it. You two always seem so damn normal."

"Maybe Lemon. I've dealt with my own misery for a long time. You know that."

"Your life's got good harmony. You get along with Dennis and make plans with Lemon. Something about Bridgeton still works. You and Virgil wrote your book and got great reviews. Your successes have always been intimidating, like I'd been left behind."

I tried to recall what happened to Jimbo after I went off to college, but those years of his life were a blank, "What happened to you after high school?"

"I tried college at Stevens Point, but it didn't work out. Wasn't me. When the war machine chased me down, I enlisted. I figured the air force offered me the most opportunity, but my vision wasn't good enough to be a pilot, so I chose fixing planes as my way out. The pricks sent me into combat most of the time anyway. I saw all that shit in 'Nam. Got hit in the knee. Realized that my PTSD from the war was just an extension of the grief of seeing Lucy die and losing my family."

"You should've kept us in the loop instead of waiting for your crisis moments."

"Well, that's just me being fucked up. Thinking if I kept it private, it would go away."

One evening he announced he'd read the stories about Bridgeton I left near the computer in his bedroom.

"Hope you don't mind me using you," I said.

"You could have asked."

"I'm not sure what I'll do with them. Besides, if I'd have asked you, maybe I wouldn't have written them."

"I know how that is."

We talked about memories and truth, but he mostly wanted to revisit his history with Beverly. "She's still around, you know," he announced.

"Where?"

"Madison."

"How do you know?"

"We talk on the phone every few weeks. Been doing that for years."

"You never speak about her. Figured you'd forgotten."

"Not for one day."

"Tell me about her."

"I thought I would when I read the story about Lucy, dead on our kitchen table. I emailed a copy to Bev. She wants you to call her."

Beverly and I talked for nearly two hours. She reminded me that Doc had paid her way through nursing school in Wausau, which led her to meeting her husband, a surgeon, at University Hospital in Madison. Their marriage lasted nearly fifty years until his death three years ago.

She remained in touch with Doc right up to his death, though Jimbo often filled her in on Doc's life through his phone calls and occasional visits. Jimbo had become her younger brother, somebody she relied on if she needed to talk about the old days. Of course, Jimbo depended on Beverly's good-will more than she needed him.

A week later she sent me a hand-written version of something we hadn't discussed on the phone. She included a short note with it:

> Mickey. If you ever get around to publishing your stories, I'd be honored if you consider this one.
>
> All my best,
> Bev

Doc's Wake

I stayed in touch with Doc over the years. He sent me birthday cards without fail, and I called him a few times a year. My family was curious about him, and I invented the story that he was "my distant uncle" for whom I cooked and cleaned when I was nineteen and still figuring out what I wanted in life.

Just after turning seventy-two, Doc was diagnosed with lung cancer, and Jimbo filled me in a month later, even though Doc didn't want him to tell me. I drove up to Bridgeton to see Doc a few days later and asked him why he was keeping it a secret. "I've always been a private person, Bev, you know that. I've only confided in Jimbo and Matt Pederson about this. They pledged to keep it a secret." He chuckled. "I guess Jimbo wasn't so trustworthy."

He hung on for two years, and I contacted him weekly, occasionally making the two-hour drive to see him. But then he stopped answering the phone calls. On a hunch, I called St. Mary's. Jeremy picked up and said Doc wasn't able to talk. I asked a former colleague at the hospital to check on him. He was down to his final days, so I phoned his room many times that day, hoping to reach Jimbo, wanting to say goodbye to Doc. Finally, Leslie picked up. Doc was somewhat alert. "How are you, Doc?"

"Going fast, Bev. Lucky you caught me."

"Can I drive up to say goodbye?"

"Not sure what would happen if you did."

"I need to tell you a final time what you've meant to me. I wouldn't be what I am without you."

"Same here."

I started laughing and crying because what he said was the most absurd notion. I figured it was the morphine talking. "I'm serious, Doc. You saved me."

"Same here, Bev."

I lost it, and he heard me crying through the speaker. "I truly mean it, Bev. I needed to help you out."

He stopped talking, and Leslie came back on. "He's in and out, Beverly. We expect him to go anytime."

"Is Jimbo there?"

"He's away for now. Taking a nap."

"Would you ask him to call?"

"Sure. But we're busy. He might not get to it."

Doc passed during the night, and I drove up to the wake through a furious April rainstorm. The people of Bridgeton were queued up beyond the doors of Jamerson Funeral Home, umbrellas extending beyond the block to the corner near the Wisconsin River. Doc looked his age in an open casket, but the undertaker created a gentle smile on his craggy face, something he wasn't always keen to show when he was alive. Jeremy muttered a perfunctory thanks for coming but barely looked me in the eye as I offered my hand. Leslie was very tearful and gracious, apologizing that Jimbo hadn't called back before Doc died. He'd forgotten to tell him.

Jimbo's face was dispassionate, and he was barely talking to people as they came through the line. He grimaced as he embraced me. Not one tear. I hugged him a second time, trying to wake him up, wondering if he had sunk into one of his blue spells. "Jimbo, it's me."

I felt a shudder under his fierce demeanor. "Can you wait a bit?"

I sat in a corner of the funeral parlor not wanting to be noticed. Memories came roaring back, more than had overwhelmed me on the two-hour drive to Bridgeton. A woman sat next to me, and I moved my chair a bit to give her more room. "I'm fine," she said.

I was remembering when Doc seduced me for the first time when I was nineteen. I was so surprised, as it was the last thing I expected from this usually unemotional and taciturn man. He was openly affectionate in bed, so unlike his usual stern manner with his boys. The woman's voice jarred me out of my reveries. "You don't know me."

I glanced at her. "Sorry. Should I?"

"We've not met, but I've known about you for so many years. I'm Doc's ex, Vera. Vera Gordon now."

I'd only seen her in photographs many years ago. While Jimbo kept me updated on her life over the years, she was never a major focus of our conversations. "I'm sorry for your loss," I said robotically, fearing the anger I assumed she still felt.

"I've wanted to apologize for years. I didn't have the courage to call you, even after Jimbo told me where you lived."

I looked at her more closely now but couldn't tell if her watery eyes were tearful. "Thank you. But it's not necessary."

"Yes, it is. I got carried away with my feelings for Doc and what his situation with you did to the family. It was a terrible mistake on my part."

"Doc didn't say much about it," I lied.

"He wouldn't. I should have done everything I could have to keep Jeremy from hating you. He poisoned Leslie, too, though Les got over it."

"I'm sure it was a shock for the boys, when Doc took up with me, and I got pregnant."

"Yes. For me, too. And when Lucy died, I let them think the worst about you and your baby and their dad, too. I've never forgiven myself."

"I hope I was good enough to Jimbo."

Those few words unleashed her tears. "More than enough. Through all his troubles, you've been more of a mom to him than I've been."

"That's not true."

"He loves you. I'm not sure he feels the same about me."

"He does. He's a complicated person."

Jimbo touched his mother's shoulder. "Mom, are you OK?"

"Fine, honey. Just chatting with Beverly. Like I told you I would someday."

He looked at me. "She's wanted to, Bev. Hope it's OK."

I nodded, still a bit stunned. His mother kissed Jimbo on the cheek and moved off, and he smiled for the first time. "I wasn't sure what would happen if she tried to apologize. Can we talk outside?"

The rain had stopped though the queue still wound westward toward the river. As we walked down the block, Jimbo was still unable to say much. "You OK, Jimbo?"

"Good enough. Need a break. Most people don't want to see me anyway. The town doesn't love me or my brothers. Just Dad."

"They remember you."

"It's been over twenty-five years since I left."

I could feel his fingers near my right hand, so I grabbed hold. "Bev, would you drive with me to the cemetery?"

"I planned on it before I went back."

He insisted I come in his shiny, new, ruby red pickup. A black camper top covered the back, and the inside was clean except for a coffee cup in the holder. I looked through the back window and saw a mattress and a quilt. "Are you sleeping in this?"

He laughed. "It came in handy at the hospital over the past month. Took lots of naps in the back. And now with Jeremy staying in the house."

"You've been here for a month?"

"Yup. Took leave from work. Jeremy and Les arrived just a few days before he died."

"When did you tell them Doc was dying?"

"He wouldn't let me until a month ago, when I moved in."

He pulled into the gravel driveway leading to her gravestone. The sun broke through, blinding us as it descended behind a string of oaks that hadn't yet leafed out. He took two folding lawn chairs out of the back and opened them a few feet from the flat stone that still reminded us that she flew away too soon.

"Do you need some private time, Bev? Before we sit."

"That would be nice."

The grass was too wet to kneel, and I wished I had brought my garden shoes from the trunk of my car. It was eleven years since my last visit, though I occasionally sat in the bedroom back home with two photos: one of her in Doc's arms at one month, the other of her well-tended gravesite both of which I kept hidden in my jewelry case. Doc accompanied me the last time I was here, and the grave-stone was surrounded by a dozen geraniums. Doc replanted them every spring, tended them all summer, and dug them up before the first frost. He watered the scarlet blooms all winter in his living room. Not all the plants had survived over the years. Three or four hardy parent plants spun off many daughters in new pots over the winters.

"Are the geraniums still at the house, Jimbo?"

"An early frost got them seven years ago. Dad was heartbroken. Left the site untended for several years. Said he didn't have the heart to start over."

Daylilies sprouted now, three inches above the moist soil, inside a freshly painted two-foot high white fence enclosing her. Her name was carved into a hardwood plaque painted a brilliant red, attached to the fence's miniature spires. I touched the letters of her name, and the sorrow came back. "Who made this garden?"

"Remember the lily root stock we dug up at your home that fall?"

"You said they were for your flower bed in St. Louis."

"I took a few back, but most of them came here. I made the fence in Dad's shop. The cemetery groundskeeper told me I couldn't put up a fence or plant perennials that would spread. I told him to take it up with Doc."

"How many varieties?"

"You gave me a dozen. It's beautiful in July. Red and golden and orange trumpets waving over her."

He took a picture of Lucy's gravestone surrounded by my lilies in bloom from his wallet. "From last summer. She's well taken care of."

"Since your dad's no longer here, maybe the groundskeeper will mow them under."

"Nah. Dad's ashes are going in, right next to her."

We sat in the lawn chairs for fifteen minutes, and there was little need to talk as we held hands and watched the sun drop.

"You should get back, Jimbo."

"Yeah. Would be the best thing."

He reached inside his sport coat. "Dad left you this."

It was a yellow envelope, addressed to Doc, my name on the return, taped shut where it had been opened—the get well card I'd sent a few weeks ago inside. "What's this?"

"Take a look."

Alongside "my best and love to you" greeting was a folded piece of St. Mary's Hospital stationary. "He couldn't write, so he dictated it to me."

> My dearest Bev,
>
> You're with me to the end. I'm unable to forget any of it even after these years. You at 19. Those few months with Lucy. Her gravesite. Watching you from afar, married, with children. Finding joy even after our great sadness. Jimbo's kept me up to date when I garner the nerve to ask, since he knows so much about you and me. Thank you for taking care of him, by the way. Nobody's done it as well as you have.
>
> I tried with other women, but I'd see you too often. It never worked out. But it has for you. That's all that matters.
>
> Your friend,
> Doc

I folded the paper before I got it too wet. Jimbo returned the chairs to his truck as I said goodbye to Lucy. We drove back in silence, and he parked behind my car. The parking lot and street were mostly empty now. “Are you coming tomorrow?”

“I’ve got to get back.”

“Mickey and Lemon want to see you.”

“Say hello to them. Another time.”

We hugged, and, this time, his tears rolled out. “I thought I’d get through it without crying.”

“No badge of honor, Jimbo.”

“It’s easy to hold back with Jeremy around.”

“Stay in touch.”

“You know I will. I have to.”

That night, I showed Bev’s story to Jimbo. When he finished reading it, I wasn’t sure if his silent reaction was from embarrassment or sadness as he recalled the passing of Doc and Lucy. “Are her words close to what happened, Jimbo?”

“Yeah, she captured it completely. Bev’s quite a woman. I’m not sure who missed out on her more, Dad or me.”

He reread her story and went out for a while. When he returned, he was all smiles. “You OK?”

“Never better. Just took me a while. That’s usually the way it works.”

I couldn’t remember him in a more ebullient state, probably since our growing up days in Bridgeton.

“How long do you think you’ll stay with me, Jimbo?”

“I can head back to St. Louis anytime.”

"Don't get me wrong. I like having you. If I had more room, I'd ask you move in."

He giggled. "That wouldn't work."

"Probably not, but it's a nice thought."

He pulled a folded piece of paper from his shirt pocket, a picture of a real estate listing in St. Paul. "I made an offer on it the fourth day I got here. The house is small, but there's a garage and a heated storage building. The owners collected antiques and restored them there. It would work as a shop."

"Hope you get it."

"I got a call from the realtor when I was out just now. It's mine."

"No kidding. How soon?"

"A few months. You could move in with me, Mick. It's big enough for two."

It was my turn to laugh.

Twenty-Six
Birds and the Bees

Two months after Jimbo moved into his new home in St. Paul, he invited Lemon and me to a housewarming supper. He was eager to please and nervous at the same time. For the most part, we'd always been the ones to host him. He grilled chicken breasts and corn on the cob and provided several types of micro-brews, though I'd mostly stopped drinking when it began to steer me into the blues too often. We dined at one of the most beautiful tables I've ever seen, maple with chairs to match—Jimbo's creations.

His woodshop was impressive, and he was halfway through building a pair of walnut end tables, a commission for one of Lemon's partners at his clinic. Between the shop and the furniture in his house, it was impossible not to be in awe of his craftsmanship, especially since he had kept it a secret from us for so many years. But Lemon and I had agreed to be cagey in our responses and scanty with our praise to see how long Jimbo could stand it. We sat on the screened porch in the dimming of the day in cushioned reclining chairs—three more of Jimbo's creations—so comfortable I could have gone to sleep. He watched us like a kindergartner anticipating our compliments. We held back until he'd had enough. "OK, shitbirds, let me know when the joke's over."

Lemon and I were enjoying the charade with "What are you talking about?" looks on our faces, but Jimbo was never one for subtle responses. “If you’re trying to make me feel bad, you’re out of luck. I’m over that crap.”

“Like hell you are,” I said. That’s all it took. We praised him to the skies as twilight shifted into dusk, and things got easy as they always did. Jimbo was full of laughter and eager to talk, so much so it was hard to believe he was ever victimized by depression. “What’s it going to be, boys, old times or something new?”

“Mickey’s been taking care of the old times pretty extensively, writing us up like we actually knew what we were doing when we were growing up. Very little of it rings true to me,” Lemon said.

“Poetic license. He’s taken it in spades,” Jimbo agreed.

I knew I’d eventually have to pay for writing about our past and sharing the stories with them. Good-natured ribbing was only fair.

“Do you remember the night we slept over in Lemon’s basement room?” I asked.

“There were a bunch of them, though usually we bunked at my place, especially after my brothers left,” Jimbo said.

“The night we talked about our dads? The birds and the bees?”

“How did we even get started that night?” Jimbo asked.

None of us could recall, but the boyhood laughs we enjoyed that long ago evening slipped into our conversation. “I think it was sometime in late eighth grade. We’d been looking at slides in Lemon’s microscope. That fancy one you had,” I said.

“Won it in the Westinghouse contest. Still have it in my basement.”

“Yeah, you had a dish of some microorganisms, and we watched them divide and separate. What was it?” Jimbo said.

“Slime mold.”

“Somehow we got to talking about how we learned about sex,” Jimbo recalled.

By the Book – Jimbo's Tale

It was the fall of seventh grade. I'd gone through puberty early and was already using Leslie's razor every other day until he told me to get my own. Dad invited me into his office, and I sat with him like one of his patients anticipating a terrible prognosis. He took down two medical books and opened each one before me. One was of a woman's sexual anatomy, the other of a man's. He cleared his throat. "It's time, probably overdue, that I give you the talk."

I didn't know a lot, but enough, including a few sessions perusing chapters in the same books he was showing me, but I played along. He explained the female first, how she produces eggs, and pointed to the fallopian tubes and the uterus. His finger drifted down to the drawing of the vagina, and he spelled out how the sperm gets deposited and one militant warrior completes the journey to create a pregnancy. He even identified the clitoris but didn't explain its function.

Then he proceeded to the male anatomy. The illustration of the penis didn't seem real as he pointed to the blood vessels within it and how they could swell up. "An erection, Jimbo. I'm sure you have them."

Then he continued on to the testicles and prostate, creating the ejaculate. He seemed to be done, though the books were still open. "Dad, is this what happened when Beverly was living with us?"

He got red-faced, and I thought he might leave the room, but, like with some difficult patient, he worked his way through it. "I owe you an explanation. Everything I've just told you is what happens biologically. But, in real life, there's also a bit of mystery."

"What do you mean?"

"The arousal thing."

He had me on new turf now and could see I was puzzled. "In some situations, a man just feels an attraction. He likes the gal or likes something about her. He's drawn to her. Wants to touch her and be in bed with her."

His eyes rolled upward, back to those months she lived with us, before all the troubles began. "We thought we were safe about it.

Wasn't Bev's fault at all. I knew better. Should have known better. But there it was. And everything changed after that."

"With Leslie and Jeremy?"

"That and more. Lesson learned."

"How could you have prevented it?"

Dad giggled nervously. "Pretty obvious, just stay away. But I see your point."

He walked over to a side cabinet, slipped his hand behind it and clutched a key. I often wondered what was in the locked drawers, besides narcotics. He reached into a large box, returned to his desk, and set three condoms in front of me. "This is one way. Know how they work?"

I was spellbound and shook my head.

"Pretty self-explanatory once you open one up. Slips over your erection. Captures the ejaculate. One size usually fits all. Effective unless you're careless."

I was unable to speak as he pushed them my way. "Keep them. You might want to experiment in the privacy of your room. When you're alone."

"By the book. Just like Doc," I said.

Lemon weighed in. "He was often by the book, but a lot more, too."

"You probably ended up knowing him better than I did," Jimbo said. "Following him around on his visits."

"Not sure about that. But he sure influenced me. He had such a curious mind. Taught me more than any teacher I had, including my professors in med school."

"I asked Les if he'd gotten the talk. He chuckled, amused by the memory."

"It's tough for any parent. Orantha did the honors with our girls," Lemon said.

He knew it was his turn.

That Just About Tops It – Lemon's Tale

Dad was a funny guy. An odd duck by today's standards. He grew up on a small dairy farm, just as smart as I am, but didn't have the freedom to go to college. He took care of his younger brothers and ailing parents right out of high school. Man of the earth. Always had a garden and fruit trees, even before Mom came his way. They met at the library in Wausau. She was right out of college and had just started working at Wausau Mutual. She told him she wouldn't marry him until he left the farm. By that time, Grandma had passed, so Dad's brothers took over the farm, allowing him to move on. She married down, as they say, but something about Dad struck her just right. Even when she was moving up the executive ladder at the insurance company, she was never embarrassed to be seen with him.

You have to know a few of those things to appreciate how he gave me "the talk." When I became obsessed with science, in fifth grade or so, he did everything he could to advance my interests, as long as it didn't cost much. He took me to museums. Hidden pockets along the river backwaters. Pumpkin Island in winter across the frozen slough tracking the coyotes. But his family farm was my biggest laboratory. He kept a second garden near the barn, and since I loved working with him, planting and harvesting, he took me out there quite a bit.

It was the spring of seventh grade, and he could see me changing physically. I spent an afternoon with him tilling and planting the early crops. His family had a few horses, and the roan mare was in heat. They'd borrowed a stallion to breed her. All afternoon that sorrel stallion chased the mare around the pasture, nipping at her, attempting to mount her, finally breeding her—the complete show. After the horses had gone off to a further pasture, Dad asked me if I'd enjoyed it. I tried to be nonchalant. "I've seen it before. With other animals."

"But never for such an extended time, right?"

I nodded. "You're a young man of science, Lem. What's going on?"

"It's what life does, Dad. Procreates to continue the species."

"You think that stallion was thinking about the next generation just now?"

"Course not. He was just...." I didn't know how to put it in words. It felt too awkward because he was my dad.

"Just what, Lem?"

"It's just what animals do. Instinct. He could smell the mare. Got whipped up."

"Could he control it?"

I knew it was a rhetorical question, so I let it be.

"Beautiful stallion like that. Reduced to sexual energy."

The two horses came racing back toward us. "Splendid when they sprint like that. They're not that far behind us in terms of evolution."

"Yes and no, Dad. They're mammals, but primates are a lot more complicated."

The stallion mounted her for the third time during the afternoon, and Dad laughed. "Relentless, isn't he? There's the difference, Lem. We can control it. Sometimes it almost hurts to hold back, but we've developed way beyond the force that's possessing the stallion and mare."

"I understand."

He chuckled at my naiveté. "If you do, you know more than me. Just because you're entranced with discovering as much as you can about the forces of life doesn't mean you'll always be able to control them."

He paused and something shifted in him. "But you can, Lem. When you meet a nice young lady, you can always treat her gently and still have the passion."

His transition left me in the dust. He could do that sometimes. "Mom and I have brought you up Catholic. The Church says the primary function of sex is to propagate the species and not for pleasure. But they're wrong about that. The pleasure is primary. And if you propagate at the same time, maybe that's hitting the bullseye."

Dad knew I was already questioning a great deal about the Church, but it didn't bother him one bit, unlike Mom. He understood I needed to do it. Telling me about the pleasure principle was deviating from the Church script, and he enjoyed it. "Lem, there's something majestic about the desire we saw this afternoon. Those huge creatures in rut. Man, that just about tops it."

Lemon looked at us. "Dad used to say that quite a bit, 'that just about tops it,' whenever he couldn't put words to something special. I didn't know at the time that Mom was in the early stages of her cervical cancer. She recovered, but I'm guessing it pretty much ended their intimate relations. At least for a while."

"What did your dad do, Lem? Never knew for sure," Jimbo said.

"A little bit of everything. Helped out at the farm. Worked carpentry off and on. Did small jobs for friends. Even filled in at the paper mill once in a while. His garden business got pretty big at one stage, when I was helping in later grade school. He was a bit of a renaissance man in terms of what he could do. He was happy being a stay-at-home dad when Mom was gone with her work. Gave him time to read."

"Was he really as smart as you?" I asked.

"I can't do half of what he could. But he never mastered knee replacements either. About a draw."

Jimbo brought in another round of beer and looked at me. "I'll take a bottle," I said. "It'll help me get through my turn."

Box of Kleenex – Mickey's Tale

My education began in the summer before Dennis went away to college. Mom was on her evening shift at the hospital, and Dad was helping Grandpa out with some telephone lines north of Bridgeton. Dennis thought I was playing baseball, I guess. Or maybe he wasn't thinking. I came into the house through the garage, and things were too quiet. I saw Dennis' wet sneakers, then a second pair that belonged to his girlfriend, Melanie, a senior-to-be he'd been seeing for a few months. They could be anywhere in the house, and I just wanted to hang out in my room. I left my sneakers in the kitchen and tiptoed around the main floor and up the carpeted steps. I heard some moaning from Dennis' room, and the door was opened a third of the way, pulling at my curiosity like a siren. Dennis' voice came at me softly. "Love you, Melanie."

"Don't stop," she replied.

I proceeded a few more feet until I had a direct view into the room. If either of them had turned and seen me, Dennis would have chased me out into the street, naked if he had to be. Their voices lowered, and the bed squeaked as Dennis shifted from the missionary position, kneeling behind Melanie, hips at her ass, thrusting, eyes closed. Melanie's face was rooted into the pillow, crying but not in pain. It went on for what seemed like an hour until Dennis collapsed onto Melanie's back and rolled over, his backside facing me now.

I furtively slipped out of the house and took off on my bike, instinctively knowing about what I'd just seen but not understanding it. I pedaled off to the river to figure it out and returned much later than expected. Dad had finished grilling the burgers, and Dennis was sitting at the table, grumbling that I hadn't been there to set it. I dashed upstairs and peeked into his room. She was gone, and his bed was half-made, but there was a distinctive smell that was new to me. Every night for the next month, whenever I heard any sounds from Dennis' room, I imagined them there.

Dennis disappeared to college in late August. His room was quiet at night and on weekends, and his bed was always trim and neat. Mom was working sixty hours a week while Dad was looking for work but usually around home when I returned from school. We developed a rhythm of coexistence, but I was spending more time in my room, and the house felt lonelier than I ever remembered it.

Several months into eighth grade, I was at my desk, racing through my homework after supper so that I could spend an hour at Lemon's. Dad shuffled in, carrying a basket of my laundry. "Where do you want it?"

"On the bed. I'll put it away."

He sat down instead, laundry still in his arms. "You're a bit neater than Dennis. I appreciate you bringing your dirty stuff down to the basement."

"Least I can do with Mom away so much."

I could feel him looking at me as I scribbled down my math problems. "Mommy shouldn't see some of your dirty laundry."

I turned around to face him. He derived great pleasure from deliberately confusing me, and now he held up a pair of my laundered briefs. "Your skivvies. And your sheets. You've been a bit sloppy expressing yourself." He chuckled. "Nothing wrong with it, just have to be more accountable with a woman in the house. Mommy probably wouldn't say anything to you. She'd just wash the hell out of them way more than I do and pretend you weren't doing things like that."

"I didn't notice."

"You're young. Why would you? Only been doing it a few years."

Actually, it was just a year, but I was embarrassed enough, wanting desperately to hide my laundry in the dresser. He wasn't done. "What do your friends call it?"

I didn't want to understand him. "What comes out," Dad clarified.

I had no reason to respond. "Cream? Jizz? Cum, most likely," he said matter-of-factly. "How about your penis? Cock? Pecker?"

"Usually just a dick."

"There are others. You should know them. So you don't get embarrassed if somebody says it and you don't know what they're talking about. Dong. Willy. Boner and woody, you know, when you're stiff. You guys must use names for it I've never heard."

"Dad, you can stop."

"You need to be much more careful with nicknames for the girl's part. To be decent. It's OK to be crude about your own. Most people can tolerate pussy. But the c-word is off-limits. You know what that is?"

I nodded. I'd heard Dennis use it when he was pissed at one of his male friends, which now seemed odd.

"You know how the two work?"

"I've seen it." I spoke of it boastfully, finally one up on Dad in this conversation.

Dad's eyes opened widely. "Should I be asking where?"

I didn't answer. "Not at school?"

"Nope."

"Can't be Lemon or Jimbo?"

"Come on, Dad."

"OK. Hope it didn't shock you."

It had, but I wasn't saying. He got up from the bed. "By the way, there's a box of Kleenex under your laundry. Use it. Better than the messes. And flush it down. Don't let Mommy see it under your blankets or even in the trash cans."

I hadn't really considered that. "OK. Thanks."

He was almost out the door. "It was Dennis."

He turned back to me, waiting. "And Melanie. In his room."

"Jesus, Mick. Should Mommy and I be worried about you snooping around our bedroom door?"

"His door was wide open."

I was exaggerating, but it was true enough. "Well, then, it's mostly on him. But you guys should be careful about respecting privacy. Someday it might be your turn."

I nodded. "Think she might be pregnant, Dad?"

He leaned against the wall. "Better not be. I gave him enough rubbers to last him a while."

"What?"

"Protection. Jimmy hats. Condoms. Figured he was having sex ... or would be soon. Told him to be careful. He and Melanie are just a short-time thing anyway."

"He said he loved her."

"Is that what you heard when you were watching?"

"Yeah. When they weren't moaning."

"Easy to say at moments like that. Be careful with those words, too. Nah, they won't be together much longer."

Jimbo and Lemon had been laughing throughout the story, even more than when I told them the first time. "Dad was right. Dennis dumped Melanie over Christmas break. Never saw her again."

"Your dad was so damn quiet when I spent that year with your family," Jimbo said.

"I never really knew him until Dennis went away. I think he got lonely and needed a friend."

"Did he talk like that a lot?"

"Sometimes. Not to Mom. Said it was military talk, from the war."

"Seems like he was so young when he died," Lemon said.

"Seventy-nine. But he always had a youthful look. Heart attack took care of that. I wish he were still around. Got to like him quite a bit."

"Same with my dad, especially before he changed after Sarah died," Lemon said.

Jimbo nodded, a look of mischief on his face. "They could be assholes at times, too, just to set the record straight."

Lemon and I welcomed Jimbo's attempt to change the mood. We both knew he missed Doc as much as or more than we missed our dads, and it was another signal that he was managing the blue elements in his personality successfully after uprooting his life and moving to St. Paul. "Do you remember what we did that night? After we told our stories?" Jimbo said, grinning broadly.

We looked at him, blankly. "Sneaking into my house?"

We smiled as it came back. Jimbo had led the way to Doc's office, unlocked the cabinet, and took two souvenirs for each of us from

Doc's condom box. "Did you ever use yours?" Jimbo asked.

"Threw them away years later. When I read about expiration dates," Lemon said.

"I used both of mine, alone in my bedroom," I said.

"That about covers your sexual exploits in high school, Mick," Jimbo laughed.

"Some of our classmates were doing it," Lemon said.

"Not you, Lem, even when you were off at college?" Jimbo asked.

"I've been more straight-laced than you two. Orantha is my first and only."

"No kidding," Jimbo said.

"Faithful. Like my dad suggested I be."

"How about you, Jimbo?" Lemon said.

"Been married twice, took several weeks in Tokyo and Hong Kong on leave when I was in 'Nam, been single with a high libido for more than twenty years. You can do the math."

"Guessing not that much, outside of your wives," I said, returning his dig.

"About right," Jimbo said. He was serious now, expecting the truth from me.

"There was Debbie Kedrowski in high school for a few months." Jimbo knew about that, but Lemon was surprised. "I had a big affair in college. Marriage to Sharon a few years after that. Not much since the divorce." I paused, wondering if I should say more.

"Never figured you to stay single, Mick. I tried to set you up but then backed off when I saw nothing would take," Lemon said.

"What happened?" Jimbo asked.

Lemon explained about the parties at his house when he and Orantha tried to be matchmakers, inviting single women they thought I'd enjoy. Jimbo was astonished. "Nobody's done favors like that for me."

"Why did you stay single after the second time, Jimbo?" Lemon asked.

"Discovered I'm not the type who should partner up. The odds of meeting a woman who could put up with me and my moods aren't that great. When I found out I couldn't make babies, part of the charm was gone anyway."

Both of them looked at me, awaiting an explanation. What did I have to lose? They'd been my friends since childhood. "I'm seeing someone right now."

"What's she like?"

"It's a man. I've been that way for a while."

Lemon looked at me like he was seeing me for the first time while Jimbo nodded knowingly. "Jesus, what's the big secret. Not like I hadn't figured it out."

I didn't know if he was bullshitting or not.

"News to me," Lemon said.

"What's he like?" Jimbo asked.

"Retired. Used to teach at Hamline."

"Does the professor have a name?" he continued.

"Hal."

"Are you going to bring him around?"

"You asking me to?"

"Of course. I can't speak for Lemon."

Lemon was still out of words.

Jimbo and I cleaned up the porch while Lemon called home. We said goodnight and agreed to have dinner at Jimbo's house once a month if it worked out. During the drive back to his house, Lemon said very little, still working through my revelation. When I pulled into his driveway, he said, "Why didn't you tell me before tonight?"

"No reason to, I guess."

"I wouldn't have thought less of you."

"I figured that but didn't dare take the chance. I was wrong. I'm sorry."

I got out of my car when he did and stood next to him in his driveway. "I've never felt it with you and Jimbo. That's always been something else. The only truly pure thing in my life."

"I know. Same here."

We hugged farewell, as we usually did, and he touched my cheek as he said goodnight.

Twenty-Seven
Endings

Two years after Jimbo moved to St. Paul, Orantha Kraig was hammered by a recurrence of breast cancer that was first treated twenty years earlier. She had undergone aggressive treatment to control the two earlier episodes, but this time, at age seventy-one, she declined the latest experimental therapy. Lemon argued with her for weeks, but she was adamant, grateful for the forty-five years she'd spent with him and the eight grandchildren their daughters had bequeathed them. Bettina, Olivia, and Jezzie were more accepting of her end-of-life decision, taking turns at her bedside during her decline and scheduling her many visitors for brief morning sessions.

I was distracted at the time. Mom was nearing ninety-six, and I was moving her from her apartment at the Oak Crest Retirement Community in St. Paul to a smaller assisted living unit. Dennis and I had sorted through her possessions six years ago when we finally persuaded her to leave the old house in Bridgeton, but this time the downsizing had a sense of finality. As Mom and I quibbled over each box of memorabilia, I could only smile at how fiercely she clung to the symbols of her past, many of which she hadn't looked at since she left Bridgeton. She fought most vehemently for the queen-sized bed she had shared with Dad for most of her life. It was too large for her new unit, and for a few days, I thought she would back away from the move. Des showed up to help resolve the dispute. He and Mom had become dear friends since he and his family had relocated to the Twin Cities at the time of her move from Bridgeton. He eagerly volunteered to store anything she wouldn't have room for—including the bed.

I called Lemon every day during Mom's transition until he told me not to, in a voice I barely recognized. Bettina and I met for coffee the next day. She was more concerned about her dad going over the edge than she feared the loss of her mother. When I stopped at the house the next day, Lemon was more distraught than I'd ever seen him, unable to sit near his beloved spouse without lapsing into tears. Bettina cautioned him about upsetting Orantha and told him to sit in the living room when two of her mother's best friends dropped by to say their farewells. Lemon and I went out for a walk, but he wouldn't say a word other than to thank me for my concern. My oldest friend had finally come face-to-face with a force greater than his vast intelligence. I'd not witnessed it, even after Sarah Ruth's suicide and the deaths of his parents, so indomitable was his determination to outthink every obstacle he encountered. I wasn't sure if he was undone more by the prospect of going through the rest of life without Orantha or enduring his remaining years alone, but every thought spinning in his disoriented mind and every sentence he uttered circled back to his wife.

A week before she passed, I said my farewell. Orantha was quite alert, her final day with that level of lucidity. She made sure Lemon was out of the house, buying groceries. "You've got a lot of work to do with that sad sack," she said.

"We've not had much luck. He just can't accept it."

"He didn't think it would come to this. Thought he'd go first. Never had a contingency plan."

"He'll figure it out. He always does."

"You and Jimbo will take care of him?"

"As much as he lets us."

"Make him let you." She grimaced as she shifted positions. "I was always envious of you and Jimbo. Especially you. The way you know him."

"Why would you be?"

"He was different when it was just the three of you. As much as I could eavesdrop on your conversations. Or get him to talk after you spent your annual weekends together. He's Lemon with you. Nobody else can claim that part of him."

"He talked about you and the girls when he was with us. How lucky he is."

"But you're still his closest friend."

I held her hand. "You've always been that."

She nodded off for fifteen minutes. When she woke, she was changed. The clarity was gone. Lemon came in from the garage with bags of groceries and peeked into the bedroom as Orantha was asking in a confused way about her grandchildren and her parents. "She's been doing this more and more. Not many days left."

"Have you said goodbye? Just in case?"

"Many times. Then, we do it over again. The girls have reached their peace."

"When will you accept it?"

"I'm trying, Mick."

She passed a week later. Hundreds of people attended her wake and funeral, and Lemon was consumed with being a good host while his daughters were overwhelmed, losing the only mother they would ever have. Lemon wanted one of them to accompany him to Kingston to bury Orantha's ashes in her family plot, but they could not do it emotionally. I told him I'd go, but he turned me down. "Maybe this will finally get me there. Allow me to go on."

He flew down on a Sunday, then postponed his return and took up residence in the timeshare condo he owned along the Caribbean. His daughters feared for his mental health and threatened to go down and rescue him. Olivia begged me to fly to Kingston. He emailed back. "I'm fine. Better than I've been for months. I don't need anybody's help. Be back soon."

While Lemon was in Jamaica, Virgil Lightfoot called me up. Virgil had earned a PhD from the University of Wisconsin in Native American Studies and taught for thirty years at the state university in River Falls. He'd become one of the most well-known Native American scholars in the country, acclaimed for his career-long studies of the tribes of the upper Midwest. We resumed our connection shortly after he started teaching at River Falls, and, most years, he lectured my history classes on our area's indigenous people. That friendship led us to co-authoring our book on the settling of the Wisconsin River.

He urgently requested that I visit him at his retirement home in Lac du Flambeau and bring Jimbo along. On the ride up, Jimbo told me he'd been in contact with Virgil quite a bit over the past few years. "Mostly through emails. Last time I saw him was just before I bought the house in St. Paul. He drove down to help me with the final inspection."

"Does he still have that power?"

"Comes and goes. But he told me the house would suit me well."

Virgil's home on the shores of Lake Flambeau was modest in size but rich in every other way. His office was overflowing with stacks of books and academic research for his current projects. The décor could have come from a museum of Native American art and artifacts. His wife had passed on five years earlier, and their six children were spread out across the country. Photographs of them at various ages filled every room, though Virgil spent most of his time alone. He was still close with his twin sister, Jennifer, a grandmother many times over living in Duluth.

We told him about Lemon's adjustment. "I'm still getting used to my wife's absence, and I've had plenty of time. You two are very accomplished loners. You should conduct seminars across the country for old guys who get shoved into solitude against their will, like Lemon and me."

Our conversation inevitably came back to Bridgeton. "How much do you remember from your year there?" I asked.

"Not so much. My sister's difficulty. Living with my aunt and uncle."

"What about the game?"

"I get confused. Do I remember it because I played in it or because people like you remind me about it every time we get together?"

He handed us a folder of newspaper clippings. A few from the aftermath of the game in February of 1965, the rest penned by Jason Stoneman, a reporter from the *Wausau Herald,* who wrote extensively about the game on its fortieth-anniversary date. His three-part story was picked up by forty newspapers as far away as Arizona, and he received thousands of hits on his website. Stoneman won several awards for the piece and turned it into a book. "Do you know how Stoneman's reporting grew legs?" Virgil asked me.

I'd read Stoneman's newspaper accounts and his book when it was published a few years later but had forgotten about them. "I was still in River Falls when Stoneman called me up. His plan was to focus on the basketball upset. Tiny Bridgeton toppling mighty Wausau. *Hoosiers* redux, spiced up by an Indian who could score buckets."

Virgil's self-deprecating humor was always amusing. "I told him very little, partly because I'd forgotten many of the details, but mostly because I didn't want to revisit that sad time in Jennifer's life. Stoneman called again a few weeks later. Said he'd unearthed some interesting details about events surrounding the game. The allegations of rape and the failure to prosecute. Did I know anything about that?"

"How'd he find out?" I said.

"Snooping around the Marathon County courthouse. I didn't want him to pursue it, but he was damn persistent. Called me three or four more times, but I was adamant he stick to the game and forget the other stuff."

"Which is when Stoneman called me," Jimbo interrupted.

Virgil and Jimbo smiled, knowing they'd kept me in the dark. "Ostensibly, he wanted my take on the two-foot push shot that won the game. On the old film, it looks like I nearly fumbled the ball out of bounds. Why was I even playing in the game? I told him about the injury to Eddie Raybold, and he asked what it was like being on the court with Virg that night. I told him to talk to the man himself, but I took Stoneman's number hoping I'd have a reason to call him back."

Virgil resumed the story. "Jimbo wanted my permission to tell the full story. Jennifer deserved it. So, I called her, and she thought it over. Finally, she agreed with Jimbo. 'Let the shit fly. Who cares where it lands.'"

Jimbo picked it up. "I called Stoneman back and told him everything. The rapes, Virgil's power to 'read' a gymnasium, the visit to his Uncle Jonny, the herbal pouch hanging near my balls during the game, and a lot about Virgil's phenomenal performance. Forty-one points, seventeen rebounds. How I played out of my mind that night, like some force beyond my capabilities was in charge of my body. That it was a magical, spiritual experience as much as getting even."

"Stoneman visited me several times after that. Even drove up to Duluth to talk to Jennifer. She told him everything about what those fuckers did to her. I continued to feed him all sorts of information. Finally, I told him I should be the one writing the damn book," Virgil said.

Virgil handed me his copy of Stoneman's book and opened it to the dedication page. "To Jennifer. She deserved more."

I hadn't noticed it when I read the book years ago. I examined the cover flap: a grainy photograph of Virgil flying through the air, his left arm spread like a red-tail hawk's wing, his right hand pinning Randy Dover's layup attempt against the backboard in the old Wausau Senior High gymnasium, with the book's title resting above it: *The Block: The Revenge of Virgil Lightfoot*.

"What did you tell him about the block?"

They both laughed as Jimbo explained. "One of Stoneman's original ideas for the newspaper article was the controversy about the block. Was it goal-tending or not? The more he talked to people who were at the game or who looked at the old film, the more he realized it was clean. Even the former Wausau coach and some of his players confirmed it. But nobody could figure out how Virgil did it, taking off at the foul line, pinning it, grabbing the ball in midair, and calling timeout. All of Stoneman's sources agreed. It was the most amazing play they'd ever seen. Even college coaches who were at the game, scouting Randy Dover for D-1 scholarships, were confounded by it. I told Stoneman it was Ojibwe magic."

Virgil giggled as Jimbo continued. "That's what made the story take off. The magical Indian revenge angle."

I looked at Virgil. "I can still see the block in my mind. How the hell did you do it?"

"I was a great leaper. When I was on the track team in college, I specialized in the long jump and reached twenty-three feet in a meet. One time in practice, I hit it just perfectly and landed just shy of twenty-five feet. Dunking was always easy for me, and I was running pretty hard up the court that night, chasing that prick. No way was Dover making the winning shot. So, I just lifted off, knowing it was me stopping him or losing the game. Uncle Jonny was there and said he was behind it. Jonny might have pulled it off. He had some real power, but more likely his claims are a bunch of Indian bullshit. Jonny's been gone for a long time, so Stoneman couldn't interview him for his book. Maybe it's the legacy of my name. I'm a Lightfoot, after all."

"You must have surprised yourself?"

"Of course. Afterward, when I thought it over. I can't remember anything about flying through the air that night. That part never made it into my memory. But I recall vividly sliding the pass down low to Jimbo. I wanted him to make the winning shot because he'd kept us in the game all night guarding Stockbridge while I was taking care of Dover."

"Stoneman ever contact Dover and Stockbridge?"

"He called me back after he became a minor celebrity with the book. Neither of those assholes wanted to be part of the story. Stockbridge was living quietly in Marshfield, selling insurance. Dover was hiding away in Madison, Indiana, retired. When people in Indiana read the story, some of them believed he was a rapist. He and his wife decided to leave town."

"Just rewards. Forty years too late," I said.

Virgil took us out to his backyard leading to sixty feet of Flambeau Lake frontage. He had a fire going, cooking some stones. "Figured you'd want to take a sweat. For old time's sake."

While we sat in the lodge, Virgil said, "The real reason I asked you up here is that I had a dream. About six weeks ago. I was soaring like an osprey above this lake, saying goodbye to everyone I knew. So, I've been having farewell conversations with everyone I need to, just in case. You're the last ones on my list."

"You believe in it?" Jimbo asked.

"As much as I believe in anything. I hope to see you over the next ten or twenty years, but you never know."

We took three sweats, jumping off Virgil's pier into five feet of cool, early September water after each one. By the time we left, Jimbo and I were renewed and exhausted. After we crossed the St. Croix River, we had to stop and take a short nap. I was too tired to drive home when we reached Jimbo's and prepared to spend the night in his spare bedroom. Before we went to sleep, I asked him if he believed in prophetic dreams. "I've only had a couple, so I'm no expert. But I don't walk in the same spiritual dimension as Virg."

"Too bad Lemon missed it."

"What have you heard from him?"

"Not much. Except we shouldn't worry."

"He's probably figuring out what to do next."

I straightened my leg to relieve the pressure on my knee. "You ever wonder who will take care of you when you can't," I said.

"Try not to. What about you?"

"Sometimes. Like next month, when I get my right knee replaced," I said.

"Stay with me."

"I won't be able to climb the stairs. You're too far from the therapy center."

"If Lemon's around, it'll be good for him."

Three weeks later, Gabe Parkinson called me up. Virgil Lightfoot was killed in a car accident, hit broadside by a drunken tourist from Chicago who ran a stop sign in Lac du Flambeau at fifty miles per hour. After Jimbo and I returned from the funeral, I emailed Lemon and told him to come home.

When he returned, Lemon was tan and fit, fifteen pounds heavier than when he'd left six weeks earlier. He knew I was headed to right knee replacement in a few days and insisted I take up residence at his house during my rehabilitation. He set me up in the downstairs master bedroom, en suite spic and span. He drove me to therapy every other day for several weeks and to see Mom when I needed to, fixed me meals and retrieved whatever I needed at my condo—everything he could possibly do except wipe my ass. After three weeks, I began to talk about returning to my condo, but Lemon insisted I stay longer. "I miss my own routine," I said.

"You can do it all here."

We were both right. "I've been thinking about the house. Wondering if I should sell it," he said.

"Jezzie stays here when she visits from Denver."

"Used to. Prefers Bettina's place now."

"Lots of memories to give up."

"It's still too big."

"What happened in Jamaica?"

"Spent time with O's family for a few days before I settled in at the condo. One day, I went out for lunch and realized how much I was enjoying my simple life on the beach. Didn't do much. Read. Walked the beach. Caught up on my sleep. It was a solitary life other than chatting with other tourists. I woke up one day, and it felt better. I was able to stand by myself again. Knowing I'll always miss O."

"No big epiphany?"

"No. Other than the shame of being so selfish in her final days."

"She forgave you for that."

He coaxed me into staying an extra week, then a week after that, until it reached nearly two months. When I insisted I had to go back, Lemon presented his final case. "I'm going to sell the house unless you move in with me."

"Why would I do that?"

"Because it makes sense. You and Dennis are scrambling to pay your mom's upkeep at Oak Crest. In my best medical judgment, she'll likely make it to one hundred. It's going to cost you. Sell your condo. Get rid of your mortgage. Save the money. Consider it my gift to your mom."

"I've got a personal life. So do you."

"I'm not getting married again. Seems like you'll be single, too. We'll close our eyes, open them, and we'll be seventy-five. Shut them again, we'll be turning eighty. Someday one of us will need taking care of. That's what friends do."

I thought of Hal, though over the past year we often went three or four weeks between dates, more likely maintaining our connection with phone calls and lunches with mutual friends. We were close friends who enjoyed intimacy a few times a month more than a couple who needed to see each other every day. I had no other prospects, nor did I look forward to a search for someone new. Lemon saw my wheels spinning.

"You can move into the apartment above the garage. The kitchenette was remodeled, and the shower stall was outfitted into a full bath. Sits empty all the time. We'd be out of each other's way as much as we need. Do as much as we want together."

"I don't want to ruin what we have, Lem."

"Won't happen. Think it over. Please. I don't want to be alone here."

"Why don't you ask Jimbo instead?"

"I did. He's in love with his woodshop. Says he's too ornery to live with."

After moving back home, I pondered Lemon's offer over the next few months. When I discussed it with Hal, he reassured me that I was welcome in his home whenever we spent a few days together. But he had lived with partners in the past, and now at age seventy-five preferred to be alone most of the time. I asked him what his plans were down the road if his solitary life became too difficult, and he dismissed any fears. He had two daughters living nearby and the savings to relocate to a retirement community if he had to.

During an afternoon visit with Mom, one of the many when she was eager to ramble on expansively about the past, she said, "Must be wonderful having the three of you together again."

"Who would have predicted we'd end up as close friends this late in life?"

"Dad would be happy to know that."

"Why?"

"He loved watching the three of you."

"I don't recall him saying much about it."

"Jimbo living with us that year when you were ten going on eleven was his idea."

"That was you, Mom. You're forgetting."

"It may have seemed like it was me because I was still friends with Vera. But when Jimbo needed a place for more than a few days, Dad suggested he move in. He's the one who forced Doc's hand."

I wondered about the clarity of her memory, which is something I did every time I met with her. "You're kidding."

"What Jeremy was doing to Jimbo was abuse. Even back then. When Dad saw the extensive bruising on Jimbo's body, he was livid. He walked Jimbo over to Doc's office for an exam and let Doc know he'd go after a restraining order the next time. I told Vera the same. They squared it with Jeremy somehow."

"Jimbo was half-scared all that year. But nothing much more happened."

"Your dad had a fierce moral compass when something was wrong. Not many people knew him well enough to understand that."

"He changed when he lost his job at the mill."

"Oh, my. He was so humbled. Wasn't sure he'd recover."

"With the drinking?"

She glanced at me like she used to just before she reprimanded me. "How'd you know?"

"I was at home with him those months. Dennis was off to Stout. Before he got hired at the mill in Schofield, you were working five or six nights a week. For several months, he went to Kennedy's Pub every night."

"I thought he was doing all his drinking at home. I told him he had to stop or he'd have to leave. I'd seen what it did to my granddaddy."

"That must have been when I noticed the change. He wanted to be friends with me after he stopped going out."

"What do you remember?"

"He was probably aimless, now that I think back, like most men, measuring his worth by his work. His days moving forward must have looked like a long chain of empty time he'd never be able to fill. I'm sure it was hard."

"He kept an upbeat sense of things when I got home from work."

"You were too tired to notice everything. He faked it with you."

She nodded, sifting through the memories. "What else happened?"

"We didn't have an easy way of talking. When we were alone, I didn't know what to say to him. Turned out, he didn't know how to talk to me either."

"Because he could be so gruff, with his cursing and frank language?"

I laughed. "A little, though most of that was amusing. Then we got used to each other. Suppertime became a talk session. He started cooking more, and I helped him. We'd clean up the kitchen together and chat about our lives most nights before I went to sleep."

"He always said it was easier when Jimbo and Lemon were around. He loved it when you boys had an overnight, and he could listen to you talk."

"Why?"

"Took him back to when he had friends. Like a lot of men, he lost most of them after the war."

"Like with Joe?"

"A couple of his friends got killed. Others came back haunted, like Joe."

"How well did you know Dad before the war?"

"We met at the hospital in Wausau. His mother was there for surgery, and we struck up a friendship. We'd been dating for almost a year."

"He told me quite a bit about Guadalcanal."

She smiled. "He mentioned that in our last year together. If I wanted to know more, I should ask you."

"What was he like when he came back?"

"On the surface, he seemed the same, so not many people saw the changes. But he'd experienced too much. Something dark and profound settled inside him. He stopped going to church. Lost any sense of believing in most things other than family. He went out of his way to help Margaret more and more. The war diminished his joy somehow, and he had to force himself to have fun. It was easy for him to become a workaholic when he got hired at the mill in Bridgeton. Then he didn't have to deal with anything personal. It was all business."

"Did you still get along?"

"Oh, sure. I figured out how to dance around his demons. But seeing you with Jimbo and Lemon released him more than anything else. One time, I think it was during the year Jimbo was with us, he told me he wished the three of you would never grow up. Lemon would move into your room, too. The three of you would stay eleven years old forever."

"When I talked to Beverly a while back, she told me you wanted more kids."

"Dad more than me. We tried. I had three miscarriages after you were born. Then life moved on."

She got up, hunched over a bit, but still close to her natural height, and reached for one of the pictures on the end table near her bed. It was of the four of us shortly after I was born. "Did Beverly tell you we were ready to adopt Lucy?"

"Not one word."

"You might remember us arguing about it during the months she was pregnant. I didn't want to at first. Figured we still had a chance on our own."

"Tell me about it."

"Beverly housecleaned for us throughout the pregnancy. Dad asked Doc what he was planning to do, and Doc said it was Beverly's decision. He wasn't going to marry her but would support the baby like his own if she kept her. Dad finally convinced me to take her baby towards the end of her pregnancy. I talked to Bev almost every day. She vacillated, one week keeping the baby, the next letting us take her. Went on for two months. Dad and I made plans but didn't tell anyone. I don't think Dennis knew either."

I was stunned. The arguments I'd overheard as a kid during that time were over adopting Lucy, not about the scandal of Beverly being pregnant or paying for her cleaning services. "Dennis has never said anything."

"I promised Dad I'd never tell you or Dennis. But now he's gone."

"What happened with Beverly?"

"Three days before Lucy was born, Bev came to us, crying. Said she had to keep her."

"Why?"

"Same reason most moms keep unexpected babies. She couldn't bear to give her up after nine months. Dad was speechless. Almost in shock. Like he'd lost one of his own. Bev had become a surrogate for our third child, and we'd agreed to everything she asked, including seeing the baby whenever she wanted. Things like that weren't done in the fifties."

"Did he want a daughter that bad?"

"It wasn't that. They didn't test for gender back then."

"I was just thinking of you guys painting my room pink in anticipation of me being a girl."

She laughed loudly. "That was my hunch."

"So, it's true. You were expecting a girl when I was born."

"It was just a silly thing, Mickey. You know that."

"Dad really wanted to go through it again?"

"He didn't think he'd put in his best effort with you and Dennis, being away so much. He was quite bitter for a few weeks after Lucy was born. Left the room the first time Beverly brought Lucy to the house. I talked to him and told him it was over. The next time Bev came, he held Lucy in his arms. It broke him in a way. He started going over to Doc's when Bev was making supper to see Lucy more. He suspected Bev would weary of being a mother, and we'd step in. In some ways, it was your dad's last big moment. You two were getting older. He wanted another chance at staying young. Can't blame him for that."

"It might have been worse if you had taken Lucy, and she died like she did."

"It would have been a terrible sorrow. We cried enough without having adopted her."

"Bev's never forgotten Lucy, even though she has kids from her marriage."

"Never do. I can remember more than a few details from each of my miscarriages."

"Jimbo's never gotten over Lucy either."

"So much happened to him that year. I didn't know he'd become attached to his sister."

"Yeah. She was the beginning of a new family for him. Turns out, he's never found another one."

"Other than you and Lem."

Mom needed a nap, so I took a walk through the flower garden areas of her nursing home, lilacs and irises ablaze everywhere. Some residents were walking by themselves, others accompanied by relatives or staff. There was a loneliness despite all the touches of beauty that had been added. I sat on a bench near a pair of flowering crabapple trees, wondering if a place like Oak Crest would be my destination twenty years down the road and who would take the time to visit me. I nodded off with those thoughts. When I woke, I saw Mom strolling toward me and was convinced I was still sleeping. But she sat next to me and smiled. "Beautiful day, isn't it, Mickey?"

I asked her what she thought about me moving in with Lemon. She was still clever enough to understand it all. "Lemon says it's for you, Mom. So Dennis and I can afford your stay here."

"Nice of him to think of me. But you know it's not that."

"I don't know what to do."

"You've never asked me about this kind of stuff before. Just went ahead and did what you wanted."

"This is different. Besides, you're the expert on this one."

"Seems like a sensible way to grow old. I wish I'd had something like it after Dad."

"It's all turned out OK?"

"As good as I could expect. But you have an opportunity for something grand in your last years. Living with a friend."

"I'd be sacrificing my privacy."

"I know about that. Shouldn't be a problem."

"What do you know?"

"About your friend, Hal. You don't have to be so secretive about it."

"How'd you find out?"

"Dennis told me."

"Who told him?"

"Your friends are looking out for you. Jimbo told Dennis. Wanted Dennis to tell me."

I started laughing. Uncontrollably. Mom was giggling, too. No end to Bridgeton watching over me.

Twenty-Eight
From the Dead

I started this project five years ago, writing bits and pieces, opening up my memory, hoping to refuel it at the same time, so it would ignite and release more of the details of what happened during the decades of our lives. Each time I came back to the sketches, more of our past emerged. Gradually, I sunk my teeth in as deeply as I could and, in the process, recognized there might be a finish line. I did not intend to dwell on any one of the stages of our lives more than the others, recognizing that what shapes us along the way usually grabs hold unexpectedly before spitting us out in an altered form. But much of the final section of this memoir is our collective assessment of time passing and death arising. We are in agreement about the potency of those inexorable forces.

Along the way, many of the people who fill these stories, who formed us most profoundly, have departed. Their voices still talk to the three of us.

Doc McPhearson

Matt Pederson and I became quite devoted to each other during my final years after my cancer diagnosis. He'd stop over at the house on his return from his solitary evening walks, and we'd sip a bit of Scotch. Ostensibly, he was checking up on me much like I did with so many patients when I made house calls. We were both feeling our age and seeking a friendly voice with whom we could reflect on how our past intersected with the present moment. Much like how our boys find sustenance in each other. Matt was a lifer here, and most people assumed I was born and raised in Bridgeton, too. But that's not accurate.

I arrived in Bridgeton in 1942, fresh out of my residency in Chicago. The population at the time was 1,246. The draft board had given me a choice: serve in the army or head out to North Central Wisconsin, where there was an acute shortage of general practitioners. Maybe it wasn't the most patriotic decision, but I took the deferment because Vera was home with Jeremy, and Les was on the way. My work consumed me, though some years I didn't earn much more than a paper mill worker on the evening shift. That didn't matter, just as I didn't care if my patients bartered for my services with food or labor or couldn't pay me at all. I wanted to get paid, don't get me wrong, and would have been damn happy to earn what physicians do now. Back then, I was willing to work all day and night. I couldn't get enough of figuring out what was wrong with my patients and helping them get through it. I figured my stay would end when the war did, but after just a few years I felt like a lifelong resident.

Everything else suffered. After fifteen years, my marriage went to shit, and I was a lousy dad on top of that. Maybe not so much with Jimbo, though you'd have to ask him. And I lost the love of my life in the process. I had a professor in medical school, who upon hearing I was headed to hunting and fishing territory and a paper mill town to boot, said, "Good luck. Maybe you'll come out ahead, but don't count on it." He just about nailed it. But Bridgeton never let me down, and I never stopped loving the Wisconsin River or the people who always seemed like creatures who had risen from the life flow of that rushing water. I was lucky to spend my life here.

Matt Pederson

Mickey, you asked me several times why I stayed in Bridgeton all my life, except for the war years and our winters in Daytona Beach after Mommy and I retired. I had just a few courses left at Stevens Point after the war, and Mommy urged me to move on to somewhere new. We nearly took up an opportunity in North Carolina, but I couldn't make the break. It had very little to do with the fact that your grandparents were still here. Grandpa was the sole owner of the Bridgeton Telephone Company at that time, and he pleaded with me to join up with him because I was a natural with my accounting background. He even promised that the business would be mine after he retired. But I didn't want to become tied to him like that. We had many disagreements over what your grandparents did to Margaret after her accident, forcing her to come back home after college because she was so scarred from the burning. They never gave her a chance.

I nearly left Bridgeton when new ownership at the mill fired me, but I got over my anger and found new work at the mill in Schofield. Mommy suggested we might as well move since she worked full-time at the hospital in Wausau, but I couldn't do that to you when you were in the middle of eighth grade. Which, my dear son, leads me to the most compelling reason I couldn't leave. I saw how much you and Dennis loved growing up here, even though neither of you came back after your first two years of college. You, especially, fell in love with the same things I did as a boy, escapading along the river with your friends. I have always been in awe of your friendship with Lemon and Jimbo. You are so damn lucky to have your boyhood pals, and that somehow you've defied the odds and maintained your love for them.

The gruff, sometimes curmudgeonly character you've creating in these stories isn't the real me. That stuff is what I became after all that happened to me, mostly before you were born. I like to think I'm the guy who sat quietly with Mommy on the screen porch in July watching the bats swoop by hunting for mosquitoes, who did all I could to help Joe find a direction, and who tried to be a big brother to my damaged sister, Margaret. Be sure you don't leave out the good stuff, son.

Joe Rebenick

I don't really deserve a place in Mickey's book, much less all the chapters he devoted to me. It's embarrassing to read about my drinking years because, by the end, I lived many more years as a sober man. Bridgeton didn't cause me to go under with the bottle. The events of the war did most of that, but Bridgeton couldn't bring me back. Mickey, Lemon, and Jimbo pulled me out of my constant state of inebriation as much as anyone, reminding me what I could have been when I was growing up in our hometown. The future seemed so limitless and pristine when I was a boy. Life reaches out and crushes us so often, but sometimes the gifts of reconciliation and resurgence find us when we least expect it. Sounds like AA talk, but I'm a child of that culture, and you must take what you can to survive.

Sarah Ruth Kraig

When I heard them calling me from that humble Catholic church in Bridgeton, I almost felt like I should return and apologize for the terrible ordeal I'd put my family through. They didn't deserve it. Just like I didn't deserve my own destiny. Bridgeton couldn't save me from being a freak, which is how I felt for most of my life, and I couldn't burden my family any longer.

I still feel a sense of relief all these years later, one I hadn't experienced since Joe and the boys rescued me from the cave when I was ten. Lizzie, Ted, and Eve have suffered, but I hurt Lem the most. He was always convinced he'd discover something to rescue me. To make me happier, at least. I never really got over him leaving home when he went off to college at sixteen, even though he called me every week and, as an adult, invited me to his home every time he phoned. An invitation I took up just once, but then realized I needed the security of my home to survive. I loved Mickey and Jimbo nearly as much as my brother. Those two were the closest thing I had to friendships growing up other than my siblings. Nothing gave me more pleasure than Jimbo calling me Little Lemon. To be compared to my brother brought me endless joy.

Lizzie Kraig

I came to Wausau from Detroit to work in the insurance industry at Wausau Mutual. It was a complete fluke that I met Ted when we latched onto the same book in the Wausau Public Library, struck up a romance, and settled by the river in Bridgeton. I spent my career becoming an expert in analyzing risk and estimating the probabilities of accidents reoccurring after they strike the first time. This is a fancy way of saying that I studied the likelihood of shit happening anytime it wants.

I wanted to believe we had beaten the odds when Joe Rebenick led the boys to Sarah Ruth's hiding place after she escaped from her abductor. Through all the years of our concern for her wellbeing, I foolishly let myself believe she was strong enough to manage her sadness. I was completely caught off guard when she ended her life on the first vacation Ted and I took by ourselves in decades. Sarah always traveled with us before that trip to New York City. Did I secretly wish something would happen to her in our absence that would free us from her care in the last years of our life? I can't say the thought never crossed my mind, as it does, I suspect, with every parent of a disabled child. But I loved her too much for that notion to take root.

Lem said our memory of Sarah would be like a pebble shifting around in whatever pair of shoes we wore, always present, rubbing that toughened skin into a painful blister, reminding us of what can go wrong when we let down our guard. The words in Sarah's farewell note were brief. "Sorry. I really tried. Over and over. Please, don't hold it against me." We never did, Sarah, but your abandonment wore us out. Your dad died less than two years later of a broken heart. I lasted five years longer, presenting a contented face to my children and friends, but my sorrow was nearly as deep as Ted's.

Orantha Chimes Kraig

Lemuel was hanging out at our beach condo in Kingston after he and my family buried my ashes, barely eating or getting exercise, so listless I began to worry he'd be unable to pull himself together and return to Minneapolis. The girls called him every day, and I listened in to his dispirited, bullshit responses to their questions, to the point where I was beyond being annoyed with him. He had no right to feel this sorry for himself. He's been blessed with profound intelligence, work that enriches him whenever he steps into surgery, and kids and grandkids who demonstrate such beauty and decency. He had me for over forty years, and I did a lot for him, dammit, more than he ever suspected. I brought him out of his depression after Sarah ended her life, and that took nearly two years.

So, I started nagging him about asking Mickey to become his housemate. He ignored me for weeks, until one afternoon we stood face-to-face on the balcony of the condo overlooking that exhilarating turquoise of the Caribbean, a view I will remember for all of eternity. We argued about his situation for an hour. Finally, I said, "What are you really worried about?" He replied that it wasn't that Mickey might say no. It was more that he'd say yes, and then their friendship would fall apart. "Do you think Mickey would let that happen? He needs you more than you've ever admitted." Lemon laughed at me and said, "If you think that's true, you've really misjudged us. I've always needed him more." Of course, just as he'd been doing for weeks at the drop of a hat, he started crying. I went into the living room and sat down, waiting for him to compose himself, and, when he came inside, he asked, "Am I wrong about Mickey? Does he need me that much?" I held his hand. "Lem, my darling, for argument's sake, let's say we're both right. You and Mickey, it's a mutual thing. Which is why him moving into the garage apartment and the two of you taking care of each other will work out just fine."

I hope I'm done with him for now. He'll be a lucky man to spend his final years with Mickey and, of course, Jimbo who'll join them for much of the ride. Life is circling back for the three of them. It was a blessing to see some of that before I left.

Doc McPhearson

My passing was not simple or easy. The cancer made for a painful exit, and at age seventy-four, I wasn't ready to fully retire. More than anything, I had unfinished work with Jimbo. He was getting close to not needing me at the time, but there were many finishing touches yet to go.

I'd neglected him for so much of his youth. In fact, he took care of me more than I tended to him during his middle and high school years, learning how to cook and maintain the house on his own. He was incredibly adept at those tasks and remarkably discreet about hiding his mental health issues until they were impossible to ignore after his war injury. But by then, I rarely saw him. His interest in woodworking came gradually, though he'd putzed around in our shop in Bridgeton throughout the years, making shelving units for the kitchen pantry and his bedroom or helping me when I needed a third hand. He was getting more serious about it during the year my cancer turned bad, visiting me for a week at a time to learn the skills, crafting a few tables for his home in St. Louis. I could feel the passion rising within him, the same love for the tools and what they could create that began to inhabit me at about his age.

I changed my will during my last months to make sure he inherited the shop and everything in it, and I watched from a distance as he moved the equipment and hand tools to his brand new shop in St. Louis. But he couldn't truly launch his real start until I returned and stood beside him, guiding him through the completion of the cherry end table I started in my final year. I was with him through many more projects, watching him interact with the wood, advising him when he needed it, slowing him down when he was rushing or getting impatient, until I knew the devotion to our craft was coursing through his soul. When he took a break and leaned back in the comfortable recliner in the corner of his shop, we discussed what we'd done with our lives and the many things I'd failed to do for him. His love for Mickey, Lemon, and Bridgeton was a regular part of those conversations. Gradually, I began my retreat and farewell.

So much of his life improved after that, though things weren't always ideal. Living a hermit's life was in his blood, and, because of that, neither of his marriages had much chance. He had bad luck trying to have kids, but if he had, his separation from them might have brought on more heartache, as happened when we lost Lucy when Jimbo was just ten. Then he pulled up stakes and settled in St. Paul near his boyhood friends, discovering a genuine and full-throated satisfaction and even joy in his retirement years, allowing me to let him go without worry. Days go by now without thinking about how I can help him. It's a pleasure to see him smile as he did when he was seven before all his troubles began.

Jimbo, my youngest and dearest, you got the very best of my healing abilities, though you can't fully comprehend how it happened. I don't even mind if you still harbor a few grudges. There's no son alive who doesn't feel a few of those toward his old man.

Matt Pederson

I began to feel the end coming after Doc's battle with cancer, which was followed a few years later by Sarah Kraig's suicide. I took stock of what I'd accomplished, which wasn't a whole lot, except to make Janice happy some of the time. I hope that little bit is true. I took frequent walks along the river. Sometimes Janice would accompany me, but the water didn't mean the same to her as it did to me. When Mickey came home five or six times a year, he'd join me. We showed each other places we discovered when we were young. Most were uniquely our own, but a few of them were spots where something memorable had happened to both of us, though often the memorable had become quite ordinary in retrospect as we'd gotten older.

When Mickey took me to the beach he and Lem Kraig named Discovery, he recounted a few of the adventures he had there with his two best friends. When I told him I used to come there with Joe when we were growing up, he recalled that Joe told him that decades ago when Joe was camping and drinking by himself down by the river. He asked me what we called it, but we hadn't named it when we were boys. It was just the swimming hole. Being a warm day in August, we stripped down and swam around the sandbar. I hadn't seen Mickey naked since he was a boy, nor he me, but neither of us had any hesitancy about gliding through that majestic water like we had done as young lads. The passage of time had reduced the size of the beach and forced us to forget many of the hours we'd spent there. But as the water ran through our thinning hair down to our chests, we were still awestruck, our amazement practically emanating off of our bodies, turning the amber water golden. This tiny beach on this isolated section of the river still glistened in the recesses of our memories as an unforgettable jewel.

While we were sitting on the warm sand, he asked me if I was disappointed in what he'd made of his life. I said, "Should I be?" He said he hoped I wasn't, that he'd tried as hard as he could to be someone I'd respect. Even if I wasn't proud of him, he wanted me to see that. I told him, "I'm proud you have the courage to ask me that question. I couldn't ever disrespect you for anything you've done or failed to do. Mommy feels the same way." He turned to me, a few tears in his eyes. "I haven't always been the best, but I've given it my best." I was quite startled as he'd always been so blessedly upbeat with us, and this was the rare moment when he revealed how lonely and bereft he sometimes felt when he contemplated how his life had occasionally skidded in a wrong direction. I kissed him on the cheek. "You've been a better son than I've been a dad. You're at least one up on me."

Janice Pederson

The boys wanted me to make it to one hundred, but I've gone on twenty years after Matt died. He was my soulmate, and it's been lonely too much of the time. I was becoming a burden to them anyway, and after a few months, they'll start forgetting. I wanted to make sure my boys were set before I left, like any mother in old age has to consider before she completes her turn. Dennis is secure. His kids and grandkids will keep him alive, even if Alberta doesn't hold up. I was always more worried about Mickey, but Lem and Jimbo promised me they'd take care of him. And Des has come back to him, magically enough. So, I let go.

Mickey wanted me to say a few words about Bridgeton before I left, since he's been thinking so deeply about what that river village has meant to him. I never thought I'd spend most of my life there. I hated it during the first years though I understood Matt's desire to be there, so he could stop in and see his sister, Margaret, when he needed to, though he could have done that living in Wausau or Stevens Point. But the town grew on me, and then it became the place I was willing to call home. I didn't fully understand why Matt wanted to come back until I watched the boys play along the river. It's what Matt knew, and it became the link that held Mickey, Jimbo, and Lemon together.

Virgil Lightfoot

Mickey said I'd get some of the last words. But then that damn drunk crashed into me, and the warning of the osprey fulfilled itself, so I'm here on my own. During the summer before the two of us began our book on the history of the settlements along the Wisconsin River, we canoed the full 430 miles of the river from the headwaters near Upper Michigan to the Mississippi. We canoed off and on for two months finally ending in Prairie du Chien on August 17. It was a wonderful lark, disrupted only by the fucking dams. We both felt it was critical research for what we'd be writing about, but it turns out we learned something more important. We got to know each other so completely sitting in that canoe, sometimes drifting with the current, other times battling against the wind, sometimes talking about our lives, other times resting quietly for an hour. It became tedious at times, and both of us thought about shortening it up once we reached the stretch of paper mills between Wausau and Nekoosa and were forced to portage around all eleven dams. But we persisted, knowing we had to pass through the heart of Bridgeton on our journey.

We're fortunate we stuck it out because the last stretch after Prairie du Sac, which does not have a single dam, was something I never forgot and was a complete inspiration for our book. It was made doubly pleasurable because his dad, Matt, and Jimbo accompanied us in a second canoe for those final six days. The rawness of the much less settled curves of the river and the backwater sloughs between the villages of Spring Green and Muscoda, and Blue River and Wauzeka, finally ending just past Wyalusing, enabled us to envision, to an extent, what it must have been like before white men settled the river in their fashion.

Among our many conversations, we talked at length about what would happen to us after we died. Mickey was mostly an atheist like his dad, though he held a slim opening for other options. We both agreed that if there was something else, we'd like each other to be there along with the people we love. Mickey, I'm here waiting for you somewhere on the other side. You and Jimbo and Lemon will enjoy our time along this body of water that looks and feels remarkably like that winding river we enjoyed so thoroughly years ago. Be well, my dear friends.

Twenty-Nine
The Flow of Life

A new flow of life swept over the shore as we turned seventy-three. I moved into the apartment above the garage at Lemon's house and kept my condo as a rental, hedging my bet. Jimbo visited us more frequently than we made the ten-mile drive to St. Paul and often spent the night in Bettina's old bedroom, which he outfitted as his own. He settled in for nearly a month with a hip replacement. Having done so many replacement surgeries in his time, Lemon was amused that he was the only one of us standing on his God-given joints.

Jimbo's lady friend, Danielle, helped Lemon and me during Jimbo's recovery. When Jimbo introduced her, Danielle shook our hands forthrightly, like she knew us well. She looked me in the eye. "You're the one who's gay, right?"

I smiled at Jimbo, no longer surprised when he outed me. "That's right."

"But he's not interested in Lemon or me. So, you don't have to worry, Danielle," Jimbo said.

Danielle was a retired nurse, and she and Lemon quickly became friends, sharing the duties of fixing meals and driving Jimbo to therapy. Jimbo was embarrassed and sometimes grumpy when Danielle helped him, more so than when Lemon did. When I cautioned him, he said, "I'm just so damn used to doing everything by myself."

"Took me a while to accept Lemon's help, too. How long have you been seeing her?"

"About a year. Didn't want to mention anything."

"Cause then we'd ask you about her."

"Now it's fair game just like you and Hal. Not seeing him as much since you've moved into Lemon's? That by design?"

"I'm more likely to be with him at his place. He gets a bit jealous when he comes here."

"Of Lemon?"

"That I've settled in here, more than Lemon himself."

Jimbo gave me an odd stare. "Because it would only be natural for him to suspect you have feelings for Lem."

"Hal knows I love Lem. Same as I feel about you. As brothers. But Lemon and I established ground rules just in case."

"What do you mean?"

"I'd never cross that line with him."

"What if Lem is interested in you? Orantha's been gone for a couple of years. He must be feeling some urges."

I chuckled thinking Jimbo would join in, but when I understood he was serious, I said, "I suggested he start dating. He's not there yet."

"It wasn't easy for either of us to kick the restart button after our divorces. Orantha meant a helluva lot more to Lem than our exes did to us. Just saying, it might be a while."

"He sometimes gets blue when he's alone, especially in the evening hours."

"What about his daughters and grandkids?"

"They don't come around as much since I've moved in. When I notice the sadness drift in, I do everything I can for him. That's part of the reason he wanted me here."

Jimbo looked at me with the audacious grin he sometimes had. "Hypothetically, what if you and Lemon slept together some night?"

This time I knew he was having fun with me. "Per our agreement, I'd have to move out the next morning."

"Where would you go?"

I paused and smiled at him. "To your place. Your guest room suits me. And I'd enjoy snuggling in your king-size bed."

Jimbo exploded in laughter. "My ground rules would be a bit more stringent than Lemon's."

"To be expected."

I couldn't recall Jimbo so amused. "Mick, your sense of humor never fails to lift me up. Where'd you get that knack?"

"A gift from Dad, mostly."

"Matty Pederson. Haven't thought about him for a while."

"Joe Rebenick was the only person who called him by that pet name."

"He stopped in at the house quite often while Dad was battling cancer. Dad started calling him Matty, and I picked it up. Gave your dad a chuckle."

"Reminded him of the old days, I suspect."

"I never told you about the gift he gave me. The day after I moved into your house when we were ten."

"After all the beatings Jeremy gave you?"

He nodded. "Matt came home early from the mill that day because Janice told him I was hurting. He shut the door to your bedroom and told me to take off my T-shirt. When he saw the bruises on my upper arms, lower back, and ribs, he said, 'Is there more?' I dropped my jeans to my ankles. Both of my thighs were black and blue like someone had smacked them repeatedly with a ball peen hammer. He examined the discolored tissue closely and said, 'What the fuck has he done to you.' He put both of his hands on my face. 'Pull up your pants. We're going to do something about this.' We marched up to

Dad's office. I was frightened to my core that Jeremy would attack me the minute I entered the front door. Dad was sitting by himself in his treatment room when we walked in. Matt shut the door and said to me, 'Show him.' I froze, not wanting Dad to see any of it. Matt looked me in the eye. 'Jimbo, we've got to show him.'

"I lifted up my T-shirt with extreme reluctance. Matt said, 'Jimbo, strip down to your briefs. He's got to see all of it.' I looked into Matty's face like he was some kind of a god who dropped down to our corner of Bridgeton to rescue me. I did exactly what he ordered me to do. It took a minute for Dad to get over his initial shock at seeing the results of Jeremy's pummeling and kicking. Then he examined me like a patient, probing at the contusions, making sure the damage hadn't reached my organs, especially the ones at the kidneys. When he was convinced I'd be OK, he took a step back and told me to get dressed. Matt said, 'Doc, this can't go on anymore. He's staying with us until it stops.' Dad was speechless, tears sliding across his cheeks, mumbling in bewilderment about losing control of his family. Matt said, 'Tell your dad who's responsible.' I hung my head and quietly told him what Jeremy had been doing. Dad shook his head. 'I'm so sorry, Jimmy. I had no idea.'"

"Is that when they made the decision you'd stay with us all year?"

"Pretty much, but at the time, I was too confused to know what that could possibly mean."

"Jesus. It all went to back to Beverly and Lucy. And Jeremy's hatred toward Doc. You were caught in the middle."

"Yeah. You remember what I was like at that age? A giant of a kid who would spout tears over the simplest things, but only in private. None of the adults in our world understood how sensitive I was, other than Beverly. They figured I could withstand anything because I was so big for my age. Matty and I were walking back to your house when I started crying, slowing down to a near halt, not knowing what would happen next. He took my hand like it belonged to you or Dennis and coaxed me along those two blocks. By the time we reached your front porch, I was bawling full-throttle, tears catching in my throat, my chest heaving, snot running down into my mouth. All the grief from Jeremy beating on me for weeks poured out of me. I haven't cried that deeply since. I was completely overwhelmed by everything, that my own flesh and blood had done this to me, in the process, rendering Dad so damn powerless. I was petrified Dad would tell Mom, and I'd be sent to her place. I was certain I'd be abandoned again once this got out. Matt sat me down on the sofa glider on your porch and positioned himself as close to me as he could, holding my right hand in both of his. I was practically his height, and my hands were already adult size. But I felt absolutely puny, like the smallest runt in school as I leaned my head against his shoulder so he could comfort me like I was a toddler who'd just fallen down the front steps."

Jimbo started sniffling as the past caught up to him, pulling me into his sorrow at the same time. "Matt said, 'Stand up, Jimbo.' I followed his command again without hesitation. Matty Pederson had absolute control over me at that moment as he tried to save my ass from complete misery. He unfolded his clean, pale blue handkerchief, wiped my face like I was his child, and placed the damp cloth into my right hand in case I needed it. 'We won't go inside until you're ready.' We stood there staring out into the early evening sky as I continued to dry my eyes with his handkerchief. He was waiting for me to calm down so I wouldn't make a fool of myself in front of you, Mick. He understood all that, about saving some face with my friend who was now going to be my roommate. After fifteen minutes, he could tell I was getting close. He put his hands on my shoulders in the most loving way. 'Jimbo, you're safe with us. It'll get better, but it's going to take a while. Janice and I will love you just as much as we do Mick for as many days as this takes. OK?' I nodded, fully believing in his words after months of uncertainty. I extended my hand. 'Here's your hanky.' He said, 'Keep it.'"

I handed Jimbo a box of tissues, and he wiped his eyes. "I still have it in the back of my underwear drawer. It's washed and ironed just like it was when he took it from his back pocket. I haven't used it since. Once in a while, I hold it and the memories come back. I was going to give it to you after he died, but I forgot, and when I remembered,

I couldn't let it go. I told myself that someday I'd tell you the story instead. And here we are, laughing and crying like two village idiots."

"Dad never mentioned any of it, and he told me lots of secrets before he died."

"Matty and I shared that one. There was no way he'd tell you. And he kept his promise. He and Janice did all they could to heal me during those months we bunked together. I always felt like I was part of your family."

Jimbo regained his equanimity, and a mirthful look bloomed on his face again. "So, Mick, if you need to snuggle with me in bed sometime, it would be my privilege."

"Asshole."

He laughed heartily. "What I mean is, I owe you and Matt. I never got to pay him back. Maybe I'll have a few opportunities with you."

He joked some more about my embarrassment at being bounced out of the closet. "When I told Dennis you're gay, he practically laughed me out of his home. And that was after I made a special trip to La Crosse to tell him. It took about an hour of convincing before he believed me. I told him he had to tell Janice but keep it a secret from you. I wanted her to shock you with the news."

"Man, you really are a prick."

He'd always been so transparent when he was pleased with himself, and this time was no exception. "You never would have told her."

"You're right. But she's still my mom."

"She suspected anyway. She asked me one time if you were, years before you told Lemon and me. She said she wanted you to be happy, and it didn't matter if it was with a man or a woman."

I got up to get him a beer. When I returned, he opened his hand for mine. I took it, and he held my right hand in a double-fisted clasp. "You're doing a good thing living here with Lem. Your dad would be proud of you. He knew how to take care of the people he loved, just like you do."

"Lem needs you, too. When you spend the night with us every few weeks, it brightens things up for both of us."

"You mean that?"

"I've never been more serious. You're part of us. You know that."

"Do you think camping out at Lem's is for the long haul?"

"Looks like it as each month passes by."

"Hal's got a big place. He could have asked you to move in."

"He might have persuaded me at one point, but living with Lemon is easier. More familiar in a lot of ways."

"Hal see other men?"

"Old friends from time to time. It's a different set of rules."

"How about you? Any old friends like that?"

"Just one. The first man I was ever with. But not very often."

"Still, something's better than nothing. Especially at our age. With our capabilities."

We talked about using the blue pill. It worked for me, but Jimbo didn't like the side effects. "So, I have to rely on nature's ability to prop me up. Not such a predictable thing. Danielle is grateful for whatever happens."

Mom was declining as she passed ninety-eight, under more care now, eating from a tray the CNAs brought to her room but not taking in many calories. On the first Wednesday in August, her heart gave out at dawn. I had visited the day before, and she didn't have much to say for one of the few times I could remember. She simply let me hold her hand as she took a nap, with a contented look on her face. As always.

We celebrated her funeral at Good Shephard Episcopalian church, where Orantha had attended for many years. It was the faith Mom had been raised in and had clung to, despite Dad's doubts. Fewer than sixty people gathered, half of them from her retirement community. Dennis, Alberta, and their two sons and their families were there. Lemon and his daughters. Jimbo and Danielle. Hal, but not at my side. Des flew up from North Carolina, where he'd moved for another job promotion. His wife said goodbye to Mom a few months earlier when they'd made their last visit. Des gave one of the eulogies expressing his gratitude for the six years he was part of her life. He stared at me as he said it, nodding, so I knew he was thankful for regaining a little of what we'd lost over the years. I received notes from my ex, Sharon, and my oldest, Ron. I had seen them a few times when they visited Des, but the chill never lifted.

Mom wanted her ashes buried next to Dad's in the family plot in Bridgeton, and I drove over the day before to make the final preparations. Jimbo and Lemon accompanied Dennis' son, Derrick, intending to return with me. Mom had outlived her siblings and everyone she'd known in Bridgeton and Wausau. But several of our classmates from high school showed up for the half-hour service at the Bridgeton cemetery. Dennis and I offered our farewells. Sally and her son, Walter, drove up from Chicago, and she added a few words of gratitude to Mom and Dad. Her husband, Stanley, was back home, confined to a wheelchair most days. Lemon and Jimbo recalled moments Mom had hosted them as boys, and Jimbo concluded, smiling through his tears. "She was the glue that held us together."

After the luncheon, Jimbo, Lemon, and I drove back out to the cemetery. We quietly greeted Lizzie and Ted Kraig, Sarah Ruth, Doc and Lucy, daylilies waving over their plots. Jimbo added a salute to his mother, and I offered one last goodbye to Mom and Dad. We drove around town, stopping briefly at the homes we grew up in, and ended up at the river near the dam. We stood at the ten-foot fence blocking us from our favorite sitting spot, where the Wisconsin River flowed through Little Bull Falls. A city maintenance truck drove up from the dam, and a young worker stopped and unlocked the gate. We approached him, and he nodded kindly, in no hurry to rush off. "I've been watching you three, staring through the fence like kids wishing you could go fishing at the dam."

We introduced ourselves. "Of course, your mom's burial. Grandpa was there. I'm Larry Mestanek."

We shook hands, thinking about our high school classmate. "You look quite a bit like Kurt when he was eighteen," Jimbo said.

"I've heard that many times. It's an honor," Larry said.

We talked a little bit about the old days until Larry finally shook his head. "Grandpa's told me the stories a million times. Life used to be so good. So simple. I'm sure some of it's true."

Larry spoke about Bridgeton like he could have been one of our boyhood friends. "Hey, Larry, would you let us sit at the dam for a while? Might be the last chance we'll have," Jimbo said.

"I'm not supposed to let anyone past the gate. They fenced it off for a reason after the drowning years back. Besides, I'm going off shift."

He didn't want to say no and lingered with the keys in his hand. "Go on down. I'll walk back up in a few hours. I'm just a few blocks away." He looked at Jimbo. "In Doc's old house."

The flat rocks near the dam hadn't moved. They weren't quite as big as they were when we were ten, but they were still imposing, inviting us to sit as they always had. The noise of the tannin-colored water rolling through the dam washed out any temptation to speak over it. After twenty minutes, Jimbo jumped down and winced where he'd had his replacement surgery. "I know you two visited Discovery a while back when you released Aggie's ashes. But I want to go back one last time."

We moved slowly over the boulders and along the river. The mullein spires still aimed skyward, flowering a brilliant ochre. We paused at the rocky overlook of the river before descending to the hidden beach. It looked much the same, though the sandbar had shifted again, this time nearer to shore, close to where it had been when we were boys. The willow was now a fully grown tree, shading half of the tiny beach.

Jimbo was already stripping down, and we joined him. I hadn't seen Lemon naked since we dispersed Aggie's ashes and her treasure of beach sand. He worked out three times a week and was close to his high school weight. Jimbo's hairy belly hung down toward his genitals a bit, but his shoulders and chest were muscled out from working with wood. His knee scars were still quite visible from his war wound. I was the least in shape, a bit of a senior citizen paunch, my leg and arm tissues beginning to sag. Jimbo looked me over, and I knew what he was thinking. "Nothing to worry about."

He laughed. "Never thought there was."

The water was running low and warm but reached our chest level near the sandbar. We dove in on the count of three, as we'd done so often as boys, and spent nearly an hour in the water and on the sandbar. The memories flowed. One of us would start. "Remember the time..." and the other two would nod. There was no need to speak of it. Time stopped as we allowed our childhood in Bridgeton to slip back in. "Damn, how could it go so fast? Seems like just a few minutes ago," Jimbo said.

There was nothing Lemon or I could add to that. I was feeling the same joyful conundrum. "We better get back. Larry might lock us in for the night," I said.

"Wouldn't be the worst thing," Lemon said.

We jumped off the sandbar and dove under, for the last time, dressed quickly and climbed up the rocks, pausing to look down at the beach. We hustled through the field and stood again near the dam. "Remember the first day we were down here?" Jimbo asked.

"Dennis was babysitting me. Mom and Dad were gone for the afternoon. We were five. Maybe six. Lemon came over to play. Dennis wanted to go fishing with your brother, Les, and was pissed he had to stay home. He decided to defy Dad's orders and led us halfway across Old Iron. He helped us climb down the ladder for the first time. You and Les were waiting for us. They fished while we played along the rocks and shoreline. After that, we came down here anytime we could get away."

Jimbo shook his head, marveling at the clarity of my memory. "Jesus, Mick, is there anything you don't remember about us growing up?"

"If I don't remember it exactly, I make it up. Who's going to correct me if I'm wrong?"

Lemon laughed. "Is that what you've been doing with your stories?"

"Some of the time. As long as I capture the spirit of it."

"Then fair enough," Jimbo said.

Lemon nodded. "We all do that when we dig into the past."

We reminisced further about our first times under the bridge as we walked up the gravel road toward the gate. Larry Mestanek was sitting just outside on a picnic table, Kurt next to him, both sipping on bottles of beer. "I called Grandpa when you didn't show up. Thought maybe you guys had done something stupid, and we'd have to rescue you."

"Sorry to keep you waiting."

"Just kidding." He opened the cooler, which contained an assortment of local microbrews. "Help yourselves."

I couldn't remember anything tasting so good, like the beer was an extension of the ale-colored river.

Kurt stared at our wet clothes and hair. "Did you fall in?"

"Took a swim," Jimbo said.

"Not by the dam," Larry said.

"We walked down to a little beach we used to go to when we were kids. Lost track of time."

"The one with the willow tree, hidden away by the rocks and the sandbar?" Larry said.

"Yup. How do you know it?" I said.

"My wife and I discovered it one day. Pulled the boat in. Spent an hour swimming. Beautiful spot."

"Happy to hear someone else loves it," I said.

"We even gave it a name. Lusty Beach." He cracked open another beer. "Cause we made our first baby there."

Grandpa Kurt busted out laughing, and we joined in. "Not sure we need to hear about that, Larry," Kurt said.

Larry was red-faced but enjoying the teasing. "Hey, Jimbo, want to see your old house?"

"We've got a long drive back to Minneapolis," Jimbo said.

"Don't have to stay long," Larry said, eager for us to join him.

Jimbo looked at Lemon and me. "We've got plenty of time. Let's go," I said.

About the Author

Michael Knoedler grew up in a Wisconsin River village a stone's throw from Bridgeton and continues to live a few miles from the river in rural Dodgeville, Wisconsin. He taught high school in Dodgeville for thirty years, during which time he published a novel for teens, *Callie's Way Home*. He and his wife, Kathy, have raised three children and enjoy the hijinks of their six grandchildren. He can be reached at: redmike50@yahoo.com.

Printed in the United States
by Baker & Taylor Publisher Services